New Coyote 2.0

To Vivian —

Michael Bergey

Michael Bergey

Michael Bergey

Cover art by Tess Garman

ISBN: 1724639714

ISBN-13: 978-1724639714

Contents

New Coyote   page 5

Tricks of the Light   page 257

Michael Bergey

New Coyote

Michael Bergey

Prologue

I was not a normal pup. Mooney's friends told each other it was something done to me in the research lab where I was born. I was healthy enough, certainly. I've always been healthy and full of energy. It's just that I didn't grow very fast, and I didn't stop growing when I should have, and I wasn't... normal. Sometimes I would forget myself and do things no natural coyote should do, and that would frighten people, sometimes. When I was nine years old I was almost a hundred pounds and still growing—still long-legged and gangling like a puppy, but no longer clumsy like one. My puppy teeth had worn out years before, and no new ones had come in. I lived with Mooney and her goats and chickens and raspberry fields and pot plants in a commune called Sunbow Farms. It wasn't really a commune any more because all the other humans had left when I was very small, but sometimes they would come back to visit or help. Mostly it was just Mooney and me. And the goats. I herded Mooney's goats for her, which is also not a natural sort of thing for a coyote to do.

I was nine years old, in the summer of 1989, when I took them out for the last time.

Chapter 1

Herding goats is pleasant work. It's peaceful. And safe, too, if no cougars come by. And when the goats misbehave, you get to chase them. Mooney and I both thought it a fine joke that her goat herd should be entrusted to a coyote for protection. Our flock consisted of two elderly Alpine nannies with bad knees named Capri and Corney, and a formidable middle-aged Saanen named Baby. Baby had been bred the previous fall and now jealously guarded a pair of male kids named Thing One and Thing Two. Capri and Corney were too old for breeding, and didn't have any use I could see except for pruning blackberries and alders, and producing fertilizer.

Mooney has accused me of being less than diligent with my herding duties, and she may have some grounds for complaint. I have been known to leave my charges unsupervised from time to time. The goats never complained, though. Only Mooney. On this day I had left them for an hour or so while investigating a party of Wynoochee River picnickers and their lunch. When I returned, I found that Baby had led the others astray and was eating the marijuana again. She knew she was not supposed to do that.

Quickly and quietly I came in from behind and a bit to the left, and slammed my shoulder hard into Baby's flank. She was caught completely by surprise this time and fell over, then thrashed clumsily to her feet and darted off uphill, bleating in terror. Thing One and Thing Two scrambled up the slope behind her, kicking dirt and gravel in my face. I lunged past the kids and snapped toothlessly at Baby's throat to keep her moving to the right and toward home. This whole area was off-limits to her. It was Weyerhaeuser timberland which had been clear-cut and planted six years before, and the new fir trees were just the right size to hide Mooney's marijuana from casual aerial surveillance. She had planted ten weeks previously, during the time of warm spring rains, and now her crop was almost ready to harvest. After I had Baby moving properly I circled back to round up Corney and Capri, but for a wonder I found those two bumping briskly along behind us as if tethered. Couldn't believe it. Mooney assures me that goats are flocking animals which naturally stay together, but she's not the one who has to run them down when they forget. Not that I have anything against chasing the odd goat from time to time, mind you. I mentioned that before. But still, the creatures can be rather trying when the mood strikes them. Even slugs like Capri and Corny could make trouble for me by pretending to be spooked by some silly little thing, and then flying off simultaneously in opposite directions.

This time my herd came together effortlessly, and stayed that way. Very strange. I snorted the dust from my nose and checked carefully for scents. Nothing directly upwind besides the goats in front of me. I would have noticed anything else right away. Downwind was the area we had just left. I worked my way crosswind and up the slope, pushing under a dense vine maple thicket to break through directly onto the ridge top. It was just a little ridge, and only took a moment to climb. A scent hit me and I froze, stomach clenched. My neck and shoulders tingled as the fur lifted. It was human urine I smelled—male human—and not from anyone I knew. I remained frozen for a minute, then relaxed. The urine scent was close by, but the man was not. Bruised fir needles revealed the path by which he had come and gone. I followed that trail for a short distance, sniffing carefully to eliminate any possibility of error, then returned to the ridge top. In typical human fashion the man had piddled away his entire allotment in one spot. I marked there too, then moved over to an area where the grass and dirt had been flattened suspiciously. There I scented gun oil and leather, old burned gunpowder, Tide detergent from the clothes, fresh sweat, fir and hemlock sap, other plant juices—all the usual one would expect from a police officer hiking through heavy brush. The man had not come to that place by accident.

I brought the goats straight home, and found Mooney out working her raspberry fields. She was sweaty and dirty and smelled wonderful. I put my paws on her shoulders and tried to lick her face, but she pushed me away so I dropped down and licked her ankles instead. They tasted as good as they smelled—rich and sour and salty, with just a trace of camomile shampoo. Humans taste the best of any animal except horses. Maybe it's the salt.

Mooney knelt down and rubbed my ears and neck affectionately. "What's up, Stinkylips? You're home early."

I don't like that name. I am very clean, including my mouth. I just happen to enjoy some things Mooney disapproves of. "Nark was here," I said shortly. Those words were easy, and came out clearly. Some other words are impossible to pronounce properly because of the *p* and *b* sounds, which come out as *pff* or worse. In those days, without my teeth, I also had trouble with *th*. Yes, I know: talking is also not a natural thing for a coyote to do. I never spoke to anyone except Mooney.

Mooney stood up suddenly. Humans always do that when they're worried or surprised. "Show me the place," she said.

I described the scents and pointed out the path taken, and Mooney agreed it had to be a government agent rather than a hiker or pot freeloader.

She had been growing grass on the Olympic Peninsula for many years, and had quite a bit of experience with these things.

Mooney's crop was a constant worry to her, and I often wished she would give it up. I couldn't understand what was so attractive about the plants. They're pleasantly musky and resinous—nice to roll in but not much good to eat. I ate a young plant once anyway, and it made me dizzy and a little sick. Then I fell asleep.

I know humans like to smoke and eat pot. Mooney tried to explain to me that our crop was very special because it was organically grown, but I couldn't see what was so special about that. Our raspberries were organic too, and they tasted just the same as Mr. Bell's. Mr. Bell was our neighbor and enemy, and his garden was very definitely not organic, although he used plenty of cow manure. Mr. Bell was a dairyman.

Mooney and I looked out over her secret fields that were no longer secret, and I could feel her distress. She was going to lose her crop, and that would be a disaster for her. I had asked her before why she grew so much, far more than she could use for herself or give away to friends. Mooney had tried to explain about property taxes, repossession, income from raspberry sales and duty to the land, and it had made no sense to me at first.

Over time I came to understand bits and pieces, and finally the whole situation, more or less. It's like this: Mooney's full name is Monica Eve Sklarsen, which means a lot to the other humans around us. It seems that Sunbow is actually part of a rather large piece of land which Mooney had inherited from her grandfather. Part of his personal estate, not the logging company he founded. The land is all surveyed now, but the original grant had specified the entire drainage of Fry Creek. That area is over fifteen square miles, and most of it old growth timber. Mooney owned the land, but the money she had inherited with it had been used up paying estate taxes and establishing the commune, and she had nothing left with which to pay property taxes. Mooney's raspberry fields earned enough for living expenses, but her tax bill was monstrous, and raspberry money was not nearly enough to deal with it. She was compelled to grow pot in order to make up the difference.

That concept gave me a particularly hard time. I couldn't understand why it was necessary for Mooney to break one law in order to obey another one. Personally, I don't bother much with laws.

'Mooney's Wood' was quite a wild place. She didn't even know it very well herself. It missed being logged in the early 1900s because it was too rugged to be attractive at the time, and also because it developed a reputation for being a place of bad luck. 'Death Creek,' they called it, and several different companies tried the land before moving on to easier country up-valley. Before the second wave of logging began, Mooney's grandfather bought it for a very nice price and decided to keep it undisturbed for possible future use. The land never brought bad luck to old man Sklarsen or his granddaughter, but then neither of them had tried to log it.

There were areas in there where I was afraid to go without a human for protection, but which were too tangled for a human to push through easily. I was afraid because of the cougars. Our undisturbed forest was the center of a highly prized territory, and was always occupied by the meanest and strongest. Cougars eat coyotes if they can catch them. I sometimes thought I might take a small radio with me so that the voices would scare the cougars away, but Mooney didn't have one like that, and she wouldn't buy me one. I was keeping an eye out on my picnic raids, but hadn't found the right kind yet. I had already checked Mr. Bell's place without success.

Enough daydreaming. I nuzzled Mooney's hand. "Will he pffe pffack?" By habit I used the proper ear positions to specify 'be back' rather than the various alternatives, but Mooney didn't bother to look. She didn't need that extra help any more. Always knew what I was trying to say.

"He'll be back," Mooney said. "And soon, too. They'll rip out the whole lot." Her voice was raw, but she was not going to let herself cry. Not yet.

I stood silently beside Mooney, shoulder pressed lightly against her hip, and waited for her to decide what to do. We had a good view from where we were standing. Fir trees studded the land below us and to our left, widely spaced and all the same size. They were twice as tall as Mooney, but rather thin and ragged-looking, and the spaces between them were thick with wildflowers, blackberries and red alder seedlings in various stages of development. All the larger alders had been cut down recently, to keep them from shading out the firs, but the blackberries were doing just fine. To our right sprawled last year's clear-cut, shocked and dry and dead, with its splintered stumps, fresh burn pile circles, and evenly spaced, almost invisible fir seedlings tucked carefully into the rubble.

Not far behind us, Mooney's Wood was so tall it was like a hill made out of living trees. When she was ready, we walked back that way.

Chapter 2

Usually I would help Mooney with her evening chores. I made sure all the chickens were locked into their coyote- and fox- and bobcat- and raccoon- and weasel- and otter-proof coop. I made sure that any spilled goat milk was cleaned up, and licked the bucket, too. I gave advice and sometimes even made a joke, although Mooney actually did most of the talking. This time we were both quiet, and worked faster than usual. It was still quite light when we finished, with summer days being so long and all.

I tried to nap while Mooney washed up and fixed dinner, but she kept banging things more than she needed to and I couldn't sleep properly, so I went outside until she called for me. We had our usual tofu and vegetables stir-fried with sesame oil and brown rice (with fish sauce for me), but this time we had a special treat: the first of our own sweet corn crop. Mooney had to slit open the kernels for me with a sharp knife, but then I could gum and lick out the insides easily enough. I love sweet corn, but Mooney's distress had caused my appetite to disappear, and I only ate to be polite. Dusk had arrived by the time we were done.

Mooney began to collect dishes and stack them on the counter, but then she stopped and became very still. Finally she straightened herself in that way which meant she was about to say something important. "We're going to harvest the crop and take it to North River tonight," she announced quietly.

Okay. I tried to look alert and respectful, and waited for further information. We always harvested at night, but it took us several nights to finish, and we usually had a little help from our friends.

"We'll need to do it without lights, so you'll have to find the plants for me, and you'll also need to help me drag them back to the van. I want to start as soon as possible. Is anyone still in the area?"

I keep track of the coming and going of cars without even thinking about it. I had heard two cars that morning, but both were gone now and no new ones had come in. "All clear now," I said, and stepped over to the dog door.

"Wait a minute," Mooney said. "I need to tie up my hair and change my clothes again. I have some special, brand new clothes and shoes I want to wear."

"I thought you said you were ready!"

"No. I said I wanted to start as soon as possible."

"Yes, Mooney."

Weyerhaeuser makes very nice logging roads. We all use them—deer, elk, cougars, coyotes, and humans. If you have the right gate keys you can go almost anywhere in a Volkswagen van.

Moon had set early, and Mooney can't see very well by starlight alone, even bright starlight. She can walk along a road by herself, but rough ground is too much for her, so she had to grip the loose skin between my shoulders and follow along while I scented out new marijuana plants for her to cut and bundle. I would hesitate for a moment when we came to things she could trip over, so she knew when to lift her feet.

There's a special look to the stars on a clear night when Moon is not out. Your eyes can really open up, and you see things that aren't there any other time. Look between the stars and there are more stars without end, so that the whole sky is clotted, glowing milk. The Milky Way itself seems solid, like you could climb up onto it if there were something tall enough to get you started. Even now I still try, sometimes.

It was full summer, so this night was short and not really that dark. Not for me, at least. Sun had barely slipped below the horizon, and the Milky Way competed with a wash of evening glow in the northwest, which moved slowly to the north and then northeast as we worked. But, of course, by then it wasn't evening glow any more, it was morning glow, and we were almost out of time.

The van was full anyway—tires nearly flat with the weight of it, and inside packed so tightly I thought the door latches might pop open. The whole roof was loaded with tightly strapped-down, canvas-covered plants. Mooney's gloves were falling apart and my fur was sticky with marijuana sap, and the thick smell of it clogged my nose, too, so that finding new plants had become difficult for me.

We had done what we could. I was lying on my side and Mooney was sitting with her back against a van wheel when I heard the crunch of a foot on loose gravel. The noise was downwind from us, so I couldn't scent what sort of animal had made it.

It might have been a deer.

It might have been, but it wasn't. I knew that from the first. We had been making a steady, subdued noise with our harvest operations, and the noise had come from downwind. I couldn't believe a wild animal would visit us in that way. I didn't stop to think, just jumped up and said something—I don't remember what—and Mooney grabbed hold of my shoulder skin again.

I pulled Mooney downslope and away from the van as fast as she would go. Half-carried her, in fact. The young fir trees were too small and scattered to provide good cover for us, but the blackberries between them still caught at Mooney's legs, several times tripping her so that her full weight slammed down onto my back. I'm strong enough for that sort of thing, but it does slow me down, and we were still uncomfortably close to Mooney's van when the police made their move.

Brightness exploded behind and around us, sending fir tree shadows lancing ahead. As one, we stepped into the closest shadow and lay down. Mooney and I wiggled under the fir tree and looked back to where we had been, and the light was so strong it hurt me. There must have been at least four spotlights trained on that van.

An amplified voice roared to life, commanding immediate surrender with hands on head and no sudden moves, just like in the movies. When no such thing happened the voice continued talking, but two of the light beams left the van to dart aggressively through the tree farm, sweeping along and then reversing or stopping suddenly in no way that I could predict. Police radios began to chatter in that intimidating way they have, and a police car edged up to our van like a farm dog inspecting one's throat. Mooney and I crouched down lower, waiting to see what would happen next, and that was a mistake. We should have been quietly getting out of there.

One of the lights happened to catch me directly in the eyes. It stopped there. My head was filled with its brilliance and I couldn't see anything else. I know it sounds stupid, but I just lay there for a moment staring straight back at that thing.

I heard voices talking: "... eyes out there, probably a raccoon or coyote or something ..." and then I panicked. I whipped around and lunged away from the lights, then found that my eyes had been dazzled and I couldn't see any more. I pushed and tripped and crashed ahead anyway. I heard a gunshot, and then angry voices, so I aimed myself in the opposite direction—away from the noises and away from the light.

The shot was not repeated, but that light clung to me relentlessly, blasting me with a brilliance so powerful I could see nothing else. I kept the light behind me, and repeatedly I threw myself sideways to shake it off, but the thing just would not be left behind. I kept trying, though, and finally stumbled onto a steep slope that felt like it might lead to safety. I turned that way, began to scramble and slide sharply downward, and then the light was gone. I was in a place where it could not reach. My eyes were still too dazzled to see anything, but this time I forced myself to stop running.

I lay down shaking and panting, head and neck pressed tightly into the dirt, ears flicking apprehensively to every small sound or imagined sound.

The light hesitated on the brush above me for a time and moved on. It did not come back.

In a few minutes my night vision and some of my sanity returned to me. I had blackberry scratches on my nose and tongue, but no other physical injuries. Mentally I was a mess. I wanted to run back to the house and wait there for Mooney, but I was too terrified even to do that. I just lay there, trembling.

After quite a long time I heard surreptitious noises approaching me through the brush. The noises were caused by a human. A single human. I could tell that easily enough, even with the wind coming wrong. Nothing moves through brush quite so clumsily as a human. This one was trying very hard to be stealthy, however. It was moving slowly, and stopping frequently, and it was not coming from the direction of the van. I kept my ears turned toward the source of those sounds and prepared myself to move on. If the man came close I would run again, but this time I would not look toward any lights, and I would not stop for anything.

The approaching human was not coming directly toward me, and it stopped whenever the lights came near. Finally, during one of the pauses I heard a very soft whisper: "Stinky, are you there?"

That name sounded beautiful to me, this time. The most glorious word ever uttered by a human throat. I glided silently to where the voice had come from and found Mooney creeping forward on hands and knees, hesitant and lost. I slipped up from behind and bumped her shoulder gently with my own, and she jerked and fell over and almost cried out, then grabbed and hugged me so hard I fell over too. She smelled as scared as I did, and her hands and knees smelled bloody.

"They shot at you!" Mooney whisper-raged. "Are you hurt?" I didn't say anything, but wiggled out of her hug and then pushed up under her arm to get her standing again. She clamped my head in the crook her arm for a second and shook me, then creakily rose to her feet, and we moved on downslope in our customary guide dog fashion. Only it was not quite so dark now. Soon the people behind us wouldn't be needing lights any more.

Normally we would have walked right up to the house without thinking about it. Mooney didn't use her yard lights because they hurt my eyes, and in my entire life we had never had a human intruder on our property. By this time we were both beginning to feel rather paranoid, though, so Mooney stopped us when we were quite a ways off, and I left her behind to make a slow spiral inward, checking for scents.

Two men were waiting there for us, both so well hidden I would never have found them except by scent. One was just inside the front door of the goat barn and the second was under the hydrangea bush by the back porch. That was a good hiding spot. One of my favorites.

I went back to report to Mooney and receive her instructions. I could help with the seeing and smelling and hearing, but I had no clue about what to do next. This mess was far too complicated for me to figure out.

Mooney explained, "If I'm caught walking around on a night when my van is found loaded to the scuppers with pot, it'll be hard to account for things no matter what I say, but if I can just get into the house or out of this area, I can claim the van was stolen and I didn't know about it. Since we never dry or store any pot here, the police may not be able to put a case together."

This seemed a bit far-fetched to me. Mooney stank of marijuana resin, and she had left her own scent all over the area we had harvested. Still, she was the boss. I kept my mouth shut and waited for more specific advice.

"If you create a diversion, I may be able to get inside without being noticed. You're sure there's no one else hidden?"

"I can't tell sthat for sure," I replied carefully. "Scents don't pffass easily sthrough windows, even when sthey're opffen, so sthere could pffe someone inside sthe house. I can make a noise at the osther side of sthe pffarn. Do you sthink sthe man will shoot at me?" One bullet had already missed me that night, and I was not eager to put myself at risk again. Bullets don't always miss. I knew that by personal experience, because Mr. Bell had shot me the year before when he saw me investigating a dead calf of his. There had been no pain at first, only a sharp slap to the throat and a whistling sound in the ears—that sweet singing whistle which means a bullet has come looking for you, and maybe even found you. A second later had come the crack of a rifle shot from the direction of Mr. Bell's house. Luckily that bullet had passed through a fold of skin and done little damage, but how many more times could I be lucky?

Mooney tried to reassure me that policemen are really not supposed to discharge their weapons at noises in the dark, and the earlier shot had been a mistake. Her words lacked conviction, but I didn't argue with her. What else was there to do? "It's not dangerous for me," I lied, "I do sthis sort of sthing all sthe time! Even if sthe man does shoot, I won't pffe where he's aiming. I pffromise."

"Yeah, sure," Mooney muttered. We began to prepare for our diversion.

I brought Mooney as close to the back door as we dared. There she took off her clothes and gloves and shoes, tied them into a tight bundle, and handed them over to me. "Bury these in a place where they'll never be found," she said. "If I'm taken away, stay nearby and keep out of sight. I'll send a friend to take care of the animals. Now—go on with you, and don't do anything stupid. And good luck!"

My mouth was full with Mooney's bundle so I didn't answer her in words—just bumped my shoulder lightly against her hip, growled once, softly, and trotted off. I've always been good at skulking, and I enjoy it. It's only the bullets that scare me.

Silently I left Mooney behind and circled around to the back door of the goat barn. I set down the bundle and stood there for a time, listening to the man. He was surprisingly quiet. All I heard were breathing sounds, and one time the faint creak of leather on leather.

Time to move. Mooney will do something stupid if you don't. I scuffed my feet on hard-packed dirt and scratched the door once, lightly. Then I grabbed the latch with my mouth and slid it back quietly, but not too quietly. Even a human would be able to hear the faint grinding sound of rusty metal on metal, followed by a clunk as the bar hit its stop. I paused for a moment, then slowly pulled the door outward, keeping my body hidden behind it in case another one of those super-powered flashlights came on. With the door half open, I let go of the latch and pressed my chin to the ground, then snaked my head and neck around the edge for a quick peek.

The man was crouched stiffly with head and body turned my way but not oriented on me. He had a gun in one hand and an unlit flashlight in the other, and both hands were shaking. I don't think he could actually see more than a vague outline of brightness where the open door was. Baby and the other goats were awake and nervous, but I don't think even they could see me. Human and goat fear-scent filled the barn.

While remaining safely outside, I shouldered the door slowly closed again, and refastened the latch. I hoped it would seem as if someone had quietly entered the goat barn and closed the door behind himself.

My plan worked. The barn exploded with brightness the instant that latch clicked shut. Light stabbed outward through every crack and knothole, and a very loud, nervous voice called out, "Freeze!" The man's voice cracked a bit at the end, making his command come out a little squeaky, but it really was quite impressive. If I had been in the barn with him I most assuredly would have frozen, but I wasn't, so I didn't. Instead I snatched up my bundle and ran very fast away from there. I was pleased and grateful to find that Mooney was right about the gunshots. There weren't any, although there was quite a bit of shouting.

When I was well clear, and had buried the clothes, I hurried over to the Bell place because it was the best spot to let me see what was going on at Sunbow. My tail was up and I bubbled with merriment and pride at my cleverness. Nice diversion! Mooney would have had plenty of opportunity to stroll on into the house.

I angled over to Mr. Bell's back porch so I could pee inside his boots again if they had been left out. After I healed from my bullet wound I had taken up the hobby of tormenting Mr. Bell in any way I could think of, and the boot trick was just one of my ideas. It was a good one except that Mr. Bell blamed his hound dog Jake instead of me. Of course, that wasn't really a problem because Jake and I hated each other too, and if he got in trouble that was fine by me. I hopped up onto the porch, and stopped. Mr. Bell's boots were there, sure enough, but they were no longer of interest to me. A stranger had been sitting on the porch swing. A stranger, but one I had smelled before. It was the same man who had spied on our pot patch.

Hastily I left the porch and moved on to a bramble-covered trash pile I knew of, and settled myself under a bent panel of corrugated metal. In that position I was hidden from every angle except for a clear view of home. I watched anxiously, no longer so sure of myself. I had never thought that Mr. Bell might be involved in all of this! Betrayal is impossible without trust, but still I felt betrayed. Silly of me.

At Sunbow, both humans were still searching the premises—waving flashlights, talking on their radios, and generally making a fuss. That meant the back porch man had left his post as Mooney had assured me he would. It had become so bright out, I wondered why they even bothered with the lights.

An upstairs bedroom window flashed into brightness and Mooney's voice came to me: "Hey! You! Get off my land this instant! I've already called the Sheriff, and I've got a dog and a shotgun in here too! You hear me? Move along! Now!"

As planned, Mooney was pretending that she had been in the house all night and was only now becoming aware that people were on her property. Her voice sounded sleepy, and scared, and angry—convincing even to me, and I had quite a bit of experience with such communications. The men should leave now, quietly and without fuss. I always did.

"*We* are the police, and *you* are under arrest!" I heard those words clearly enough, but after that the voices quieted down so I couldn't make them out any more. I began to worry. What if Mooney had made a mistake? Our house could be a trap for her!

Cars raced up our driveway and skidded to a halt in our yard, and men jumped out to crouch behind them with guns drawn. The voices became loud again, and I heard Mooney say something about a warrant. One of the new people replied that if Mooney continued to resist arrest they would be forced to use their weapons.

Mooney came out of the house with her hands on top of her head, and almost every man had a gun pointed at her. She was grabbed and handcuffed, and pushed into one of the cars. She didn't struggle.

It was not supposed to happen like this! Not like this. I found myself whining softly with each breath. I kept licking my nose in distraction— couldn't make myself stop. My neck hurt, and I shook all over, and I just didn't know what to do. Men ran into our house with guns still drawn, and more cars arrived, and Mooney was taken away. The men were there for hours, and no one even let the goats and chickens out. Finally all but one of them went away.

Jake could smell that I was nearby, and kept sniffing around and wuffling, but the numb-nose never did find me. I stayed where I was all through that day, confused and shocked—lay there in the dry dirt, watching the farm and panting from the heat of the roofing tin close above my head. I hardly even snapped at the deer flies—mostly just let them bite. There were no tears, of course. Tears are for humans.

At dusk another vehicle came. One I recognized. It was John Cultee's old white International pickup, this time with the camper shell on it.

John was my favorite of Mooney's friends. He had never actually lived at Sunbow, but he came to visit almost every weekend, and he had been around as long as I could remember.

John was tall, even for a human, and towered over me. He was heavy, too, and he had straight black hair he kept in a ponytail. He had a tremendous force of personality. When I was very young I would show my belly when we greeted, and even piddle a bit despite myself. That was something I never did for anyone else besides Mooney.

There was something about John and Mooney that distinguished them from other humans. It was not simply that they were family. They both had a Presence to them that sometimes made other humans uncomfortable. The other humans didn't seem to be fully aware of it, but I was. I could sense either of them from several yards away regardless of sight, sound, or scent. I was not uncomfortable, though. They were mine, and I was theirs, and that was all I needed to know. I think there may have been something about me that affected them in much the same way.

Hearing John's truck was the first good thing that had happened to me since dawn. I straightened up and whined quietly, but stayed where I was. I needed to remain hidden until he made the Sheriff, or deputy, or policeman, or whatever, go away. Besides, I was very close to Mr. Bell's house, and I didn't want to play the target practice game any more. Better to wait until dark.

John's truck bounced to a stop at the police barricade, and he stepped out to talk to the man for a moment. Then he got back into his truck and drove away.

He drove away! John didn't wave his arms or shout, so I didn't have a clue about what was said. He just left.

Depression paralyzed me again. Listlessly I forced myself to review exit routes one more time as if it really mattered, but then a new thing caught my attention—brought my head up and ears stiffly forward. It was not a sound, but rather the lack of a sound. I couldn't hear the International any longer.

John's truck has a distinctive sound suggestive of a much larger vehicle, and it always seems in need of a new muffler. On a quiet day I can hear it for a couple of miles, sometimes farther. I had been subliminally aware of the sound fading away in the usual manner, but then it had stopped abruptly. John had shut down the engine and he was still nearby. He wanted me to find him!

I forgot my clever escape routes and popped straight out into the open, tearing across Mr. Bell's south pasture in flagrantly full view. Jake saw me and gave chase, but he didn't have a chance of catching me. In a couple of minutes Jake and the dairy and Sunbow had all been left behind.

I'm a very good runner. John has clocked me at forty-six miles per hour, and on dirt roads with chuckholes I can beat a car—sometimes for just a couple of minutes, sometimes forever. It depends on how many chuckholes there are. I knew where John had to be, and I was halfway there before I began to slow down. I left the road then and continued overland and in concealment the rest of the way. I had a decidedly mixed reputation at Wynoochee Wildwood, and never showed myself there by daylight.

Wynoochee Wildwood is a private campground which is always partly empty, even when the weather is warm. When I found John he was setting up camp in one of the more secluded rental spaces. He had already started a fire, and was pitching a tent even though he usually slept in the camper or on the ground. The tent and his truck had been cleverly positioned to provide a very effective privacy screen. He really was expecting me!

As John tightened the last tent line I slunk in from behind and rubbed up against the backs of his legs. It didn't seem to surprise him. He turned around and knelt down to greet me but I just stood there and looked at him with head, ears, and tail down.

John shuffled forward on his knees, then settled himself cross-legged and reached over to stroke my neck and chin. I put my head in his lap and collapsed.

"Sin-Ka-Lip, Sin-Ka-Lip. You will be okay. Mooney will be okay. Be patient."

John began to sing quietly, one of his shaman songs. I don't remember his words now, but at the time they seemed utterly interesting, and they went on for a long while. When the singing ended I remained motionless with my eyes closed, finally at peace. Perhaps I slept.

"Are you thirsty? I have water in the truck."

Those words snapped me to alertness again, and I scrambled hastily to my feet.

"Sorry, Coyote. I didn't mean to startle you like that."

Thirsty. How could I have forgotten that? John fetched water and a bowl, and it was good. Very, very good. I drank as he poured—took in a quart before stopping to breathe properly.

I settled myself upright with the pan between my front legs, and watched John while he finished making camp. When he brought the grocery bag into view, I lost interest in the water and pushed my head inside as soon as he set the bag down. My nose had already told me what was inside.

Fresh bread and raw steaks—plenty of both. I took mine straight from the wrappers. John cooked his meat.

While waiting for John to finish his meal, I began to lick myself clean —first time that day I had felt the urge to take care of myself. Had to quit, though. Too much marijuana sap. Better to start with a swim in the river. As usual, John seemed to know ahead of time what I wanted, and when the darkness had grown deep enough we slipped off to an empty stretch of riverbank far away from any lighted campsites.

My summer coat is not as nice-looking as I like, but at least it's easy to clean. John helped me with my head and neck, washed himself, and then challenged me to a game of water tag. I won, of course. After that I led him back to his tent, groomed myself properly, and curled up for sleep. Slept in the tent this time.

I awoke well before dawn, rested and strong. Ready to think again. John was asleep so I edged over and nuzzled his neck, just behind the right ear. He pushed my head away and burrowed deeper into his sleeping bag, but I found the zipper and pulled it slowly back all the way to its end, then gave a quick tug to lay the bag open like a razor clam shell, with him the meat inside.

John cursed me competently but without anger and then sat himself upright, rubbing his eyes. He smelled like clean, warm human. No soap, no deodorant, no smoke, and no bug repellent. Too bad they're not like that all the time. I pushed forward to lick his face enthusiastically, then presented myself for an ear scratch. John complied.

"So what are you going to do now, Stinky? I gave goat and chicken care instructions to the deputy when he wouldn't let me in, and I told him an Animal Control officer and reporter would be coming by later to check on him. I don't think he believed me, but it should motivate him to do at least some sort of care. Mooney is going to be pissed." John lifted my chin until our eyes met, and paused as if waiting for an answer from me.

I didn't answer, but I did look him in the eyes for a time. Then I sagged down and presented my belly for rubbing. I had never talked to anyone besides Mooney. I let her teach me to read but I never talked, no matter what the temptation. I don't know why. It's one of the things that made Mooney so crazy. Mooney shared our conversations with John and a few others, but I think only John actually believed her. He had always treated me as a thinking creature, and I appreciated it. If I ever got around to talking to other humans, I would start with him.

"Mooney wasn't able to talk to me in private," John continued. "All she would say was that she had been feeling bad the day before, got a little drunk, and went to bed early. Then at the crack of dawn a small army of police and federal agents assaulted her home and arrested her at gunpoint without a warrant. The ACLU attorney is lapping it all up."

"So what really happened—hmmm?" John was rubbing my belly way down low. One of my favorite spots.

What the hell. Now seemed as good a time as any to break tradition. I rolled to my feet and nudged open the tent screen zipper. "I need to go pffee," I told it softly.

I didn't talk again until John had taken me far away from Wynoochee Wildwood. We were walking Sklarsen Company land, well north, near the Matlock turnoff. Some fine trees there, maybe seventy years since the last cutting. John and I pretended not to notice the brand new survey stakes we passed. Those trees would be gone soon, but there was nothing we could do about it.

When I'm walking with humans I like to splash through and lap at all the puddles we pass. It's something to do while waiting for them to catch up. This time all the chuckhole puddles were dry, but there were a few scum-covered seeps and springs along the roadside. Mooney hates to see me drink dirty water—says I'll catch all sorts of horrible diseases. John is much more reasonable, and he walks faster too.

John walked, and I ran ahead and sideways and back again until I felt tired enough to be comfortable with his pace. I was panting a bit, and had mud and foam on my chin, so I slipped up behind and nuzzled him to rub it off on his shirt.

"Someone found our pffot pffatch," I said at last, walking beside John and looking straight ahead to avoid his eyes. We were on a straight, level stretch of road with fir and hemlock branches from both sides meeting far overhead. The road smelled of dust, and dry moss, and old coyote shit. No one I knew.

"Mooney said we needed to harvest right away. We worked all night and filled sthe van, pffut sthen we were almost caught. I sthink it was a trapff."

I moved my ears forward for *p* and backward for *b* in the usual manner, hoping Mooney might have explained about the ear positions as pronunciation aids. I was hoping even more that John would forbear from asking those stupid questions movie-humans come up with when an animal first talks to them.

John did well with that part, all in all. He kept on walking, also looking straight ahead, seeming quite calm except for the sudden sharp thrill-spike in his scent. After a time he murmured "Traff? Sorry, but I didn't quite catch that. What's a traff?"

"Not traff. Trapff."

"Sorry guy, still can't quite—"

"***Trapff***. Tra...pfffff. A trick."

"Ah. Got it now. Why do you feel it was a trap?"

"I didn't hear any cars coming. Sthe men were just sthere. Sthey must have pffen hiding somewhere. Maypffe sthey were at Mr. Pffell's house. One of sthem was on his pfforch. I could smell it."

"Mr. Bell doesn't love us. That's for sure. I guess this means Mooney will have to give up her pot business."

No more marijuana for Mooney to fret over! My tail lifted at the thought, but then it sagged back down to touch the ground. "Mooney is in jail! Who cares apffout sthe damn pffot?"

"Oh, don't worry about Mooney. She'll most likely be out today or tomorrow. From what I could tell, they found a few good clues but blew it all when they arrested her without a warrant. The Sheriff had gone to her house earlier in the evening, but assumed it was vacant when no one answered the door. He put two deputies in charge of guarding it, and they reported that one person attempted to approach the house just before dawn, but got away. Mooney came to the window when they started making noise with their search, so she must have been there all night after all. Good thing, too! They have men and dogs searching the whole lower valley." He paused a moment, then asked, "You're sure there were no helpers?"

"Sthere were no helpffers, just me and Mooney. We heard sthe men coming, and ran away. Mooney said if she could get pffack inside sthe house wisthout pffeing seen, she would pffe safe. Pffut sthey took her aaanywaay!" I was starting to whine a little, so I stopped talking then. John doesn't like whining.

"But Mooney's plan did work! They've weakened their case by arresting her improperly, and there are two police witnesses who will have to testify that she was in her house the whole time when the pot harvesting was going on. How did you do it?"

Bewildered, but beginning to feel more hopeful, I explained about our diversion tactic and my removal of clothes and shoes and gloves to a safe place.

"You said Mooney used all new clothes and shoes for the harvesting? That's perfect! Mooney is no dummy. She knew footprint and fiber analysis would lead to dead ends that way. DNA analysis and fingerprints will show Mooney used things in the van, but not when she did so."

John continued to discuss our situation in considerable detail, but I was soon lost. I wasn't completely sure what DNA was, but it didn't seem very useful to me. Mooney had left a strong body scent all over everything, and now John said they would have trouble proving she was even there! This was all a bit beyond me, so I didn't say any more about it. John was here, and he seemed pleased enough. If he was satisfied, so was I.

Mooney would be coming back! John had said so. All I had to do was wait and be patient. I walked on in silence but with a bounce to my steps, and with tail held high. High for a coyote, anyway. We tend to be somewhat modest that way. John walked silently beside me, and after a time he asked if I had any more questions.

"Can we eat lunch yet? And... can you tell me a story?"

John stopped walking and stared down at me. "I didn't know you liked my stories."

"You know I always listen when you tell stories for Mooney. I never make noise or leave sthe room until you're done, and I watch you sthe whole time. Sometimes I tell Mooney what stories to ask for. She's told you sthat herself."

"I thought it was a game she was playing with me," John replied sheepishly. "I should have known better. What story would you like?"

"I need to hear a story apffout Coyote. Sthe first one. Mooney says sthat I'm sthe original, real Coyote. If she's right, I need to know what I'm like."

"You don't need a story for that. You are what you are. Besides, you've heard them all before." John was smiling now, like he had made a joke of some sort.

"I might have forgotten something, or want to ask a question. And anyway, you never tell sthem sthe same way twice. Maypffe sthis time you'll get one right." I was smiling now too, and I bumped my shoulder playfully against his thigh. John bumped back, so I whipped around and nipped at his ankles until he couldn't walk properly any more.

John stopped walking, but otherwise ignored my teasing. He selected a particular spot in the center of the road, brushed it smooth, shrugged off his pack, and sat down cross-legged. It was shady there, and had an acceptable breeze. Seemed as good a spot as any. I sat down on my haunches with tail curled around my feet and tried to look attentive and respectful.

John held silence to himself for a time, then began formally:

"This World was not empty when humans came to live here. It was occupied by the Animal People. We call them Animal People because they often took the shape of animals, but they could take on other forms as well. Often they looked much like humans do today. Often they acted like humans, too—foolish and quarrelsome.

"Sin-Ka-Lip was the worst of them. Even his name was a term of contempt. It means 'The Imitator'. Sin-Ka-Lip didn't choose that name for himself, of course. Others called him that.

"Sin-Ka-Lip was lazy, vain, selfish, gluttonous, and far too horny for his own good—probably the most human-like of all the Animal People, although his preferred form was the coyote. He probably looked just like you, except that his eyes were not slanted then, and his mouth was filled with lovely, smooth, strong teeth."

John leaned toward me and flaunted a wide, toothy smile. Then he settled back and continued with his story.

"Spirit Chief was keeper of the creatures of our own World, including the Animal People. He was often presented with problems to judge, but he was wise and patient, and was usually able to show the Animal People how to solve these problems for themselves. Over time, most of the Animal People learned that one of the best ways to stay out of trouble was to stay away from Sin-Ka-Lip.

"Sin-Ka-Lip was not well liked, and for good reason. When troubles were brought to Spirit Chief for solution, Sin-Ka-Lip was often involved. He often played cruel jokes, which would sometimes even result in the death of the victim. Sin-Ka-Lip thought those were especially funny. It should be added, of course, that people in those days didn't take death as seriously as we do now. Sin-Ka-Lip himself died many times, and was always brought back to life again by his brother, Fox.

"But I'm getting ahead of myself. This story is not about Sin-Ka-Lip getting killed. It's about the end of the World as it was when only the Animal People lived here. Spirit Chief called a council meeting to announce the news.

"'A new kind of people will be coming soon,' he proclaimed. 'They will look much like you do now. You are all in your soft, weak forms out of respect for this meeting. For now you have no claws, or beaks, or sharp teeth. The New People will be like this all the time. They will be very easy to kill, but you must not do that.

"'Hear me! You are commanded to help and protect these New People when they come. Some of you have names now, and some do not, but tomorrow all will be required to choose. You will hold forever the names and animal forms that suit you best, and your children will fill the Earth.

"'Tomorrow at dawn you will begin choosing names and natures. I will give each of you Medicine Power and show you the work you must do. Choose well, for you and your children will live with this choice forever.'

"The Animal People were astonished by this news, and talked of it endlessly. Most were excited and curious, and eager to take their assigned places in the new World, but some were jealous and angry, and vowed they would destroy the New People when they came.

"Sin-Ka-Lip had no wish to destroy the New People, but he certainly had no desire to be called 'Sin-Ka-Lip' forever. He hated that name, and the way everyone avoided him and said bad things about him. He vowed he would be first to meet with Spirit Chief, and would choose a different name.

"'I will become Eagle,' he proclaimed loudly. 'I will soar above the mountains and none will be able to follow. I will be ruler of the birds. Maybe I will choose to become Grizzly Bear, who will rule the four-footed people, or Salmon, who will be chief of all fishes.'

"Fox made fun of Sin-Ka-Lip's grand words. 'My dear Brother, I know you too well. You'll probably sleep late and get last choice of all the names. But don't worry. People despise your name, and no one will take it. Your proper name will be waiting for you, no matter when you show up. You had better go to bed now if you want to have any hope of getting up early.'

"Sin-Ka-Lip became angry then, and stalked off home. He decided he would not sleep at all that night. That way there would be no chance of being late. He was determined to be the very first one to see Spirit Chief in the morning.

"Halfway through the night Sin-Ka-Lip became very sleepy. He would stand up and walk around, but his eyelids drooped downward again the moment he stopped moving. 'I will *not* let myself sleep!' he muttered fiercely. He whipped his head around and bit his tongue and paws to keep himself awake, but his eyes still kept closing whenever he stopped for a moment. Finally, in frustration, he picked up two small sticks and jammed them between his eyelids to keep them braced apart. The sticks hurt terribly, but Sin-Ka-Lip forced himself to endure the pain. Soon his eyeballs began to itch and burn from drying out, so he put some grease on them.

"'There is no way I can fall asleep now,' he said to himself, and settled down to be as comfortable as possible. The sticks didn't hurt as much when he kept his eyes very still. After a short time Sin-Ka-Lip's breathing became soft, and quiet. He had fallen asleep with his eyes open.

"When Sin-Ka-Lip awoke it was bright outside, but too foggy to see where the sun was. He flicked the sticks out from between his eyelids, wiped away the grease, and looked around in sudden panic. What time was it? Frantically Sin-Ka-Lip ran to Spirit Chief's house. He arrived panting and wild, with foam on his muzzle. His eyes felt sore and very strange. The outer corners were still tucked upward where the sticks had forced them during the hours he had slept.

"Sin-Ka-Lip found Spirit Chief sitting all alone at the entrance to his house, and he spoke to him right away, without waiting for permission. Sin-Ka-Lip had never been very good at manners. 'I have come to choose a name for myself,' he proclaimed. 'I wish to be... Eagle!'

"'That name has been taken already.'

"Sin-Ka-Lip was stunned. He had thought he was the first to arrive! Where were all the others?

"'In that case, I choose the name Grizzly Bear.' Sin-Ka-Lip spoke more respectfully now, with his head and tail lowered a little.

"'That name also has been chosen.'

"A terrible suspicion was creeping into Sin-Ka-Lip's heart. 'Salmon?' he whispered apprehensively. His tail was on the ground, and he had lowered his ears completely.

"Spirit Chief replied gently, 'That name is taken as well. All the names except one have been claimed, and I think you know which one that is. You must keep your name, Sin-Ka-Lip. It is the right one for you. I made you sleep because I wanted you to be the last one here. You and the New People deserve each other. You have been chosen to be their Chief and Guide, for they know nothing of this World.

"'Protecting the New People will be a difficult job. Already they have enemies. I have called very strong Medicine for you, different from that which I have given to the others. This Medicine will aid you in ways none may expect.'

"With these words Spirit Chief extended his hand toward Sin-Ka-Lip to touch his heart and give him his Medicine Powers, but Sin-Ka-Lip was startled by the gesture. He thought for a moment Spirit Chief was getting ready to strike him, and so he threw himself onto his back, exposing his belly in submission, and the Medicine Powers sank into his bowels and genitals instead of his heart.

"Spirit Chief laughed. 'So that is where you wish to keep your Medicine Powers! So be it; that place is as good as any other. Go now with my blessing, and try to grow up a bit.'

"Sin-Ka-Lip slunk off, utterly speechless for once. It took him several minutes to realize that he had achieved his wish after all. He would be a Chief! A Very Important Person! And he would be chief over a naive and highly favored people entirely unaware of his reputation. Things were looking up.

"From that day on, Sin-Ka-Lip's eyes remained slanted up at the corners. He was upset by that at first, but soon he decided that on *him*, slanted eyes looked quite attractive.

"So... what do you think?" John interrupted himself. "Do you like your eyes the way they are now, or would you prefer them round and bulging, like a Cocker Spaniel's?"

John's voice had become hoarse, but I could tell he was faking it so he could use it as an excuse to end the story early. John's voice never gave out unless he wanted it to.

I shuffled forward and lay down with my head in his lap, looking straight upward with my attractively slanted eyes.

"You know what I like," I said softly. It didn't work this time. Story was over.

John stroked my head for a minute or so, then reached an arm back to drag his pack into view. "I have a phone call to make," he explained. "I promised Mooney's attorney I'd call at two for an update, and we still have to eat lunch, walk back to the truck, and find a phone."

"I can helpff wisth sthe lunch," I offered. I hoped John and Mooney really did have things under control.

We ate our lunch and walked back without further conversation, but when we reached the truck I braced myself to ask a question I had wondered about for a long time.

"Am I really magical?" I asked. "I mean, I can talk, and only humans can do sthat, so does it mean I have some sort of spffirit inside me sthat makes me sthe way I am?"

John leaned his back and neck against the truck and gazed up at the treetops for a time. "Do you believe in magic?" he asked carefully.

"Yes, of course. Doesn't everypffody?"

"Have you ever done or seen magic?"

"I don't sthink so. What is it like?"

"What do you dream about? Try to describe any conversations or encounters that you think might help me answer your question."

"I don't have any dreams. Everyone else talks apffout stheir dreams, pffut I'm not even sure what a dream is."

"You have dreams, Sin-Ka-Lip. You just don't remember them, and that is as it should be.

"I will tell you something about yourself. Before you were born, when you were still just a single cell, some extra DNA was inserted into you. This new material was intended to override certain segments of your original DNA, resulting in delayed maturation and aging, along with extra time for brain development, in a pattern similar to that found in human children. In fact, it was human DNA that was adapted for the purpose. The intent was to give your brain more time and opportunity to grow, possibly resulting in greater intelligence. An incidental effect would be a greatly increased life span."

The concept of DNA detection at crime sites was confusing to me, but I had watched enough cartoons to know all about super heroes with altered DNA structures. If that wasn't magic, it was just as good. The exact meaning of John's words had escaped me, but the reference to 'greater intelligence' seemed relevant enough: I already knew I was the smartest thing on four legs. I thought John was saying I didn't have Medicine Powers, but did have Cartoon Super Hero Powers. Would I begin to develop other special capabilities? Invisible would be nice, for starters.

I continued to fantasize until a new question came to me. "What apffout sthe osthers? Sthere must pffe osthers like me! Was sthe expfferiment hard to do?"

"There are no others," John replied in that same careful voice. "Many scientists worked on this project for many years, but without success. It is especially ironic that you, the only surviving product of the program, were not actually authorized. The intended test animals were beagles, not coyotes."

"Sthen where did I come from?" I asked in puzzlement. This was getting more confusing instead of less.

"I performed the DNA insertion and implantation into a beagle host mother myself. That part is relatively simple once the insertion virus has been developed. I made sure I was on duty and alone when you were born, and I took you away, replacing you with a stillborn beagle pup from a different mother. Lucy was very sad to lose you, but faking your death was the only way to get you away without suspicion. You wouldn't believe the security they had in that place! Fortunately for both of us, I was in a position of trust, and I was very careful. They still don't know."

29

I horror I whimpered, "My mosther... my mosther is... a *pffeagle?*" This was not so good. "You're not teasing me, are you John?"

"I'm trying to answer a complicated question as simply as I can. All you need to understand right now is that Mooney and I are trying to do our very best for you, and that it would be bad luck indeed if you're ever found by the people I took you away from. I developed much of their research plan, but I quit my position as research director once I had you, and I haven't been back since. Haven't wanted to."

I felt overwhelmed. "Let's not talk any more for now," I said plaintively, and we didn't.

Chapter 3

John was allowed back on Sunbow the next day, but it was almost a week before Mooney came home, and I never saw her van again. John bought another for her.

Mooney hates to accept valuable gifts, but she had nothing else to drive, and John told her the van was not worth much anyway.

It wasn't, really. The thing was even older and more broken down than her previous one, and it smoked.

John and Mooney were constantly talking about money now, and the talks were not happy ones. All they could agree on was that Mooney was out of the pot-growing business for good. As if we had a choice! Mooney had been released from custody, but she had very much not been forgotten.

Our money problems were no closer to solution when summer ended and the autumn rains returned. As always they started out warm and rare, but gradually became cold and constant, so that dryness ceased to exist outside of heated human dwellings.

Cold and damp were not a problem for me, of course. My winter coat had come back, and I hardly noticed such things. My winter pelt is thick and glossy. It hides my boniness, and makes me look bigger than I am, and humans tell me it has red-gold highlights that are quite gorgeous. I can't quite see the color in the highlights—but I can see colors a little, and I know what red-gold is. It's the color of campfire coals and Sunsets. I like that.

The autumn rains were nothing to me, but autumn also brought hunting season, and that was a real pain—the worst time of the year. The log road gates were unlocked during hunting season and the hills became infested with men carrying high-powered telescopic rifles. The men were noisy and clumsy and easy enough to avoid, but their bullets carried so far that another man clear over on the next ridge could be aiming at you too. Weyerhaeuser opened its land for deer hunting only, but when a human has a rifle in his hands you can never be sure what he'll do with it. Mooney was well aware of this danger and wouldn't let me leave her land except at night.

Mooney's Wood had no roads and was posted against trespassing, so it functioned as a sanctuary. At night the deer ventured out to browse on young trees, and the predators ventured out to eat deer guts and wounded deer. I ate tofu and rice, with sometimes a few deer guts on the side.

The dry days of summer were just a memory, and my fur was always muddy when I came home to Sunbow. Mooney required me to jump in the creek and rinse off before entering the house, but she always gave me a good towel rub afterwards. I liked that. Sometimes I would contrive reasons to go back outside so we could do it all over again. When I came home after Mooney was asleep I had to jump in the creek anyway, and then stay off the carpets and bed. Mooney had a special wet fur mat I was supposed to sleep on then. When I was clean and dry, and when John was not visiting, I slept on the bed with Mooney.

Hunting season passed without incident, but something quite unexpected happened in late December. A good thing, for once—something very special for me.

John was visiting again, and I had talked him into taking me for an outing. Mooney was going to come along too and I couldn't quite keep myself from panting as I stood by the truck waiting for them to get organized. It was going to be crowded in the cab with the three of us, and I was afraid I would be told to ride in back, so I decided to get in early.

The door latches on John's truck were rusty and very stiff, but I grabbed one anyway and wrenched it roughly open, bruising my gums a little in the process. Then I jumped inside and wedged myself securely into the center of the seat. The humans arrived shortly, and we had a good time, but that evening my mouth was still sore, and it didn't get better during the next few days.

Finally I asked Mooney to take a look and tell me if something was wrong. She pulled my jaws wide open and prodded the sore spot with her finger. "What's this? Stinky, I think…" Mooney ran her finger all along the gum line, poking and pinching excitedly, then she pushed my head to arm's length so she could look me in the eyes. Mooney's own eyes were shining with new tears. "Sin-Ka-Lip, my dear… you're teething!"

I held absolutely still for a moment, then began to tremble. Silently I backed away from her and slunk into the bathroom, where I put my front feet up on the sink and stared at the mirror. The upper gums were slightly puffy and discolored in front, and Mooney's probing had produced a smear of blood, but I couldn't see anything more than that.

Mooney came up beside me and reached over to press on both sides of the spot where the blood was coming from. It hurt and felt good at the same time. "Look now, Sin-Ka-Lip," she said.

Between her fingertips, gleaming like a tiny hailstone, shone the tip of a tooth.

The top incisor teeth came in all at once, and rather quickly, too. By the end of January they were completely exposed, and the lower incisors had begun to appear. One of my speech impediments vanished, and I could say *th* sounds at will. After that it seemed a new tooth was showing almost every day. I had a full set up or started by my birthday in the middle of March, and other parts of me were beginning to develop as well. Not just teeth. The fangs were nice to look at, but the shearing teeth in back were the ones that gave me the greatest pleasure. I used them to demolish quite a number of sticks, bones, and deer hooves, although in the house I had to content myself with Nylabones. I also had to slow my speech to keep from biting my tongue too often. I'm still astonished and jealous when I watch a fast-talking human rattle the words away. A few seconds of that would put me on soft food for a week.

I was so proud of my new teeth that sometimes I would stand up in front of the bathroom mirror and curl back my lips to expose them all, turning my head from side to side for the best view. One day Mooney saw me doing that and laughed so much she had to sit down. Then she went to the phone and began calling our old commune members. Before I knew what was happening, she had organized a full-scale Sunbow reunion in my honor.

I was intrigued and terrified by the prospect, but mostly terrified — especially after Mooney admitted that the group would include some new people. Strangers! I told Mooney I was going to run off and boycott the whole production.

Mooney gave me to know that such behavior was unacceptable. "Just because our friends are bringing a few spouses and children doesn't mean you have to go all to pieces! Yes, I know you're shy and your instincts are hard to control, but we humans can control our instincts enough to get by, and you can too. Now—you have almost two weeks until spring break. I want you to pull yourself together and grow up. Remember, you won't have to see them all at once. Take your time, and meet them out in the woods if you have to. It's not so hard—you can do this!"

Prepare to face a crowd of humans? What a thing to ask! There was no way I could prepare for that. I would just have to do my best when the time came. I knew Mooney would forgive me if I really did have to run away, but some of those people were important friends of mine, and in a bizarre sort of way I was looking forward to the event. I certainly wouldn't be bored! And it might take my mind off another thing that had been bothering me.

The problem had started just after Christmas, but the real trouble had not begun until a couple of months later, when Broke Ear entered her season.

Broke Ear and her mate Fluff Tail were the coyotes living closest to Sunbow, and we got along just fine together. They let me run with them and I helped take care of their pups. Pup, singular, this year. It had been a hard year for pups, and only one was still alive. I called her Princess.

It's kind of strange, when you think about it. Broke and Fluff would drive away their own pups as soon as they were old enough to care for themselves, but they never did that to me. I was always welcome to come back. Almost always. This time I wore out my welcome, just a bit.

I had always admired Broke Ear in a respectful sort of way, but with springtime my feelings had suddenly become very much warmer. I cuddled up to her whenever she would let me, and I was constantly trying to think of ways to please her. Of course the surest way to please any coyote is to bring food, and I did that. They all took the freezer meat I stole for them but Broke Ear still had eyes only for Fluff Tail, and eventually he had to drive me away. I lost my appetite at home, and kept wandering off to follow the coyotes' trail at a distance, checking scent marks and sighing. It was a strange feeling, and completely new to me.

John and Mooney only laughed when I told them about it. They said it was the spring rut, and all male coyotes go through it every year, and I should pity the poor male dogs. They're horny all year long if the humans let them keep their testicles.

Chapter 4

The reunion was not what I had feared it would be. Mostly I stayed out in the woods, the yard, and the goat barn, and my old friends came to greet me a few at a time. The new people had all been carefully coached, and they didn't come rushing up or make any fast moves. In fact, several of them smelled rather scared, which surprised me at first. My new teeth had helped to give me confidence, but I hadn't showed them at all. Not once. We all got over our fears, though, and before they left I could count them all as friends. Except the very young ones, of course. I suppose they don't remember me.

During this time I met one human who became very important to me. John brought her, which surprised us all. He had never come with a companion before.

She was shy. I heard John talking with her gently for a long time before he led her out through the rain and into the goat barn. I felt more confident because of her shyness and John's Presence, so I padfooted right up to them after rolling in hay to make my fur sort of dry. The girl's head was already turned my way but her eyes didn't follow me as I approached, so I stopped in puzzlement a few feet in front and to the side. She was about my size, rather bony-looking, and with straight, very short hair which I thought was probably brown. Medium-colored, anyway. She smelled of fear or anger but her basic scent was quite nice. Rich and complex, and with components I couldn't recall ever encountering before.

"You'll have to come a little closer," John said. "Mouse has had an accident, and she can't see you."

I was shocked. I had never seen a blind person except on television. As John spoke to me the girl's eyes turned in my general direction, but they didn't focus. I sidled up to John's far side while inspecting the girl apprehensively, and her eyes still failed to track my movements.

"You two don't need to be scared of each other. I know you both, and I think you'll get along. Now—who wants to come forward first?"

The new human and I were both silent. John smiled, then pulled the girl's hand forward to press it down into my shoulder fur.

We both held ourselves absolutely still, and I became aware of a powerful Presence about her—not quite like any I had ever felt before. Startled again, I shook myself free and skittered away.

The girl spoke for the first time. "I don't think he likes me, Dr. Cultee. Maybe we should go back inside." Her words hurt John. I could feel that too.

I'm not always a coward. Before things could get worse I circled around behind John to the girl's other side, and gently nuzzled the hand she held there clenching her shirt. The girl snatched her hand away and rubbed her fingers on the shirt front, but then she brought the hand back and began to stroke the top of my head, and later the rest of me. Her touch was delicate and trembling, and it still had that special feel to it. Quite pleasant, actually. More than pleasant. When she was done I returned the compliment—sniffing and tasting her carefully until I had her memorized. She held herself rigidly motionless while I did that, but after a time her trembling stopped, and slowly her stress scent began to fade as well.

"He's really big!" she said, finally.

It was true. I probably outweighed her by a pound or two, and I would have been taller if we had both been standing on our hind legs. I turned toward John and opened my mouth to make a joke about that, then froze.

I had been about to talk in front of a stranger! I snapped my mouth shut and turned my head away—stared off intently at nothing in particular. The barn doors were open, and on the far side of Fry Creek I could just make out Mr. Bell walking his fences, with Jake stumping contentedly along behind him. They both looked old and not very dangerous from where I stood.

Later that day the rain stopped, but when I went up to the house to see who wanted to go for a walk, they were all laughing and talking so loudly no one noticed. The party was in my honor but they seemed to be doing quite well without me. If I had made some noise I could have had all the attention I wanted, but I preferred to turn away so that I could feel abandoned and melancholic. I went back to the goat barn and began climbing the stairs to the hayloft. It was one of the driest places outside of the house, and I spent a lot of time there.

"Who's that?"

It was Mouse's voice, somehow sounding annoyed, guilty, and slightly scared at the same time. She was in the loft. I backed down slowly and began to walk away.

"Coyote, is that you?"

I paused. I liked that name better than the 'Sin-Ka-Lip,' 'Stinkylips,' or 'Stinky' Mooney persisted in calling me. Mouse's question deserved an answer, so I whined softly in response.

"Coyote! Here, boy!"

Annoying words, but I wasn't really offended. Mouse didn't mean them that way. Still, I didn't go up to her. If you start coming when called, people expect it of you. Eventually Mouse appeared at the loft edge, felt carefully for the treads, and worked her way down to me. I was waiting at the bottom and got a rather nice hug for my troubles. Then she sat down beside me, put an arm over my shoulder, and began to talk.

"There were too many people there, and they kept asking me about my accident, and could they get anything for me, and what did I think about El Salvador, and have I tried a Homeopath. You're much better company because you can't talk. Everybody loves you. I wish I was a coyote like you. I wouldn't have to talk or answer questions or explain anything. I wouldn't have to explain anything at all." Mouse put her other arm around me, buried her face in my neck fur, and began to sob quietly.

One of Baby's kids bleated for attention and Mouse started, and pushed herself away. "Sorry about that, Coyote. You probably think I'm just a helpless little kid who doesn't know how to do anything except cry and complain. Come on—I'm done blubbering. You can show me the goats. Was that Thing One or Thing Two?"

Mouse stood up, still with one hand on my shoulder, and pulled politely at my fur until I got up too. I think she just wanted me for support, but I led her along directly to the stall. If she was going to waste her time playing with goats I might as well help her get it over with.

Thing One and Thing Two weren't really kids any more, and they had been assigned a stall to themselves. They were still affectionate, but now prone to belligerence that was only partly play. Mooney would have to get rid of them soon. Mouse visited with the Things, and with their mother, and with the two old ladies, but she didn't try to get into the stalls. That was good, because she would have been knocked over into the manure, most likely, and me to blame for it.

The last stall in line was layered with diatomaceous earth for me to roll in when I had fleas, so it couldn't be used for anything else. Mouse stopped there for a few seconds and listened, then moved on to the open back door while I stayed close beside her. We stopped at the exact spot where I had fooled the Sheriff's deputy. How long had that been—only eight months? Time is a strange thing.

Mouse hesitated with one hand on the doorjamb and one on my back. "This is the goat yard, isn't it?" She was speaking half to herself and half to me. I moved forward slowly, so she would have to follow me or let go, and she came along while I skirted the puddles and most of the manure on my way to the paddock gate.

Our walk was short and slow, but fun. Mouse sped up when she found how good I was at guiding her around the rough spots, and she gave many satisfying and accurate compliments. We got back to the house without anyone even noticing we had been gone.

I led Mouse up onto the back porch, then stuck my head through the dog door to see if anyone was in the kitchen. The room was empty, for once, so I pulled my head back outside and grabbed the doorknob with my mouth. I didn't want to leave my guest behind, and that dog door was getting rather small for me. I could barely squeeze my chest through it any more.

There was bread cooling on the counter. I wanted some, but thought maybe I could get Mouse to steal it for me instead of just taking it myself. I could tell she wanted some too. She was sniffing and turning her head, but the whole kitchen was filled with the aroma and she couldn't focus on the exact location. I helped her.

Begging is a pleasurable, natural function. Some might call it an art form. I'm a master, of course, and we had one of the loaves almost finished when a knot of my less well known friends came in.

The humans began talking at me right away—friendly, but too loud. It doesn't matter what they said—words all sound about the same when you're not listening to them. I had to get out of that place! I began to edge away... then became aware that Mouse was standing behind me, holding on as if for protection.

She was standing behind me!

No one had ever done that before.

We turned toward each other in gentle, mutual panic, and then a magical thing happened. True magic.

I shifted position to stand tall, and when Mouse felt what I was doing she joined me, giving a surreptitious one-armed hug and thump on the chest. I smiled at Mouse and at the visitors, and carefully took the last of the bread from her fingers. This was *my* house, and it was *my* bread. Mooney had baked it for me as much as for anyone, and I was only pretending to steal it.

The visitors came forward for greetings, still too fast and too loud, but I met them with head, ears, and tail up. Mouse did well too.

More people came, better behaved this time. The attention was split between me and Mouse, and that made it easier for us both. I knew each one of those humans individually, and it helped if I thought of them that way instead of as members of a group. Finally John and Mooney came in. They looked very pleased with me, and perhaps a bit drunk as well. Not stoned, just a little alcohol. We had converted our home to permanently drug-free status. Mooney raised her glass and proposed a toast: "To Coyote: our mascot, and the soul of Sunbow!"

A ragged but respectful response filled the kitchen and hall, and someone called out, "Speech!"

There were some chuckles, and then most of the room was watching me anxiously. I suppose they were waiting for me to skitter out through the dog door and disappear. That's what I normally would have done, but not this time. Instead I felt the same energy and confidence I knew when playing in private with John or Mooney.

The eyes were still on me. Probably would be forever until I did something.

Slowly I raised my head, tilted it a little to the side, and half-closed my eyes. Then I filled my lungs and began a sweet, pure howl—wolf style with no yipping. Mooney and John joined me almost immediately, and then the rest so that my whole body thrummed with the sound of it, and I couldn't tell my own voice from the human voices around me. We continued until it seemed like the right time to stop, which we all knew together. There was long silence, and then they all broke into the gabbling individual conversations humans are so fond of. The tone of the room was happy, and excited, and a little embarrassed.

I reached up to lick the tears from Mouse's face, then turned to the dog door and jammed myself through slowly and with dignity, for old times' sake. I needed a good, long run.

Chapter 5

When we were alone together again, Mooney told me about Mouse's accident. She had hit her head and almost died when running away from a police officer in Seattle earlier that winter. Bleeding inside of her brain had damaged part of it so that she couldn't see, and she claimed she couldn't remember anything either. No one was sure if the blindness and memory loss would be permanent, so she was a ward of the City of Seattle until a relative showed up to claim her, or her memory came back enough to allow her home to be found. The police officer who had made the report thought she was a runaway, since he had found her wandering the Pike Street Market area aimlessly and without adequate clothing. No one there had seen her before, and no identification had been found on her.

The girl had picked up her 'Mouse' nickname at the University Hospital where she was treated. She seemed constantly fearful, and tended to run off when things became confusing or hectic. John had met Mouse and learned about her case during medical rounds, and later offered to help out by taking her to Sunbow for a change of environment. Her counselor was surprised by John's interest, but quick to take advantage of it. Special trips were one of the best possible treats for the foster children, and not to be spurned.

The Sunbow visit was considered a great success, and John began to bring Mouse with him almost every time he came. I was pleased because she was good company, and someone I could be dominant over.

I had never been dominant over a human; just the goats and coyote pups. And the chickens, of course, but they were too dumb to be worth the trouble. John explained to me once that part of the contract between humans and dogs is that all humans are dominant over all dogs, with a few minor exceptions such as guard dogs on duty. I was not a part of that contract. In Mouse I found someone even shyer than I was, and I naturally drifted into a leadership role. I took her on progressively longer walks, and we got to moving pretty fast on the smooth sections. It was the only way she could run. The exercise helped Mouse a lot. I could feel her growing stronger. She became very fond of me and would often cry when it was time to go back to Seattle. I missed her too.

Mouse talked a lot on our walks, and I soon learned that she was faking her amnesia. The blindness was real enough, though. It bothered her a lot more than she let on to the other humans. Several times I almost spoke to her, but each time I held myself back. I needed to know if she was going to stay with us.

We touched frequently, enjoying our resonance, and when I was with Mouse I didn't think about Broke Ear so much. In early May my rut faded, and I didn't think about Broke Ear at all.

In June, Mouse told me her school would be coming to an end soon. I was astonished. Had it been two months already? Mouse also told me there was talk about a field trip to let her classmates see the wonderful place she had been going to every weekend. Mouse and I tried to communicate our disapproval of this plan, but somehow it happened anyway.

Chapter 6

I was familiar enough with school buses, but I had never thought to see one in my own yard before! The thing looked weirdly out of place there, and much larger than I had expected. Far too large for my liking, and the noise coming from inside was spine-chilling. Mouse and I watched through a crack between the hayloft loading doors. Or rather, I watched and Mouse listened.

"That's Bruce," she explained after an especially loud and nasty laugh drifted up to us. "He's gross."

Mouse shuddered, and I could tell she was imagining what it would have been like to sit beside Bruce for the whole three-hour drive from Seattle. Fortunately, Mouse had convinced the authorities so thoroughly of her instability that no one had considered sending her over that way. John had brought her the previous day, and she was well rested and almost ready to do her duty.

"Now remember. You promised you wouldn't run away! If you do, I'll run away too. Or something. You *will* stay with me, won't you?" Mouse was starting to blubber a little, so I pushed up against her and licked her face to comfort her.

I was terrified, too, but tried to hold onto the memory of that strange confidence I had felt at Mooney's reunion party. Maybe we could do it again.

"I can hear them getting out now. Come on, Coyote. It's better to meet them in the open."

My feelings exactly.

Silence took them all when Mouse and I moved into view. By then I was the size of a young Great Dane, but I don't think I looked much like a dog. I tried, though—even managed to fake a pleasantly mindless 'doggy' expression, and some approximation of a tail wag.

Mouse was clutching my shoulder skin harder than she needed to. "Hi everybody," she began bravely, "I'd like you to meet my friend Coyote. He's very smart! Show them what you can do, Coyote. Shake!" This part was not my idea, but Mouse had really pushed for it, and John and Mooney had backed her up.

I sat down carefully on my haunches and raised my right front foot, but my ears were back, and perhaps my expression was not quite so pleasant as it had been. No one tried to shake hands with me, anyway. So far, so good. I had been afraid the whole busload would come up and want to touch me.

From a spot safely in the center of the knot of kids, Bruce called out, "Does he do any other tricks?"

I put my foot down and glared in his direction, trying to look unpleasant without actually showing my teeth. I think I must have succeeded because one of the teachers interrupted and said that maybe Mouse's dog wasn't in the mood for tricks right now. It might be shy from all the people.

Good guess!

Mouse looked annoyed, but moved on to Stage Two: bathroom break and tour of the premises. Fortunately the adults had some experience with these things and had pulled the bus into a freeway rest stop not long before. Still it took quite a while, and some of the more active had begun to give themselves a tour of the yard before the official one started.

As the group separated into individuals, I noticed that many of them were not very healthy. Some had twisted or missing limbs, or appeared only partly aware of their surroundings, and had adults attending them closely. There certainly were a lot of adults! In my nervousness I hadn't realized quite how many.

But they were happy! Young and old seemed delighted to be there. The young ones were impressed by the (cool) goats or (gross) goat shit. Adults discussed the wonderful scenery and quiet, or the large and pungent manure pile beside which the bus was parked. Sunbow didn't seem very quiet to me just then, but I suppose it was an improvement after three hours in that bus.

The tour began shortly, and ended only a little while later. To my intense relief I learned that our job was no more than a token presentation of the yard, pens, barns, chicken coop, and creek bank. Mouse and I were done after that, and the adults took over with Supervised Activities. In the transition there was a short time in which no one seemed to be noticing us. I nudged Mouse with my shoulder so she could grab hold, then drew her into the goat barn and over to the hayloft stairs. We swarmed up rapidly as soon as the last child was called away, then pushed the hay around to make a warm, invisible nest in the back.

I peered through a crack in the boards as the more ambulatory children were formed into lines, issued an assortment of raincoats and umbrellas, and then marched off into the drizzle on a Nature Excursion. The others disappeared into the house, and Mouse and I took a nap.

A barbecue had been planned for the afternoon, to take place outside if it was not raining or in the machinery barn if it was. It was raining, of course, so we were left alone while the hot dogs were cooking. We woke when our names were mentioned, but no serious search was started until the food was about ready, and suddenly there we were.

It was easier to make myself appear friendly when approaching kids with food, so I got a good taste before Mouse did. She became annoyed then, and said she needed me to help her stand in line. John was cooking, and asked with a mock serious expression how many hot dogs I wanted. I yipped five times and looked to the grill to show I wanted them cooked. The kids were all staring at me again, but it didn't matter. Nothing was going to get between me and the food.

John called someone over to help us carry our plates, and Mouse and I settled into a corner where she helped me get at the bottom half of my cup of Coke, while I helped her finish the food she didn't want. Afterward I skirted the less crowded areas, looking for leftovers and more handouts. Handouts were plentiful, and I was able to greet some of the kids properly. They were really quite nice, mostly.

I probably would have taken a dislike to Bruce even without Mouse's hints. He was the tallest one with relatively normal intelligence, and he was fat. Not that I care about fat, mind you. It was the way he acted that annoyed me. Others avoided him, but he pushed himself into their personal spaces as if unaware of this. He was aware of me, however, and watched intently as I made my rounds. Finally he held out his half-finished hot dog and called to me. As I approached cautiously he spat on it, then held it out again. I have nothing against saliva, but I didn't like his attitude so I moved off. I was full, anyway.

Later, when a ragged line was being herded together to get back onto the bus, I let myself into the Things' stall and rolled in the dirty corner, soaking up as much goat piss as my fur would hold. I got some manure mixed in with it too, but that was okay. When I was well saturated, I left the barn and circled around to the end of the bus line. Smiling and waving my tail gaily I slipped up behind Bruce and gave him a long, affectionate body rub before trotting off to the creek for a dip. Male goat urine can be a great protector of personal space. I kind of wondered where he would end up sitting.

Chapter 7

With school over, Mouse came by more often, sometimes staying for a week or more. She explained that John didn't really have custody of her, he was just borrowing her. That was puzzling. Did anyone have custody of me? The idea of trading pack members around had never occurred to me, and soon faded from mind. John liked her, so he brought her with him. Nothing more to it than that.

It was still raining most days, so we spent a lot of time in the hayloft. It had been my special place, but I was happy to share it, and it seemed to give Mouse a great deal of comfort to hide back in our den and pretend no one could ever find us. One day after we had been napping I woke to find Mouse facing me with a hard-to-read expression. She didn't smell upset, but she was very keyed up.

"You were talking in your sleep, Coyote."

She sounded like she expected me to contradict her. I put on an inscrutable expression and began to clean myself. I wondered how far she would take this.

"Mooney said you can talk, but I thought she was teasing me. She teases me a lot. If you can talk, why haven't you said anything to me? You haven't told them where I came from, have you? Please say you didn't!"

Inscrutable wasn't working—and she couldn't see it, anyway. I reached over and licked her neck where the big vein is. "I didn't tell anyone. Not even Mooney."

If she liked that answer, maybe she would give me a belly rub. I flopped myself over to find out.

Later we ran over to Mooney and proudly announced our new understanding, but I still didn't say anything about Mouse's pretend amnesia.

I shouldn't have been surprised when John showed up one Friday with a Seeing Eye Dog harness. He had offered before, but Mouse and I had declined because the loose skin above my shoulders made a perfectly comfortable handle, and we enjoyed the contact. When we were going fast, it was as if she saw obstacles as soon as I did, and moved to avoid them even before I could signal by shift of balance.

This time John insisted that Mouse really did need to have some official training in Guide Dog procedures. I didn't realize it at the time, but what he really meant was that I could use the practice at being a Guide Dog. We could make a game of it, he said.

"Don't walk under ladders."

"Don't abandon your human to investigate interesting things."

"Don't walk out in the street and get run over, even if you're ordered to."

All that was just common sense, but the traffic light business was new to me. I knew about traffic lights, certainly. We had one right over in Montesano, where Mooney did most of her shopping. It's the county seat, after all, and has lots of special things. This light was at the place where Main Street crossed the Old Highway, and I had seen it many times. Apparently it made a very big difference which of the three lights was shining. The top light is called 'red,' the middle 'yellow,' and the bottom 'green'. Car drivers are supposed to stop or go based on which light is shining, and pedestrians are supposed to cross the street during the 'safe' period.

Very clever, but not relevant to me. I would never be afoot in a city big enough to have traffic lights. When I was in the truck or van, I would wedge myself down on the floor when we entered congested areas and just lift my head to peer over the dashboard from time to time.

I didn't take John's game very seriously, but I paid attention anyway and learned all the rules in a couple of hours. John and Mooney even staged a short graduation ceremony where Mouse and I received diplomas marked "M.S.E.T." (Master of Seeing Eye Trivia).

We played with the harness often enough to become familiar with it, but mostly we left it behind. John didn't make us use it more often until one day in July when he invited Mouse and me for a drive, and threw the harness in back while we were fighting for position up front.

John drove us south to the freeway, turned west toward Aberdeen, then pulled off in Central Park, which really worried me since that's the way to the vet. Central Park is not a real park, by the way. It's just a place where people live. Not even a town, really—just some roads and houses. And a veterinary clinic.

We didn't go to the vet this time, but stopped instead at a public building I had never seen before. Marked 'Central Park School,' it was really two buildings, with a covered concrete yard between them and a large, fenced, grassy area behind. The buildings were almost as large as Mr. Bell's dairy barns.

The place had a parking lot with no cars in it, and playing fields with no one playing in them. Eerie. I stayed in the truck with my ears back until John grabbed me and tried to drag me out. Mouse could feel my mood, and held onto me from her position in the center of the truck cab.

After a few seconds John stopped pulling and started laughing. "Okay. I give up for now, Stinky. You can rest a minute, but you do have to come out and investigate this place. It's called 'Central Park School,' and it's the closest grade school to Sunbow. Mouse will be coming here this fall if she continues to stay with us."

"I know what it's called," I told him. "I can read. Why did you pffring me here?"

I should have figured it out first, but Mouse was the one who spoke. "You want Coyote to be a Seeing Eye Dog for me! That's dumb. He could never do that!" Mouse was angrier than I had ever seen her before. She wasn't faking, either. I could tell by her scent, and the way her arms quivered as they held me, and by that other way we have.

John tried to soothe her. "We won't try to make him do anything he's not capable of. Couldn't if we tried. But Coyote has shown more courage with groups these last months than I've hoped for in a long time. We need to see if we can take this all the way—teach him how to be comfortable with any group of strangers. You could use the help too."

We both knew what John was referring to. Twice now I had felt a confidence totally out of character as I faced Mooney's reunion and Mouse's end-of-school field trip. It had never occurred to me that John would take that as potentiality to enter human society. Such a joke!

While I was thinking, John tugged gently at the scruff of my neck and I jumped down out of habit. Forgot to resist. Then my curiosity took over and I trotted out to check and mark the premises.

This place was no stranger to canines. Most of the scent marks were several weeks old but still I could discriminate at least six individuals of different ages and sexes, and that was just from the urine. All the droppings had been picked up. In fact, the facilities were distressingly clean and well maintained, although the southwest playing field was soggy and had a distinct septic tank smell. The grass was very lush there, and I had a nice roll and strut.

I felt much more at ease when I rejoined John and Mouse. They were on a tour of their own, with John leading Mouse around the buildings, pointing out doors (all locked) and dangers such as support posts or bike racks. I let John do the talking.

When John had finished with his orientation he brought over the harness and strapped it on me. "All right, kids, it's your turn now. Show me if you remember anything."

We went through our drills then, showing off and being silly, and that was the end of our lesson. That day John didn't say anything more about the craziness of Mouse and me trying to go to school together.

I didn't go on many picnic basket raids that summer. I didn't have the time, for one thing. Mouse was around almost every day, and she was good company. Also, Mooney had sold her goats. She said they didn't pay their way. She was clearing land to expand her raspberry fields and didn't have time for anything else.

That's what Mooney said, but what she meant was that she was afraid for my safety. After the pot raid we had lost our feeling of privacy—kept encountering strange people in places they should not have been. Mooney and I had felt uncomfortable about resuming the herding business, and she didn't want to just leave the goats in their pens every day.

I had never liked the goats much, but the barn smelled strange without them. We had to change our whole daily routine, and Mooney really did devote all the extra time to her new berry fields. All that time, and a considerable amount more. She seemed to have little time for me any more, and none at all for herself. I grew to hate the new fields, and wished the river would flood and take them away, they seemed such a burden to her.

Chapter 8

They were all staring at me. I felt it as a tingling in my neck. They were not hostile, but they couldn't keep themselves from staring. No one at Central Park School had worked with a blind student or Guide Dog before—certainly not a Guide Dog like me! Montesano was the school where blind students went. It was bigger, and had more resources, and they knew what to do. John was the one who had wanted us to go to Central Park. He had told them a smaller school would better meet Mouse's special needs, and had persuaded them to take us on through promises of teaching grant money from Seattle. By August he had already attended several orientation meetings, and now Mouse and I were required to make our appearance as well. Our resistance had been argued and cajoled into abeyance, for the moment, but it was a close thing.

Mooney had come along to help give us courage and we formed a tight little pack as we followed one of the school people down a long, newly carpeted hallway smelling of chalk dust, disinfectant, Xerox machines, and fresh paint. My nose told me no dog had ever been there before, and even the human scent was muted. I was wearing my harness and had an extra-large floral bandana around my neck, and I tried to project a feeling of confidence and friendliness for Mouse's sake. Mouse was right there with me but her hand was on the harness, not on me, and I felt cut off from her.

Halfway down the hall we turned left into a very large room with very small furniture. In the center of the room was a long, wide table, so low I could look down onto it, and lots of sturdy, small chairs which fit beneath. Several official-looking adults were already seated there. It looked like a tight fit for all of them, and some couldn't get their thighs under the table at all.

As I had been taught, I led Mouse to one of the empty chairs, then sat down on my haunches behind her. My eyes were level with all the human ones. Nice furniture!

Preliminary greetings were quite sketchy—just quick verbal acknowledgements with nothing tactile at all. I was included in the presentations, but no one spoke to me directly. The head human introduced himself as Mr. Sawyer, the principal. He was as tall as John, but leaner, and he smiled a lot. He was clearly dominant, but not a brute. The others deferred to him without fear.

"I'm sorry I had to schedule our meeting in Mrs. Dellship's first grade room, but with the painting this is the only one available. These seats are not so bad when you get used to them. Is everyone comfortable?"

Quite a few humans talked, but I remember only three of them clearly. The first one was Mrs. Stanford, who would be Mouse's sixth grade teacher. She was average to short for a human female, about Mooney's height but much heavier, and looked very uncomfortable in her silly little chair. She was one of the people whose thighs didn't fit under the table. Mrs. Stanford was welcoming to Mouse, a bit cold to Mooney, and wouldn't acknowledge me at all.

The second person was Mrs. Seeley, in charge of the Resource Room and Library. Mrs. Seeley was also in charge of 'Special Education' and would be spending a lot of time with us. Mrs. Seeley was tall and light-haired, and her legs didn't fit under the table either, but that was not from being fat. She was just too big, like Mr. Sawyer. I recognized Mrs. Seeley. I had seen her before, and through my own carelessness she had seen me too. Her whole family had seen me. Mrs. Seeley and her family had provided me with my first taste of liverwurst, on one of my picnic raids. But that had been almost a year ago, and they had not actually seen me with the sandwiches, and they had thought I was a wild animal. Mrs. Seeley wouldn't recognize me in my role as a Guide Dog. I hoped.

A rather small, wiry man introduced himself as Mr. Burrey, the new school district psychologist. He would be monitoring Mouse's amnesia and checking on her to see that she adapted well. He smelled delightfully of smoked salmon, and had a smooth, controlled way of moving not common in humans. He also had a tendency to watch me closely when the others were busy talking.

The meeting was hard on Mouse, with a lot of questions which she didn't answer very completely. I know for a time she was even thinking about running from the room. She wouldn't get far, of course, but at least it would be an end to the torment of the meeting. I licked Mouse's ear to remind her I was with her, and she settled down.

There was a great deal of talk concerning schedules, lesson plans, special projects, and so forth, but I didn't listen very carefully. I just watched and sniffed and felt the tone. These people represented the Real World, or Civilization, or whatever you wish to call it. I hoped we were ready for each other.

After the meeting we had an impromptu greeting session in which I was polite but not affectionate. That could come later for those who deserved it.

Mouse and I were called on to give a Guide Dog Demonstration, which we performed flawlessly. Our memory of the school grounds had not faded.

Mr. Burrey just happened to be near the van as we were getting ready to leave, and drew John into a full-scale conversation which then somehow turned to me. He said I looked just like a coyote, except I was way too big and confident, and he wondered what sort of dog I was. John replied that I had a rather mixed heritage, but it shouldn't affect my suitability for Guide Dog work. I was the product of a new training program, which was experimental but seemed to be producing excellent results so far.

Mr. Burrey persisted. "I'm somewhat familiar with Guide Dog training programs, and this one's performance is far superior to any I've seen. There's some real intelligence at work here, not just good training. Is he neutered?"

As is proper for my kind, and as I've mentioned before, I'm a bit seasonal when it comes to sex. Coyotes have no business birthing pups at the wrong time of year and in summer my interest—and my testicles—shrink down to just a little bit more than nothing. I recognize the sense of that now, but at the time I was still coming to terms with the idea, and Mr. Burrey's question annoyed me. Before John could answer him I flopped down onto the pavement and began licking myself to give them all a good view. John and Mooney laughed, and John said he'd ask me what I thought about stud service next spring.

Mr. Burrey didn't laugh. Instead he knelt down beside me and reached out to touch my shoulder with a tentative hand. I sat up so he could rub my back properly, and while he did that I sniffed him over. Beneath the smoked salmon scent on his clothes and skin, his own personal scent was rather unusual. There was a strong canine component to it. Humans who live with dogs have a canine tang to them, but that's a surface scent, strongest on clothing and hands. With Mr. Burrey the scent seemed to be coming out of the skin itself, just as my own did.

The canine scent was unfamiliar to me, but I didn't spend much thought on it just then because Mr. Burrey had a Presence about him similar to what I felt from Mouse, Mooney, and John. More like Mouse, actually, but different in its own way.

No one with that special sort of feel had ever tried to hurt me, so I was willing to accept Mr. Burrey as friend. And my humans seemed to like him. I've often found human reactions to be a useful guide when judging character.

Mr. Burrey appeared quite touched when I accepted him—as though I had given him a gift of some sort.

Chapter 9

Our first day of school was rough, but not as bad as it might have been. At Mr. Burrey's suggestion we had been given permission to enter the classroom early. Mouse and I greeted Mrs. Stanford when she came in then waited—alone and grimly tense—as she left the room to form up her new class in the covered area between the buildings. I cringed at the muted roar of two hundred human children simultaneously laughing, yelling, and talking excitedly while a dozen adults strove to intimidate them into obedience. At the time I truly thought there was killing going on—but when I went out later I couldn't even smell blood.

The noise outside faded to a steady murmur with adult voices rising above it, and then the marching started, one group at a time. Eventually a surge of footsteps came to our door and didn't pass it by. Instead the footsteps stopped there and we heard Mrs. Stanford explaining our presence to her new class. The knob turned, and the door opened, and a couple of dozen small humans were herded in and made to take their seats.

Mouse and I had been helped to set up a small work alcove in the back of the room between the encyclopedia shelf and the fish tank, and we were spared close contact as the room filled up from the front. Each student stared at us shyly and excitedly as it searched for its assigned chair, but soon Mrs. Stanford required them to turn their eyes to the front, and we could relax.

Almost the entire morning was devoted to rules and other forms of talk. Unending talk. I had never thought that fear and boredom could be merged into one feeling, but that is what I was experiencing. Mouse whispered to me at one point that things seemed to be starting out pretty typically. I answered with one of my best sighs, and pressed myself down onto the floor.

Mouse and I tried to skip the morning break but were ordered firmly outside, where we instantly found ourselves surrounded by curious kids wanting to make friends and help us with things. They were all much smaller than Mouse, although Mouse was the shy one. She wouldn't talk at first, but finally admitted that she really did need to use the restroom. She took a hand for guidance but kept her other hand firmly on me, even when our escort began to cackle gleefully that Mouse couldn't take a boy dog into the girls' room.

The teacher on yard duty came over then, and proclaimed that Guide Dogs were allowed to go anywhere, even inside the restrooms. Then she escorted Mouse to a stall and hurried back out to her station.

Mouse stayed in that stall until the bell rang and the room emptied, then unlocked her door and let me lead her back to class. No one told me what I was supposed to do when I needed to relieve myself, but I had a feeling the hallway walls and floor were off-limits, so I just held on.

Lunchtime showed definite potential. Mouse's new circle of self-appointed helpers (all girls now) swept in immediately to guide her to the lunch line and tell her what to do, but they seemed even more interested in me. We were escorted gaily to the front of the line, where Mouse was served, and a sudden bubbling group inspiration produced a tray for me and a servant to carry it.

The Guide Dog video had made it quite clear that I was not to accept food while on duty—but was I on duty during lunch break? I chose the more flexible interpretation and enjoyed myself fully, eventually consuming three extra portions of spaghetti after my own tray was empty and before the supervisor made them stop bringing me more. These kids were looking better to me all the time!

It turned out that we weren't supposed to go directly back to the classroom after lunch, but had a chunk of 'free time' that consisted of talking, jumping rope, talking, hopscotch, and talking. I began to make my way toward the outer fields, and Mouse stuck tenaciously with me until she realized what I needed.

"Oh! I'm sorry, Coyote! I forgot there's no restroom here for you. Come right back when you're done. Please." Then she let go and I ran off to the soggy area. No one played any games there, so it was a good spot for me.

After lunch we were escorted to the resource room where Mrs. Seeley greeted us both warmly, seated Mouse, and presented me with a liverwurst sandwich.

Liverwurst! She *knew*. I took the gift delicately from her fingers, set it down on the carpet, and gazed up at her with my expressionless, neutral look that drives humans so crazy. They can't tell if I'm about to lick them or bite them.

Mrs. Seeley wasn't fooled, though. I had been too polite when I took the sandwich. "You have spaghetti sauce on your bandana," she said matter-of-factly, and stretched her hand right past my nose to untie it. I held myself absolutely still. She had called my bluff by reaching directly through the fear-bite zone. On purpose, I thought.

Mrs. Seeley took the bandana to a nearby sink and began to wash it, so I picked up my sandwich and moved over to lie down close beside Mouse.

Carefully I set the sandwich down and cradled it between my front paws for safekeeping. I was full of spaghetti, and on duty, but I would definitely be wanting that sandwich later. Liverwurst is a glorious food—mostly pork liver but rich in fat as well, and with a sour-fermented, almost rotten tang to it. Mooney would never buy me liverwurst. It's not a vegetarian food.

Mrs. Seeley finished with the bandana and came over to kneel on the carpet beside me. Close, but not too close. "We'll just let that dry for a while, and then you can put it on again when you go home. You look much more handsome without it, you know." Then she cautiously reached out her hand and began to stroke the top of my head. I edged toward her and leaned into the hand, groaning softly. Mrs. Seeley had a way about her that inspired trust.

Mouse snaked an arm around my neck and pulled me back toward herself, just a gentle tug, explaining "Coyote doesn't like strangers very much."

Mrs. Seeley withdrew her hand but I nudged it with my nose and rolled my eyes up at her in a friendly sort of way. She hesitated, then reached out to cradle my head between both of her hands. "But we're not strangers! We've met before. Isn't that true? You wouldn't believe how much time I've spent trying to figure out how you got those sandwiches out of my car last year! The doors and windows were all closed. But now I know." Mrs. Seeley looked toward Mouse significantly, then turned back to me.

"Don't try to deny it. I found the wrappers you left, and I'd recognize you anywhere. I thought you were a wolf! But that's silly. The wolves are all gone now." Mrs. Seeley seemed sad when she said that.

Mrs. Seeley was wrong about Mouse helping me steal those sandwiches. I hadn't even known Mouse back then. She was wrong about the wolves, too. There are quite a few wolf crosses in the Wynoochee Valley, and even some pure-bloods. They all live with humans, though, and they're usually fenced or chained to keep them out of trouble.

Mouse spoke sharply, "Were you stealing from Mrs. Seeley? You have to stop that! You could get hurt."

It seemed like a good time to change the subject so I wiggled free and flopped over with belly exposed and front paws crossed on top of my head. I made my eyes very big and peered up piteously at Mrs. Seeley. It was all a game, and she knew it.

Mrs. Seeley laughed. "You are forgiven, Coyote," she proclaimed solemnly. "But enough of such silliness. It's time for us to get to work. Today we'll begin memorizing the Braille alphabet."

I quickly lost interest in Mouse's lessons, but the sandwich became steadily more attractive to me. I decided I was not quite full after all, and ate it. Good sandwich! Exactly like the ones I had stolen before. There was the liverwurst, of course, but also fresh home-baked bread and just the right amount of mayonnaise, hot mustard, and thin slivers of sweet onion. Mrs. Seeley was definitely someone worth knowing. Good cooks are always worth knowing.

Resource room was scheduled for the whole afternoon, and Mrs. Seeley didn't throw us out for break time, so we finally had a chance to settle down and actually feel comfortable. Mrs. Seeley had other duties besides taking care of us but she stopped by every few minutes to chat with Mouse and keep her working smoothly. Just before school let out Mr. Burrey came by, and this time he smelled of smoked ham. He had even brought some for me, which somehow I managed to find room for. Good ham.

I scented him thoroughly during our greeting, and the canine scent was still there, although much fainter than it had been before—too faint to determine exactly what type of dog I was smelling.

Guessing a dog's breed by scent is usually fairly easy. Hound dogs like Jake are sour and musty, Chows acrid and musty, Malamutes and wolves sort of light and dusty, with almost a sawdust smell to them when they're healthy. Wolves are not dogs, they say, but to me a Malamute smells more like a wolf than it does like a hound, and that's the sort of smell Mr. Burrey had. An intriguing puzzle, and I suppose I spent more time with him than was polite. Finally he pushed my head away. "If you haven't figured it out yet, Coyote, you'll have to try again later. Anyway, I came here for Mouse, not you." He was rubbing my ears and smiling even as he pushed me away.

The conversation moved on to Mouse's feelings about how this new school was working out, and what sort of suggestions she had that might make it easier for her. Mouse couldn't bring herself to voice any suggestions, but Mrs. Seeley spoke on her behalf. "I'm not really sure she should even be in sixth grade," she said at one point. "She's bigger than all the other girls, and she seems to know a lot of this material already." Mouse objected vigorously to that, saying she was almost sure sixth grade was right, and anyway there was no way she could even think about going to junior high just yet. Mr. Burrey and Mrs. Seeley exchanged quick glances then, and changed the subject.

When the dismissal bell rang, Mr. Burrey concluded our meeting by suggesting that we continue the current schedule for now, including the early entry into Mrs. Stanford's classroom. As he was leaving, Mr. Burrey remarked casually, "I've just made an offer on some land in your area, Mouse. It's a beautiful spot right by the river, just up from the Wynoochee-Wishkah road. If the deal goes through we'll be neighbors."

Mooney was waiting for us in the parking lot, looking and smelling very worried. She had a million questions, and I think she was astonished that we hadn't run away or been kicked out first thing. Mouse still wasn't in the mood, so I did most of the talking.

"I don't think I like Mrs. Stanford very much, pffut Mrs. Seeley and Mr. Pffurrey are okay. Mr. Pffurrey still smells like a dog."

"Stinky! What a thing to say! Mr. Burrey doesn't even have a dog. How could he smell like one?"

"Oh, I don't know. He just does. I guess I should have mentioned it pffefore."

"Well, he must have just sat on something and got it on his clothes."

"Yes, of course," I said.

Later that day I woke up from my second afternoon nap with a limerick in my head that sounded kind of neat:

I think that I like Mr. Pffurrey.
His voice makes me come in a hurry.
He treats me real well.
Pffut I fear that his smell
Should pffe something to make us all worry.

I shared the limerick with Mouse, but she said it was dumb so I didn't tell it to anyone else.

School continued, and we became very popular despite our shyness. We didn't do well in Mrs. Stanford's class, though. Mrs. Stanford seemed to have trouble thinking like a blind person, and Mouse wouldn't ask for help, so she just looked stupid instead. One time I overheard Mrs. Stanford whispering to another teacher that she thought the brain injury might have affected Mouse's intelligence as well as her vision and memory. I didn't tell Mouse about it because I knew it would hurt her feelings, but I did ask John later. He said Mouse's injury was in the wrong part of the brain to affect her thinking ability, and her doctors were quite puzzled about how it could have caused amnesia. John looked at me intently when he said that, but I turned away and wouldn't meet his eyes.

Chapter 10

At home the cycle of the year continued to move along, with old routines crammed beside astonishing changes. The rains returned and my winter coat came in, but the goats were gone from Sunbow, and so was I for much of the day. Mouse and the school kept me busy during the daytime, and hunting season was hardly a burden at all.

My night life was less affected by all the changes. Mouse didn't like me to go out so much, and she worried that I might be in danger from cougars or whatever. Mooney tried to reassure her that it was my nature to do these things, and I couldn't help myself, and I *would* be careful, wouldn't I?

I really couldn't help myself. Mooney was right about that. I lived for the woods at night, with no friendly humans stumbling along to hold me back, and no unfriendly humans to get in my way. There was so much to keep track of, and not everything was an enemy.

There were the coyotes, of course. I spent a lot of time with them, but I had also become quite friendly with a young bitch at the Gunderson ranch. She was considered to be three-quarters wolf, but I thought they must have been mistaken because she looked and smelled pure to me. She had long, elegant wolf legs, and a gorgeously lazy wolf tail, and wolf eyes: shining-pale, knowing eyes that saw to my heart, and liked it. The humans had named her Balta, but I didn't approve of that name so I called her Lazytail. At night I would release her from her pen so we could run game together.

In November we actually brought down a deer, but I suppose that one doesn't really count, since she was gut shot and rather slow. I expect we were doing her a favor by killing her. We both gorged ourselves and waddled back to Lazy's place so I could lock her up, then I went on to Sunbow and carefully washed off every bit of blood before going inside. The next morning Mooney thought I was sick because I wouldn't eat my breakfast, and she made Mouse and me both stay home from school.

That was nice. Kind of like a surprise Saturday. I spent most of the day napping, and was thoroughly 'cured' by evening. I loped over to Lazytail's pen first thing so we could visit the deer carcass together, but she was not there. Her humans must have taken her inside for the night. It was cold outside, and Lazytail would have skipped breakfast too. No doubt they thought they were being kind to her.

Oh, well. Maybe next time. Resignedly I trotted on to the site of our kill, and was disappointed again. The carcass was gone, and the place stank of cougar.

One thing is certain: coyotes don't argue with cougars about anything whatsoever. We may hang around and pester them at a safe distance, but that's about it. I could think of many safer and more worthwhile things to do with my evening, so I trotted off in the opposite direction from the way the cougar had gone, which just happened to aim me toward Mr. Burrey's new home and smokehouse.

The weather was one of those glorious, frosty lulls between rainstorms, and the ground had sprouted a thick covering of grass-like ice needles which lifted small pebbles, dead leaves, and other debris an inch or more into the air. Steam gushed from my mouth with each breath, the stars were thick and close, and Moon was so bright I had to squint when looking at her. She happened to be perfectly full, too, which reminded me to be especially alert.

Moon is funny. She's quite pretty and yes, I do sing to her sometimes, but mostly she's an inconvenience. Humans can see me far too well by Moonlight, and the light also seems to stimulate them into all sorts of crazy behaviors, such as walking out in the woods without flashlights to help me keep track of them. In the summertime, when it's warm and dry, I've even seen humans mating by Moonlight—generally on blankets at the gravel bar just downstream from Sunbow. Of course, I'm much more likely to see groups of males drinking beer there and pretending to fish.

On this night I didn't encounter any humans, and it was still quite early when I reached Mr. Burrey's house. It was a mobile home, actually. Mr. Burrey had seemed a little embarrassed about that, as if a mobile home were not as good as a regular house, but I couldn't quite fathom the distinction. A house is a house. They're warm inside and they keep the rain out. I could smell that his smokehouse was in operation, and that was something I could relate to. Venison, this time. I moved closer to test the door.

The smokehouse door was unlocked, but I couldn't make myself go inside at first. My eyes were burning and nose clogged just from poking my head in, so I pulled the door wide open and moved back to wait for things to air out. New smoke kept coming up from a tray of glowing coals and wood chips on the floor, but with the door open the smoke would not stay inside, and soon most of it was gone.

Treasure revealed itself to me with the dissipation of that smoke. Above those coals the smokehouse was filled to capacity with dangling joints and strips of venison. True wealth, just waiting to be harvested, and to reach the lowest rack I wouldn't even have to jump. Holding my breath and stepping gingerly inside, I selected the largest piece within easy reach, and took it. A simple sharp bite and pull, and it was mine. My eyes were burning again, so I squeezed them shut and scuttled on out of there. I ran off a few yards and set the meat down so I could cough and snort and paw at my eyes, but soon I felt better, and was ready to properly investigate my prize: a short haunch, crusted with salt and herbs, and the smoking process had only just started to work on it. I suppose it smelled wonderful, but my nose wasn't working very well just then, so I couldn't tell. No matter. It was sweet and salty and juicy and stolen, and that was good enough for me. I lay down right there and began to eat. The lights in Mr. Burrey's place were out, his property was nicely secluded, and I knew he didn't keep dogs. Nothing to worry about. I devoted full attention to my work.

I heard a low growl directly in front of me, and I was startled.

Startled! What a pitiful, weak word that is. Startlement doesn't even come close to describing my feelings. My chest froze so that I couldn't breathe, and I swear my heart stopped too, for a moment. Carefully I lifted my gaze to the source of that growl, and beheld a wolf. Not just any wolf, mind you: no, this was the largest and most formidable canine creature I had ever in my life encountered, and it was not pleased with me. It crouched in leap-ready position, and its lips were curled back nastily, and Moon-fire burned cold in its eyes. I am not small, but this thing made me feel small, and I never even considered fighting it. Slowly and carefully I began to back away, leaving my meat lying where it was. Maybe it could be distracted by food.

No such luck. The wolf followed my retreat inexorably, stepping over the venison haunch as if it were a rock. This encounter was looking distinctly territorial, but I didn't dare try a full submission posture. If you expose your throat to someone who's really irritated, it may get ripped out anyway.

Flight definitely seemed the best choice, but even that posed a bit of a problem for me. I never doubted I could outrun the wolf given a proper start, but it was too close. My flank would be exposed as I turned around.

I had been in situations like this with farm dogs, and some time previously I had stumbled onto a unique strategy to break the deadlock.

"Hey! Get outta here, you sonafish!"

I shouted as loudly as I could, trying to keep my voice human-sounding. My natural voice is higher-pitched than I like, but I have no shortage of volume, and those words rang out on the night air.

The wolf could see that I was the source of the noise, but couldn't resist looking away for an instant to make sure there was no human behind it. That was all the chance I needed, and I took off down Mr. Burrey's driveway and onto the main road in a burst of pure, panic-driven speed.

After a few hundred yards I risked a look back to see how much I had gained, and found the thing close behind me.

Close is too mild a word: it was *there*. Could have bitten the end off my tail any time it liked. Oh, and I was exaggerating when I said my first burst of speed was panic-driven: I had never known true panic before that moment. I hurled myself down the center of the road then, faster than I had ever run before, and the wolf caught up and ran beside me on the left, smiling now around its tongue. It didn't even seem to be working hard.

I couldn't keep up that speed for long, of course. My lungs were burning already, and soon my legs began to drag despite my uttermost force of will. The wolf stayed with me, then without warning it darted sideways to bump its shoulder hard against mine. Somehow I kept my balance the first time that happened, but the second bump was too much for me. I rolled and skidded for quite a distance before I managed to regain my balance, but then I popped up and slashed instantly sideways as the coyotes had taught me to do. The move was little more than a reflex, really, but by pure chance I did manage to make contact. I felt one fang tear through fur and skin, but it was not enough. Just a little nip. I was answered by the shock of teeth striking to the bone in my left thigh, and my body was dragged backwards and flipped over with overwhelming force. I was too busy to notice any pain.

I didn't have to expose my throat. It was already done, and the jaws were already there, clamping down so I could hardly breathe. Total surrender was my only option, if I could be said to have any options at all. I had no strength left, and not even breath enough to scream.

I forced myself to lie still—to breathe, nothing more. The wolf could have killed me already, but it had not. If we both held still for just a few seconds longer the encounter would change from deadly battle to discipline session, and it's bad form to kill a passive subordinate during a discipline session. That's the rule, and we both knew it.

The seconds passed, and the wolf let its option pass with them. I would live.

Under tense conditions like these it is common for the victor to hold on for a long time in case the 'subordinate' decides to change its mind. I prepared myself for a long wait, forcing myself to remain still. I caught up with my breathing, and my nose recovered from some of its smoke-dullness so that my captor's scent began to pull at my attention. Nothing enhances one's scent like a fight, and even with a less-than-perfect nose I eventually came to recognize this one: it was the same canine scent I had detected in Mr. Burrey's skin.

I suppose John and Mooney didn't do very well in their attempts to give me a 'normal' upbringing, because I was immediately convinced that this wolf and Mr. Burrey were the same. I was just a youngster, after all. What did I know? Werewolf movies were as real to me as anything else.

When the teeth were eventually withdrawn, I stayed down and performed the best greeting ritual I could manage from that position. The wolf accepted it, and I finally felt safe enough to turn my attention away from him and investigate my wounds.

Such a mess! My leg was bruised and bleeding, and it seemed every tooth had penetrated deeply. The numbness of fresh injury was beginning to wear off, and my hip hurt too. Felt like the leg had almost come out of its socket.

The wolf took an interest in my leg then, sniffing and licking at it gently. After a short time his ears and tail went down and he nuzzled my face in what I would have to describe as embarrassment.

Cautiously I pulled myself up onto three legs, and tested the fourth. It failed, and I would have fallen over if the wolf hadn't supported me with his shoulder for a moment. I regained my balance, pointed myself toward home, and tottered carefully forward. The wolf kept himself close beside me the whole way to Sunbow, and even onto the back porch. He showed no fear of human things.

My bad leg caught the edge of the dog door as I went in, and the pain was so great I yelped despite myself. It was the first noise I had made since telling the wolf he was a son of a bitch.

I turned around and saw his head poking through the dog door behind me. He examined the kitchen, paused, and began pushing forward as if to come inside, but Mooney called out to me then, and he froze into stillness. The wolf gave one last look at me, then carefully withdrew his head from the door and was gone.

Chapter 11

Dr. Benton was not on emergency duty that night, but Mooney knew where he lived. She strode right up to his front door and made noises until the lights came on and the door was opened a crack. A short, low-voiced conversation followed, but I didn't pay much attention to the words. Mooney's body language was much more interesting. She really is quite good at these things when she lets herself go completely, and of course the doctor couldn't resist her. Within minutes we were all at his clinic, and I was being examined.

"Ms. Sklarsen—this *is* Sin-Ka-Lip, isn't it?"

"Yes, of course he is. Why?"

"You *did* notice he has teeth now, didn't you? Most people would have picked up on a thing like that and mentioned it to their veterinarian."

"Oh! The teeth. Yes. They look nice, don't they? Last spring they all just sort of started coming in all at once, like for a regular puppy. I was going to stop by and ask you about them, but with one thing and another I never got around to it. Money has been a little short lately."

"Yes. I see. You do have enough to pay for tonight's work, don't you?"

"Uh, well... uh, not really. Not exactly *with* me right now, but... we've known each other for a long time, and..."

"Never mind. I know you're good for it. And anyway, one doesn't come across a patient like Sin-Ka-Lip just any day. Are you sure you won't let me present his case? He's fascinating! And these new teeth just make it better! If... oh, very well. Yes. Perhaps we can talk about it again some other time. I'll get to work now. I'm sure you didn't come here to talk."

In typical contrary, veterinary fashion the man began his exam by looking at my teeth and ears. Any idiot could have seen that my ears were just fine. The blood was dripping from the other end of me. But I suppose we all have our little rituals. Dr. Benton murmured soothingly to me and Mooney and Mouse as he massaged my head and neck, working carefully backwards through skin and fur. He complimented Mooney effusively on its excellent condition and total absence of fleas, which seemed very important to him. I had never suffered from fleas at Sunbow, but I saw what they did to the farm dogs, so I understood his obsession.

The front half of the exam really took only a few seconds, and then it was time to start messing with the wounds. I flinched away at the first touch of his fingers, despite my promise to hold still. That leg *hurt!* Dr. Benton backed off then, and wrote some notes in his folder.

"If you need a muzzle, Sin-Ka-Lip will let you put one on," Mooney volunteered. "Or I can do it. He won't be offended."

Curiously, I really wasn't offended by the idea of a muzzle. It was a compliment, in a way. No one had bothered to suggest a muzzle back when Mr. Bell shot me. I had been toothless then.

Dr. Benton paused in his writing to thank Mooney for her offer, but declined it for the moment. He was planning to drug me before even commencing work.

"He's in good shape but I need to probe the wounds, stitch some of them, and infuse them all with antibiotics. I can't do that with him awake. We'll give him an intramuscular injection of ketamine and xylazine, which should last long enough to get the job done. I'll use gas if I need extra time. I'm pretty sure the leg isn't broken or dislocated, but I'll need x-rays to make sure. You are available to help, aren't you? He's too big for me to lift by myself."

Mooney assured him that she would stay as long as necessary and do whatever she could to help. No one asked my opinion.

The drug injection was somewhat like a vaccination but it went deep into the muscles on my back, and the syringe was a lot bigger, and it hurt more. At least he didn't try to jab the needle into my sore leg. I might have objected to that.

Dr. Benton had explained to Mooney that I would soon begin to feel very strange, and she should kneel down to hold me and comfort me as I fell asleep. She did that, but nothing happened at first and I wondered what all the fuss was about. And then—the world began to change. I had expected to fall over in a wave of overwhelming drowsiness but instead everything just sort of faded away, sideways, very slowly. Mooney was stroking and talking to me but her words and touch were no longer important. Nothing was important.

I became aware of vague shapes around me—some quite close, some embedded in the walls and furnishings, still others somehow present beyond the walls. At first I tried to swing my head around to see them better but each shape would disappear when viewed directly, and I didn't really care about them anyway. As I lost interest in turning my head, my eyes rested without volition on one of the closer ones, and it gradually became clear.

It was a wolf.

The wolf was standing just a few of feet away, staring straight back at me. Suddenly its jaws parted in a pleased smile, and it spoke.

"He's aware of me now. This would be a fitting time to move in."

An irritated, higher-pitched voice answered from another nearby figure and I forced my head to turn that way. This time I could see it. It was a coyote, and its eyes were on me too. Its lips were curled back like it had just stuck its nose in something very disagreeable.

"Just kill it. Its spirit is weak and useless. I'll take it back and try again some other time, maybe."

The wolf spoke again, and once again I managed to swing my head around and look at it. Couldn't seem to focus on both at once.

"Thank you for your concern, Little Brother, but I think I'll wait. Useless or not, all your power is tied up in him while he lives, and now he's mine. This is going to be very interesting!"

The coyote began to speak again but the wolf ignored its words and moved toward me, then around and behind to where I couldn't see it any more.

Pain burst suddenly from my injured leg as if teeth were stabbing back into it—grinding down tooth-for-tooth into the wounds already there. I tried to scream and whip around but my body would not obey me—merely twitched and jerked ineffectively. I may have made some sounds, though. I think I felt Mooney's hands trying to hold me still, heard her voice crooning over and over, "Hush, child, everything is fine."

The pain went deeper—ate into my belly like a lamprey in a salmon—but the drug also had increased its hold and the pain was no longer important to me. Nothing was important to me. I don't remember anything more.

I awoke before dawn feeling dizzy and sick, and there was some sort of smooth plastic thing around my neck and head that made it hard to move or see properly. I stood up and pawed at it vaguely, then stopped for a moment to vomit up nothing. I held still when I was done, and tried to focus myself.

I was in a veterinary hospital and the thing around my head was an Elizabethan collar. A memory of the wolf and coyote came back to me, and I shuddered. It must have been a dream—my first ever. Dreams were not as much fun as I had been led to believe. Maybe the drugs had been to blame. Resignedly I forced myself to lie down and try for more sleep, and after a time I succeeded.

My stomach and the rest of me felt a lot better when I awoke the second time. It was lighter outside, almost dawn, and dogs were barking all around me. There certainly were a lot of them! The scents mingled and crawled over each other so it was impossible to sort them out completely. There was some odor of sickness, but mostly just a lot of bodies—too many to be in the same building. There was plenty of fresh fecal and urine odor, so it was clear quite a few had not bothered to wait until the humans came to let them out. I could sympathize with that. I needed to go out too.

The kennel latch was crude, and I had it open from the inside with a few seconds of clever paw work. I hobbled down the hallway and found a side door, which also opened without difficulty except for the rim of my stiff plastic cone-collar getting in the way. I exited the building, took care of necessary duties, then went back to my kennel and locked myself in again. The leg gave me some trouble, but it was endurable as long as I didn't bump it. I fidgeted on the blankets until I was as comfortable as I was going to get, then dozed off again until the humans came.

Mooney was the first human to greet me. I think she must have been waiting in the parking lot to be let in. She made much of me and my wounds, and I returned the compliment as best I could. When we were alone I asked her if we could go home yet, but she said we had to get Dr. Benton's permission first. I said something rather rude which I won't repeat here, and Mooney told me to hush. When Dr. Benton finally did arrive he came right over to us. I think he wanted to get Mooney out of his way as quickly as possible.

"As you'll remember, Sin-Ka-Lip didn't react well to the anesthetic last night—but he's looking great today! I don't think I've ever seen such a nasty wound look so well the next morning. If he shows a good appetite we might even be able to send him home."

Mooney looked at me and winked. "Did you hear what he said about showing a good appetite? How about a bit of breakfast?" Dr. Benton nodded to an assistant, who hurried off and then came back with a large bowl of canned dog food. I could smell there was medicine in it.

The better brands of dog food are actually pretty tasty, and this was one of those brands. I was still a little queasy but I pretended to be delighted by the food, eating it rapidly and licking the bowl, too. That's not easy when you're wearing an Elizabethan collar.

Dr. Benton was pleased, and Mooney soon had us out of there with a bottle of pills and a promise to come back in two days for a recheck. As soon as we were clear, she took the collar off and I had my first chance to look at myself. I was shocked and heartbroken by what I saw. The leg was puffy and discolored, and completely shaved. Somehow that nakedness was more appalling than anything else. That fur was supposed to last me all winter! The larger holes had been stitched shut but they were all oozing a thin, bloody fluid, and the wound area stank of iodine.

And *this* was the work Dr. Benton was so proud of? I was not impressed, and said so.

The wounds healed rapidly. Dr. Benton remarked on it during our first and only recheck visit.

"I've never seen a deep wound close up like this! Sin-Ka-Lip here has quite the constitution! But then, there are a lot of things about him that aren't quite typical, as we've discussed before. I was planning to see him every four or five days until the drainage stopped and the wounds are well granulated, but I guess we're already there. These stitches will need to come out in a few days, but I know you like to do that yourself. Shouldn't be a problem this time. Just finish up the antibiotics and keep Sin-Ka-Lip away from whatever it was that bit him, and he should be fine.

"Oh, I almost forgot. He's looking so good today I think we can update his vaccinations. What do you think?"

Chapter 12

Fur is funny stuff. Sometimes it comes back in days, sometimes not for months. It was past the fur-growing season, but somehow I got lucky. The wounds had hardly closed before they were hidden by a layer of dense, vigorous new growth, and the pain and stiffness faded almost as rapidly. I apologized to Mooney for my criticism of Dr. Benton's veterinary skills.

Mouse and I went back to school as soon as I could walk properly, and after a week or so I started going out at night again. The coyotes were suspicious when I returned to visit them—sniffed me diligently and persistently from one end to the other. They seemed puzzled and uneasy about something, but eventually they got over it. Lazytail was just glad to see me any old way.

Mouse had refused to go to school without me, but since I was back on my feet so fast, she only lost a few days. We were smothered with attention from our fan club, and several boys began hanging around too, despite themselves. Mouse and I were getting so used to attention that we even enjoyed it a little. That feeling did not include enjoyment of 'meetings' however, and we were both very glum when we brought the news home with us.

A progress meeting was due, to see if Mouse's 'mainstreaming plan' was working properly, and also to address some concerns voiced by parents about me and Mooney. It was scheduled for the second Monday in December, which was a conference day so there were no classes. No classes on Tuesday either. I could definitely do without the meeting, but the two free days would be nice.

One good thing about the meeting was that it brought John back to visit. He and Mooney had been having a series of rather nasty arguments about money, and John's work load in Seattle had suddenly become much heavier, so he couldn't come over as frequently. Even my injury had only prompted an overnight stay, and he hadn't been back since. John must have been feeling guilty about that, because he negotiated a couple of extra weekdays off this time, so he could stay longer.

Mr. Sawyer started the meeting with a compliment on how well Mouse was doing with Mrs. Seeley, and how nicely she seemed to be adapting socially. Then he invited Mrs. Seeley and Mrs. Stanford to give more detailed reports.

Mrs. Seeley was enthusiastic about Mouse and me, Mrs. Stanford rather less so. After they were done, Mr. Burrey presented his impressions of Mouse's progress, which were quite favorable. Finally Mr. Sawyer spoke again.

"I want to congratulate Mouse once more on her excellent progress this term! Her stay here has been a pleasure and an education for all of us. However, as the administrator in charge of this school I have to deal with many things outside of the classroom, and I'm afraid I have to address an issue now that may be a bit sensitive. It has to do with Mouse's Guide Dog 'Coyote'.

"Coyote and Mouse are inseparable, and his behavior here at the school has been flawless. He is obviously a highly trained and extremely valuable animal, and we all enjoy his company. The problem has to do with Coyote's genetic background. Dr. Cultee, would you tell me again just what breed of dog Coyote is, and where he came from? You did say he was a stray of some sort, didn't you?"

John replied smoothly, "Well, he's not exactly a stray. I found him in front of a Safeway store in Tacoma. I was attending a conference, and stopped by to get some coffee, and there he was in a big cardboard box with about a dozen brothers and sisters. A little girl was just giving them all away. I stopped to say hello, and she handed Coyote up to me and said he was her favorite, but her mother told her they all had to go. She didn't seem very happy about it.

"I held Coyote for a minute, and he took to me like I was his best friend in the world. I just couldn't put him down."

I had heard different versions of this story before, but John was really hamming it up this time. I liked the part about the little girl, and we had never made it to a dozen littermates before. John doesn't lie all that much, but he's not bad when he sets his mind to it.

"Did the girl tell you anything about the parents? Are you aware of any coyote or wolf blood in his ancestry?"

John tried to look puzzled and innocent, but I could smell he was getting tense. "Oh, nothing like that. The mother was a purebred white German Shepherd, very large. The father they were not so sure about, but I doubt there are many wolves wandering around Tacoma looking for a good time. Except near the Navy base, of course."

No one looked amused.

I was surprised at John. He had never talked like that in public before! Even I could tell it was the wrong thing to say if he was trying to soothe feelings.

Mr. Sawyer continued without comment, "State law does not specifically prohibit the keeping of wolves, coyotes, and their crosses if they are securely contained on private land, but I have a mandate to protect the students in my care from dangerous situations of any kind. Several parents have claimed that Coyote is clearly a cross of some sort, and therefore inherently dangerous. I can't say that I completely disagree with them. Can you think of any way for me to resolve this situation, short of prohibiting Coyote from coming to school?"

John was trembling now, and his body had grown tense and stiff. He answered in a quiet, controlled voice, but there was a power to it that made the fur stand up on my neck.

"Coyote is a dog because I say he is a dog. If any private citizens feel differently, I suggest they contact me directly. In addition, I would like to suggest that the school district keep well out of any such dispute. I guarantee that you will regret it if you don't.

"Now, I hope this concludes any discussion about my dog's genetic background. Are there any other matters that need to be discussed?"

The room was utterly quiet now, and no one would meet John's eyes. Finally, Mr. Sawyer spoke.

"I'm sorry, Dr. Cultee. I never meant to make this meeting into a confrontation. My job is to settle disagreements, not start them. I'll tell the concerned parents that I'm satisfied with things as they are, and further complaints will have to be directed elsewhere. Is that satisfactory?"

"That will do nicely. I've been expecting trouble about Coyote's physical appearance, and I'm prepared to take legal action as needed. All I ask is that you make your evaluations based on what you actually see, not what people tell you."

The meeting broke up rapidly after that. We all seemed in a hurry to get away. I kind of wondered why Mouse and Mooney and I had even been there.

Mr. Burrey did manage to encounter us in the parking lot again. We were in a break between showers, so the humans stopped to chat for a minute instead of scuttling along to their respective vehicles.

Mr. Burrey congratulated John, and promised his full influence in keeping the bureaucracy at bay. "Getting nasty was a good strategy. Public employees always favor the side that seems most likely to raise a fuss, but I guess you know that already."

Mr. Burrey moved over to greet me and I took a submissive position, which I had not done with him before. Mr. Burrey's canine underscent was clearly present now, and it was clearly identical to that of the wolf who had attacked me. "Don't worry, you old son of a fish. I won't bite you," he whispered to me, then stood up and returned his attention to my humans.

On the way home I had trouble sitting still, and kept jumping up on the seats and then jumping down until Mooney told me to cut it out and sit still. Mooney and Mouse and John were already sitting still. They didn't talk much, either, so when we reached Sunbow I opened the door myself and left them all behind. A good, long run was what I needed.

The rain was heavy at times and my outer fur was quickly soaked, but I felt completely comfortable. The new growth on my leg was already thick enough to do its job. The leg itself seemed completely healed, and didn't slow me down at all. Pretty darn good for just shy of a month! After dark the sky cleared again, and when the glow told me Moon was about to rise, I sat in an open space and watched her come up—watched more closely than I ever had before. I've always admired Moon, but that night she was especially beautiful. Full, and perfect. I felt strange and dizzy when she first showed herself, but only for a second.

I still wasn't a bit tired, so I raced Moon northward up the valley, drunk with the speed of my passage. I could have run like that forever, but the clouds came back so I stopped my race and called it a tie. I was already well beyond Mr. Burrey's place—an astonishing distance for so early in the night! The valley was narrower here, and there weren't so many riverside pastures and fields. A little farther and I would pass the last house, a small one with antlered elk skulls nailed up all over it.

With Moon hidden by clouds the night was dark enough for me to approach the house closely. I would never have done that in good light! Anyone who had killed that many elk and then put their bones up for display had to be a good shot, and not shy about the trigger.

Lights on—dinnertime—beefsteak and potatoes. Hunger struck me then—sudden and powerful. The irresistible scent drew me closer and I put my paws up on the kitchen windowsill so I could peer inside.

A man was in there. An older man, partly bald, sitting at table with his back to me. He was wearing blue jeans with suspenders, a checkered flannel shirt, and shoes. He was wearing his shoes inside the house! Mooney never let anyone do that. The human was alone, and I thought he didn't have many visitors because every level surface was loaded with those small household items humans accumulate so readily. Even the dinner table was covered over, except for the part he was using.

I remained at the window, jaws parted slightly, watching the man eat. My mouth felt strange. Not sore, just strange. Heavy, perhaps. I felt a tickle on one paw and looked down to see that a thread of saliva had spun down onto it. That was unusual. I don't let myself drool much, but I had been thinking about other things—thinking about ways to enter the house without being detected. I directed my gaze back to the human and he turned quickly to face me. Some humans are sensitive that way. We locked eyes for an instant and I felt his shock and fear.

I dropped down from the window in confusion, and moved off to a spot where I could continue to watch the house without being seen. Shortly the man emerged carrying a heavy-looking rifle with a flashlight attached to it. Time to leave for real! I was hardly clear before a side-thumper of an explosion shook the woods, followed rapidly by another one. Even the ground beneath my feet vibrated with those shots! That was one big gun the man was using, and he was firing at shadows. I must truly have frightened him.

I was pleased with myself, and danced along with my rocking horse gait for a time, flipping my tail up in the air with each stride. Then I crossed fresh deer scent and my hunger rushed back again—stronger even than before.

I tracked the deer, caught it, killed it. A mature blacktail buck over twice my size, and he wasn't even sick. I shouldn't have been able to do that.

And another thing...

I'm a coyote. It's in my nature to kill things and to enjoy the killing. That's the truth, and no sense trying to deny it. Human hunters enjoy killing too, or they wouldn't go to so much trouble. Still, the death of that buck brought to me a level of pleasure beyond anything I had ever experienced before. Very strange.

A visitor came to join me as I was eating. It was the wolf who had bitten me the month before. Hastily I backed away from my kill and took a submissive posture. The wolf came over like an old friend, acknowledged my respects, then moved on to sniff delicately at the carcass and begin work on one of the haunches. That left the belly for me, which is where all the best parts are. Very considerate of him.

We gorged ourselves, but had to leave most of the carcass behind. Such a waste... and my coyotes too far away to hear my sharing-howl. I was not surprised when the wolf left me in the vicinity of Mr. Burrey's place. He pushed me over and grabbed my throat in a friendly sort of way, so I popped up and nipped his hocks when he turned away, and we had a pretend battle until I was vanquished again. Being beaten by a recognized superior is kind of fun for both parties.

I took the scenic route home and arrived there shortly before Moonset, which was easy to see because a cold wind had come through and blown away all the clouds. Our kitchen light was on, and Mooney was sitting at the table, but she was asleep with her head pillowed in her arms. I made it past without waking her, which is harder than it sounds. The dog door squeaks, the floorboards squeak, and my claws have a tendency to click on the linoleum. Still, I did manage to get by and into Mouse's bed without waking anyone. I was damp from my mandatory dip in the creek, but I had been diligent with my washing, and felt sure there was no blood left on me.

It was time to go to bed, so I went to bed, but I didn't feel tired. I was burning with energy, and felt I could have started the night all over again. As I curled up behind Mouse I had an urge to nip her on the back of the neck. Not enough to hurt her much, but enough to taste the blood. I restrained myself and the feeling passed.

Mooney's voice woke me just after dawn. She was angry, of course, and beginning to work herself up into a proper state. Then she stopped cold.

"What happened to your leg?"

I lifted my head and dared to look into her eyes. There was no anger in them. Only puzzlement, and a touch of fear.

"Your leg. What's happened to it?" Mooney stepped over and began to run her hands through the fur of my thigh, parting it to examine the skin minutely. Mouse woke up blearily, and leaned back against the headboard to get out of her way.

"It's all gone! No scars, no clip marks—nothing there at all!" Mooney left me to find John, and I jumped out of bed hastily. Felt too vulnerable up there. If they were going to start a big investigation, we might as well do it in the kitchen.

Mooney presented me to John with some trepidation, as if she had already half-convinced herself the whole thing was her imagination. Mooney was leaving herself wide open for teasing, but John didn't do anything of the sort. He simply examined the leg carefully, then pronounced that this was clearly the result of a magical process of some sort. No other explanation would serve. "Mooney and I were hoping it wouldn't happen this way," he added.

Mouse came into the kitchen and stood with her hand on the door jamb, looking confused and worried. "What's the matter with Coyote? Is he hurt again?"

"I'm fine, Mouse. Something strange has hapffened to my leg, pffut I don't think it's pffad."

I turned back to John, "I've asked you apffout magic pffefore, pffut you never tell me anything. Can you tell me now?" I tried to make myself sound meek, and reasonable, and disconsolate. That always helps.

"It's definitely time for more lessons, but first I need some time to sort things out and make a plan. This has taken me completely by surprise. For now, just promise me you won't do it again unless I tell you to."

"Won't do what again?"

"Whatever it was you did to change your leg like that. Think over what you did last night, and then don't do anything remotely like it. If you'll excuse me for a minute, Mooney and I need to make a phone call. Don't go away."

I had never seen John so rattled! Not even when Mooney was arrested. I sat down beside Mouse so she could comfort herself by playing with my ears, but instead she reached down and ran careful fingers over my leg. "Coyote—what's going on? Your leg is okay, isn't it? It feels fine to me."

"They're upffset pffecause the scars are gone and the fur is pffack like new. It just hapffend overnight, and they think it must pffe magic."

"Well, they're probably right, but I don't see why they need to have a cow about it. You can talk, too, and they're used to that. Adults can be so dumb sometimes."

"Thanks, Mouser. It's nice to hear someone talking sense. Pffelly Rupff?" I begged, and sagged down close beside her.

"Rub your own belly, you old goat. Just use your magic. I need to use the bathroom." Then she kissed me on the nose and left. Mouse wasn't as shy as she used to be.

I lay down by the stove and settled myself for a nap. No particular place to go until John and Mooney finished their call, and it had been a long night.

"Sin-Ka-Lip?" That was Mooney, speaking. I scrambled to my feet, and pretended to look alert.

"Sin-Ka-Lip—we've decided it's time for you to know a little bit more about yourself. Maybe it'll help us all figure out what's going on." Mooney was speaking in a diffident, almost embarrassed manner; unlike her usual bossiness.

"So... well... it's like this: some years ago, in the mid-seventies, I was really into Native American world views. Nothing new about that. My family has been that way since Grandpa Sklarsen's day. When I was little Gramps told me stories about how he'd once met Coyote, and Fox, and other crazy critters... and how he'd been cursed for a lark to be part jackalope. Claimed I was cursed, too, most likely, since we shared the blood, but you could never tell when Gramps was pulling your leg. He had tribal connections, anyway, and when I showed an interest he set me up with a Shaman friend in Colville to be guided on a purification fast and spirit quest. It was a lot easier than I thought it would be! A few days of fasting, sweat lodge sessions, and meditations, and right away I slipping into that state where you're dreaming while you're still awake. Shaman said I was a natural, just like Gramps, or maybe my hippie drugs had taught me a thing or two worth knowing. He said he didn't care, the Power flows where it likes. He said it was not his place to judge... until I told him my first dream. Shaman didn't like that dream at all. He said "Poor girl! You don't deserve this. I should never have led you down this path."

I had dreamed of Coyote, you see. Or 'Sin-Ka-Lip' as he's sometimes called in that area. That's what put the Shaman off.

"Coyote was waiting for me in the Spirit World. He didn't make himself hard to find at all, just walked right up to me and told me he was willing to be my Totem. He said he liked me; I was his kind of human. He also told me our family land was a place of strong Power, and might prove useful to him in an endeavor he was contemplating. Coyote visited my dreams several times during that quest and afterward, and I learned that he was getting ready to undertake a quest of his own. This is what he told me:

"'I am a powerful Totem,' he said. 'I serve my own kind most of all, as it is with all of us, but I have a duty to you humans as well. Or at least, to the humans who were here before your kind came. They call themselves the People, and they call your kind the White People. It makes little difference to me, except that your kind of human is harder to get along with than the others. You tried to kill us all, but we coyotes were too clever for you and now we're stronger than ever. Still, you've brought a new magic with you that is difficult to deal with. Some of you are comfortable to be around, but others—arrgh! Their aura is harsh, and alien. We call it *ixhicoláha*, or improper belief, and my Medicine is weakened when too much of it surrounds me. Many times I've unexpectedly lost my ability to change form or maintain illusions when walking among you. It's difficult to describe how embarrassing that can be!

"'The greatest indignity came in nineteen-oh-three, when I was shot and killed by... someone I trusted. It was an accident, really, but the man was a scientist so he preserved my body, not wanting it to go to waste, and sent it off to his homeland for further study. Sent it to *Berlin*, for pity's sake! My skeleton is still there, on display, and pieces of my flesh are also still there, in neatly-labeled glass-capped glass jars. No, make that neatly *mislabeled* jars. 'Apparently extinct subspecies,' indeed! I *am* my species. My body encompasses all coyote-kind!

"'But never mind about that. That is not the point. The important fact is this: my spirit cannot fade while my people live, and while humans dream of me, but in your World I'm helpless now. I have little power when I'm dead.'

"That's what Coyote told me, or close to it. But he told me more than that. Coyote is not entirely without friends, and several recovery attempts had been made over the years, all unsuccessful. It was hard for those of the People who knew the old ways to accomplish anything in Hitler's Germany, or later in East Germany, so recovery was taking longer than expected.

"Coyote told me that a new effort was being made to bring his body back from East Berlin. A part of it, anyway. Only a little piece would be needed. In fact, this plan required only a single cell to be revived by magic. That cell would be used to grow a new body, and that body would be Coyote's. In addition, Coyote would allow only part of his spirit to enter the new body and return to our World. Without memories, he would be born and raised in the society of the White People, so he could finally master our way of thinking and learn the secret of our power. Coyote had offered to be my Spirit Guide, but what he really wanted was for me to guide him.

"Coyote may be lazy, untrustworthy, and sometimes malicious, but old 'Imitator' is actually the most creative of the Animal People, and quite brave in his way. He told me that in all the histories of the Worlds, this has never been tried. I couldn't turn him down, and I've devoted my life to his experiment. Devoted it to *you*, Sin-Ka-Lip."

"Hold on!" I yipped. "Are you trying to tell me I'm *Coyote?* The real, magical Coyote, like in the legends?"

"Yes. But I've told you that before. Did you think I was lying to you?"

"What am I supffpffosed to think, Mooney? John told me I'm the result of a DNA expfferiment!"

John answered that one. "Both statements are true, Coyote. The DNA experiment was done exactly as I told you, but it would never have worked without Medicine Power.

"I am Shaman, although not greatly advanced. My training in that direction was slowed by my decision to go to college and medical school. You know all that, but I don't think I've ever told you who my Totem is.

"Fox is the one who speaks to me in my visions. In fact, he's the one who directed my steps to the universities. He had a plan that could only be accomplished in that way, if it could even work at all. He told me of this plan on his very first visit. 'Coyote is dead,' he said. 'His spirit speaks to me and asks for help. I will call to the Powers to recreate his body as I've done before, but this time he wants more than that. Coyote would learn the White People's Medicine. He wants that power which let them conquer this land so quickly we're still dazed from it. Coyote is crazy to try this, but he has always been crazy, and he has almost always talked me into helping him with his schemes. I have tendencies in that direction myself.'

"Fox smiled then, and he smiled in a way that did look rather demented. But maybe he was just teasing me. I was quite young then, and even in my dream state I was speechless at the honor of being so addressed by a Spirit of Power. I was terrified that it should be sharing these personal thoughts with me, and I had no idea why it chose to do so.

"That first vision encounter with Fox lasted for a long time. Fox asked me many questions about the White People and what they believed most strongly. Finally we concluded that this thing called 'Science' was their greatest strength. It is a fanatical belief that the World operates in only one way, with rules that cannot be changed under any circumstances. This belief is false, of course, but when held firmly enough, by enough people, it has often vanquished us. The guns and the well-fed soldiers beyond count didn't help either.

"Fox knows many things, and he has great power, but museums and laboratories and universities are saturated with thoughts and beliefs that are alien to his kind. Fox has trouble with that sort of place, just like Coyote does. He required help to get a part of your body back from Germany, and guidance on how to apply his Medicine Power in the right way. It took me almost twenty years, but in the end I gave him what he needed."

John laid a hand on my shoulder gently, perhaps even reverently. He looked straight into my eyes with an expression that made me turn away in embarrassment.

"The result... is you," he continued softly. "My old colleagues at the research lab are still working on their super dog, and they may even succeed some day. Fox and I just used a little magic to beat them to it. The talking was not my idea, by the way. You figured that out on your own.

"You are one of the more magical beings alive in this World today, Coyote. Like the others of your kind, you have an innate magical ability that can never be taken from you. But you are not here to play with magic. You are here to put magic aside for now, and learn to do things the other way. It was your own idea, even though you can't remember it now." John stopped talking and looked at me expectantly, as if waiting for some kind of response.

I was speechless, for once—just stared back dumbly with my jaws agape and my tail drooped down to the floor.

"Well, don't you have any questions?"

"I don't know what to say! Why didn't you tell me this pffefore?"

"It wasn't time for you to know."

"What *else* is it not time for me to know? I need to think apffout all this," I said, and slipped away through the dog door before anyone could stop me.

I've been told that long, steady running causes the body to release morphine-like chemicals called endorphins, resulting in a 'natural high'. If that's true, then I'm an addict. The fear of cougars, hunters, and farm dogs just seems to make it better.

I headed north, up the valley. That's the way I go when I want to get away from humans. The cold front had made the world cloudless and windless, with a sweet, tangy smell made up of snow, spruce, hemlock, and a hundred other scents I don't know the human names for. I didn't skirt the Burrey place this time. It's right on the most direct path north, and I figured the wolf wasn't so dangerous for me any more. And it was daylight, so he wouldn't be out anyway.

Mr. Burrey was out, though. He was butchering a deer. *My* deer. I recognized it by the scent, and by the missing portions. I recognized Mr. Burrey's canine scent too. His wolf scent. Mr. Burrey smelled more wolf than human this morning.

Some of the hunters I've seen can't even strip out the guts without splattering their shirts, but this man seemed to know exactly what he was doing. His movements were smooth and unhurried, he never cut twice in the same place, and only his hands were bloody. After a time he sat down for a rest, and glanced around idly. His eyes passed over the bushes I was hiding in, then snapped back and locked onto me. "Coyote! So glad you could come to visit. Have you had breakfast yet?" Mr. Burrey returned to the carcass and gathered up a double handful of the nicer scraps, then set them out neatly on a patch of undisturbed grass halfway between us. "Help yourself. It's your kill anyway." Then he turned his back to me and resumed work.

I slunk over cautiously and bolted the meat, then continued to watch from my closer vantage. Mr. Burrey began talking to me as he cut, still keeping his back and side to me, and his eyes politely averted. Finally I crept over and nuzzled his legs, and accepted the morsels he handed back from time to time.

I had never watched a human-style carcass partitioning from so close before. Mooney didn't approve of meat, and I didn't feel welcome enough at the other places. Mr. Burrey's knives and saw were much more efficient than teeth, but perhaps not as much fun. I wasn't complaining, though.

Mr. Burrey finished the cutting and began to wash his tools and hands. When that was done he fetched another bucket, filled it with clean water, and presented it to me.

"Thirsty? Help yourself! I'll let all this set a bit, mix up some salt and herbs, and get it straight into the smokehouse. Are you sure you don't want any more?" Mr. Burrey looked over his work and selected another choice morsel to tempt me with, but I was too full. All I could do was sniff and take it from his fingers, and set it down on the grass. Maybe later.

Mr. Burrey knelt in front of me and reached cautiously forward to scratch between the ears. I kept those ears forward in a friendly sort of way, so he knew he was welcome to do that. "So—what did you think of last night? A bit of a surprise for both of us, eh? I never thought you could be affected that way, or I would have tried harder to warn you."

I attended to Mr. Burrey politely—as politely as I could manage—but his words rolled over me and my eyelids kept closing themselves despite my best efforts to keep them open. What I really wanted was a nap—maybe even right where I was. Mr. Burrey noticed my condition and gave in to it.

"All right, my friend, I get your drift. The party's over, and now I'm talking too much. We can speak again later." He rose to his feet and left me.

Old nature books will often have the wily wolf captured or killed while resting after a big meal. They called the condition being 'Meat Drunk,' and it is not a superstition. Just then a fine, long nap seemed the most luxurious of all possible pleasures, and I sauntered off until I found a Sun-warmed rock to lie down on, then flopped belly-up and gave full attention to digesting my meal. It was still frosty in the shade, but the day was absolutely wind-free, and Sun's diligent work had made my spot almost too hot for me.

I slept heavily until my nose was assaulted by wood smoke, and I woke to find myself immersed in billows of the stuff. I jumped to my feet and tried to decide which way to run, then relaxed when the source became apparent. Mr. Burrey had started the fire in his smokchouse, and the alder smoke was oozing onto the ground like fog instead of rising up in the air as it's supposed to. Smoke does that sometimes on a cold still day. I sneezed and shook myself, then trotted down to a smoke-free part of Mr. Burrey's yard, where I could supervise.

I had slept through the salting and loading process, and the fire adjustment was almost done already. I felt too lazy to go out running, but I wasn't quite ready to nap again, and the thought of food was not appealing. Truth to say I was sort of bored, so I just stayed put. Mr. Burrey finished his work and came over for greetings, and I remembered one thing that is always worth doing if the human is trustworthy. Rolling ostentatiously onto my back, I exposed my belly for attention.

Mr. Burrey leaned over and gave it a perfunctory pat, then squatted down and cautiously poked at my thigh where the wound had been. Finally he grabbed the paw and tugged at it until I kicked out irritably to make him let go.

"Your leg looks good, like it was never injured." He was gazing at me earnestly, the way humans do when they want to talk about something and can't quite figure out how to bring up the subject.

I was pretty sure I knew what he wanted, and I was feeling mellow enough to make it easy for him, so I rose to my haunches and returned his gaze politely. Not threat-style, just attentive. Humans seem to like it when you look at them while they're talking. If he had something to say, this would be a good time.

Mr. Burrey seated himself cross-legged and straight-backed, then began speaking carefully and respectfully, as one human would to another of equal rank. He was dominant, so he couldn't really mean it, but I appreciated the gesture.

"One night about a month ago I saw you here, eating some of my smoked venison. The smokehouse door was open, and you were lying down right about where we're sitting now. You were enjoying yourself so much you didn't even notice what was going on around you, so you were surprised by a rather alarming visitor. What you did then was quite remarkable. You told your visitor to get lost in very loud, reasonably clear English. I was looking straight at you in bright moonlight, so I know what I'm talking about.

"Now, some people call you a dog, and some call you a coyote. The smarter ones don't know what to call you at all. Whatever it is you are, it is not generally considered to be a talking kind of creature. We humans tend to think we have a monopoly on that sort of thing.

"I can see how you may be reluctant to discuss this capability with most humans, and if you choose not to talk to me now, I'll try not to be too disappointed. But still I have to ask: will you talk to me? I think we have a lot to discuss."

I looked back at Mr. Burrey with ears forward. I might talk to him, might not. There was no hurry. He waited for a minute, then smiled wryly. "Oh, well. I guess I'll have to do all the talking myself for now. I know you can understand me perfectly well, and there are a few things you need to realize.

"First, I'm sure you've figured out by now that I have a bit of a magic problem. A curse, if you will. These things are not well accepted by the more educated humans, but the term 'lycanthropy' is often used to describe my condition. It's not painful or dangerous in itself, but it can put me in situations which are quite deadly for me and those around me. I've learned to deal with it by living as far out in the country as possible, and by keeping a close eye on the calendar. Still, when this condition is active I can have quite a temper, along with other behavioral problems that I find hard to control. I've studied psychology to try and deal with the situation, and the training does help, but otherwise I've made no progress.

"This condition is considered to be transmissible under certain circumstances, and it now appears the curse has affected you too. We need to talk so that I can give you advice about how to keep it from getting the best of you."

Mr. Burrey paused for a moment, then continued when I didn't say anything.

"The change always occurs on the night of the full moon, and often on the night before or the night after, but never more than those three nights. It doesn't wait for midnight, but gets to work at moonrise, regardless of where the sun is, so during the summer months it starts and ends in daylight. The process is so gentle I can hardly feel it. I just get kind of dreamy for a bit, and it's over. It doesn't even matter if I'm moving or standing still, except that when I'm moving I always lose balance and fall over from the sudden shift in body proportions.

"The real problem comes just after the change to wolf form has occurred. I'm immediately overcome by a hunger so powerful I can't even describe it properly. I'll have a desire to kill and eat literally anything I see, even humans. The feeling passes after I have a good meal, so I try to keep something nearby when my time approaches.

"There's a lot more to tell, but I'm not sure I want to continue with you just staring at me like that. I've told you my secret, and I think it really is your turn to speak now."

Mr. Burrey did have a point. His secret was just as delicate as mine, if not more so.

"Okay. I'll talk. What do you want me to say?"

Mr. Burrey's mouth sagged open for a second, then snapped shut. "You really *can* talk!"

"You convinced me," I responded mockingly. "Was I too gullipffle?"

"Was that last word supposed to be gullible? I couldn't quite catch it."

"I have troupffle with the pffes and pffes," I answered irritably. "Those sounds don't fit into a pffropffer mouth. They were invented pffy creatures with tight, round little lipffs, like I have under my tail."

"Maybe you could give some sort of visual signal to help discriminate them," Mr. Burrey suggested helpfully. "Your ears would be good. You could just move them forward or backward to show what you meant."

"I'll think apffout it," I replied a little coldly, but then I remembered he was dominant, and had to be treated with better respect than that. "Thank you for the idea," I added dutifully.

Mr. Burrey had lost his customary poise. He was trembling slightly, and had leaned toward me so that I felt uncomfortable. I shuffled back a few inches.

"Who taught you to talk? Did Dr. Cultee do some surgery or something?"

"No one taught me. I did it all myself. I think anyone could talk if they wanted to, pffut they get annoyed with me when I try and teach them.

"Excepfft for Pffrincess. I just got her to say 'unlock,' and I'm making pffrogress with the word 'more'. Excepfft she thinks it's easier to just whine and nuzzle my chin."

"Who's Frincess?"

"*Pffrincess*. Pfrinnn... cesss. She's a coyote pffupff from the spffring pffefore last. She lives near Sunpffow. Pffrincess won't grow upff, and looks just like the new pffupffs from this year, pffut she's really smart. I hopffe she's not sick."

"Could you teach me?"

I guess he didn't care much about Princess, which was too bad. I did. She and Lazytail were my best non-human friends. I put those thoughts aside to try and answer Mr. Burrey's latest question.

"You already know how to talk. What could I teach you?"

"But I can't talk when I'm a wolf."

"Have you tried?" I answered meekly.

"Of course not. Wolves can't talk!"

"Yes, of course, Mr. Pffurrey. I think I need to go home now." I began to edge away. This man was beginning to annoy me.

Mr. Burrey saw what I was doing, and tried to change the subject. "Wait! Forget about the talking. There are things you need to know about tonight!"

I ignored him and danced off. Mr. Burrey called after me: "Yesterday the moon was not completely full. That is tonight, so we'll both be changing again. Get away from your house as quickly as you can, and meet me here. I'll have meat ready for you."

"Mr. Pffurrey thinks I'm a werewolf," I told John when I got back to the house. "He says he's a werewolf too."

"You can't be a werewolf, Stinky. Only a human could be a werewolf, if there even are such things. Or, did Mr. Burrey say you would change into a human when the moon is full? The proper term for that would be 'coywere' I suppose. Why does he think that?"

Suddenly I didn't want to tell John about my night's activities. There was a nagging feeling that some of them might have been less than appropriate.

"Oh, nothing in pffarticular," I replied evasively. "He looked at the pfflace where the wound was, and didn't know what to think apffout it." I had never told anyone about how I was injured, except to say it was from a fight. They all thought it was a dog, even though I had never said that specifically.

"I wish you hadn't let him look at you like that," John replied in a worried tone. "I don't want anyone paying special attention to that sort of thing. Maybe we should clip some of the fur down the way it was before, so it's not so noticeable."

"No! If anyone tries to mess upff my fur again I'll pffite them!" Then I remembered John's status, and shrank down into submissive posture.

John grabbed my throat fur and rolled me over gently to acknowledge there were no hard feelings, then began to scratch behind the ears. "What are we going to do with you, Coyote? None of us has a clue, you know. Even Fox and OldCoyoteSpirit are just guessing. I can tell by the way they ask about you. OldCoyoteSpirit seems especially strange this last month. It's almost like he's losing interest in the whole plan."

"Who is OldCoyoteSpffirit?"

"Didn't I mention that? OldCoyoteSpirit is the part of your soul that was left behind in the Spirit World when you were born. He's been keeping an eye on you all your life."

"Really? I had a dream last month, and I think OldCoyoteSpffirit was in it. He didn't seem to like me. He said my spffirit was useless, and he wanted to take it pffack."

"You saw Old Coyote in a dream? You're not supposed to be able to remember your dreams!"

"Maypffe it was the drugs. Dr. Pffenton gave me a shot to make me sleepff while he fixed my wounds, and when I was almost asleepff I saw a coyote and a wolf standing in front of me. They were arguing, and the coyote said my spffirit was weak and useless. He asked the wolf to kill me so he could take it pffack."

John stared down at me, his head cocked in astonishment. "Wolf and OldCoyoteSpirit working together? That's hard to believe! I was taught they don't get along these days. Of course, it could all be just a regular dream you made up—not a vision dream.

"You know, Stinky, I'm just a mortal but I think there's more to you than OldCoyoteSpirit gives you credit for! But never mind my opinion; OldCoyote's experiment has hardly begun, and you have years ahead of you to work it out. For now you need to keep to the business at hand, which brings us clear 'round to our conversation from this morning. Have you figured out what you did last night to grow your fur back and make the scars go away? That sort of magic requires a full Totem's powers, but Fox says he had nothing to do with it."

John deserved at least some sort of a story, so I obliged him. "I ran north upff the valley after I left Sunpffow. I kepfft on running after dark, racing with Moon. I pffothered the man with the elk skulls on his house, and then I caught a deer and ate some of it. Then I went home. I don't remempffer any magic at all."

"You killed a deer by yourself? That's quite an accomplishment! I know Mooney doesn't like that sort of thing, but it *is* part of your nature, and you should be proud if you do it well. What you kill should not be wasted, though. We need to find it and bring it home. It's probably half-frozen and in good condition... or... I forgot. It was sick, wasn't it?"

"Yes," I lied. "I don't think you would want any, pffut I think I should go pffack tonight and have some more. If that's alright with you."

"Don't make yourself ill."

Mooney came out to us then, and offered me lunch and breakfast. "I ate at Mr. Pffurrey's house. I'm full right now," I replied politely.

"What did he give you? You're never full!" she teased. "Well, you can come on in and watch us eat. Maybe your appetite will come back."

You know, it did. I sometimes wonder why I don't get fat.

By unvoiced consensus we didn't talk any more about magic and special destinies. We just gathered around the kitchen table and chatted about nothing in particular. The wood stove was roaring busily and the house was too hot, but humans need it that way and I had long ago learned not to complain. I just panted discretely from time to time. Through the kitchen window I could see wispy, almost transparent mare's tail clouds coming in from the east, and I knew the weather would change again before nightfall. And besides, Mooney had heard on the radio that snow was likely. That would be nice, although it hardly ever stuck so early in the season. Sometimes we would have a whole winter with no snow at all.

Mouse was excited, and remarked that she had never played in snow before. John and Mooney glanced at each other for an instant, but they didn't say anything. They had already figured out that Mouse didn't really have amnesia. Now they knew she was from a place where it didn't snow.

I knew exactly where Mouse's old home was. That was our secret. Why she left she had not told even me, but she still cried about it from time to time, and she was terrified by the thought of being sent back there.

After lunch I wandered off to the hayloft for a nap, and awoke at dusk with the scent of new snow and old hay around me. I felt excited, bubbling with energy. Definitely needed to run.

There were no snowflakes yet, but the clouds were still thickening. It would be a comfortably dark night, even with Moon behind them. I wandered idly through vacant goat pens, and peered into the living room for a time before starting. My humans were arrayed on chairs in front of the television, faces intent in the flickering light. Mooney would be turning on the living room lamps soon.

I didn't feel like getting wet just then, so I crossed Fry Creek by taking our driveway down to the main road with its culvert, then following Mr. Bell's drive back up. His cows were inside already, but I passed several elk who were borrowing the south pasture. We ignored each other as we usually did.

It was pretty much dark by human standards as I strolled into Mr. Bell's front yard. He was watching television too—same program. Jake was asleep with his head under the footrest of the recliner, ready to be pinched there when Mr. Bell put it down. Jake appeared to be spending a lot more time indoors these days, which was rather tolerant of his master since Jake always stank of manure and general hound-dogginess. I had never known him to have a bath, although Mr. Bell's cow dip kept him free of fleas.

I stood on the front porch a bit longer, front feet on the railing and head cocked around so I could view human, dog, and television clearly. After a while I lost interest and wandered out into the yard again. Time to leave all this behind and begin my run in earnest. Maybe Mr. Burrey would have some food waiting for me as he had promised.

The overcast sky to the west still had a bit of light to it, but now there was light to the east as well. Moon was just rising, trying her best to penetrate the snow clouds. My eyes were drawn and held by that faint wash of light and I stood bemused for a time, thinking of nothing in particular.

A cow snorted in the loafing barn and I jumped and looked around guiltily. Really should keep more alert in hostile territory! I turned toward the barn and began to slink cautiously closer.

Halfway there I stopped in puzzlement. Mr. Bell had forty-seven full-grown Holsteins in that barn, and I had been about to enter with the intention of killing and eating one of them! That went so far beyond stupidity I couldn't think of a word for it. I was very hungry, though. Painfully hungry. I turned away from the barn and ran off in the direction of Mr. Burrey's place.

He had promised to have meat for me, and if he had forgotten that promise I could always break into his smokehouse and take some for myself.

The wolf was waiting for me on Mr. Burrey's driveway, gnawing on a deer femur. He was crushing the bone casually, effortlessly, then carefully licking out the rich marrow. My own leg bone is a quarter that size. He must have really been holding back when he bit me the month before.

A good part of the deer skeleton was laid out neatly on the driveway, cut into convenient pieces with quite a bit of meat left on. Mr. Burrey must have been planning for this meal the whole time he was butchering. The wolf greeted me courteously though rather briefly, and we both went single-mindedly to work.

I had a late start but I ate faster, so we each got about half of what was there. I thought maybe the buck had been sick after all, since my bones also cracked open with little effort. They tasted and smelled just fine, though. Mr. Burrey's driveway was littered with bone fragments when we were done, and we both sprawled contentedly among them, licking our muzzles and pads.

I really do like to keep myself clean, so I began licking my front paw and drawing it from the back of my head forward and over the muzzle to wipe away any last flecks of food. That brought my ear forward as usual, but something was not quite right. The ear tip barely touched my eye. It should be much longer than that — should cover the eye completely and extend clear out to the bridge of my nose.

I checked the other ear and it was exactly the same, more than two inches shorter than it should have been. Not up to coyote specifications at all! The ears felt perfectly normal; they lifted and turned just the way they were supposed to lift and turn, and there was certainly nothing the matter with my hearing. Nothing was wrong with those ears except for their size. Strange. More strange than you can know, if it has never happened to you.

The wolf had been watching my facial explorations intently, and now he was smirking. The expression is hard to describe, so you'll just have to take my word for it. Smirking he was, and not trying to hide it.

"What's so funny?" I muttered irritably, in English. I'll do that sometimes when I can't figure out how to express myself in proper canine body language. And anyway, that wolf was dominant, so I had to be careful about snarling or showing teeth.

The wolf stood up and approached me, still smirking, so I lay down and exposed my belly to be sure there were no hard feelings. He ignored all that — just looked down at me for a moment, and then began to contort his face and move his chest strangely. I thought he was going to vomit, so I rolled sideways to get myself clear.

What came out of his mouth were sounds, not the slightly used venison I was expecting. First whines and squeaks, then something very much like the human vowel sounds *ay, ee, eye, oh, yew*. The wolf appeared immensely pleased with this accomplishment, and began to struggle with new groupings.

"K-k-k-oyy...*ta*," he finally produced, after considerable effort and experimentation.

"You mean 'Coyote'? You're trying to say my name?"

He smiled back at me and told me yes by his posture. He even appeared to wag his tail, but I've been told that wolves don't wag their tails, so I guess he was just moving it back and forth.

The wolf repeated his new word several times, polishing the edges until it sounded pretty good. Then he started on another one, which went faster.

"W-ooll-ff."

"You're saying 'wolf'!" More agreement.

"K-oyy-ta... woolff," he proclaimed proudly, and nudged my ear with his muzzle.

My mythological namesake is famous for his pigheadedness, and I suppose I'm well endowed with the trait myself... but there is a limit.

"You're saying that my ears are shorter pffecause I've turned into a wolf," I stated flatly.

More agreement.

"You really are Mr. Pffurrey, aren't you?"

Agreement again.

"You told me wolves can't talk."

"Wrrronn-ga." He was learning fast.

We worked out more words together, but Mr. Burrey really didn't require my help. He already knew the words, just needed practice teaching his throat how to form them properly. I gathered that different muscles were involved when he was in human form, and he had to start from basic sounds. It had never even occurred to him that such a thing was possible. After a while Mr. Burrey became tired from contorting his mouth and throat to produce human words, and he was biting his tongue too often. I was accustomed to speaking English, but I was having my own troubles. My voice sounded funny now—low-pitched and strange—and I had almost bitten my tongue too. We decided we had had enough of talking.

We should have been sleepy after such a big meal, but it just seemed to give us more energy. With no trouble at all I lured Mr. Burrey into a race westward along the Wynoochee-Wishkah road, and we were streaking up the stretch of switchbacks called 'Thirteen Corners' just as the first snowflakes began to fall.

The road straightened after we climbed out of the valley, and there we could go full speed without skidding on the gravel. I'm not sure how fast we ran, but the snowflakes stung when they struck my nose and tongue, and my eyes were pinched almost shut against them, and the roar of wind in my ears drowned out all other sounds. Mr. Burrey had been toying with me on our previous race.

I'm pleased to report that I beat him decisively, this time. The thought occurred to me that another fight might have a different outcome as well... but we canines don't necessarily go picking fights just because we think we might win. Dominance is based on more than physical strength. It's a matter of respect and tradition, too. And anyway, he still was bigger than I was.

I don't think Mr. Burrey had played much with dogs or wolves before; certainly not with coyotes. Several of the games seemed new to him. We had a good time and covered a lot of ground.

The snow was coming down so thickly I couldn't see far or scent much, and the frozen ground from our cold snap was letting it accumulate after all. There were several inches on the road by the time we got back to Mr. Burrey's place, and it showed no signs of slowing. Moon wouldn't be setting quite yet, but Mr. Burrey seemed to have a fear of being late home. Understandable, considering his condition.

We settled ourselves on the snow in Mr. Burrey's yard, dozing and waking while fresh snow covered us like a blanket. We still weren't tired, but neither of us wanted to go inside the house, and we were done with running. Finally Moon's glow began to sink and fade into the western half of the valley, although dawn was not quite ready yet in the east. I kept myself awake, with an eye fixed diligently on my companion. I wanted to see the transformation.

I missed it. Probably always would. I was distracted by my own transformation just when I should have been paying attention.

A transient wash of dizziness and there I was, virtually unchanged except for my ears, jaws, and fur markings, but with a naked, snow-covered human curled up close beside. Immediately he staggered to his feet, brushed the snow from his shoulders, and turned to face me.

"Gloat on, you son of a dog." Mr. Burrey had already begun to shiver violently, and his voice was thick with cold, and with amused envy. I shook myself and followed silently as he picked his way painfully over to the back door. He hissed sharply with each step, and kept blindly bumping into things. I think his dark-vision had disappeared with his wolf form. He opened the door and reached inside to grab a towel that happened to be hanging there, dried himself, and put on a heavy robe and slippers that also just happened to be there, then turned to me and offered breakfast.

"Yes, thank you," I replied politely as I had been taught. I was planning to have a good breakfast at Sunbow, but there was no sense wasting such a convenient opportunity.

Just like John, Mr. Burrey knew how to put on a proper breakfast. Scrambled eggs, sausage, buttered toast, and lots of it. Mooney says a man could get a heart attack just looking at a breakfast like that, but she read somewhere that dogs are immune. I guess that counts for me as well. Mr. Burrey would have to take his own chances. Maybe he felt his monthly transformations would help clear out the gunk from his arteries.

"Would Monsieur like his meal served on the table—or on the floor?"

"On the floor, pfflease. Mouse thinks I should eat from the tapffle pffecause I'm a mempffer of the family and it's disrespffectful to treat me differently, pffut the floor is a lot more comfortapffle."

"Yes, I know."

Mr. Burrey ate much more slowly as a human, and he had to clean things up too, so after I finished my own breakfast I lay upright, sphinx style, and watched him. His back was turned to me as he washed the dishes, so that was a good time to discuss sensitive subjects if we needed to. Easier for me, at least.

It was Mr. Burrey who spoke first. "I've been really worried you might hurt somebody. Was there any trouble?" He was hunching his shoulders like he was afraid of the answer I might give.

"No troupffle. For a minute I wanted to kill one of Mr. Pffell's cows, pffut that was stupffid, so I didn't. It was strange, though. I never wanted to do anything like that pffefore."

"That's the way it works. You get these killing urges that seem so reasonable; then later you wonder what got into you." Mr. Burrey paused, then continued earnestly, "Well, something really did get into you. The curse is not a passive thing. It varies in intensity, and I believe there's some sort of demon or spirit that controls it. The spirit will control you, too, if you let it. Sometimes it talks to you during your dreams. Have you heard it yet?"

"I don't have dreams."

"That's funny; I thought everyone dreamed, even animals. But excuse me. I guess it would be more polite for me to say 'non-human beings'."

"Call me what you like; I don't care apffout that sort of thing. Pffut pfflease tell me more apffout this spffirit. Can it really make me do things I don't want to?"

"I don't really know for sure, but I think so. So far I haven't injured any humans, but a couple of times I've come awfully close. I try to stay as far out in the country as possible during the full moon time. There are fewer people around, and somehow it's easier to control myself. Out here I feel more like a real wolf and less like a monster."

Mr. Burrey didn't say anything more for a bit, but his words had got me to thinking about the elk skull man. I had been watching him with intense concentration, then felt something was wrong. Now I remembered: it was the man I had been drooling for fully as much as the food on his plate. The feeling had been so natural that only a vague disquiet had persisted to warn me.

This was not cool. It was not right for something to get inside my head like that! I was silent until Mr. Burrey asked what was bothering me.

"The night pffefore last, I looked at a man in the wrong way, like he was food. I didn't even notice what I was thinking!"

"Yeah. Scary, isn't it? I could handle any part of this except the business of losing control of myself like that. Just remember—food is the key! Keep yourself fed, and you won't get in trouble. Also, don't bite anything you don't plan on killing."

"Does that mean you're sorry you pffit me, or sorry you didn't kill me?" I teased. We were both taking ourselves too seriously.

Enough talking. Breakfast was done, and the snow was falling faster than ever—almost a foot on the ground already. Looked like time to go home.

Humans seem to find great beauty in the sight of a coyote bounding through deep snow, but I say it's a lot of work. I was quite warm and tired when I got back to Sunbow, and it was later than I wanted it to be. The humans were sitting down to breakfast, but their eyes kept turning anxiously outward through the kitchen window. I got a good view of that because I came up from a direction they weren't expecting.

I was in through the dog door before anyone saw me (Mooney had enlarged the opening again, so I fit nicely).

"Hi. I'm pffack," I offered cautiously, keeping prudently close to the door. "What's for pffreakfast?"

Mooney compressed her lips and lowered her eyebrows, but didn't say anything at first. That gave Mouse a chance to scramble out of her chair and come over to hug me. She had the house memorized, so she could move pretty fast when she felt like it.

"Don't you ever stay home at night any more?" she asked plaintively. "We all worry about you."

"I'm a wild animal. I need to go out at night."

"You're not wild, Coyote! You've been with people all your life, and you'd never hurt anyone."

"I am so wild," I insisted. "The coyotes let me run with them, and I don't have any morals. Mooney said so herself. You can't trust me. I might do anything. Anything at all. And you can't make me stay when I need to go out. So there!"

"You sound more like your father every day," John observed. Then he and Mooney chuckled, and everything was okay. I had a suspicion they were making fun of me, though.

Breakfast was oatmeal with raisins, and a melon slice on the side. I liked Mr. Burrey's version better.

Chapter 13

Snow came heavily all through that day, and I never heard the snow plow. John couldn't leave for Seattle at the time he was planning to, and of course there was another school-free day for Mouse and me. Just before dusk the electricity stopped, and Mooney brought out candles to have ready. I went out for a run so I could be alone at Moonrise in case the wolf curse hit again.

I didn't feel anything special, but still I pushed an ear forward to cover each eye in turn before I was convinced. Moonglow in the sky, ears still long. Seemed safe enough. I was through for the month, and could go back inside to be with my family.

I was hungry enough for dinner, but didn't feel any homicidal urges whatsoever. Even so I felt unsure of myself, and kept aloof. Mooney thought I was mad at her for some little thing, and came by later to find out what she had done wrong—even volunteered a belly rub! We all went to bed early, and I actually slept through most of the night.

In the morning the snow was much deeper, although it was not coming down so fast any more. The flakes were like powder, some so small I could barely see them. The plow still hadn't come, but it didn't really matter because our driveway was a quarter mile long, and John's truck was parked by the house. It looked like we might not go to school all week, and by then we'd be into Christmas vacation.

The phone was still working and John managed to get a call through to work. He came back smiling. "Seattle's a mess. They told me to just stay away until this is all finished. Most of the businesses are closed, and the hospital is on emergency services only. What a bunch of wimps! In Spokane we could get a snow like this and hardly notice it."

"And how would you get your truck out?" Mooney countered. Her voice sounded a little irritated.

"Oh, I'd never take my truck this far from the road if I thought there'd be a heavy fall. I'd park it by the curb and hope the plow didn't hit it. Everybody has old junkers so they don't have to worry about being hit. Nice cars are kept in the garage for nice weather."

"Since you have this snow business worked out so well, you've doubtless noticed that we're almost out of split firewood. You can keep yourself productive while I make breakfast. Stinky will most likely be wanting to help you." She looked at me pointedly, and I got up promptly to go with John.

Wood chopping was not such a bad idea, actually. It was much cooler and more comfortable outside, and my part of the work was quite simple. It consisted of pawing log rounds down from the stack, then rolling them over to the splitting block with my nose. I made a game out of it, and used them like bowling balls to try and knock John over, but he was too quick for me. He even complimented me on how close to the block I was delivering my loads. When John was done chopping, I let him carry the split pieces to the door while I lay down in the snow and admired the day.

The clouds had grown much brighter, and John commented that they were so thin the blue sky was showing through from behind them. I couldn't see such a faint shade of color, but I could tell the snowstorm was almost over. The flakes were so small and rare I couldn't see them at all, just felt their touch on my nose and eyelids. And the air was becoming rapidly colder.

We were called to breakfast then, and the clouds were gone before we finished eating. Mouse was outside as soon as she could get ready—waddling and pushing herself along with too much clothing. She started out by making a snowman.

Humans are always making snowmen, but no one can tell me why. When Mouse was done with hers she called me over to admire it. We were alone in the yard together. "Here, Coyote, let's back up a little and check it out." She grabbed my scruff and hauled me off a few paces, then turned me around, still holding my shoulder skin.

"What do you think?"

"It looks great," I lied.

"No it doesn't. There's too much dirt and leaves mixed in with the snow."

What I wanted to say was, 'What difference does it make? You can't see it and I don't care,' but fortunately I stopped myself in time. Instead I told her the snow was perfectly clean, and everything looked fine.

"Don't lie to me, you. I can tell. We'll just make another one."

"How could you tell I was lying?" If I was giving myself away, I needed to find out what I was doing wrong so I wouldn't repeat the mistake. Lying is an art that requires constant practice.

"Don't worry, you old fur ball, you haven't lost your touch. I just knew the snow was dirty, is all."

"You could smell it, right?" I knew she was capable of that. Humans can use their noses a lot more than they think they can, if they'll just put their heads to the ground and try. Mouse was a good pupil, and I had taught her a lot.

"Yes, I could do that I guess, but I forgot. I only noticed when we stepped back and looked at it together."

"You mean you noticed my tone of voice when I said it looked great."

"No, I just knew when you looked at it." Mouse sounded embarrassed, as if she thought she might have done something bad.

"I don't think I understand."

Mouse was silent at first, then took a big breath and began talking all in a rush. "When we're touching, I can sometimes see what you see. Not really seeing it but just sort of like remembering it, like I just know what's there. It's been going on for a long time, ever since just after we started going on walks together. That's how I can keep up so well. It's not like I'm reading your mind or anything. I can't tell anything else... Except, maybe some of your feelings, sometimes," she added after a short pause.

That explained a lot. As I thought about it, I realized the communication was not just one-way. There were times when I had shifted my body to help Mouse keep from falling even before I could have felt the change in her pull on me. And I could sense her feelings too, sometimes. I stood silently where I was, staring straight ahead and considering what Mouse had said.

"Coyote?"

"Yes?"

"Coyote, you're not mad at me, are you?"

"Mad at you? Why should I pffe mad?"

"You don't think I've invaded your privacy, or anything like that? My mother said I shouldn't ever do that any more because it's... No. Never mind about that. But I was afraid to tell you! I thought you might not let me touch you any more."

"No, Mouse. I don't care apffout that kind of pffrivacy. You should have told me long ago. Maypffe if we pffractice, we can get pffetter. Now... apffout that snowman. Yes, there's some dirt in the snow, pffut he looks just fine. Let's do something else."

The 'something else' looked for a while like me pulling Mouse on a sled, but I discouraged the idea, and finally refused flatly. On packed snow that might be kind of fun, but no way on fresh, deep powder. I did agree to her plan of constructing an igloo.

We started by trying to cut the snow into blocks, but it was too light and fluffy, and the blocks fell apart. Even Mouse's snowman had been hard to stick together. We were going to give up, but John had been watching us, and came out to share advice.

"You need to keep the snow in place with boards or something, then pour water on it. The water will freeze and hold everything together."

The well pump was not working due to lack of electricity, so I got my exercise carrying buckets of water from the creek while John and Mouse scooped up snow and pushed it between the board forms. Each bucket of water made the snow slump down drastically, but the humans kept stuffing in more snow, and I kept fetching more water until the walls rose despite themselves. Mouse objected to the use of broken fir branches to hold the roof up, but John said when you're making a snow shelter you use what is around you. We had no hard-packed snow like the Eskimos did, but we had plenty of wood, which Eskimos are happy enough to use when they can get it. It's just that wood is not available in the places where igloos are made.

Our snow house was square instead of round, and it had a flat roof, but it was ours. From inside you could see the walls glowing from Sun's light shining through them, and it was very quiet and peaceful.

It was past lunchtime when we finished, and all of us were good and hungry. Mooney met us at the kitchen door. "You're taking all that stuff off right where you are! I'll not have you tracking snow and dirt from one end of the house to the other. Stinky is bad enough."

She looked at me critically, but for a change I was clean. Carrying water over fresh-fallen snow doesn't mess you up much, and I had shaken myself vigorously just before coming up onto the porch.

"You can come in the way you are," she told me.

"By the way, the electricity came about an hour ago. You can both have your showers after lunch."

Lunch consisted of chili and fresh baked bread. Our stove was propane, so the lack of electricity had not affected it.

I slipped back out to our snow house for my after-lunch nap. I wanted to appreciate it by myself, without a lot of talking around me. Not a bad job. Not bad at all. Inside I curled myself into a ball and fell asleep fantasizing about what it would be like to dig a den of my own, and have someone to share it with.

The cold snap lasted only a day and a half, and our normal weather came back with vicious force.

First were the mare's tail clouds, from the southwest this time, rushing in very fast. The sky turned from clear to overcast in an hour, and a southwest breeze started up, smelling of the sea. Gulls came with that breeze, and settled on the gravel bar in a tight, squabbling flock. By dusk the breeze had become a wind that rattled windows in their casings, and our electricity had failed again. Phones too, this time.

I went to bed with Mouse to comfort her, but I didn't want to go out anyway. The wind had been frightening at dusk, and it continued to rise during the night. Sometimes it made a hackles-up crooning sound like a cat before a fight, and our house would shake or even seem to crawl and tilt beneath me with the stronger gusts. In the distance I heard branches and whole trees crashing to the ground, and flying leaves kept tapping sharply against the bedroom window, startling us. Sometimes twigs struck too, and they slapped the glass so hard I thought it would break. A heavy rain came with the wind, and in the morning most of the snow was gone. Our snow house had collapsed into a jumble of sticks and slush, and Fry Creek was beginning to crawl up into Mooney's new berry fields.

Ceaseless, hard rain all day Saturday. It was what we call a 'warm rain' here. About fifty degrees, I guess—warm enough to melt snow on contact, even on the lower mountain slopes. By evening the wind had almost stopped, but that relentless rain was stronger than ever.

On Sunday our driveway went under and Sunbow was nearly surrounded by swirling, debris-choked water. Mr. Bell's place looked the same, except that it was detached from the nearby high ground and formed a true island. Rain was still pouring down, and I wondered if it would ever stop.

All the berry fields were covered now, new and old. Mooney kept saying she had never seen the river come up so high before. She was acting very strangely—drunk or numb is the best way to describe it—always staring through one window or another at the dark water surging past, way too close. We all caught her mood, and skulked about trying to avoid notice. The radio played softly and ceaselessly on a local channel Mooney didn't like, and she turned the volume up whenever a new flood report came in. Mooney had plenty of batteries on hand, so she didn't need to worry about conserving them.

We were in the evacuation zone, but the river had gone up so quickly we were cut off before anybody knew it. I don't think either Mooney or Mr. Bell would have left, though. Our homes really were above flood level, even this flood. The chickens needed tending, and I know Mr. Bell would never have left his cows. They all had names, and some looked rather old to be giving much milk.

Mr. Bell had a generator for backup power, so for him it was business as usual except that the pasture was gone, so his cows had to stay in the barns and eat hay.

I was bored, and the humans were crabby, so on Sunday I took off during daylight to explore.

Fry Creek was wide and deep near Sunbow, but that was mostly back-up from Wynoochee, and without much current. I swam across where the water became narrow at the start of the old growth area, which was all above flood level.

The flood really was confined to the valley bottom, but that was so full it looked like a lake. Normally we could get two days of hard rain without even noticing it, but all that snow melting overnight had overloaded our river. It was still raining steadily, but in the highlands where I was the water ran off rapidly in the customary small rivulets and creeks. Nothing unusual about that. I decided to go south this time, and soon I was able to move on down and use the road quite a bit, since that section was built on higher ground. Wynoochee Wildwood was pretty much completely under water, though, and even had a current sweeping through parts of it. Everything was so quiet! Nothing human there at all.

The Gundersons had stayed, of course. I think they would have drowned before abandoning their horses. The Gundersons' farm didn't have as much high ground as Sunbow so their house, horses, and movable possessions were all crowded together on one small island. Lazytail's pen was under water, and it was the kind with a wire roof on it so you can't climb out.

Alarm shot through me when I saw that, but I tried to ignore the feeling. Lazytail's humans would have taken care of her! Surely they would have. Desperately I longed to swim over and investigate more closely, but that would have been a bad idea because the Gundersons were very much in evidence. They bustled from here to there making temporary fences, and comforting their horses, and dragging expensive equipment further back from the still-rising waters.

My viewpoint was too exposed, so I slipped into heavier cover and paced anxiously, just out of sight. Finally I risked a soft, tentative howl. Immediately Lazytail's voice rose to join with mine and we sang together, but then she stopped early, before we were finished. I heard shouting, and a splash, and peeked through dripping fern fronds to see Lazytail swimming straight toward me, trailing a short length of rope.

Lazytail surged out of the water and we rushed up chest to chest, had one joyful boxing match, then streaked off down the road together. We headed northwest, for higher ground and better privacy. That land was all Weyerhaeuser tree farms, and this was not a good day for logging.

We had the country even more to ourselves than I had expected. Trees were down everywhere, some of them rather large. It would take weeks of heavy chainsaw work to get those roads open again. The downed trees didn't bother us, of course; we just swarmed over or under them. I was getting sap on my fur from the broken branches, though, and that would rub off on the carpets later if I wasn't careful. Mooney might have a thing or two to say about that.

On impulse I led us to the ridge behind Mr. Burrey's place so I could look down and check on it before going farther north. That property was set right on the riverbank, much lower than Sunbow or the dairy, and it might not have done so well, flood-wise.

Mr. Burrey's home had not done so well. It was half under water, and not slack water. More than a little current was at work on it. There was no sign of Mr. Burrey or his van.

We slid and scuttled down the slope to get a better look. Or at least, I did, and Lazytail followed to keep me company. I found something for her that made it well worth her while, though: Mr. Burrey's smokehouse still had meat in it!

I swam back with the first piece in my mouth, presented it to her proudly, then went back to get another for myself. We glutted ourselves happily all through that afternoon, with me swimming back to fetch more as needed. Lazytail was a good swimmer too, but the muddy water and half-submerged buildings spooked her, and she wouldn't go in. It was just as well. That current was tricky, and there were fences and things under the water that could hold you down and kill you if the current pressed you against them. It was all quite dangerous, actually, and foolish of me to go there, but the meat was delicious.

It made me very happy to bring food to Lazytail, and I felt a thrill whenever she nuzzled my face, so that I couldn't help sticking out the tip of my tongue like I do when my belly is rubbed. Soon we let the meat drunkenness have its way with us, and nestled together contentedly in the best rain shelter we could find—a trifle damp, perhaps, but still perfectly comfortable. Wolf and coyote fur works well enough under such conditions.

We were startled awake by the crash of breaking glass and jumped up in panic. I located the source immediately, and relaxed. It was only a floating tree shattering Mr. Burrey's living room window. A hemlock, I think.

The tree had penetrated deeply and was still jammed in place, with the root end extending into faster water. Tree and trailerhouse were both shifting visibly as the current pulled at them.

The trailer was anchored well enough for a windstorm, I suppose, but not for something like this. Wynoochee had hold of it now, and he was not going to let go. The trailer continued to move, sometimes silently, sometimes with a loud grinding and popping sound, but every moment faster as the water got a stronger and stronger grip on it. The dead electrical lines and their support cable held for a short time, causing the utility pole to snap and Mr. Burrey's trailer to swing around and crush his smokehouse, but then everything came loose and spun into the main channel and around the bend. Mr. Burrey didn't have a garage, so that left nothing standing above water besides the alder trees that had been present when he arrived. It was like he had never lived there.

I was sad to see the smokehouse go. It was not empty yet. And Mr. Burrey would be unhappy about his trailer. Anyway, it looked like the party was over. No more meat to be found here, and I knew Mooney would make a fuss again if I didn't head home soon. I retraced our trail to the Gundersons' place to drop off Lazytail.

Night had arrived while Lazytail and I slept, but it was not really that late yet. Sixteen-hour December nights give you a lot of time to work with. The Gundersons were still diligently busy, with a generator roaring away, and lights on everywhere. Their house was still an island, but now a small boat was tied up to it so they could get off when they wanted to. It looked like the water level might have dropped a little, but I couldn't tell for sure.

Lazytail and I stopped at the place where I had met her earlier that day, and I gave her one last body rub and lick on the face before turning back for Sunbow. She stood by the water for a few seconds, then whipped around and ran past me to lead the way.

We argued for several minutes, but Lazytail couldn't talk in words, and it probably wouldn't have made any difference. I even started out across the water as if swimming to her house, but she wouldn't follow me—just stood there and watched until I came back.

"She followed me home. Can we keepff her?"

"She's lovely! Don't you know where she lives? I thought you had every dog in the valley memorized." Lazytail and Mooney were making friends enthusiastically while she said this. I noted that Mooney was letting her put mud all over her clothes, which she would have yelled at me for doing. I didn't say anything about it, though. At least Lazytail had distracted Mooney from her depression.

"I've never seen her pffefore," I lied. "Maypffe she got lost from the flooding."

Mooney looked at me suspiciously for a moment, but I guess she decided it wasn't worth making an issue over. She was just glad to see me back safely. "You must both be starving. Stinky—why don't you go push her in the creek and get some of that mud washed off. I'll start something heating. Mouse! Get some towels and meet me at the back porch please! We have a visitor."

Fry Creek was muddy, but not as muddy as we were. Washing Lazytail consisted of pushing her over in the water or jumping on top of her and rubbing her with my body. She was just my size and strength, so it was a lot of work, especially when she decided she liked this new game, and jumped on top of me instead, then grabbed me with her front legs and used the mating position and movements, which are also for playing. After a time I switched places with her, and took my turn at that until I pushed things a little too far, which made her yip and sit down suddenly.

Lazytail and I both had bellies full of venison, so we weren't very hungry for dinner. Lazytail ate a bite or two of her food, but she seemed uncomfortable in the kitchen and wanted to go out again right away. She wouldn't explore the rest of the house at all, even with the humans encouraging her. Maybe the flickering candlelight put her off. In the end I took Lazytail out to the hayloft for our nap, which seemed to bother Mouse for some reason. Jealousy, I suppose. I knew she'd get over it, so I didn't let it worry me. Mouse was always taking things too seriously.

When I awoke from my nap the house lights were out, rain was rumbling on the shingles above my head, and Lazytail was cuddled up against me, still asleep. Mouse would be wanting me in bed with her, but it was so nice right where I was. I rested my head on Lazytail's flank and drifted back to sleep again, immersed in her fragrance.

We slept until daylight, which is a lot of sleeping. I guess we were both kind of worn out. Through the loft window I saw a patch of clear sky and a ground fog or mist over the river and banks. The rain had stopped.

Smoke was already coming from our chimney, and I could smell oatmeal cooking, so Lazytail and I went in as soon as we were finished with our morning duties. We ran the perimeter together, and Lazytail helped me mark as if we both owned the place. Later, if I felt like it, I might spend some thought on just who had abducted whom, but right now food was calling, even if it was only oatmeal.

Wynoochee is a short river, prone to rapid changes. The flood waters began to back off that same day, and by evening the road was open. Mouse and I could get to school again, but now it was vacation time, and we didn't have to. John could have left, but he didn't want to go just yet. He did make a trip out to pick up supplies, though.

Mooney's berry fields were starting to show above water. The older fields were on higher ground, and just had a thick layer of mud all over them. Mooney made herself smile, and said the mud would increase soil fertility and make them bear even better next year. As she spoke, her eyes kept scanning her new fields, trying to see through the turbid water and assess the damage.

Mooney's suspicions were confirmed the next morning. There *were* no new berry fields, just a new gravel bar. The waters had stripped away every cane, and even the soil beneath them. A year of Mooney's work was gone.

We all tried to comfort her, and I know we did help, but how much can you do? Mooney said she didn't want to talk about it.

A thing happened then which was so remarkable it made Mooney forget all about her fields. For a while, anyway. We were still looking down at the site of the disaster, not doing anything in particular, when Mr. Bell went out to his tractor and started it up. He was right in view, of course. His house and barns were just a quarter mile from our house. He could see us clearly too.

When Mr. Bell got his tractor started, he didn't go pushing manure around like usual, but instead drove into the milking barn for a few minutes, then emerged and set forth along his driveway, which was still under water, along with most of his land.

A car would have stalled, but not that old tractor. I saw it out of sight but heard it continue down to the road, then realized with a shock it was coming back up our own drive.

"Mooney! Mr. Pffell is coming here!" My voice squeaked when I tried to say 'Pffell,' so it sounded more like a high-pitched bark. Mooney and John looked at each other in bewilderment. There was no way the man could blame this flood on us!

Lazytail and I made ourselves disappear for the confrontation, but not too far off. I had never attacked a human, but there's always a first time. Mooney and John walked with Mouse to the main yard and waited.

Mooney was ready for a fight, but that's not what she got. Mr. Bell had not brought trouble, but rather a gift. His tractor's manure scoop held a generator, boxes of electrical parts, and two large cans of gasoline. "I know we haven't got along so well these last few years, but I couldn't stand to see you folk sitting here with no power when I got this extra generator just lying around taking up space in the barn.

"Y'know, it ain't right for neighbors to be feuding," he added in a much quieter voice. "I never had the stomach for it, and I might need your help someday."

Mooney answered in the only sensible way. "Why, uh, thank you, Mr. Bell! That's very neighborly of you." Then she got stuck and couldn't think of anything else to say. Mr. Bell smiled and took over for her.

"The old thing is a trifle tweaky, so I better show you how to treat her right. And you'll have to oil her now and then. She's from the time before they put sealed ball bearings every damn place they could think of. I'd throw her out, but it's nice to keep something around in case the new one craps out on me. You don't want to have forty cows to milk, and no power!

"Now, we'll need a spot with a roof over it, not too far from the meter box. I'll just put in a permanent tap outlet at the box, and wire up a heavy cable you can keep out of the way when you don't need it. I'm afraid she ain't powerful enough to run your water heater, but at least you can get the well and lights working. Candles and lanterns get kind of old after a couple days, eh?"

John had been unable to buy more candles, and my humans were drinking nothing but rainwater. They were still using the toilet, though. Buckets of river water flushed it just fine, but they were a lot of work to carry. The humans hadn't bathed since Monday.

Mr. Bell didn't stay long after he got the generator working, and he didn't talk about anything much. The last thing he said was a wish that the milk truck would get through soon. The tank was getting awful full, and even with refrigeration it would soon be too old to sell. As he left, Mooney thanked him again, and gave him one of the loaves of bread she had just baked for us. She did that later, too—continued to bake things for him and take them over every couple of days or so. I know he appreciated it, and it eased a lot of the tension between our farms.

As soon as Mr. Bell was gone, Mooney loaded the stove top with pots of water, and lit all the burners. Our new generator could operate the washing machine, but the dryer took too much power, so before long the humans had damp clothes hung everywhere. It was way too hot and steamy in the house, and I mostly stayed outside with Lazytail. She would only go inside to eat.

The humans seemed totally absorbed in their cleaning frenzy, the house was possessed by drying laundry, and our new generator filled the air with a hammering racket. Seemed like a good time for another outing, even if it was full daylight.

Lazytail was amenable, and I raced her up the slope into Weyerhaeuser land, beating her easily. She had never been able to get enough exercise before, but we could fix that.

I was curious about Mr. Burrey's place, so we retraced our previous day's trail to check it out. When we arrived, we found Mr. Burrey poking about in a dazed, desultory way, like he didn't know where to begin. The water was mostly gone, but his driveway and trailer foundation were so covered with mud and broken trees that it was hard to see what had once been there. The clouds had come back, and it was raining again, gently.

I don't bark much, but I did this time—bounded joyfully and yip-yap-noisily down the soggy slope to greet him. I had been worried about that man.

"Hey! Stay away from those cables! You can never tell for sure if they're live or not." The power cables trailed slackly from their pole, and disappeared under a tangle of slimy debris. It was hard to imagine that any electricity could be lurking within them, but I was not about to argue. I circled them widely, and Lazytail followed with me as usual.

"It's good to see you, Coyote. I worried you might have been trapped by the water. Barely got clear, myself. I had no idea your little river could do all this!"

He gestured vaguely at the devastation surrounding us, looked for a place to sit down, then thought better of it. I pressed up against him enthusiastically until he lost balance and sat down anyway, then I licked his face until he pushed me away. Lazytail kept her distance.

"Mooney was surpffrised apffout the flood too. She said it has never hapffend like this pffefore. We're all okay, pffut she lost her pfferry fields, and she's not sure what she'll use for money."

"I'm not sure what I'll use for money either. I'm not exactly wealthy, you know. At least I saved all my books and other personal things." He glanced over to his van then. It was as close to his lot as he could safely get it, and its tires were squashed-looking from the weight inside. "That van is so packed I haven't been able to get at anything. There's no room to unload at the shelter."

"I didn't know there's a shelter. Where is it? Are there lots of pffeopffle in it?" Mr. Burrey would want to talk about his new temporary quarters. Humans are very particular about keeping a roof over themselves, and will go to extraordinary efforts to do so.

"They've opened up the National Guard Armory over on Clemons Road. There are people everywhere—Red Cross, Guard, police, and just folks like me. The flood was so bad it even covered the freeway! There's been a lot of damage, but I don't think anyone's been killed."

"You mean no humans have pffeen killed."

Mr. Burrey caught my point instantly. "No humans have been killed. I don't know for sure about any other animals, but I don't think it's been too bad. There are patches of high ground all through the valley, and most of the people with animals ignored the evacuation order so they could take care of them.

"I can't help noticing your new friend," he added after a pause. "Is she from the flood?"

"Sort of," I evaded, then changed the subject back to Mr. Burrey. "Where will you stay now?"

"She's really good-looking. Nice and wolfy, and I think she likes you." He winked at me and called to her, but she only came halfway.

I knew Lazytail wasn't really that shy. She was only pretending. "Her name is Lazytail. She'll come to you if you have some food. So will I."

"Well, I did throw a few pieces of that smoked venison in the van before I left, and I think I might even be able to get at it without moving the rest of the stuff. But you must be tired of venison by now. I have some granola, though, and a little cold coffee. Oh, and I have some peppermints in there too."

"I think we'll take the venison, if that's alright with you," I replied expressionlessly. "I don't think Lazytail would like pffepffermints."

Mr. Burrey used several small pieces of meat to buy his friendship with Lazytail, and he was good company. The loss of his trailer hadn't seemed to damage his sense of humor. I couldn't help contrasting that with Mooney's depression. She always took everything so hard—I wished I could help her some way.

"Well, it's getting dark and there's nothing I can do here. Nothing to salvage, and I don't think I'll be putting another trailer or house on this spot. I guess I'll just go back to the shelter for tonight, and start looking for an apartment in town tomorrow."

Mr. Burrey turned away from the place where his home had been, and something about the way he did that made my throat catch. Oh, yes; Mr. Burrey felt his loss, all right. He had just been hiding it with his jokes. Without thinking, I blurted out an offer of Sunbow as a place to stay. He thanked me for the sentiment, but reminded me it would be unfair to my humans to invite a werewolf onto their premises. Of course that got me to arguing against him, and I repeated my offer more emphatically. Finally Mr. Burrey did agree to use our property to store the things on his van.

"That's a thought, alright. A lot of my things were crammed in there wet, and they'll be ruined if I can't get them dry soon. Some of them are probably already ruined. If Mooney agrees, I'll take you up on your storage space offer. But that's daylight work. For now I'll head back to the shelter and check out the newspaper ads. You two enjoy your night out!"

As it happened, we didn't spend the night out. I was feeling rather sorry for Mooney and I didn't want to add to her stress, so I led us back to Sunbow in time for dinner. Anyway, Mr. Burrey hadn't given us enough venison, and I was still hungry.

It was good we went back. John was trying to cheer up Mooney by making a semi-traditional dinner using the new supplies. He was tending an open alder fire on the concrete floor just inside the main doors of the machinery barn. Two big salmon were spread open on sticks propped up with concrete blocks to lean just the right way over the coals, and an oil pot for fry bread occupied the other half of the same fire. Thin ribbons of fragrant, choking smoke crawled deep inside the barn and then circled back out into the rain, but the floor level was pretty clear.

John greeted us enthusiastically. "Good timing! You're gone so much these days I decided to start everything without you, but it's all about ready to eat now, and suddenly here you are. Most remarkable!"

I rushed up for a hug while Lazytail hesitated for a moment, then joined in when John called to her softly. We got mud all over his jacket, but he took it well. It was his chore coat anyway.

"You don't happen to know if your friend has eaten salmon before, do you? I'm cooking it clear through, which should kill everything, but it's always good to know."

John was referring to the disease dogs and coyotes and wolves can get from eating raw salmon. It's not too dangerous if you have tetracycline on hand to treat it with, and you can only get it once, so I was immune, but John was concerned about Lazytail.

"I don't know if Lazytail has had salmon pffefore. I never saw them feed her anything excepfft... uh, I don't know," I finished lamely. I had just blown my story of Lazytail being a poor, lost flood victim, so I tried to change the subject quickly.

"Mr. Pffurrey is coming here tomorrow to unload some things and dry them out. He lost his trailer, and doesn't have any pfflace to pffut them now."

"Mr. Burrey? He's welcome, of course, but who invited him? Mooney hasn't left Sunbow all week, and the phones are still out."

"I invited him. His trailer is compffletely gone, and I felt sorry for him."

"You talked to Mr. Burrey? I thought you didn't talk to anyone except Mooney and Mouse and me."

"It was an accident. He heard and saw me spffeak when I didn't know he was there. Later he asked me very nicely to talk again, so I did. Mooney is always telling pffeopffle I can talk."

"Those are Sunbow people, and I've finally persuaded her to stop mentioning it even to them. Mr. Burrey is a complete stranger."

"Mr. Pffurrey won't tell anyone," I stated with conviction. "He just wants to pffe left alone like we do."

"Well, it's too late to change any of that now. What were you saying about Lazytail? I thought you didn't know where she lived! Tell me the truth or I'll eat your dinner myself, and have Mooney fix you some more rice and tofu."

John could never be so cruel, and his stomach wasn't big enough anyway, but I wasn't going to test him. Besides, the Gundersons would probably be posting notices soon.

"She's from the horse ranch, but she doesn't want to live there any more. Lazytail likes it pffetter here."

"Well, unless they're abusing her, there's not much we can do about that. She'll have to go home tomorrow. So will I, for that matter. If I'm not back at work soon there'll be some tough explaining to do. Try to keep up Mooney's spirits, will you? I worry about her."

"I worry apffout her too. I'll do what I can, but I don't understand this 'money' pffusiness very well. Isn't there some other way of getting money pffesides growing pffot or raspfferries? Maypffe you can give her some."

"I'm already helping Mooney every way she'll let me, but those taxes are over eighty thousand a year. We keep working on it, but the only thing we can think of to generate that kind of money is logging, and Mooney refuses to cut a single tree. It's her land, and that's her decision to make, but the county will eventually seize it all for back taxes if she doesn't do anything at all. I've been hanging back to let her come to terms with the idea, but she's not moving very fast."

"I've pffeen keepffing quiet apffout it too, pffut maypffe it's time for me to talk to her. Mooney's no fun the way she is now."

"Good luck! But let's drop that subject for tonight. Learning about Mr. Burrey will be more than enough for her, on top of everything else that's happened.

"You say he just started talking to you—didn't come unglued or anything? That man is weirder than I thought!"

"He did have some troupffle at first, pffut he got used to it. Mr. Pffurrey understands what it's like, I think."

"Interesting! I'll enjoy talking with him tomorrow. Maybe he'll have some ideas about how to get you to stop lying so much. But then, I suspect getting Coyote to stop lying would require a change in the very structure of reality. Maybe that's a bit beyond us.

"But enough of that. I need to get moving now or all this food will be ruined. You keep Lazytail away from the fish while I get Mooney over to help carry things inside."

While John was gone I looked over the fire appraisingly. Fire frightened me, a little, but I was drawn to it as well. Such a very human thing! Raw power—but so common they don't even think about it. Gingerly I grasped a small log with my teeth and tossed it in, then skittered away from the sparks that burst back toward me.

The fish aroma distracted me then. They were just perfect—dripping juice and oil slowly onto the edge of the coals. I tried to see how I could steal a bite without leaving a mark, but couldn't do it so I licked off some of the juice instead. Lazytail wanted to help, but I wouldn't let her. Wolves are not trustworthy when food is involved.

It was a fine dinner—a memorable dinner—delicious, and sufficient for all. Lazytail had trouble with the fish bones, though, and I had to show her how to deal with them. She still wouldn't sleep inside the house, but Mooney set up a foam pad and blankets for Mouse in the hayloft, and we all curled up together for some serious resting. No night jaunts this time.

The cold front was back by morning. Frost on the ground, clear sky, and no wind. My favorite kind of winter weather. Mouse woke me. "Do you think Lazytail can learn to talk like you do?" she whispered.

My eyes snapped open, then half-closed again as I indulged myself in a leisurely yawn and stretch. "I don't know," I told her in a fake sleepy voice. "Give me a pffelly rupff and I'll ask her."

"Forget the belly rub. I'll ask her myself." Mouse turned her back to me and reached for Lazytail, who was yawning and stretching on her other side.

"Has this jerk taught you any words yet?"

Lazytail rolled over to expose her own belly. Mouse felt the movement and reached over to stroke her instead of me. Lazytail's touchable area was much larger than mine, with the long double row of nipples just visible through pale, soft belly fur. The nipples were all standing up firmly, and seemed bigger than I remembered. Humans could stroke those all they liked, but my favorite parts were off-limits. I was jealous again and nuzzled Mouse's neck. Finally she rolled on her back so she could stroke both our heads at once, and no one got a belly rub at all.

I don't know why, but it's always the male humans who work with gasoline engines. Or perhaps it's petroleum products in general. Lawn mowers, chain saws, outboard motors, even barbecue starter fluid—the females do a perfectly good job with all of them, but become suddenly helpless if there's a male around. That's why John and I were given generator duty.

Mooney hated the generator noise as much as I did, so it wasn't started until after breakfast. I didn't hate the generator, by the way, just the noise from it. Even the fumes were a mixed sort of thing. They smelled horrible, and made me want to vomit if I got too strong a whiff of them, but engine exhaust was often associated with an outing in the truck or van, and so was shot through with pleasurable associations for me.

I had never seen a generator like the one Mr. Bell brought us. Lots of places had generators, but they were all store-bought units with all the parts connected directly together and cunningly enfolded in a compact welded-steel frame. Mr. Bell's rig was a massive wooden plank with a grease-encrusted and really old-looking engine bolted securely to one end and connected to the generator shaft with a short piece of stiff rubber hose. The generator itself was the size and shape of a large watermelon and had its own four separate cast-iron feet. The words 'Sears-Roebuck' were molded into the cast-iron housing and showed clearly through the grime. John and Mr. Bell together had not been able to lift the thing. Only Mr. Bell's tractor was strong enough to do that.

The thing was obviously homemade, but it worked just fine—wasn't really 'tweaky' at all. With John's coaching, I actually started it myself. Setting the choke and pulling the starter rope were easy. With the rope in my teeth I was able to pull with my whole back, and I have a lot of strength that way. I broke the rope on my first try and John had to replace it, but after that I was more gentle, and the engine fired right up. The hard part was forcing myself close enough to disengage the choke after that mind-numbing exhaust noise had begun. Lazytail stayed far away through it all, and looked at me like I was crazy. Probably right. My ears rang for several minutes afterward.

With generator started, the humans went into an abbreviated version of our previous day's cleaning frenzy. Lazytail and I were about ready to wander off when we heard Mr. Burrey's van approaching. We ran out to greet him in the driveway and see if he had any smoked venison left, and we pounced on him the second he opened the door.

"Glad to see you too!" he managed to choke out from under us. He hardly tasted very canine at all any more. His scent followed Moon's phases, I suppose.

"Do you have any venison left?" I asked hopefully, looking down at his throat from my position astride his chest. I could still smell smoked venison in his van, but that might just be old wrappings.

"And what will you do if I don't have any? Eat me?"

"Maypffe," I replied, and nibbled his ear, then let him roll me over and conquer me again. Lazytail kept dancing just in and out of his reach, which distracted him from me, so I jumped up and began nipping at his ankles and the hem of his jacket.

We arrived at the house in a tangle, and Mr. Burrey had to steady himself with one hand on the porch rail before he could climb the stairs. I burst in through the dog door to announce his arrival.

"John—Mooney—Mouse! We have a visitor!"

Mooney was already there, washing dishes. John had told her Mr. Burrey might be coming, and we had made a lot of noise, so she was not surprised. I'm not sure she knew quite what to say, though.

"Good morning, Mr. Burrey. Come on inside! Would you like some coffee?"

Much later, after John and Mouse had come over, Mooney took up the subject of me.

"I hear you've been, uh, speaking with Coyote." Mooney hesitated for a moment, then added, "It's rather unusual for him to talk to people outside Sunbow. He's still rather shy, you know, despite his progress at school this fall. You didn't have any, uh, trouble, did you? Some people might have a hard time accepting him."

Mooney was talking like I wasn't there. I hate that.

"I have a lot of experience with things that are hard to accept," Mr. Burrey replied with a tone of considerable understanding. "I must admit I did act rather badly on the occasion when I first heard him talk, but he has forgiven me, I think. Is that true, Coyote? Are you still mad at me?"

At least Mr. Burrey had the courtesy to include me in the conversation. I went over and sat down beside his chair, then thought better of it and took a position behind him, near the door, where he had to twist his head around to see me.

"No, I'm not mad at you, Mr. Pffurrey. We all get a pffit excited sometimes. Next time you get excited that way, I think I'll run away a pffit faster... Or maypffe not," I added boldly, after a moment's pause.

"I'll try to see that the problem doesn't come up again," Mr. Burrey assured me. "And by the way, I'd like you all to call me Peter, or Pete, if you will. Mr. Burrey sounds too formal."

"Pffeter." I tested the name. A hard one, but interesting.

"Pffeter Pffurrey... Pffeter Pffurrey. Pffurrey Pffete! Furry Feet!" I yelped delightedly. Mooney glared at me.

"Furry Feet is far too fleet. 'Spffecially when he's seeking meat." I was being rude, but the rhyme had burst into my head suddenly, and I couldn't let it go to waste. Mr. Burrey looked angry and pained, Mooney just angry.

"That will be quite enough, Sin-Ka-Lip! Show a little courtesy and respect, will you please?"

I edged closer to the dog door and bowed my head and tail. "Sorry Mr. Pffurrey... Feet!"

I hurled myself through and skidded to a halt in the yard.

"Furry Feet, Furry Feet, Furry Feet is fond of meat!" I sang back toward the house, then charged into Lazytail and bowled her over. I nipped her here, there, all over, and fled into the frozen woods. She put her whole spirit into catching me. Gave me a good chase, too.

Mr. Burrey's van was by the machinery barn when we got back, and thin, hot smoke was pouring from the barn's chimney. It was almost dark, so lights were on in the house and barn, but the generator was not running. Power was back on.

Lazytail and I went over to the barn first, which was closed up now to keep in the heat. John's cook fire had been cleaned away completely, and heat was now pushing out from the wood stove in the center of the building. Every surface was carefully layered with books, clothing, and small personal items such as humans are fond of. They smelled damp and slightly moldy, but that would soon be fixed. The building was already uncomfortably warm. There was no sign of Mr. Burrey or his venison.

Some of Mr. Burrey's things smelled rather interesting—especially a set of very old books and one wooden chest set up on shelves well out of my reach. I was just pushing a chair over to let me climb closer when Mr. Burrey came in with a load of wood.

I jumped and whipped around as the door banged open, then tried to relax and not look guilty. Lazytail was startled too, and backed into a workbench layered with damp textbooks, which sent some of them sliding down onto her. Lazytail bolted out the door, and Mr. Burrey dropped his wood to rush over and rescue his books. He didn't appear to notice what I had been doing.

I went over and sniffed politely as he was bending over to put all aright. He was newly showered, and smelling of Mooney's favorite bath soap, and wearing John's clothes. The clothes were far too big for him, and he had the sleeves and pant legs rolled up.

"Welcome back, Coyote. I guess I can always count on you and your friend to get into trouble if the opportunity presents itself. No harm done, though.

"Thanks again for offering your place to help me sort things out. There was more water damage than I realized. Good thing I didn't leave it any longer!"

Mr. Burrey knelt down and reached over to tousle my ears, so I pushed up against him and then slumped down into the belly rub position. I did get a belly rub then. A good one. Mr. Burrey was not so particular about what areas he touched.

"Alright, you letch. That's enough." He rose from his knees and gathered up the wood he had dropped, set it down neatly beside the stove, then threw in a couple of pieces and poked them around. As he headed for the door I was still lying on my back hopefully, following him with my eyes.

"Cut that out," he chided. "Some wild animal you are! I've been getting quite an earful about your habits and general character, and I think an evening at home is definitely indicated. If I were you I'd turn on all the charm and courtesy I could muster. You have no idea how lucky you are to have the family you do!" Mr. Burrey's tone of voice was very serious when he said those last words.

Actually, I already did know how lucky I was. Neighbors throughout the valley would have been shocked to discover how much I knew about them. I was not particularly impressed.

"Yes, Mr. Pffurrey," was all I said. Then I got up and followed him dutifully to the house. Lazytail joined us in the yard, and went inside readily enough. She had progressed to the point where she wasn't actually uncomfortable in the house any more. Or at least, she was not uncomfortable while I was with her.

John would be driving back to Seattle soon, so an early dinner was almost ready. Macaroni and cheese, with spinach frozen from last year's garden. I hate spinach. I told Mooney once that I shouldn't have to eat any because I'm a carnivore, but she told me, "Forget it. If you want to be a carnivore, you can pretend you're eating stomach contents from your prey."

Spinach is not so bad with lots of fish sauce on it. I ate mine like a man, but Lazytail wouldn't touch hers. She liked the macaroni, though. Afterward John put her in the truck cab and drove off. He would be leaving her with the Gundersons on his way out.

With John and Lazytail gone there were just me, Mouse, Mooney, and Mr. Burrey. He would be spending the night with us in one of the extra bedrooms. It was strange to have a new person in the house, even one I knew already.

Phone and cable were back on too, so we sat down to watch television after the dishes were done. Mr. Burrey had done most of the work, almost forcing Mooney out of the room. I could tell he really didn't want to do the dishes, and Mooney didn't really want him to do them, but they both felt obligated somehow. One of those 'human things,' I suppose.

I didn't usually have a preference about what show to watch. I would wait for someone else to turn on the television, then either stay or leave the room, depending on my mood. This time I left the room. I could hear something much more interesting going on outside.

Lazytail was standing in the driveway, howling softly for me. I answered her from the porch, then rushed over for greetings. She smelled like herself, and John, and the truck, and the woods, but she didn't have any of that heavy kennel smell on her fur at all. She must have wiggled free before she was locked inside.

I glanced through the window as we headed out together. The humans were watching a documentary on wolves. "Is it true what they say apffout wolves mating for life?" I asked Lazytail playfully in the talk of men. She didn't pay attention to my words, but in her own way she asked me if I cared. I told her yes.

Clouds were putting out the stars one patch at a time. The weather would be breaking soon, but for now it was still cold and dry. Good weather for holding scents.

Wynoochee was completely in his banks now, although still running furiously, and still heavily laden with mud and logs. The humans were all back in their homes, cleaning up the wreckage, or congratulating themselves on not having any damage to deal with.

Lazytail took the lead first, and we raced each other north, up the main road. We were almost up to the elk skull cabin when we finally stopped to rest.

The cabin lights were on, and a new mercury floodlight had been installed in the yard, but I was feeling feisty from the race, so I crept over anyway to put my paws up on the kitchen windowsill and peer through as I had before. Lazytail got up beside me.

The kitchen was still messy, but things had been moved around so the empty chair was now facing directly toward our window. The flashlight-rifle was lying right there on the table top ready for use, but there was no man in view.

I like to think of myself as a proper coyote coward, but sometimes I suspect living with humans has corrupted me. I keep finding myself doing really stupid things, just to see what might happen. I was already doing one of those things by even being there, so of course I had to make it worse by scratching at the window sill to attract attention.

It worked. That old man was not deaf, certainly. He was not slow, either! Within seconds he was there in the kitchen, staring at us and reaching for his rifle. He might have got one of us if he had been willing to fire through the glass, but I suppose he didn't think about that until later. Instead he snatched up his gun and threw himself at the back door in one smooth movement, and we had just enough time to get out of view before the bullets came.

I heard several strike trees and frozen mud close by, and then we were safely away—exhilarated by our stupidity and daunted by the shots and echoes still coming up from behind. Those noises kept on for some time, like a thunderstorm.

By mutual consent we quit for the night then. There was no way we could top that encounter. Lazytail's scent was a fascinating, hard-to-sort-out combination of terror and excitement, and I expect she got the same from me. The long lope home gave us plenty of time to relax, though, and we slipped into Mouse's room without incident, settling down together on the floor beside her bed. Best to be getting a bit of sleep, if possible. Tomorrow was a special day.

December twenty-first: Winter Solstice and shortest day of the year. In the days when Sunbow was still a full-scale commune, Mooney and the others had tried to transfer most of our Christmas celebrations to the Solstice, but it had never really caught on. Instead the Solstice had become a more solemn time for us—a time to share memories of the year past, and hopes for the year to come. I was disappointed that John had been unable to stay the extra day, but he had explained that he'd be coming back in three days for Christmas, and he might get in trouble with his boss if he never showed up for work at all.

I had trouble visualizing John as submissive to anyone, and said so. He replied with a chuckle that his boss was actually not very dominant, but she was still his boss, and had to be obeyed. Another one of those 'human things,' I guess.

After breakfast Mooney took Lazytail back to the Gundersons' place, and Mr. Burrey went out to the machinery barn to sort through his belongings. Mouse and I went with him to help.

Books, papers, lots of kitchen utensils and herbs, other items I couldn't identify so easily—Mr. Burrey went over them all, item by item, but ended up tossing quite a few of those items into the trash. At one point I asked why he was discarding those particular possessions after going to so much trouble to save them. Surely there were other things he would rather have preserved? Mr. Burrey became irritated, and told me he had been in a hurry. I already knew that.

"You sure have a lot of stuff!" Mouse observed much later. She was holding a small stone that Mr. Burrey had told her was a trilobite fossil. It looked rather like a squashed, petrified, mouse-sized sow bug. Small mouse, no tail.

Mouse's comment sounded strange to me, and not very tactful. Not typical of her. Mr. Burrey had a lot more personal things than I did, but for a human he had very little. Even his trailer had been uncluttered before he lost it, and now he was down to a great deal less. Just one van full, counting the trash.

Of course, Mouse had even less than that—only the things she had made or been given since her accident the previous winter. Maybe Mr. Burrey's treasures seemed like a lot to her.

"I've had that since I was a kid," Mr. Burrey replied gently. "It's an agate fossil. All the original structure has been replaced by silica crystals. Very hard. Pretty, too." He didn't sound irritated any longer. "I stole it, you know."

I had been lying beside a stack of berry flats by the north wall, half-listening, but not looking in Mr. Burrey's direction. I was tracking the sounds and scent of a rat, actually. A little closer and I might even have gone for him. Big male. Fat. Worth the trouble. Mooney didn't mind so much when I killed rats, although she preferred to believe I didn't eat them.

I turned my full attention to Mr. Burrey, staring at him in surprise. He returned my gaze, but not quite straight on.

"Don't look so shocked! I did it, and I'm sorry, but not so sorry I can't deal with it. My friend hardly noticed it was gone, but I've cherished it all these years, even though I could buy others just like it for not very much money. It's kind of hard to explain, I guess."

I guess so. He stole a rock thirty years ago, and he was still thinking about it?

Mouse answered for me, "I know what it's like to really want something bad, even when you shouldn't." She held out the trilobite, which Mr. Burrey took back and placed carefully on the workbench.

"What do you want really bad?" His voice sounded so casual, but he was staring at Mouse intently.

"I want my old stuff. Some of the things I left behind."

"What's so bad about that?"

Mouse started, guiltily. "I mean, I wish I could remember what it was like before I came here. I probably had some toys and books and stuff. Maybe even some friends who would want to know what happened to me."

"You have friends here," I interjected quietly. If Mouse really wanted to keep her secret, it would be best to change the subject immediately. Maybe she needed some help. "If there's a spffecial toy you want, try asking John. He pffrings me things all the time. Maypffe he has something for you already. It's almost Christmas, you know."

That got Mr. Burrey and Mouse talking about Christmas, toys, and other things I didn't find all that interesting. Mr. Burrey let the subject change without objection, but if he had any belief left about Mouse's amnesia, it was probably all gone by then.

The rat had stopped moving when I spoke to Mouse, but now he was becoming bold again. Sometimes steady talk would leave them unfazed, so they just went about their business as if no one were there. This one was putting far too much faith in the protection of a few flimsy old berry flats.

"So what do you think, Coyote?"

"Huh?" The rat was startled by my voice, and skittered off a little. I looked to Mr. Burrey in confusion and annoyance, but tried not to let the annoyance show.

"Do you believe the Solstice is a time when magic is more powerful? I was telling Mouse how the Church kept having trouble with people celebrating pagan mid-winter rituals, and established many of our current Christmas customs to distract them from the old ways."

"Yes, I know apffout that. Mooney tried to pffring pffack some of the old rituals, pffut it was too much troupffle, so she quit."

"Really, now! Has she ever heard of the *Neulebskar* ceremony? I'm told that if it's done properly and the spirits are pleased, they can sometimes be persuaded to provide protection from enemies for the next year, or even grant wishes. I've done a lot of research into that one, but I've never tried it because it requires a blood sacrifice, which has to be performed by a virgin. I've never been that comfortable with people who are willing to do blood sacrifices."

"I've never heard of that one, and I don't think Mooney has either. She's mostly interested in Earth Mother things, which she learns apffout from her friends. She doesn't want anything for herself, just healing for the Earth."

"Don't we all."

"Would you really kill something just to see if you could get magic from it?" Mouse looked fascinated and disgusted by the thought.

"I might, under certain circumstances. The sacrificed animal is generally eaten after the ceremony, and we eat meat all the time when we could be just as healthy with a vegetarian diet. Just ask Mooney."

Neither of us needed to ask Mooney. She had made her opinions on the subject quite clear. Mouse and I agreed with her in principle, but not very well when it came to specifics. I preferred to think that the vegetarian ideals were not really meant for coyotes. I had been provided with sharp teeth, so I must be meant to use them sometimes.

The sacrifice thing was rather intriguing, in a way. I asked Mr. Burrey to tell me more about it.

Mr. Burrey found a stool and set it under the high shelf that held the old books and chest I had been interested in earlier. He took down one of the books and moved to set it on the workbench, then tucked it under one arm while he got a clean shirt to lay down first. When he spread the covers, the book fell open to the page he wanted.

"This book is printed in German, but the passage here is Old Danish. I had a language scholar teach me the proper meanings and pronunciations, so I can read it to you, if you like."

Mr. Burrey sounded like he really did want to read it to us, so I told him he could if it wasn't too long.

"Your tact could use some brushing up, Coyote. Still, here goes. Don't worry, it really isn't that long."

Mr. Burrey began to read in a stately, measured cadence somewhat similar to the way John spoke when he was telling one of his stories. The words sounded much different, however. I couldn't understand any of them, of course, and there were a lot of 'g,' 'b,' 'd,' and 's' sounds. It seemed to me that Mr. Burrey's Presence became much stronger while he spoke them, but now I think it may have been a different Presence I felt.

After a short while I was distracted by the rat again. He was scratching about between the flats right beside me. I tuned out Mr. Burrey's words once again, so that when the rat came out I was ready for him—crushed his spine without fuss, and almost silently.

Almost silently.

Mr. Burrey had finished reading at that moment, and both humans heard my sudden shift of position and the snap of my teeth. They turned toward me in startlement.

"What are you doing?" Mouse asked.

My mouth was full of rat, but he was only kicking and twitching helplessly. Couldn't get away. I set him down gently and answered, "It's just a rat. He came out from between the flats, and I caught him."

"Coyote! Shame on you! Put it down this instant!"

"He is down."

"Good. You didn't hurt it, did you?"

Mouse was being silly. She knew I killed rats. Maybe the talk about blood sacrifices had got her to feeling squeamish. "I think I pffroke his pffack. He's just lying there and kicking right now. Should I finish him off?"

"Don't you dare! Honestly, Coyote, don't you have any kindness in you at all?"

Mouse rushed over to me and started feeling for the rat so she could pick him up. Mr. Burrey told her to be careful, it might bite her, but she ignored him and continued her search. The rat was mine, and he was lying right there under my nose, but I let her take him away without protest.

Mr. Burrey stepped over and tried to take the rat from her. She wouldn't let go, so he led her over to the bench and they wrapped the rat in the shirt that was lying there. The whole scene was silly, since the rat was kicking more slowly all the time, and blood was trickling out of his nose and mouth. Soon he wouldn't be able to bite anybody.

"Careful of the trilobite!" Mr. Burrey protested as she bumped it while gathering up the shirt. Mouse reached out automatically and grabbed the fossil in one hand, then held the rat, shirt, and stone bug together to her chest. She began to sob quietly.

"I think it's dead," she finally admitted.

Mr. Burrey took the bundle away from her and spread it out on the workbench. "Yes, it's dead," he confirmed. Mouse excused herself and went back to the house.

Mr. Burrey fetched a bucket of water and began to rinse the blood from his shirt. "I need to get this out in cold water before the stain sets, or the shirt will be ruined." He gave the shirt his attention for a short time, then began to wash the trilobite instead, lingering over it bemusedly. The movements of his fingers looked to me more like stroking than cleaning, and he appeared to have forgotten I was there. I reclined by the berry flats, watching him work and also eying the dead rat. Finally I brought myself to speak about it. "You don't need this any more, do you?" I inquired diffidently.

"Hmm..? uh... Oh! No. Of course not. Go right ahead, Coyote. Mouse is gone now, and I certainly don't care. Never fancied rat much myself, even when the moon is full." Mr. Burrey turned his attention back to the trilobite fossil.

The rat was a nice one. Juicy, and so big I almost had to swallow him in two pieces. My temporary distress finally caught Mr. Burrey's attention.

"Are you going to choke on that, or what? I'm sure the rat's spirit is watching you right now and hoping."

I couldn't speak just then to answer, but he didn't deserve one anyway. Instead I finished swallowing, licked my chops, and sidled over to Mr. Burrey so I could nuzzle him and finish cleaning up.

"No, you don't! These may be work pants, but they're not that dirty yet."

I opened my mouth widely. "See? I'm clean. I just wanted to share scents with you."

"We'll save that for later, if it's alright with you.

"You know, Coyote, this little episode has been rather strange. If interpreted in a certain way, one might say that we just performed the

116

Neulebskar ritual without realizing it. Immediately after I finished reading the invocation, there was Mouse, holding the rat as its blood fell onto this ancient stone that has great significance to me. I assume Mouse is a virgin, so that completes the picture. Mind-boggling coincidence, isn't it?" Mr. Burrey was still holding the trilobite—seemed reluctant to put it down.

"You know, Mr. Pffurrey, I'm not so sure apffout coincidences any more. I don't think they work very well when I'm around."

Just after lunch, Lazytail came to visit us again. I didn't hear her howling this time. She was just out there in the yard, waiting, and when we noticed her she shuffled toward us in the most ingratiating, submissive way she knew. When I rushed over to greet her, I smelled blood and found several little cuts on her gums and face which I licked clean for her. I could smell and taste fresh metal with the blood, so I knew the cuts were from tearing her way through one of the chain-link sides of her kennel. That's a dumb, painful way to get out of someplace. You can break a tooth or lose an eye that way. Or get tangled in the wires and choke yourself to death.

Mooney's feelings were hard to interpret. She was irritated, but I think flattered as well. Lazytail had obviously gone to a lot of trouble to get back to us. Nevertheless, Lazytail had to go home. No other options were acceptable.

"Lazytail! What are you doing here? What sort of lies has Stinky been telling you?" Mooney stepped over to the van and opened the side door. "Come on, Lazy! Back inside! It's time to go home again."

Lazytail moved closer and took up the submissive position again, but she wouldn't get into the van, even when Mooney went to the house and came back with fresh bread to bribe her with. Finally Mooney got some rope to use as a leash, but Lazytail moved off even farther when she saw it. Mouse and I just stood back and waited. I certainly didn't want to be involved when Mooney was being thwarted.

Mooney turned to me. "She likes you best. You get her into the van."

"I can't do any pffetter than you can," I protested. "She never does what I tell her, and I don't want her to go anyway."

"Don't talk to her, just run around with her a bit, then jump inside. Maybe she'll follow you. If that doesn't work, I'll call the Gundersons and let them figure it out."

"Why don't you call them first?"

"Stinky, just do it. Now."

"Alright, I'll try," I responded dubiously, "pffut I think she's too smart for that trick to work."

"So do I, but I need to be able to say we did our best. Go on. Give her a workout!"

I needed to stretch my legs anyway—didn't waste any time, just streaked past Lazytail and dared her to catch me. Who could resist?

I led Lazytail in a loose spiral around the main yard area to get warmed up, then cut straight through between the goat barn and the machinery barn, where the manure pile used to be. The mud was deep and pungent there, and she almost caught me as I sank in, but then she hit the soft area and slowed down too. I broke through and got up to speed again, streaking right past the humans and splattering them nicely. By accident, of course. Lazytail did the same. Mooney shouted something uncomplimentary and untrue about my ancestry, and told me to "get on with it."

Okay. I was still in the main yard area, so I doubled back to the van and hurled myself through the open door. Mooney was already moving to slam it shut as soon as Lazytail followed me inside.

She needn't have bothered. Lazytail wasn't going in that van for any reason whatsoever. She skidded to a stop and stood there panting up at me and smiling, while I returned the compliment and then shook myself vigorously.

"Sin-Ka-Lip! Stop that! You know better than to shake inside the van. Get out of there and wash yourself off before I turn the hose on you!"

Lazytail wouldn't go into the creek with me, so she was still covered with manure mud when Mr. Gunderson arrived. When he eventually left, they were both muddy but she was still loose at Sunbow. She could damn well stay there forever, as far as he was concerned. He didn't want anything bad to happen to her, but if Mooney felt like adopting the ungrateful bitch, that was fine by him.

I looked at Mooney pleadingly, but I think she had already made up her mind. "We like her, and I'll be happy to take care of her," Mooney said. "I just want to be sure you understand that we didn't steal her away or anything. She just got this idea in her head that she's going to stay here, and we can't make her go away."

"That is abundantly clear," Mr. Gunderson replied. "I really do like Balta, but if this is what she wants, I won't stop her. She's all up on her shots and worming—shouldn't need anything until spring. I'll get the records to you when I can find them."

Mr. Gunderson had calmed down quite a bit, and moved closer to Lazytail so he could pet her one more time before leaving, but she shied away suspiciously and wouldn't let herself be touched.

"You *do* know about wolf crosses."

Mr. Gunderson made that into a half-question, half-affirmation, looking at me as he said it. I had forced myself to remain in full view beside Mooney during the show, so there had been plenty of opportunity for him to see me. Probably his first good look ever.

Mooney glanced down and patted me on the head. "Yes, I've learned a thing or two. Flaky, aren't they?"

I put my ears back, and Mr. Gunderson chuckled. "Good luck! I think you'll need it. Balta chewed right through the side of her kennel today, you know."

Mr. Gunderson graciously declined an offer of coffee and coffee cake, got into his truck, and started the engine, but just before driving off he opened the window and added, "By the way, you should know that since she's a high-wolf cross, she goes into heat only once a year. January or February most likely, and she'll probably show a split heat. Be sure to keep a close eye on her. Also, don't let her near any stock, especially young ones like lambs or calves. The temptation might be more than she can handle."

He put the truck in gear and started it moving, but just then Mooney asked him some sort of a question, and he put it in neutral to answer. After that they got into a regular human-style 'chat' which lasted over half an hour, with the truck idling the whole time. Mouse got cold and went back into the house, while Lazytail and I slipped off into the brush to watch from concealment. I still can't understand humans. If Mr. Gunderson wanted to stay and talk, why wouldn't he go into the kitchen for coffee and food? And why did Mooney just stand there in the rain, talking to him? She had forgotten to put on her heavy coat, and I knew she was freezing.

Chapter 14

Back in school again—so strange to be there—like walking through a dream from long ago. Everyone was pouring out stories of flood experiences, and the noise level was even higher than usual. Mouse and I were especially popular because we had actually been living in the flood area. Most of the others lived outside the valley, and school had remained open except for the snow days and vacation.

Even Mrs. Stanford seemed glad to see us, or at least Mouse. She had never warmed to me—always smelled a little scared whenever she came close. It hadn't helped that when she was near me I would sometimes growl, ever so softly, deep down in my chest—so softly she couldn't be sure I was really doing it. I hoped. It was a bad habit, and Mouse kicked me whenever she caught me at it, but I pretended I couldn't help myself.

We were both rather confused about what was being taught, but I could tell the feeling was shared by others in the class. I've since learned that disorientation is the normal feeling when school resumes after even the shortest of vacations. This time, however, I sat close beside Mouse and paid strict attention, bringing every word on the blackboard into the sharpest possible focus. I think the humans could see it better, but I did well enough, even from the back of the room. Our snowman conversation had got me to thinking that if I really looked at the visual aids, perhaps Mouse would understand them too, and it might help her to keep up with the other kids. Mouse had her hand on my neck all through first session, and I could feel how hard she was concentrating. In fact, it seemed at times I could sense an echo of Mrs. Stanford's words through Mouse's ears. Whatever it was, we did very well on question and answer, so that Mrs. Stanford seemed pleased, and rather surprised.

Second morning session went well too, although I was quite tired by the end of it. A nap would have been nice, but there was never any nap time scheduled at school. A pity.

"You know," Mouse said toward the end of second session, "this is the first time we've been alone together since before the flood. You're so busy with that wolf friend of yours you don't have any time for me any more."

We didn't seem very alone to me. The room was filled with humans. That meant I didn't have to answer her.

Mouse brought up the subject again during a private moment in Mrs. Seeley's room that afternoon. She was supposed to be practicing fractions in Braille, and it was slow-going for her. I wasn't much help, since all I really wanted to do was lie under the table and sleep.

"Don't you sleep at night any more?" she complained, slouching down so she could reach me with her toes and jab them into whatever part of my anatomy she could reach. This time it was my left shoulder. Plenty of fur and muscle there for padding, so I didn't bother to move away. She had kicked off her shoes and the soft human toes felt almost pleasant.

This sounded awfully familiar. "I've always gone out at night," I protested. "I'm just a wild animal, so I can do whatever I like. And pffesides, I'm in season now, and Lazytail is too, almost. She needs extra attention right now."

"That's still not the right answer. You're Coyote, and you're on a magical quest. I heard all about it from John and Mooney. You're supposed to be going to school to learn about Science, remember?"

"I don't feel magical, and I don't see the pffoint in most of these pffropfflems we're working on, and I still need a napff. You're the one who has to pffass all the tests. I just go along to keepff you out of troupffle." I got up halfway and dragged myself to the far end of the table where she couldn't reach me, then settled myself again.

"Well, you just go lick your rear end and go to sleep then! I don't need your help anyway. And you can just go do whatever you like with Lazytail, too. I don't care about that either!" She was really mad and hurt, but I knew she'd get over it, so I turned my back to her and prepared myself for sleep.

I couldn't do it.

Napping is generally an easy thing for me, especially in a quiet, carpeted, overheated classroom. This time all I could think about was how silent Mouse had become. Just sitting there and fuming, most likely. After a while I got up and padded over to her. The nap wasn't worth it. Cost too much.

"What should I do, Mouse? I really like Lazytail, and you could never keepff upff with us out in the woods. It's more fun running at night, and safer too."

"I know, Coyote, but you've been gone so much! You must be gone all night, you sleep so much. You hardly even stayed awake for Christmas presents! I don't see why Mooney puts up with it."

Mooney wasn't exactly 'putting up with it,' in my opinion; but if Mouse hadn't noticed, I wasn't going to say anything about it.

"I'm with you now," I offered.

"Yeah. Just barely." She was mollified, but not to the point where I could nap again. I hardly napped at all that day.

When Mouse went to bed, Lazytail and I went with her, but Lazytail was gone when I woke later that night, and her sleeping cushion was cold. I began to worry immediately, and went outside to find her.

The trail led straight toward Mr. Bell's place, and I began to trot faster. I wasn't sure Lazytail really understood the difference between game and stock, but I had always been with her, keeping her in line. If she decided to attack one of Mr. Bell's calves, we would all be in big trouble.

I swam the creek anxiously, listening for sounds of a disturbance, but heard nothing unusual. That, at least, was a good sign. And Mr. Bell shouldn't be leaving the cows outside at night much this time of year. The air was moving the wrong way for me to check the pasture by scent, but I began to relax. Lazy had probably just passed through on her way north.

I heard Jake growling, not far off—a strange sort of growl I had never heard from him before.

Jake is not among the better watch dogs, and certainly was not in the habit of patrolling the outer pasture fence late on a winter night. I broke into a run and found them both together, but they were not fighting.

They were... *playing.*

I skidded to a stop and froze motionless, staring in disbelief. How could she do this to me? Jake and I had been enemies together all our lives!

The sluggish air took my scent to them, and Lazytail rushed over for greetings. I was cool to her, eyes only on Jake. He was standing there doing nothing. Trying to take it all in, I guess. Finally he decided that belligerence was the appropriate response, and shared it with both of us. Lazytail seemed surprised, but I was not. Jake had been after me for years, and any friend of mine had to be an enemy of his. I backed off prudently, and after a brief hesitation Lazytail followed me away, with Jake barking along ferociously, also at a prudent distance. Jake and I had never actually fought with each other, which was just as well. When I was younger he could have killed me or hurt me badly. Now the opposite was true. I outweighed him by about thirty pounds and was in much better shape.

Jake followed us to the edge of his domain, then stood and barked us away as only a hound dog can, sounding appropriately fierce and competent, but maybe just a bit lonely too. He didn't wander like I did, and Mr. Bell had even fewer visitors than Mooney. I had never thought of it before, but Jake knew me better than any other canine in the world. Too bad we hated each other so much.

My heart was not for roaming that night, and I was able to persuade Lazytail to come home before too long. It was only when we swam the creek that the last traces of Jake's sour mustiness disappeared from her fur.

The second day of school went more smoothly. Kids had settled in, and I was better rested for daytime work. The weather remained clear, cold, and still, which is normal for much of January. The rains would start again soon enough.

Mouse and I breezed through Mrs. Stanford's class, there was spaghetti for lunch, and Mrs. Seeley's class went well too, as it generally did. Mouse and I were in good spirits when we got to Sunbow.

That all ended when I greeted Lazytail. She had been visiting Jake again. I could smell it.

English is very good for some purposes. With it I could have told Lazytail exactly what I thought of her behavior, and how I wanted her to behave. As it was, I could only do the first half.

Our language conveys feelings like no other can. Feelings are what it's for. A lift of tail or ear, a trembling muscle, change of eye position, or even subtle alterations in scent can mean everything. Lazytail knew how upset I was, and I knew she was concerned and supportive, but I simply couldn't convey to her what was bothering me. In the end I rushed absently through our evening routine with the humans, then took us out for a relentless, fast lope that ate up dozens of miles and much of the night. We came home lame and exhausted, but I was proud of Lazytail. She had kept up well.

School didn't go so well the next day. I was tired and irritable, and my feet hurt. I even showed my teeth to one of our admirers when he inadvertently stepped on my toes. He looked shocked and fearful when I did that, and I hastened to make up for it. Mooney was always drumming into me how careful I had to be. She said lifting my lips was like one human pulling a knife on another one. I tried not to make that mistake, but it was so hard, sometimes.

Mouse was disgusted with me by the time we got home, and she tattled to Mooney. I told Mooney all about Lazytail and Jake, and she smiled sadly. "Now you know what it's like."

"Know what *what* is like?"

"Now you know how I feel when you go out and do who knows what, and there's not a thing I can do about it besides locking you in a cage, which wouldn't work even if I had the nerve to try it."

Mooney generally didn't use such long sentences, even when she was mad. She was sounding sort of like Mouse.

"So what should we do?" I prompted after Mooney had wound down sufficiently.

"Do? Why, we don't *do* anything! Just let them play. Maybe we can be friends with Mr. Bell again. I think, if I work at it, maybe I could forgive him now for that time he tried to kill you."

"Pffut Lazytail will pffe going into heat soon," I blurted incautiously. I had developed a wealth of plans and fantasies about that, none of which involved Jake.

"She will now, will she? So we could end up with a dozen of Jake's puppies tumbling around Sunbow this spring. Wouldn't that be fun? We could call them Wynoochee Wolfhounds."

She looked at me challengingly. "Or did you have other ideas?"

I lowered my ears and head and tail, and rolled my eyes upward to gaze entreatingly at Mooney. "I'm in season already, just like you said would hapffen. And I'm ten years old now. I'll pffe eleven when the pffupffs are pfforn. Most coyotes are dead pffy that age! Isn't that old enough for me?"

"Oh, you..." Mooney left her sentence unfinished and reached over to rub my ears. I sat down on my haunches and leaned into her hand, groaning with pleasure and dreaming about Lazytail.

Mooney laughed suddenly, and pushed me off. She was looking down at my belly, where the sitting position and my romantic thoughts were making me show quite a bit.

"Put that thing away, you dirty old man. Can't you think about anything else?"

"No, not really," I admitted. "I know it's too early, pffut I think I can almost smell her already, and her nipffles are getting pffigger."

"It looks like you've done your homework alright, Stinky. But honestly, I'm really not ready for this. Maybe we'll just have to get Lazytail spayed."

"No! I'll leave her alone. I pffromise!"

"Sin-Ka-Lip, my sweets, you couldn't keep that promise even if you meant it. Don't worry though. I was just teasing you about spaying Lazytail. Mr. Burrey has suggested a better idea. He'll be going on a trip to Pullman soon to do some research, and he's offered to take you along. Lazytail will be out of season when you get back, and we'll have another year to figure out what to do about you two."

"Pffut what apffout Jake?" It had never occurred to me that I might be sent away. This ruined everything!

"Just you let me and Mr. Bell worry about Jake," Mooney told me firmly.

"And remember this. Whatever else happens, John and I are not going to let you become a father at your age. Ten years may be over the hill for a regular coyote, but not for you. And you have a job to do that's going to put some pretty rough demands on you. You don't need one more burden."

Mooney didn't understand at all. Lazytail wasn't a burden! I tried to explain this to her but she just didn't seem to get it. She kept saying yes, she understood, and I would too some day. "It's only puppy-love," she told me at one point, and smiled like she had made a joke. I was not amused. This was not a joking matter.

It was not a negotiable matter either, and when the time came for Mr. Burrey to leave for Pullman, I was with him.

January ninth. Moon two days shy of full and Lazytail just shy of full heat. A scent to die for, and so affectionate, but still not quite ready. Not quite ready, and now miles behind us.

Cheated.

Miserable and sullen, I perched on the front passenger seat of Mr. Burrey's van, waiting for him to talk at me. It was a bucket seat on a pedestal. Not very comfortable for me, but I always sit in front when I can. It's a canine thing, I suppose.

The back of the van was all empty space except for the small pile of camping things we had brought with us, so the heater fan blew our scents around and back to us mingled with goose down and water repellent and ripstop nylon. Mr. Burrey's wolf scent was strongly present now—stronger than his human scent.

"Don't take it so hard, Coyote. It's probably better this way," he finally remarked.

"If one more human tells me, 'It's pffetter this way,' I'll pffite a chunk out of him and eat it!"

I muttered those words quietly, head turned away. It's hard to threaten someone who's dominant over you, but I was feeling desperate, and besides I knew old Furry Feet wouldn't take offense. He was quite mellow when human.

"Excuse me, I didn't quite catch that?"

"Oh, nothing," I replied resignedly. Humans don't always hear very well. Good thing, too.

"Well, as I was saying, it's probably better that we're spending our full moon time far away from Sunbow. The curse affects me in more ways than I care to admit, and I'm afraid with your new friend so close to going into heat... well, you know what I mean. It just wouldn't be smart for me to be at Sunbow right now."

"Not you, too! Won't anyone leave her alone?"

"I was just speaking hypothetically. Dogs generally run away or try to kill me." He turned toward me with a slightly scary smile and added, "That second choice is not a wise one."

"Well you just leave Lazytail alone, then! I don't care what she does to you, don't you dare hurt her!"

"Oh, Coyote. Don't worry about Lazytail! I would never hurt her, and I can always run away if she gets mad at me. It's just that I find her very... attractive. Most humans wouldn't understand, but I think you do."

"Yes. You're right. Maypffe it is pffest if we stay away for now."

We were both silent as Mr. Burrey wove us through the congested area around Olympia. Much later he turned toward me briefly and cleared his throat, then put his eyes firmly back on the road. "Tell me now, Coyote. Speaking man to man. What is it like?"

"I'm not a man, and I don't know what you're talking apffout," I evaded.

"Come on. You can talk to me, at least. I'll understand better than anyone else would."

This was embarrassing for me. I didn't mind talking about sex, just hated to admit my lack of experience. I even thought about making something up, but finally decided on telling the truth. It's less work.

"I don't know. I've never done it," I replied finally.

"What? You've been wandering the valley for years now. You can open doors and gates. Surely there have been plenty of opportunities for you!"

"Yes, pffut most dogs don't like me, either, and I wasn't really interested until this last year. At least, not for myself. I watched a lot. Humans too. I think dogs do it pffetter. Humans finish too quickly, like horses. The dogs take their time and apffreciate it more."

"Oh."

Long pause.

"That's an interesting way of looking at things. You do realize most humans would take exception to that statement, don't you?"

"Yes, I know. You humans think you're the pffest at everything. You even think the World was created for humans."

"And who was it created for?"

"Coyotes, of course. We just don't have it working pffropfferly yet."

Chapter 15

Pullman is a strange little town, not like the others. You drive all day through rangeland and then get into empty wheat fields near the end—really nice, open land with very few humans. Suddenly the road slices down from the edge of the Palouse and you're in a spider-shaped human settlement with a huge university in the center. Actually the town is little more than a layer of houses and businesses clinging to the university and feeding off of it like fleas or ticks. I disliked the place from the first, but then I don't really like any towns or cities.

We stayed the first night at a 'pets okay' motel in Pullman, having arrived well after dark and both exhausted from driving. The departure had been late, hectic, and unpleasant—no one satisfied with the arrangement, but no one able to agree on an alternative.

I had never been on such a long trip before and was not the best of company, but Mr. Burrey didn't make it any easier. There was a lot of ice on the road so he wouldn't go very fast, but he didn't stop often either. Our only major break had been just beyond a single gas station called the town of Washtucna. It was a day before our first possible transformation but Moon was almost ready to rise then, so Peter pulled his van over to wait for her. No sense taking unnecessary chances.

Patches of crusted snow covered most of the ground with stiff, dry grass blades poking through and quivering to a sharp breeze from the northeast. The sky was wide open and cloudless, with no trees or mountains or clouds to challenge it, and the land began to blaze with light the moment Moon appeared. I longed to go running, even tired as I was, but Mr. Burrey said he was cold, and wouldn't let me. We did howl together, though, and he taught me to sing Greensleeves:

Alas, my love, you do me wrong
To cast me off so discourteously...

I like that song. It has a sort of canine feel to it, and the words flow smoothly from the throat. Mr. Burrey told me the author is unknown. Perhaps he's unhuman, too.

Mr. Burrey didn't even pretend to work next day, just drove us out sightseeing and looking for a good camping place. Before we left Pullman he stopped at a supermarket and stocked up on chuck steak and soup bones, along with sausages, eggs, and bread. Starving was not part of our agenda.

Kamiak Butte is rocky, solitary, and steep—thrusting high above the endless Palouse hills north of Pullman. It has trees on it. The place is a park and wildlife sanctuary with no overnight camping, which suited us just fine once we had the van hidden. No need to worry about running into humans after dark. Not that any sane human would be out camping in such weather, Mr. Burrey told me.

As it turned out the Butte was a nice spot, but far too small to hold our attention for long. The snow there was deeper than at Washtucna, and colder —so cold it made an unpleasant squeaking sound when stepped on, and the loose surface flakes puffed forward like Styrofoam crumbs when scuffed. There was no stickiness to them at all. The snow extended outward as far as I could see to form an unbroken cover on the plowed and seeded hills, with a thin crust that could only just bear our weight. We spent most of the night running those hills, and ended up meeting humans after all.

The Palouse is totally devoted to farming. It's not flat, but they plow it all anyway because the soil is rich with volcanic ash and very fertile. Everywhere you go there are old, abandoned houses or foundation stones, but there are fewer farmers now. They drove out the Nez Perce and Palus in the late 1800s, put it all to wheat, and called it the 'Inland Empire'. Forty years later the Great Depression came and most of the small farmers went bankrupt. They took their kin to the cities but they left their houses behind, and the big agribusiness farmers plow around them still. Or so Mr. Burrey had told me earlier while he was still in human form. Now he wasn't talking much.

We were checking out one of those old houses. Not looking for anything in particular, just looking. Wheat fields really did come right up to the door. The night was mostly gone, and so were my five chuck steaks. I couldn't believe I was hungry again already, but there it was. I was growing irritable, too. No wonder werewolves have such a bad reputation.

"Come on out, Furry Feet. There's no game in there. If you want something to eat we'll have to go pffack to the van, or maypffe raid a farm." The air was bitingly cold and dry, so that my breath exploded into huge clouds of steam which dissipated instantly after I stopped talking.

There was a real farm not far from where we stood. Three houses, and huge machines everywhere. Many of them lay rusty and untended in the snow, and appeared to be non-functional. Some even had bushes or small trees growing up through them. The newer, larger machines were parked neatly in a series of open-sided metal stalls, each one of which would have held our goat barn with room to spare.

We had skirted the farm widely when first passing, since it was brightly lit and smelled of more than one dog. That prudent attitude had faded as my hunger increased, and now the thought of a visit there had begun to intrigue me. I suggested a side trip. Mr. Burrey was not so keen on the idea.

"Fffet-terr g-go ffvan. Go ffvan."

He was concentrating so much on his pronunciation that his words came out more like a suggestion than an order. I chose to interpret them that way.

"Furry Feet! You're not scared of a coupffle of farm dogs, are you? We can eat *them!*" The curse must have been working on us pretty strongly just then, because I was more than half serious, and Mr. Burrey didn't stop me.

I wasn't looking for farm dogs or trouble, though. It was freezer meat I wanted, and that is often found on farmhouse back porches or in workshops. I chose the largest house first, and immediately found what I was looking for —a chest freezer almost as big as Mr. Bell's. Nothing was locked, of course. Whatever for? Our only problem was how to carry off the quantity we wanted.

I finally struck on the idea of loading all the meat onto a big hooded jacket which I took down from the wall nearby, then gripping the cloth with my teeth while Mr. Burrey pulled at the other end to make a sort of hammock or sling. It would have worked, too, except that one of the pieces fell out onto the porch boards with a resounding thud, and woke the dogs.

There were two of them; a brainless Springer Spaniel and a more sensible Labrador. All they really had to do was stand off at a distance and bark. We were already leaving. That's what the Lab did but the Springer came up much closer, lunging viciously and then turning away while working himself up to do more. His barking had started off rapid, frantic, and high-pitched, but became deeper and more forceful as his confidence grew. Not that his voice could ever get that deep. He was only half my size.

Mr. Burrey and I kept our haunches down and tails curled tightly between our legs—concentrating on dragging off our booty as efficiently as possible while still being ready to defend ourselves. It was easy in the farmyard, where the snow was packed down, but the undisturbed snow was more of a problem. We kept breaking through the crust while the Springer danced along on the surface, coming closer with each little rush. He picked on me for some reason.

I was becoming really irritated. More angry than I really had a right to be. Just the curse working again, I suppose. When the Springer finally mustered the courage to actually touch me, I lost my temper and bit his head off.

Yes, you read that right. I bit his head off.

When I felt that dog's teeth in me I dropped my burden and whipped around so fast he didn't even have time to face me squarely. He seemed to be moving in slow motion. Almost his whole neck fit into my mouth so I snapped down as hard as I could, shook him with all my strength, and he just... fell apart. The body landed yards away to kick and spray blood on the snow for a time. The head snapped its jaws twice and went still as I held it. The Labrador stopped barking and disappeared.

I dropped the head. "We should go now," I suggested softly, dazed. The killing had filled me with a pleasure greater than any belly rub. Only once before had I felt this way: when I killed the buck.

Mr. Burrey didn't answer me—didn't need to. It was definitely time to go. He did walk over to sniff tentatively at the Springer's body, and I knew what he was thinking. That dog was much more appetizing than the frozen chunks of cow meat we were trying to carry off.

Mr. Burrey restrained himself, though, and he was just turning away when I heard the porch door open and saw a man lifting a rifle into firing position. I didn't waste any time staring or thinking, just barked once and fled lightly across the fragile snow crust, unburdened and impossibly swift. Mr. Burrey followed close behind.

I longed desperately for trees, then. That lovely open country didn't seem quite so wonderful any more, since we stood out by Moon's light like the bullseye on a target, and nothing to be done about it besides reaching the rise ahead as quickly as we possibly could.

The first shots missed, and we were close to our goal when Mr. Burrey was struck. I felt rather than saw him go down, felt it through my feet on the snow.

I wanted to keep on running, to circle back and kill the farmer, to do anything besides what I actually did, which was to rush back to Furry Feet and try to help him.

His left thighbone was shattered, I think. The leg flopped uselessly and wouldn't bear weight, and now his blood lay steaming and eating its way into the snow just like the Springer's had. Way too much of it. I nudged him up and we staggered forward together, breaking the crust with each step rather than skimming on top. Too clumsy. Two more bullets sliced down close beside us, and each time I thought it would be me, but then they stopped for a while. Time to reload, I guess.

The shots started again as we topped the rise, and then we were over. Safe, for the moment. Okay to rest. Only that one shot had touched us, but it was more than enough. Mr. Burrey was still bleeding heavily and his Presence felt wrong—sort of loose, and unstable.

John had taught me all about blood loss and shock, but that knowledge was of no benefit to us just then. It was miles back to Kamiak Butte, and I didn't know where to turn for help. Staying where we were was not an option, though, and I nudged Mr. Burrey onto his feet again, aiming him generally away from the farm and toward the butte.

I was really rattled, or I would have remembered about the Moon change. Mr. Burrey had been doing this longer, though, and remembered for me. He tried to take control of the direction we were going, and when I wouldn't let him he spoke laboriously, "Nneeed... housse." Nicely formed words, for him, but those two are easier than most.

He was trying to remind me that his injury made it impossible to reach the van before Moon set, even if he had the strength. He would be left stranded and naked on the snow, and would surely die from the cold, if nothing else.

It soon became clear that Mr. Burrey was trying to get back to the abandoned farmhouse we had visited just before the meat raid. It was not far off, and a good thing, too. He collapsed, finally, and I had to drag him over the snow for the last part of the trip. Made better time that way anyhow.

All the house's windows and doors were missing, but in one of the upstairs bedrooms was a kid's nest with mattress, blanket scraps, and an impressive collection of trash/treasures. Mr. Burrey revived himself enough to climb the stairs and lie down on the mattress, but that was it for him. He was in a bad way—staggering and shivering so that he fell down twice on the stairs, and on the mattress he just collapsed and trembled. Considering how much blood he had lost, I was surprised he was alive at all. That leg was truly a mess.

I gathered up the blanket scraps, along with some burlap bags and old newspapers—layering them carefully on top and to one side of him, and putting myself on the other side. It was all I could do.

The shivering stopped after a time, but the breathing slowed down too. I wasn't sure that was good. Furry Feet would no longer respond when I spoke to him, and his Presence felt even more diffuse and poorly centered, like it was falling apart.

The Presence continued to disperse and weaken, like fog on a summer morning. It was hardly anchored to Mr. Burrey at all any more. I felt drawn to it, more aware than I had ever been before, but when I reached out somehow to touch a part, that part disappeared, and I felt a trace of the killing pleasure again. The thought came to me that I could take it all that way—

should take it—it was my right. Mr. Burrey had proven himself unworthy, and...

Now, where had *that* thought come from? It was not mine, certainly! I admired Mr. Burrey. If being shot makes one 'unworthy,' then I'm unworthy too.

I may lie, cheat, and have a subnormal moral sense by human standards, but that's not necessarily the same as being weak-willed. Mr. Burrey was my friend, and I began to fight this new danger as soon as I recognized it.

First, the draining. I tried to keep myself from doing it, tried to reverse the process. I knew I had energy to spare; I could feel it inside of me. All I had to do was figure out how to share it.

What is the opposite of pleasure? Pain, nausea, tiredness, depression—those were the feelings I sought—the guides I followed to help me do the right thing. The process was quite disagreeable, and now I could clearly feel something fighting my efforts. The thing was alien, not a part of me. Don't ask how I knew, but there was no doubt. I shoved it roughly aside—enough to accomplish what I needed to, anyway—and felt my own life energy begin to flood out from me like blood from a deep wound. My breath caught in shock, and I suppressed a panicked reflex to stop what I was doing. The reflex was my own, not something forced on me by that other thing. This was a dangerous magic I was attempting! I could die from it.

The energy slammed roughly outward, uncontrolled and disruptive, doing as much harm as good. Some was absorbed but the rest was tearing at the last connection with Mr. Burrey's body—pushing him away from it.

Inward again. Hold it... here! I found I had some sort of control over the energy-stuff, my own at least, and managed to pull it together into a crude sphere around us. Mine on the outside, Mr. Burrey's on the inside, and our two physical bodies in the very center. I held it that way by my will alone—battling my ignorance, my pain and nausea, and even that other thing that crept around trying to stop me whenever I tired. It seemed to speak to me sometimes, whispering urgently that I was risking myself on a hopeless cause, I must quit before I damaged myself any further.

I don't know what the Old Ones would be able to do with their Medicine Powers, but Mr. Burrey's body was still bleeding and dying, and I could only hold things together for a limited time. I was learning control, but I could also feel myself weakening. My own substance was fraying and dissipating while keeping Mr. Burrey's together. Still, I persisted. I had a clear, compelling reason to do so which I no longer fully understand. I suspect the knowledge has been taken from me.

Mr. Burrey's breaths had become shallow and tremulous, and the pauses between had grown so long that each new breath came as a dull surprise. I had given up hope for him, but from pure stubbornness I held on anyway. When Mr. Burrey was truly dead I would let him go, but not before then.

Without warning the change-magic tickled my spine, then surged swiftly through me. When it passed I found myself curled protectively around a naked human, who was curled himself into the tightest knot he could make. He was not wounded, and neither was I. The bite wound left by that Springer had disappeared, and even my fur was free of blood. Mr. Burrey was clean too, but all the rest of the blood was still there—in the blankets, on the floor, and a great puddle still unfrozen in the mattress beneath us.

Mr. Burrey lifted his head from under my chin and peered around blearily. He didn't look very well. Kind of like I felt. "Could you move over a bit, please? You're lying on the only spot... not soaked with blood."

Mr. Burrey shifted over to the warm, dry spot I vacated for him, then brushed at his thigh and groin area distastefully. "Bullet fragments. Every speck is pushed out... during the change. Wish I could passen... patent it... somehow. I'd be..." A violent spasm of shivering locked Mr. Burrey's jaws together and took his voice away. He curled himself back into a tight ball, and I began to cover him, and after a few minutes he was able to speak again. "More, please," he said through clenched teeth. "There must be something downstairs you can use."

I did find more stuff, mostly newspaper, along with some torn garbage bags and a pillowcase which had contained walnuts before the rats got to them. Mr. Burrey was embedded in the center of a rather large, fluffy rubbish pile before he was satisfied.

"Thanks, kid. You've saved my life. Now it's time for you to get out of here. You saw the trail we left. No one could resist following something like that, and they'll be here at first light. Wait for me at the van. I'll get back there somehow. And don't you dare eat all the steaks!" Mr. Burrey's voice came muffled from inside his cocoon—still strange from weakness and spasmodic trembling, but much better than it had been. He would be safe, I thought. Still I hesitated.

"Go on! What are you waiting for?"

"Are you sure you'll pffe okay?"

"Yes, I'm sure! The only one in danger now is you! Get out of here."

"Yes, Sir, Mr. Furry Feet, Sir. I'm leaving right now. And I'll save a steak for you. Maypffe."

Mr. Burrey arrived at the van around mid-day, driven over by the same man who had nearly killed him. Mr. Burrey told me that later. Personally, I have trouble telling humans apart by sight when they're wearing a lot of clothes, and I hadn't been close enough to the farmer to smell him properly the night before.

Mr. Burrey was warmly dressed, and he wasn't wearing handcuffs. Good, so far. What a talker! Here he is: found naked on a blood-soaked mattress in an abandoned house, with wolf prints leading up to it but no human footprints at all. They dress him up, drive him where he wants to go, and don't even call the police! I wonder what the farmer thought about all the paw prints around Mr. Burrey's van.

I did notice him surreptitiously copying down our license number. Kamiak Butte has brush and trees to hide behind, and the farmer would have been quite alarmed, I think, if he had realized that one of last night's visitors stood at leap-distance from him at that very moment. I allowed Mr. Burrey to see me, but of course he didn't say anything about it—just took the van key from its hiding place under a rock and used it to open up the side door. The farmer peered inside, then watched impassively as Mr. Burrey located his parka and boots and exchanged them for the ones he was borrowing. Mr. Burrey tried to give the farmer some money, too, but he wouldn't take it. He wouldn't even take back the clothes Mr. Burrey was wearing. He just stood silently beside the van until it was successfully started, then got back into his own truck and drove on ahead.

Mr. Burrey called to me as soon as the farmer had moved far enough along, and I leapt in through the side door he opened for me. Mr. Burrey slammed the door closed and jumped back into the driver's seat, then jerked the van into motion and followed the farmer out to the main road. We turned north toward Spokane, and I watched through one of Mr. Burrey's spy holes as the farmer waited for us to start away, then turned back south toward his own home. I never saw him again.

I climbed up to join Mr. Burrey in front. "How did it go?"

"Don't ask. I don't think I've ever been so embarrassed."

I didn't really want to pry, but professional curiosity was getting the best of me and I persisted. "Did you use any tricks I should know apffout?"

"Unlike you, the people out here have a highly developed sense of privacy and good manners. I admitted that I had been caught making love to a married woman, and the husband had abducted me and left me to die of exposure. They didn't see the bloody mattress because I covered it over with trash before they came upstairs. They asked me if any large animals had come into the house during the night, and I said yes, but they ran off when I yelled. No one asked how I got there without leaving any human tracks. I wonder if they thought of it and were afraid to mention anything.

"They were definitely a scared bunch, poor folks. The farmer didn't even believe himself when he described how fast we ran, and that dog you killed was quite a sight. The Labrador is jammed way back under the house, and she won't come out for anybody."

"Why aren't they more curious? That's a terripffle story! It wouldn't last for two seconds against Mooney! And what apffout us opffening the freezer and dragging the meat away on a jacket? Wolves don't do that."

"It's the best story they're going to get, Coyote. Regular people are funny that way: no one can lie to them better than they lie to themselves. Now if it's alright with you, I'd rather drop the subject."

What a concept—people actually *helping* you lie to them! Too bad all my friends were so smart.

We wanted to get far away from Kamiak Butte, but not all the way north to Spokane. Tekoa Mountain was just right. It was about the same elevation and had a similar snow type, but it was much larger than Kamiak. We had a big dinner and then set down to nap until Moon was ready to rise— left the fire burning to maybe thaw out our steaks and bones for later. We were both deeply exhausted.

That night was uneventful in the sense that we didn't kill anything or get in trouble. We ate our meat, ran off into the woods as far from humans as possible, even napped a bit near the end. We passed plenty of tracks—deer, fox, even coyote—but we forced ourselves not to follow any. Mr. Burrey made nice progress with his language lessons, and he showed me how to crack rocks with my teeth. What a body! Too bad it's so hard to control.

Our eggs were all frozen, so we boiled them for breakfast instead of frying, but they tasted just fine that way, and there was plenty of bread and sausage. We liked the spot so well that we came right back, after going into town for more meat.

The third night passed much like the second. We still were subdued from our first night's experience and didn't want to try anything new. I realize now that we both had spirit injuries which would take some time to heal, and resting was the best thing for us. Fortunately, that's just what we felt like doing.

We had a visitor in the morning. He walked like a man and looked like a man, but he wasn't human, not even a little. His Presence was of a power beyond anything I had ever felt, and he smelled of male fox. Just fox. Nothing else. Not even clothing and laundry detergent and deodorant. Mr. Burrey recognized his strangeness and importance too, and invited him to breakfast with extreme deference. The visitor said he could not eat with us. He must speak.

He looked sick, and angry, and sad. So sad. Like Mooney when Wynoochee took her berry fields. "You have become a soul-eater," he accused me. "How could you do this thing?"

The visitor was addressing me directly. Mr. Burrey tried to answer for me, but was waved into silence.

I abased myself and attempted to formulate an answer—didn't even try to pretend I couldn't talk. I knew exactly who this person was, and what he was talking about.

"I... I didn't want to. I couldn't helpff it. Sir." I felt he should be given a title of respect, but wasn't sure which one to use.

"I see you really are weak and useless. I was hoping we had done better." He let silence grow the way John did when he was angry, and I waited quietly and extremely submissively, just as I did when John was angry. Saying more could only invite more criticism. Mr. Burrey remained silent too, for once.

"So what are you going to do now?"

"I don't know, Sir. I think I need some helpff."

The visitor was evidently expecting this response, because he paused only long enough to pretend to think. "I expect the only thing I can do is to destroy the both of you. No one who has chosen to follow your path ever gives it up. In a way it's our fault, for trusting you. All that power, and no discipline to control it." He went to one knee and sniffed me from nose to tail, which was tucked tightly between my legs. For Mr. Burrey's benefit he ran his hands along the fur and pretended to examine it closely. I kept myself absolutely still and stiff, although I couldn't prevent myself from trembling. After a short time he withdrew and looked me in the eyes again. The anger was still there, but no longer directed at me, and a look of relief, or maybe hope, was mixed with the sadness.

"I see now: you're not a soul-eater, after all. It appears you have a little 'guest'. Nasty. You had a taste of what it took, but it will take you as well, in the end."

He stood up and looked to Mr. Burrey, then back to me again. "You're right. This really isn't your fault, which is good news. I'll still have to kill you both, but it may not be necessary to destroy you utterly."

We were both staring at the visitor, unable to think of anything to say. Finally Mr. Burrey ventured to speak.

"Ahm... it looks like you and Coyote already know each other, but I'm a little lost. My name is Peter Burrey. And you?" He reached forward very cautiously, offering to shake hands. Our visitor was unarmed, and that probably gave Mr. Burrey a little confidence. Misplaced.

The visitor shook hands without hesitation. "Call me Fox. I am ancient and wise. More ancient and less wise than you may think. Too much wisdom makes one tired, so I let myself forget things. And what are you, Peter Burrey? Do you make things, grow things, kill things? My Brother Coyote seems very fond of you. It will be a shame to kill you."

"I'm not really sure I want to be killed just now," Mr. Burrey proposed carefully. "Could you perhaps explain for me? Slowly, please."

Fox looked slightly impatient, but also amused. "Very tactfully put, Peter Burrey. Most humans of your race would have taken offense by now. I'll try to return the courtesy.

"So, to begin. I've been observing you and Coyote for three nights now. Each night you've become wolves when Moon rises, then changed back into your customary forms when she leaves the sky. You have become not just wolves, but something else as well, something much more powerful than normal wolves. You did this not through Medicine Power, but through the magic more typical of your own people, Peter Burrey. The difference can be clearly felt by one like me.

"On your first night, one of you destroyed, or I should say consumed, the spirit of a farm dog.

"Now, you should realize that I have nothing against killing dogs when they're in the way. Dogs can be a great nuisance, or worse. The problem is this eating of souls. At first I thought you were doing it deliberately, but now I see you're a victim as much as any other. You and Coyote have both been possessed by a very powerful spirit—powerful from the many souls it has eaten in the past, and eager to grow stronger through your actions. In the end it will consume you, too, but not while you're still useful to it.

"Very few spirits are capable of possessing two bodies simultaneously, but that is what this one has done. I can feel the linkage between you, even though I can't determine the precise nature of the spirit. It's a soul-eater, though, and an old one. I can tell that well enough."

Mr. Burrey replied carefully, "Yes. I've been aware of this for a long time, and I've been fighting it as hard as I can. Isn't there some less drastic way of getting rid of it? Can you drive it out some way?"

Fox smiled, just a touch of maliciously. "Exorcisms are a specialty of your own people. Perhaps you should try a Catholic priest."

"I have, several times. There is a bit of professional rivalry in that field, and I gave them all their chance. No luck. I've even sought help from Islamic and Buddhist and Hindu leaders. The best of them can sense my problem, but no one has been able to cure it."

"Just as I told you: the most we can do is save your soul, Peter Burrey, and even that won't be easy or sure. It may well perish during our efforts to destroy what is locked into it. You are a son of the invaders, but for the sake of your friendship with Coyote we'll do the best we can. Anyway, your people are not quite so bad these days, and they did bring chickens with them. We foxes thank you for that, at least."

Mr. Burrey was listening with rigid attention. I couldn't tell how much he believed, but I accepted every word.

Fox!

Matchless in cleverness, and one of the most powerful of us lower-plane folks. One of my fathers, too, in a sense. I had never thought of him as a flesh-and-blood person before. And a shape-changer! Just like in the old stories. No one who smelled like he did could spend much time walking on two legs. I sat with mouth half-open, gazing at him in awe. I was glad he wasn't mad at me any more, but this killing business had me worried. Mr. Burrey was not keen on the idea either.

"You mentioned 'we' several times just now, Mr. Fox. Who is working with you? Maybe I can talk with some of them. No one is more motivated than I am when it comes to curing my condition. I'll take any kind of help I can get."

"Not 'Mr. Fox,' if you please. Just Fox. Or in this place you may call me *Wyaloo*. You needn't concern yourself with who is helping me. There will be enough of us to do the job, you can be sure of that! I'm afraid that's all I should really tell you about our plans. There's nothing you can do about them, and knowing the details will just make it harder for you."

"Excuse me, but if I were willing to commit suicide I could have done that years ago. I think Coyote and I will have to decline your help if you can't think of anything less drastic. We'll work this out on our own somehow."

Fox smiled sadly, and made to leave. "Do what you like. Neither your permission nor your cooperation is required, but it would be a good idea to have your affairs in order before Moon is full again."

"Excuse me, Fox, Sir?" I interrupted diffidently. I didn't like his death threats any more than Mr. Burrey did, but I was more used to such things and tried not to let them get under my skin. Fox could answer a lot of important questions for me if he felt so inclined, and it was a shame to just let him go.

"Yes, Brother?"

"What does OldCoyoteSpffirit say? Does he really think I'm no good?"

"Well, yes. I wouldn't take it personally, though. He's criticizing himself as much as you when he says that. Besides, he's only been talking that way for the last couple of months. Before that he was very proud of you. And himself, too, of course."

"Really? What did I do to change his mind? Do you think I could make upff to him some way? I don't think he's given me enough time to pffrove anything at all. I'm only ten years old, you know."

"Of course I know that. I was there. But yes, I do agree with you that OldCoyoteSpirit is being more than usually unreasonable. Hopefully you can be a mellowing force for him when the two of you join back together."

"Fox-Uncle, why is WolfSpffirit doing this to me? I like wolves. At least the ones I've met so far."

"WolfSpirit? What are you talking about? Wolf is not a spirit right now. He's one of the people who will be helping me kill you and get rid of your curse."

I told about my dream then, but Fox still seemed puzzled.

"That sounds like a True Dream, but OldCoyoteSpirit never mentioned it to me. You're not supposed to be remembering any dreams at all, but I suppose one could slip through from time to time. Why would you be seeing a wolf?"

"I don't know. I was hopffing you could tell me."

"No, I can't answer that right now, but I'll check into it. I expect the spirit-eater entered you during that dream, but why it was in wolf form, and why it causes these transformations, I don't know. I'll see you soon."

He walked away before I could ask more questions—walked off into the woods, not toward the road. Mr. Burrey and I sat together silently for a few minutes, then I slipped off to follow the trail. The deep, punched-through human tracks were soon replaced by faint, almost invisible fox paw scuffs on the snow crust. I was not surprised, and I didn't follow them any farther.

"Well, Coyote: what do you think of that old geezer?" Mr. Burrey prompted me when I got back. "He gave me quite a turn there. I think we should probably move camp again today. It's time I got to work anyway."

He didn't really want an answer to that one, so I didn't say anything except to suggest that a second course of breakfast might be indicated. I ate it all. Mr. Burrey had lost his appetite.

We broke camp under the same cold, clear sky we had enjoyed all along. Mr. Burrey had been wearing layer on layer of clothes, and would often huddle over the fire or a propane burner he kept in the van. When we got the engine warmed up he put the heater on its highest setting, so that I had to move into the back to keep from passing out from it.

We headed south to Pullman, went straight through it, and continued on to a really little town named Colton, then kept on going until we reached the bluffs above the river called Snake. Mr. Burrey had some friends there he wanted me to meet.

The male was a student at the veterinary college in Pullman, older than most of his classmates. He differed from them in other ways, too. He kept broken animals.

It was Saturday, so Ernest and Naomi Papillio were both home when we reached their place. Mr. Burrey told me if they had not been there he would have gone into the house anyway, to wait for them. They were that kind of people. Nothing was ever locked.

Their house was on rangeland, and we had to open and close two welded-steel cattle gates to get to it—one to keep the landlord's animals in, one to keep them out. The driveway ran down near the bottom of a gulch for some distance before rising back up onto tablelands where the house was located. It was the only way to get there. I had never been to this place before, but it felt so familiar... and I knew all about it from John's stories. The whole area was a lacy, ragged edge of the Snake River Gorge, where the southern half of the Palouse had been ripped away. It consisted of relatively flat, fertile bits of Palouse land cut by steep, wooded gullies that could be difficult to cross, especially for humans. Exciting country that I longed to be out running through, and beautiful. John sometimes said the river made it through millions of years of erosion. Other times he told me I had created it myself during a great battle in my other life, in the time of legends. The Snake River Gorge, that is. The land was always here, even before legends.

The first broken animal I saw was a wolf. Young male, pulling in terror at his chain because Mr. Burrey's van was strange to him. Ernie had told Mr. Burrey to drive past the wolf and park without looking at him directly. We could try greeting him later after his fear had faded, but visitors were hard on him and it was best to go slowly. The wolf's name was Smokey, and he had a healthy body but no place to live properly. Too fearful to be a pet any more, too naive for the wild, and the good zoos were all full.

Mr. Burrey and I went straight up to the door after we had parked. The snow was patchy and much thinner here, and it was warmer, but nowhere even close to melting. Smoke poured fast, thin, and hot from the chimney of the house, which was rambling and ragged-looking, with little sheds and wings built out from each side. There were paddocks behind it with three horses in them. Nice-looking ones, pressed up against the rails in curiosity.

Ernie and Nana each had a strong Presence. I should have guessed. Ernie's jaw opened in pleased surprise when he saw me, and he dropped to his knees to try for a respectful greeting. I obliged him, and Nana too, a moment later.

"Where did you find this monster?" Ernie marveled. "He looks like a coyote on steroids. They don't get nearly this big, but no way could he be anything else."

"Don't ask me," Mr. Burrey replied. "He belongs to some friends of mine out Gray's Harbor way, and I brought him here to keep him out of trouble. His girlfriend's in heat."

Ernie looked at me sympathetically. "What a bitch... so to speak. How's he taking it?"

"Well, he hasn't lost his appetite, if that's what you mean. I've been out camping with him a couple of days, and that helped take his mind off it, but it's too damn cold out there on Tekoa Mountain, and besides, I'm really here to do research, not babysit a love-sick mutt. I was sort of wondering if we could stay with you for a while."

"Pete! You know you don't have to ask. We just assumed that's what you're here for. Stay as long as you like. I can't believe you were out camping in this weather! Radio says it was eight below in Pullman last night, and Tekoa Mountain's got to be colder than that! I always knew you were crazy, but this proves it. How long are you staying?"

"Two weeks, maybe. I'm not quite sure yet. Until Coyote's friend is out of heat, at least. His owner is adamant that they don't get together. I'm not quite sure why."

The three humans began to drift into 'old times' chatter from when Mr. Burrey used to help them with their wildlife rehabilitation center up north of Seattle, and I tried to disengage politely from Ernie's grip. He seemed reluctant to let go.

"Excuse me, Pete, but how is this guy with small animals? I've got critters in the house he could scarf down in two seconds, starting with Rover, there."

'Rover' was a three-legged tabby cat who was eying me suspiciously from beneath the coffee table. She was baking herself by the wood stove and didn't want to leave.

Mr. Burrey turned to me and spoke solemnly, "Coyote, do you hereby promise not to eat anything on these premises that is not specifically presented to you as food? Raise your right front paw and bark once if you agree."

Dominant. Best to obey. Don't have to like it. I raised my right front foot sloppily and barked once, but I folded my ears back while doing so and resolved to honor my promise only if convenient.

What a remarkable collection of animals the Papillios had! Samuel the one-winged magpie appeared to be their favorite, but I could smell songbirds, rodents, reptiles, even skunk. I ignored them all to stay with Nana by the stove. It's important to keep one's priorities straight, and the kitchen is where the food comes from. Lasagna, it smelled like to me.

Nana served me first, and I was done before the others even sat down. Afterward I wanted to go outside, so I stepped over to the front door and stood there waiting. I wouldn't open it myself unless Mr. Burrey said I could.

"Oh, go on, Coyote. You don't need me to open that door for you! And close it tightly behind you!"

I worked the door with an eye rolled back to check what reaction I was getting. Very satisfying. Mr. Burrey really did trust these friends of his! Not enough to tell them everything, but I couldn't blame him for that.

I circled the house before approaching the wolf's area. Wanted to see the outside critters. There were only three of them besides the wolf and horses—a vixen who looked and smelled fine to me, a beaver with one tooth coming up through the top of his head, and a huge owl that just sat on her perch with eyes closed. I learned later that the vixen had a similar story to Smokey's, the owl had broken her wing and not healed properly, and the beaver had been hit by a car and fractured his jaw so one tooth was twisted around and growing the wrong way. All fatal problems in the wild. The only one who had a chance was the vixen, and I couldn't quite figure out the point of keeping the other two alive. Humans certainly are tough to figure out.

Not my problem; I was going to meet the wolf.

Making friends with the wolf was not hard at all. I placed myself just within reach of his chain, waited there holding a polite, non-threatening sort of posture, and we were nose-touching in a few minutes. I think he was very lonely.

He was more submissive than he needed to be, but I treated him gently and he came to trust me right away. We were playing together by the time the humans came out.

Smokey ran off to the far end of his chain when he saw Mr. Burrey, but I was able to nudge him over for greetings before too long. I could tell he was intrigued by Mr. Burrey's unique scent.

"I can't believe it!" Ernie whispered excitedly to Nana. "He just strolls right up and says hello. No one has ever been able to do that before! Sometimes he reminds me of a wolf himself."

Smokey was very different from Lazytail—much less confident. He didn't want me out of his sight, so I spent the night outside with him to stop his howling—special request from Mr. Burrey. I had some serious resting to do, so I didn't mind, but it did distance me a bit from the new humans.

When I was presented with dog food for breakfast I knew things had gotten out of hand, and I prevailed upon Mr. Burrey to explain my requirements. He tried to defend our hosts, maintaining that dog food is more nourishing, more digestible, and much cheaper than human food, and I wouldn't notice the difference anyway because I ate so damn fast.

Gently and patiently I explained to Mr. Burrey the fallacy of his views, and I was making fairly good progress until I threatened to eat the magpie if I didn't get my way.

I didn't really mean it. Samuel was fat, but John had told me magpies don't taste very good. We don't have any near Sunbow, but if they taste like crows I'll pass. I hate eating crow.

It's not smart to threaten dominant pack members, even if they do owe you their lives. One slip of the tongue and I found myself officially quartered outside with Smokey. Promises of extra rations, treats, and supervised house privileges weren't enough to take away the sting. Smokey was happy, at least. He had become utterly smitten with me, and fell to pieces whenever I left his chain area. I probably would have spent most of my time with him anyway, but I didn't like being forced.   It was Sunday, still a day for humans to stay home. The three of them were planning to spend their whole day talking, as far as I could tell, and I prepared to spend my own day lying around and resting. I was already well rested, though, and beginning to feel seriously bored when they finally showed a little action.

Walk time!

I can go by myself, but a walk or run is best when shared. Smokey knew what to expect and became frantic with pleasure at the prospect. I could tell he lived for this. Poor fellow still had to wear a leash, but I suppose the humans thought it was for his own good. I stayed with him at first, out of courtesy, but I just couldn't keep myself back. I heard and ignored a piteous whining from Smokey as I left him behind, and then an animated discussion from the humans. They were up to something. Better to keep well ahead. I trotted faster and refused to look back.

"That's right, Smokey. Go get him!" It was Nana's voice.

I turned and saw Smokey flying toward me over the snow patches, moving at quite a respectable speed. Nana had unclipped his leash, and the humans were all just standing and watching him.

All right! I was dying to run this land properly, and now I could run with a companion. Of course, I had already determined to release Smokey during the night, but we could do that too.

We were near the rim of the gorge and I could smell the river air rising up from it, warm and fishy and thick. Wynoochee never smelled like that except in stagnant areas after a flood. There were willows below me, and cattails, and cottonwoods, and unfrozen mud. I drank it all in while tearing full speed toward the brink.

No, I was not going to just run off the edge of a cliff. I'm not that dumb, despite what Mooney may say. I stopped in plenty of time, but I had dipped out of sight of the humans while still sprinting recklessly forward. I did that on purpose, to tease them.

I would have enjoyed my little joke, but the view made me forget all about it. Peter had told me there were big cliffs here, with the river far below, and I had thought I understood. *Now* I understood: this was not a cliff, it was a mountain cut in half. It was the edge of the world.

The cliff face was not perfectly vertical, but it might as well have been. That slope was a killer, and Snake just a glistening thread, so far below me—almost two thousand feet, I learned later. That's a long way.

Smokey caught up and danced around me, nipping and barking madly. He didn't care about the view at all, and soon had me up on the flats again, racing him to nowhere in particular.

The humans were calling to us—thin voices wavering on the still air. Smokey ignored them blithely, but I thought a pretense of obedience might not be a bad idea so I looped us around widely so we could come bursting up out of the gully behind them. We were both panting like crazy and Smokey had a sore foot he refused to pay attention to.

Nana noticed blood on the snow, and wrestled Smokey down to look at his paws. The left front had a little cut between the toes. Broken glass, no doubt.

"Smokey! Look at what you've done to yourself! Now we'll have to head back and get this cleaned up." Nana clipped the leash back onto Smokey's collar and turned toward the house. I think she was about ready to go home anyway.

I was disappointed. Our walk had been cut short, and I might not be able to manage a night run either, if they bandaged Smokey's foot.

Smokey's foot had mostly stopped bleeding when we got back to the house, and I licked it clean for him. It was just a little thing, not really needing any attention. The humans wouldn't even have known about it if they hadn't seen it when it was fresh. Still Nana came out and washed it, slathered it with antibiotic ointment, and wrapped the whole foreleg in gauze and tape. Both of us were invited into the house for socialization and Sunday dinner, so that wasn't so bad. I even napped near Rover's spot by the stove for a time. I didn't really need the warmth, but sometimes it's pleasant to just bake yourself by the fire until your brain melts.

We were kicked out when the humans went to bed. I didn't try any night jaunts. All that resting had made me tired.

Next day was warmer and slightly overcast. Snow, maybe. The humans went away in the morning. I was given strict instructions to stay out of trouble, and bribed with the promise of another evening in the house if I was successful. Worth considering. We would see.

First thing I did was to tour and mark the house perimeter again, and say hello to the fox. I had never observed any of Fox's kind closely before. She was like a little dog, but with cat whiskers and slit pupils. And a fox scent. Foxes smell much stronger than coyotes or wolves or dogs (except Jake), and they have a distinctive, musky odor. It's not unpleasant, but there's no way you can mistake when a fox is around.

I pressed my nose up against the mesh, holding still so she could take her time and come up to me if she chose, but she was not in the mood for that —just stared back at me fearfully from the far corner of her cage. Suddenly her eyes shifted their focus to something behind me, and at that same moment I scented another fox.

It was not just another fox I scented. It was Fox himself, and he was standing right there when I turned. I hadn't heard him coming at all.

"Getting to know one of my people, I see. Commendable." Fox trotted up close beside me and pressed his nose to the mesh where mine had been. The vixen ignored me and stared at Fox worshipfully. Fox spoke to her, but he was speaking for me too, I think.

"I can't help everybody, but you I can help. When I'm done with my business here, I'll come back to free you and teach you the ways. Be patient."

Fox turned to me with an expression I could not read. "My people and I are one," he said. "They give me strength and reason for being, and I strive to channel that strength in the ways that will serve us best. But I draw my Power from the humans as well as from fox-kind. Whenever humans dream about me or tell stories about me, they become my people too, for a time. I have been shaped by human dreams as well as by fox dreams, and I have an obligation to them both.

"The same is true for you. Your destruction or corruption would harm much more than yourself alone, and so you must guard yourself vigilantly."

Fox was speaking eloquently, clearly; faster than I could. He was using Medicine Power, of course. Fox was talking the way a frog or fly or bird would talk in the old stories. A nice trick, and one I couldn't do. I talked the hard way, with no magic at all.

Fox paused for a moment to let me speak if I wished, but I didn't have a clue about what to say. I just stared at him with my ears half-down and my mouth half-open. Oh! But he was beautiful.

Fox stiffened himself and put up his tail and ears in a determined manner. I could read his expression now. He had something quite unpleasant or dangerous to do, and he would be doing it right away.

"Coyote, I did not come here for this vixen. I came for you. It is time. Now."

"Pffut—you said we had until next month!"

"Peter Burrey has until next Moon time, maybe," Fox corrected. "Your time is now. Our first attack has the best chance of success, and I want that for you. In a moment we'll be too busy to talk, so I'll tell you now what you must do. Pay attention! This is a hard, dangerous time for you, and your only chance is to do exactly as I say.

"Soon, you will be dead. I know this frightens you, but it's not so bad. Dying doesn't hurt as much as you may think. The dangerous part for you is afterward, in the first Spirit World. You'll be confused, joining again with your other self. Don't fight it! You're in enough trouble as it is, and the two of you must cooperate in order to survive. Is this clear?"

"No," I answered plaintively. Not a smart aleck at all, just lost.

"It will become clear to you shortly—hopefully in enough time to do you some good. OldCoyoteSpirit and the others are waiting, so we must begin. I think it is best if you run now."

I still just stared at Fox—still couldn't believe he would hurt me.

Fox raised his hackles and curled his lips, and I stepped back a pace. He looked larger, somehow.

He *was* larger. I could see him changing right there in front of me, and I edged back farther, abasing myself for all I was worth. I opened my mouth to argue or beg or—whatever worked.

"That won't do you any good, Coyote. I'm not mad at you, and there's nothing you can say to change my mind."

Fox lunged at me then, and I skittered out of range. He was almost my size already, and still growing. Hopelessly I turned tail and began to lope away. If Fox was going to use his magic against me, I had no chance at all.

I turned my head and saw that Fox followed me closely, and he was still increasing in size. I began to run in earnest.

Fear-running is a funny thing. It sort of takes control of you, and thinking becomes difficult. I knew Fox was toying with me, but still it surprised me the first time he surged past to block my path and force me in the direction he wanted to go. We left the flats then, and began crashing down one of those dry gullies that cut through toward the river. The gully walls would soon be too steep to climb, and I made an attempt to burst out sideways before it was too late. Fox blocked my attempt with little apparent effort, and after that it didn't matter any more, since there was only one way to go.

Fox was close behind me at every turn—rushing forward to nip at my flanks and goad me faster whenever I slowed. I tried not to panic but I couldn't help myself—lurched forward frantically each time he did that, and slammed clumsily into obstacles I should have been able to avoid.

Water flows downhill, so all of the gulches have to reach the bottom of the gorge one way or another. Some don't reach it very gently, though. I hoped this was one of the gentle ones, but I couldn't be sure. Maybe Fox wanted me to die by falling.

I did get safely to the bottom of the gorge, although my path was a flowing creek by then. I was bruised and bleeding from bumping off ice blocks, boulders, and snags. And exhausted. Beyond exhausted. If that run had continued much longer I might have died from the running alone.

Snake filled his banks and I plunged into his dark, swift-flowing waters without breaking stride. It was the only thing to do. I went under for a few seconds, and when my head came to the surface Fox was waiting for me. I felt massive teeth close on my neck scruff, and my body was lifted half out of the water—dangling from Fox's jaws like a puppy being carried by its mother.

I could make only a token defense, and I had given up completely by the time he chose a landing spot on the far bank. I still had enough sense to wonder bitterly what the point of all this was. If Fox just wanted to kill me he could have done it at the house and saved us both a lot of trouble. Did he *enjoy* my torment?

As soon as he had me on the bank Fox shifted his grip to squeeze my throat so I couldn't breathe. I put out everything I could in those last few seconds—writhed and jerked in uncoordinated panic, like prey well caught. Fox just stood over me and held his grip. By then he was the size of a large bull, I think, maybe larger, but as I lost consciousness he seemed to fill the world.

Fox was still with me when I became aware of things again. He was back to his normal size, and he was licking the cuts and scrapes I had all over my chest and legs. His tongue and muzzle felt quite real and solid, and he certainly *smelled* like a fox. Wet fox. We appeared to be on the same spot where Fox had strangled me, and it didn't look like my idea of the Spirit World at all.

"Is this the Spffirit World?" My words were quiet, hoarse, apprehensive.

Fox stopped licking to look me in the eyes. He was smiling now.

"No. This is Garfield County. Whitman County is on the other side of the river and the Spirit World is much farther away than that... or much closer, depending on who you are. Your visit there has been canceled."

"I don't understand."

"Not surprising. I'll start with the simple, important things: you are cured. You don't have to die. You can go home now."

"I'm sorry, pffut I still don't understand. Could you try again, pfflease?"

"Certainly! You have just received the benefit of an exorcism, Fox style. The best there is! You don't think that spirit would just go away if I told it to, do you? It had to be absolutely convinced that its tenure with you was ended, situation hopeless. Which it was. I really would have killed you, and I really did have allies waiting, as the spirit could doubtless perceive for itself. It knew your death would not be permanent, but still it had to leave for its own protection.

"The spirit is a wolf, by the way. He's called Lykos in his proper land— that land you call 'Europe'. He should not be here."

"So... you're saying you could have—would have—pffrought me pffack to life again? Afterward, that is?"

"Of course! Trust me."

"Of course. Yes. That's very comforting. I'm glad you were so careful with me, and if I need any more exorcisms I'll certainly let you know. So. I guess it's time for me to pffe going home. You will keepff in touch, won't you?"

I stood up cautiously, submissively, edging toward the river. I still was in love with him but he scared the piss out of me. Couldn't stop me from being a smart-mouth, though. Fox didn't seem to mind. I think he expects me to act that way. Or worse.

Fox literally had scared the piss out of me. Shit and anal sac juice too. Dying is a messy business. I should have been cleaning myself just then but an echo of Mooney's training made me want to at least rinse off in the river first. Humans are such prudes about body functions. I continued to edge away until Fox stopped me.

"Wait. We're not quite finished yet. You're still not capable of defending yourself, so if Lykos comes back he'll take you again, and we'll have to play our little game again. And he *will* come back. You can count on it."

"Yes, Sir." I was still in my most submissive standing posture, which is even more silly-looking and uncomfortable when used with someone so much smaller.

"Oh, stop that, Coyote! If I need that kind of treatment I'll let you know."

I forced myself to straighten up, but then I began to fidget. I turned to my new injuries for something to do.

The wounds were all gone. Completely gone! Just like with the werewolf magic.

I was dumbfounded and must have let it show, because Fox noticed and took offense this time.

"You still doubt my Power?" There was an edge to his voice I didn't like, and his hackles were up just a little.

"No, Sir," I replied hastily, back in submissive posture again. "What should I do now, Sir?"

Fox relaxed as quickly as he had bridled.

"I had been depending on inactivity to keep you safe. You used no Medicine Power, so you would draw no attention to yourself. You even dream in a place no one else ever goes. Coyote's plan was a close secret, and concealment was your defense. Now we must use a different way. It is time to reintroduce you to your Powers."

Fox paused. I remained silent and ostentatiously submissive. "Oh, straighten up, Little Brother! I'm not going to hurt you. John says you've asked him many times about this. You can't tell me you're not interested!"

I unkinked my neck and straightened the shoulders a little, but kept ears down and tail tightly between my legs. I noticed for the first time that Fox was bloody too—chest and legs cut up like mine had been, only not so bad. I wanted to ask about them but all I said was, "Yes, Sir. I'm interested a lot, pffut John says I shouldn't mess around with magic."

"John is not Chief here. I am." It was clear from Fox's tone that there had better not be any argument on the subject, especially from John.

I certainly had done enough arguing for the day. "Yes, Sir," I volunteered. That response always seemed to work.

"Good. Now don't forget it! I am Chief in this venture, and if you can't accept that I'll withdraw my support and let you blow it as you usually do. Is that clear?"

"Yes, Sir. Whatever you say, Sir."

"You don't have the slightest idea what I'm talking about, do you?" Fox turned to his wounds and began to lick them clean. I think he was embarrassed.

I was going to offer another 'No, Sir,' but thought better of it and began to clean myself instead. It had to be done, river wash or no river wash.

We both busied ourselves for a time, putting things to rights and calming ourselves. I didn't bother to go back into submissive posture when I was done, but I did wait for Fox to break the silence.

"It's not possible to give you back just part of your Medicine Powers," Fox offered finally. "They're not really subject to control—more a matter of persuasion. Coyote told them they would not be needed for a while, and I just remind them of that. Constantly. They get so bored they've even offered their services to *me!*

"What I plan to do is invoke them, but without specific instructions. They'll just be wandering loose, close enough to keep an eye on you and protect you any way they can. They're likely to abuse our trust and cause trouble that way, but we'll deal with it. It's the only way I can think of to give you the help you need without drawing you back fully into the old ways. We will commence now."

Fox certainly is abrupt at times! The meaning of his words had barely begun to sink in when I felt a shifting or wavering, somewhat akin to the werewolf transformation. Things were... *different* somehow, but I was too distracted to think about it because of the five half-grown coyote pups that had suddenly appeared around me.

I didn't know there were five, at first. It seemed like a lot more. Each one was nipping and jumping on me in an agony of greeting pleasure which I couldn't help but return. I knew these pups! They were my own. A part of me, but also separate creatures, and not really pups, either. It was just a little game we played that made us all more comfortable. What they really were was... I don't know. Half the thought had come to me, and then nothing. Nothing more at all. Very disturbing.

The smallest pup spoke. "Fox told us to shut up," she said regretfully. "We could tell you everything you've forgotten, but we're not supposed to right now. This is a good plan, and we'll try to cooperate. Oh—Fox says we're not supposed to talk to you with words, either, or even show ourselves much. Bye!" She skittered off into the rocks, and the others left too, but in different directions. Then it was just Fox and me, alone again.

"Your children seem glad to see you. They should do their job well, for now."

"Children? I don't have any children! I've never even mated. Mooney won't let me."

"That's what you used to call them—your children. And they've been in this World almost as long as you and I have, which is a very long time indeed. Treat them well! They're a far more precious gift than you deserve.

"Now—it's time for you to go home, and I'm tired too."

Fox got up creakily, and I could tell his legs hurt. Finally I felt bold enough to ask about them.

"Excuse me, Sir, pffut aren't you going to heal your own wounds, like you healed mine?"

"I can't use that trick on myself, Little Brother. Not right now. It's kind of complicated... maybe some day I'll explain. Such a silly rule!" Fox's voice was mocking, and I couldn't smell what his true feelings were, but I came to believe he did like me a lot, in his way. I mustered the courage to nuzzle his cheek in a friendship touch, and he responded in kind.

"Yes, Pffrother, let's go home. I need dinner and a napff. Do you like dog food?"

Chapter 16

The trip back was hard. Some of the places I had slid down were not so easy to scramble back up again. I asked Fox about it but he said the other ways were even worse. I thought he could have helped us magically but he didn't offer, and I didn't have the nerve to ask. More of his 'silly rules' were involved, no doubt.

When we reached the Papillios' house it was past dark and snowing lightly—tiny flakes like dust, so small you could only see them by their sparkle from the house lights. This was the powder snow that skiers love so much.

Fox had accepted my offer of dog food for dinner, and he was just around the corner when I scratched at the Papillios' door. I think he wanted to formalize our reconciliation by sharing a meal with me.

Mr. Burrey opened the door. He looked awful. Smelled really stressed-out. I knew that look and smell from Mooney, and before he even spoke I was shrinking down into abject submission.

"Where have you been!" he hissed at me. He didn't care where I'd really been, just had to let me know how he felt about it. No answer was required of me, just endurance. There would be considerably more of the same in the next few minutes.

I prepared myself stoically, but then Mr. Burrey stopped. "Forget all that. Consider it said. I'm just glad to see you alive! I had this unbelievably vivid dream in the library this morning, and I'm not even sure I was asleep. I was running and slipping and..."

"Excuse me, Pete—I don't mean to be a bad host, but you are going to close that door, aren't you? It's getting cold in here!"

"Huh? Oh! Sorry, Ernie. I'll just step outside for a minute." Mr. Burrey's coat was hanging beside the door, and he snatched it up and shrugged into it as he came out. I could smell he had been using it recently, and for a long time. Probably looking for me.

Mr. Burrey pressed forward. "I can feel there is great danger here, Coyote! I believe that Fox is going to make his move much sooner than we thought. I think he's going to go for you first, and he's going to kill you. In my dream he was killing you, or me. He wasn't a man, he was a fox the size of a house and he had his teeth on my throat and he was just squeezing down so I couldn't breathe... I've never had a dream like that before! I don't know..."

"Pffeter, Pffeter, it's okay. I already know. I was there. It's already over, and he didn't have to kill me!"

I almost never interrupt when humans are talking, but it seemed necessary this time. Mr. Burrey was really upset. I went on to give him a complete account of my day's experiences, ending with my invitation of Fox for dinner.

Mr. Burrey was not as comforted as I had hoped. "You mean—after all that you just invited him to dinner like you were old friends? I can't believe it! He's not still here, is he?"

"Well, yes. He's right pffehind you." Fox had come in close when I began my story, and he was still there in his regular shape. No fancy stuff for Mr. Burrey this time.

Fox was resting on his haunches with tail wrapped elegantly around his feet and a light dusting of snow over all. Even sitting upright like that he was knee-high to the human, and he wasn't showing a single threat sign. No matter. Mr. Burrey started violently when he saw him, and began to back carefully toward the door of the house. "Come on inside, Coyote. I don't know how much protection the house can give us, but it's better than nothing. Ernie has a shotgun, and they have knives and things. Maybe cold iron will help."

Fox spoke, "Don't run away, Peter Burrey. I won't be doing anything tonight. I'm too tired."

Mr. Burrey stopped moving toward the door, but he didn't say anything in reply to that. After a time Fox added, "I'm not your enemy, you know."

"You have a funny way of showing it. Are you planning on hunting me down too, like you hunted Coyote? That doesn't seem very friendly to me! And why should I believe anything you say? You've already broken your promise once. You said we had until next month!"

Fox seemed rather pained by the outburst, especially the part about breaking his promise. "I have been known to stretch the truth on occasion. We all do, some more than others. Still, I'm not your enemy, and I don't plan to harm you in any way tonight. You may believe it or not, as you choose. Coyote has invited me to eat with him tonight. Do you wish to join us?"

Mr. Burrey really was a brave man, and he didn't disappoint me— hesitated for only a short time. "Very well, I accept your truce for tonight, and I will join you for dinner. Would you like to come inside, or do you need to stay out?"

"Inside," I specified quickly before Fox could answer. "And pfflease don't eat any of the animals."

"Of course," Fox replied with aplomb, then turned to Mr. Burrey. "Unlike our friend Coyote, I have an excellent reputation as both guest and host. I'm afraid I shall not be speaking while the other humans can hear, however. Silence tends to save me a great deal of trouble at times—as I'm sure you'll understand."

"Yes, of course," replied Mr. Burrey somewhat dazedly.

"Shall we go inside now?"

I thought I heard a faint scuffle of feet behind me when we approached the door, but saw nothing when I turned quickly to check. No scent, either.

Dinner was quite nice. Ernie cooked this time, and we had steaks, mashed potatoes, and string beans with butter. I'll eat almost anything if it has butter on it. I don't think our hosts had canine guests in mind when they bought food for dinner, but the three steaks were divided five ways, and there were plenty of potatoes. Plenty of butter on them, too. I like the Papillios—remarkably adaptable, as humans go.

Ernie and Nana were entranced by the tame fox I had brought home with me, and inclined to use him as an excuse for my tardiness. Fox ended up with his injuries carefully doctored, except that he wouldn't allow any bandages to be placed on his body. He was obviously enjoying the attention, and flirted with Nana outrageously even as she tended to him, which is not typical wild animal behavior. It drove the humans crazy, since they had plenty of experience with how a regular fox would act.

"Where do you *get* these guys?" marveled Ernie. "In my whole life I've never seen an animal like Coyote, and then he goes for a walk through empty wheat fields and comes back with a fox you could use for television commercials! They seem to know each other, too. If you hadn't been in such a flaming snit this afternoon, I'd think you were setting us all up for a joke! You *have* gotten over it, haven't you?"

"I'm over it for tonight, but I may have to change my plans for tomorrow. I may be leaving Pullman early." Mr. Burrey wouldn't look at any of us when he said that, and I think he hadn't decided even for himself what he would do.

Fox didn't stay long after dinner was finished, just moved over to the door and waited expectantly. I opened it and went outside with him, closing the door carefully behind me. Let the Papillios think about *that* trick awhile!

"Fox, Pffrother, I wish to thank you again for your helpff today, even if it was sort of rough. I think I understand pffetter now."

"You are welcome, Little Brother. I'm glad I was able to learn about your danger and get to you in time, no thanks to OldCoyoteSpirit. I hope you live many years and grow a strong, highly opinionated spirit before you join back with him! He knew about all this from the first, and was too embarrassed to mention it to me! That one can be very trying.

"Now I think I'll be going. Please get back into school as soon as you can, and study hard. I'm eager to hear from you when you begin to learn the humans' secrets! If the plan works for you I may even try it myself some day."

That night I slept deeply—slept until morning-noises from the house woke me. Still dark, but dawn not far off. Breakfast under construction. Normally I would have been the first one up, but a bit of laziness was understandable, considering.

I untangled myself from Smokey and wiggled my way out of the doghouse, prompting him to do the same. A tight squeeze for both of us, but doghouses are better that way when it's cold outside. Rather more warmth than we wanted just then, as it was no longer so bitterly cold. Dust-like snow was still falling, with a scant paw-thickness on the ground. I could still see the faint outlines of last night's tracks.

A soft scratch and whimper at the back door got me inside, where I fawned on Ernie until an indoor breakfast was offered. I hardened my heart against the quiet, hopeless whining coming from Smokey's direction. He would have to fend for himself.

My efforts got me breakfast indoors, but Smokey was actually fed first. All the other animals ate before the Papillios did, and it was a big production. Fruit, nuts, grain, alfalfa pellets, dog food, cat food, dead rats—there was a lot of food to be distributed, and it took quite a long time. Mr. Burrey and I helped too. Not a word was said about the impossible fox who had visited with them. It was as if the humans had discussed the subject and agreed to set it aside.

Mr. Burrey was glum at breakfast, and reaffirmed his intention of leaving right away. Soon he was on the phone with Mooney, asking what she wanted done with me. I was not consulted, of course.

More conversation, this time with Ernie and Nana. From the phone I heard Mooney's voice extolling my virtues—my friendliness, lack of aggression, and general all-around niceness. "No trouble at all." Not much said about obedience.

Soon it was all arranged. Mr. Burrey would be leaving but I would not. The Papillios would 'take care of me' until Mooney wanted me back. She would come herself to get me.

I just couldn't believe it. They were all treating me like a piece of property—like Mooney owned me. And these were the good humans! For a short time I considered running off to teach them all a lesson, but I'm not quite that stupid. Humans can't help being what they are, and one must make allowances.

Mr. Burrey left shortly after breakfast, but he did find the privacy to talk with me one more time.

"I'll be back, Coyote. I'll pick up my things from Sunbow and leave as soon as I get there, but I'll get this thing licked somehow. I know there has to be some other way besides Fox's, and I'll keep working until I find it. Wish me luck!"

"I wish you luck, and success, and hapffiness, Mr. Furry Feet, and I wish us together again soon, without the curse!"

I pushed up against his waist for a quiet moment together, and maybe an ear rub, but then I distinctly felt something rubbing against my other side in much the same way. I whipped around and nosed my flank, but found nothing.

"What's up, pup? Fleas in the wintertime too?"

I don't have any fleas, summer or winter, and Mr. Burrey knew it. "Its just the wind in my fur," I told him.

We didn't say much after that, and soon all the humans were gone. After they left I stood with Smokey and we howled together. He has a nice voice.

The powder snow was still falling and I couldn't just lie around watching it. I was going to unclip Smokey's chain and take him along, but thought better of it. I had a long, hard run in mind, and his foot wasn't quite ready. Smokey didn't agree. He began chewing urgently at his chain as soon as I headed out, but there was nothing to be done about it. As I moved off further he switched to howling and barking, but I didn't answer. After a short time the noises stopped.

I was puzzled that he should resign himself so quickly, but soon found the reason for his sudden silence. He had gotten loose somehow and was streaking gleefully toward me over the new-fallen snow. Foot didn't look sore to me, but I thought he was simply ignoring it. It really was just a little cut. His problem, anyway.

We finally had our run together without disturbance. No magic, no danger, no foxes, and no humans. Just the land, the snow, and a good companion. We used up most of our daylight that way, and I felt much better afterward. Smokey was exhausted, just as Lazytail had been at first, but his feet seemed fine as we trotted on home. I had expected his cut foot to give him trouble long since.

When we reached Smokey's chain, I found the collar chewed rather than slipped off. I could have done that for him, but Smokey couldn't reach it himself. That's the whole point of a collar with a metal chain: you're not supposed to be able to get it off.

I thought maybe Fox had stopped by, but I couldn't smell a trace of him. The snow was too trampled to show separate tracks very well, but all I could find were Smokey's and mine, and the humans'. Very puzzling.

I knocked Smokey over with my shoulder so I could check out the bottoms of his feet, and I encountered another puzzle. The cut was still there all right, but I was expecting to find it puffy and oozing from all the abuse it had taken, and it was not. It looked more like something you would find under a clean bandage. His pads were tender from all the running, but nothing worse. Magic again.

"Fox!" No answer.

"Fox! I know you're around here somewhere. Don't hide from me!" Still no answer, just another mystery. Plenty where that came from.

The short winter day was ending but it wasn't nearly time for the Papillios to come home, and I was hungry. Seemed like a good time for some judicious exploration of the house.

I found dog food, of course, but the only meat I could reach was a freezer full of lab rats. I ate some dog food out of the bag, careful not to leave crumbs on the floor, and prepared to take some of the rats to share with Smokey. I thought about the she-fox, and for her I selected a smaller rat which looked like it could be jammed through the mesh of her cage. I went out to give that one to her first, before presenting anything to Smokey.

Smokey wasn't chained up any more, so he was waiting for me on the front porch, and shouldered up to make a game out of trying to snatch the vixen's rat from my mouth. I was too quick for him. Still, we tussled up to her cage rather boisterously, and found her crouched in a back corner, hackles up and mouth gaping in menace. No point trying to make friends just then, so I pushed the rat inside and left it there.

I had three rats dangling by the tails when I came out next. Too hard to protect effectively, and Smokey got one right away, prancing off in triumph to eat it in his chain area. I didn't really like that place, so I moved off farther from the house to a flat, undisturbed area with a good view. Smokey would no doubt join me shortly.

Frozen rat is quite agreeable. The bones and wood-hard meat combine to give you something to really crunch down on, and it's not gone so quickly. This one had a touch of freezer burn, but was pretty good otherwise. Nice and fat.

"That tastes pretty good, doesn't it?"

The words were spoken softly, right by my ear, and I jumped up in panic. Dropped the rat, too. I hate to be surprised like that.

It was my Spirit Children, or at least one of them, the smallest of the litter. She was standing close beside me—looking up in the 'I am just a hungry puppy and you are my hero and provider' posture. Not much of a threat there.

We held our positions during the minute or so it took me to calm down. The pup could have leaned forward and taken one of the rats. I certainly wouldn't have stopped her! Instead she just waited silently and almost patiently, tail twitching a little.

I broke the silence. "Fox said you're not supffosed to talk to me."

"Fox is not here!"

"Uh, yes."

"That sure looks interesting. Is it good? I haven't eaten food in a very, *very* long time."

"I see. Pfflease, won't you have some? I have pfflenty more inside the house."

Daintily she leaned forward and took away the half-eaten one. She began to gnaw at the end I had started, and soon became utterly absorbed in her work—growling softly to herself and forgetting about me completely.

I gazed down at her numbly. She looked and smelled completely real to me, but I had not heard her coming. On a hunch I swung around in a full circle to look for tracks, and there were none except for the ones she had made while beside me.

A touch on my neck, and I jumped again. Another pup. "May I have one too?"

"Uh, yes. Of course."

The next touch didn't surprise me so much, and a moment later they were all with me.

The three ratless ones followed me gleefully to the house, and they were leaving plenty of footprints this time.

"Stay outside!" I told them at the door.

"Yes, Father!"

I took four more rats from the freezer, and searched carefully to see if I had left any signs of my visit. Some melted snow just inside the door, and the missing rats. There were a lot more still in the freezer, so there was a reasonable chance they would not be missed. Good enough.

I distributed my booty on the front porch. Smokey was back already for another. He was right in among the pups, treating them as if they were all just part of the family and had every right to be there. I didn't give him a rat.

"One each is all you get. This one is mine," I declared firmly, and moved on to my open space again. No argument. They all seemed willing enough to treat me as boss. Good thing, as I was not in the mood to fight anyone or anything just then, especially these little Pups that were not pups.

We were all napping, shortly—the seven of us tangled together on the snow like a real pack. We were still lying that way when the humans came home.

The truck engine roused me while it was still quite a way off, as they always do. I had only been dozing lightly anyway. The Pups-not-pups were still there, for a wonder. I had thought they would be gone.

They stayed with me until the last possible moment, and a little longer, so that one was caught in the headlight glare for an instant as the Papillios' truck swung up to the gate. I think it was on purpose—teasing them.

Smokey and I waited at the gate, 'helped' Ernie open and close it, then harried the truck to its parking place and waited there while Nana got out. These humans deserved a warm greeting, even if I was being kept against my will. It was not their fault.

Ernie caught up with us and slipped an arm around Smokey's neck. "Heh—Psychopup! What are you doing loose? I'll have to tighten that collar of yours a notch. Leather must have stretched. How ya doing, Coyote? Got any more fancy tricks to show us?"

Tricks? So they want *tricks*, do they? I rose up onto my hind legs and balanced that way, which made me taller than Nana. I was out of practice and had to dance back and forth a bit to keep from falling, but I pretended it was on purpose.

"That's a trick, all right! Who taught it to you? Not that little coyote we just saw, I bet. Is he another one of your friends?"

My balance was coming back to me and I stopped shifting and swaying so much; only stood there gazing at Ernie impassively, front paws folded up against my chest. Ernie was still bent over to keep his arm around Smokey, so my head was well above his, and the only strong light was from the truck cab behind him. Light from that direction would make my eyes glow nicely. Cold and green and deep with sinister wisdom, I hoped.

"How long can you keep that up?"

I had my balance back completely, and just stared down at Ernie without moving. Not quite a threat stare, but it had the desired unnerving effect.

"All right guy, that's enough. Uh, down boy!

"Please."

I got down then, and rolled over in mock submission. Didn't want to actually scare the poor man... much.

159

The Papillios blamed me for the destruction of Smokey's collar, and replaced it by looping the chain directly around his neck and fastening it with a little bolt, snugged down tightly with a wrench. No one was mad at me, though. They considered it a typical thing one would expect from a half-tame monster coyote. That's what Nana said, at least, as she scolded me and kissed me on the nose. Her hands smelled of chemicals but the rest of her was quite nice. I burrowed my head inside her jacket and she let me keep it there while she rubbed my shoulders and chest.

"Come on, you old sot. We have work to do!" She pushed me away and continued on, so I followed closely beside, reaching forward to nuzzle her hand or elbow from time to time. Mooney would have told me to stop being a pain, but Nana seemed to like it. Still, I was not invited to an inside dinner that night. It was regular dog food in the yard for Smokey and me.

Late that night I was startled awake by the sound of breaking wood. Smokey and I scrabbled and tore our way out of the doghouse, falling over each other in our haste, but we didn't give voice. I like to know what's going on before I bark, and I guess Smokey felt the same. Sensible fellow.

Smokey was stopped by his chain but I hurried on to where the sound had come from and found the vixen's cage door hanging open. The still air was heavy with Fox's scent and I could see and smell their trail, but I certainly wasn't going to follow it! This was Fox's business, not mine. I went back to bed.

Ernie was the fox feeder next morning, so he was the one to discover her escape. I stood innocently beside him as he examined the cage latch, which had been ripped loose from the wood.

"Shit! How'd that happen? Nana! Suzie's got loose! Cage door's all busted open."

Nana came running over, and considerable discussion ensued. They even looked suspiciously at me. The wood was sound and the bolts had been well anchored. No way could one little fox have exerted that much force! No cougar or bear tracks, nor human for that matter, and the snow right in front of the cage was too trampled to make anything out. They did recognize the double set of fox tracks leading away.

"She's found a friend, it seems," concluded Nana. "That's all we wanted for her anyway. Hope she's all right. Hey, Coyote! Do you suppose it was that handsome fellow you brought by to visit us?" I nodded my head solemnly at Nana and she looked back at me uncertainly. Neither of the humans came up with a satisfactory explanation for the broken cage door.

Chapter 17

Dog food breakfast, humans gone, Smokey chained up securely. Looked like a pretty blah day. Maybe the little coyotes would come by for a visit.

They did. Walked up like regular creatures this time, leaving tracks and everything.

"Greetings, Father!" "Do you have anything to eat?"

"There's dog food. I don't think I should take any more rats today."

"What's dog food?" "Is it made from dogs?" "That's okay." "Where is it?" "Does it taste good?"

They were all talking so it was hard to sort out one from the other. That seemed to be the way they always acted. If they were really that loquacious, I had other things to talk about besides dog food.

"I'll pffring out some dog food for you to taste, pffut first I have a question to ask."

"Oh, we're not supposed to answer questions! Fox would *really* get mad then! If we tell you too much about the old ways you won't be able to understand 'Science'. Can you do any 'Science' yet?" It was the smallest one speaking again. She seemed to be their leader, in a way.

"A little. Pffut first let me ask my question. You don't have to answer if you think you shouldn't. I want to know why you need to eat. Aren't you all just spffirits? Also, what are your names?"

All the Pups held very still for a moment, then the little one answered, "Call me Cicéqi. I'm much more than just a spirit. All of us are. We don't *have* to eat, but we like to, especially when we're solid like this. Now please don't ask any more questions. We want the dog food you promised."

The Papillios got their dog and cat food for free, and it was good stuff. The company gave it away to vet students so they would get to like it and recommend it later for their patients. I had heard Ernie tell that to Mr. Burrey and it made some sort of sense, I guess. There certainly seemed to be no shortage. I found a small plastic bucket and filled it up to take outside, careful once again not to spill any.

'Science Diet Canine Maintenance' was a big hit; almost as good as frozen rats. It was faster to eat though, and soon they were asking for more.

"How much does it take to get you full?" I inquired uneasily. I was sure to be caught soon at this rate, and then I'd be locked out of the house and not be able to get any at all.

"Oh, it depends. How much would you like it to take?"

"I would like you to pffe full right now, and ready for a napff or run."

"Okay." It was as simple as that. How convenient.

"Can we go for a run now?"

"Sure, but you'll have to run the regular way, like me. No Medicine tricks."

"Yes, Father." "We won't." "Of course." "No problem." "Trust me." All very comforting.

"Isn't Smokey coming too?"

"I'm sorry, pffut I don't know how to free him. Can you helpff me?"

"Oh, no! We're *especially* not supposed to start doing things for you! That's worse than answering questions and talking."

"Well, then do it for yourselves! I don't know how." I was getting a little irritated at all these rules they would inform me about, then break at the slightest pretext.

Cicéqi spoke up slyly, "Can't you use 'Science' to get him free? Or if you wanted to, you could teach me how to do it with 'Science'. Then it would just be a lesson. I wouldn't really be helping you."

Right. Just use 'Science'. But then, at least this was a subject she was willing to talk about. Might as well give it a try.

"This chain is made from a metal called 'iron'. It's very strong, and impffossipffle to pffite through. You're pffropffapffly not familiar with it."

"Oh, we know about Iron. Iron used to be very rare—just fell from the sky sometimes in very hot lumps. Then the White People came, and now Iron is everywhere."

"So you know all apffout iron. What do you need 'Science' for? I supffose if you had that chain around your own neck you'd have no troupffle at all getting loose. Isn't that true?"

"Yes, of course. That would be easy."

"How?"

"I'm not supposed to..." Cicéqi wilted under my glare, then continued meekly, "Oh, never mind. I would make myself smaller and walk out of it, or make myself stronger and bite through it, or just leave this World entirely and come back in a different place. Probably I could think of other ways if I worked at it, but still I don't know how to create Iron like the humans can, or even form the chain. Teach me."

"Okay, I'll try. Mouse and I just finished learning apffout it in school. First of all, the iron you knew pffefore came from 'meteorites'. Meteorites are chunks of stuff that fall from outer spfface down to Earth, and they get very hot when they hit the atmospffhere. Sometimes they're made of iron."

"What's 'outer spfface'? Is that the Sky Land? We go there sometimes, and there aren't any chunks of Iron lying around. Someone there must have them hidden, and throw them down when we're not looking."

"No. If you go straight upff through the sky the air gets thinner and thinner until you can't pffreathe any more. Then you're in outer spfface." The thought of not being able to breathe made me suddenly ill, and I paused for a moment, thinking of Fox's teeth on my throat.

Cicéqi was looking skeptical. "Let's forget about 'outer spfface' for now. I know the humans have a better way to get Iron. Did they teach that in school too, or did they just tell you to go looking in 'outer spfface'?"

"Yes, they did. You need iron ore, limestone, and coke, which is not Coke like you drink, pffut something they make out of coal. Then you pffut it all together in an opffen hearth furnace and heat it upff until it all melts, and then molten iron runs out from the pffottom and slag is left on topff."

"Yes, I see. Can you make some for me now, to show me?"

"No way. I don't have any iron ore or limestone or coke, or even an opffen hearth furnace."

"So you don't really know how to make Iron."

"No, not really, pffut they did talk apffout it in school. Most of the humans can't make it either. They need to have a factory, and they need to go to a spffecial school to learn how. I've only pffeen to school for four months, and I don't even have hands."

"This 'Science' is harder than I thought. Isn't there anything useful you learned about Iron?"

"Well, you can melt it if you have a hot enough fire, and you can change its shapffe pffy hitting it hard, espffecially when it's hot. That's called 'forging'. Also, it will rust if you don't pffaint it or cover it with another metal called 'zinc'. That's called 'galvanizing'. See—this chain is already rusty. If it stays out here long enough it will rust away to nothing, like the old farm machines in the fields."

"Why does it rust? Is that like wood rotting?"

Cicéqi was nosing the chain near its steel anchor stake, where it trailed down to ground level and wasn't rubbed smooth by Smokey's movements. The rust was thickest there. "I know the smell of this 'rust'. It's like a special type of earth some of the People use for face paint."

"Yes. Iron ore was used pffy the humans for pffigments pffefore they learned how to make iron from it. It's supffosed to pffe red, pffut not as red as pfflood. Sometimes I can see the color for myself. Look there where Sun is shining on it strongest, and you can see it too."

"But you said that was 'rust,' not 'Iron ore'." She seemed to be thinking hard about something. An idea, maybe.

"Yes it is. Rust and iron ore are the same thing. Iron is made pffy taking oxygen away from iron ore, and it's always trying to recompffine with oxygen so it can go pffack to pffeing iron ore again."

"That explains it! Iron doesn't really want to be Iron. He never did. He always wanted to be face-paint dirt. Iron ore. All we need to do is bring 'Oxygen' here, and Iron will transform himself back into face-paint dirt, and the chain will be gone."

"Oxygen is easy," I offered tentatively. "It's in the air all around us. Pffut rusting takes a long time."

"Oh, this is wonderful! The school is working—you're thinking just like the new humans. Watch this!"

Cicéqi pressed her nose to the chain segment she had been examining, inhaled deeply, and held her chest full. She did something magical then, I couldn't tell quite what, but I felt it with my whole body and I wanted to join her. In a moment I *would* join her. She began to breathe out softly and sing or hum and—something else. I was just beginning to understand when one of the other Pups pushed himself between us, turned around to face me, and sat down. My view was blocked, and I no longer heard the singing, no longer felt it. "Sorry, Father," he said. "She forgets herself." Smokey was standing right beside me, but no one moved to block *his* view.

After a minute or two the Pup stepped away, and I went over to investigate the chain. Cicéqi was standing proudly over her work, and with good cause.

The chain beneath her was thickly crusted with fresh rust. Flakes peeled back and crumbled away even as I watched. I moved over to sniff closely and received another shock. The rust was spreading rapidly, and the snow beneath it had begun to melt.

"The magic is still working!"

Cicéqi favored me with a toothy, knowing smile. "Your children can be very persuasive," she replied.

"I never realized you were so powerful!"

"Yes, we are. Or rather, you are. All our strength comes from you. But this was a Teaching Song, not a Power Song. Only the Quickening came from me, and now Iron is using the Power of humans'—and your own—belief in 'Oxygen' to help free himself. In fact, this Song actually *generates* Power. Very dangerous magic! Too bad we didn't think of it back when they were building the railroads."

I was listening to Cicéqi, but with only part of my attention. Mostly I stared fixedly down at the chain section she had first sung to. On my face I could feel heat from it, and the snow had melted back to a distance of several inches.

"Cicéqi, when will the spffell pffe finished?"

"Oh, when all the Iron in the chain has found his Oxygen. Don't worry. I sang softly so that only this chain could hear properly. I think."

"How hot will it get?"

"I don't know. I've never done this before. Does Oxygen get things hot when she joins with them?"

"Yes. When wood or other things pffurn, that is from oxygen joining with them."

"No. Fire has nothing to do with Oxygen. He is... never mind. We're supposed to be doing this by 'Science,' so I'll listen to you. Are you trying to tell me Oxygen will make Iron burn? I've seen Iron in Fire many times, but I've never seen him burn! Why should he do so now, just because I showed him how to attract Oxygen more quickly?"

"I don't know. I get confused sometimes apffout all this. Still, that chain looks awfully hot! It won't hurt Smokey, will it?"

The rust line had extended a great deal while we talked, and the original section was putting out heat of an intensity that forced me to back off a bit. It was in Sun's full light, but I think in the dark it would have been glowing. Rust was flaking off at a furious pace, and the solid cores of the links were getting distinctly thinner beneath it all.

Smokey moved back with me, then retreated further, dragging at the chain so the hot section was pulled across a fresh patch of snow. There was a loud hiss and popping sound, and the snow flashed instantly into steam, startling all of us.

Smokey threw himself to the end of his chain, and kept on going. The thin, heat-softened links had parted with little resistance, but still made a lot of steam as they hit fresh snow, and Smokey decided he wanted to leave them behind.

We caught up with him in seconds, but then Smokey wasn't really scared. His chain was dragging along in a very ordinary way now, except for the dark line of rust and half-melted snow it left behind. All that fresh snow was keeping it cool, but the rust spell was working as hard as ever.

"Cicéqi! What do we do when the pffart around his neck gets hot? Can't you stopff it now?"

"You're the one who knows about Science! You tell me what to do. It would have been nice if you'd mentioned about Oxygen getting things hot before you asked me to destroy the chain."

That's not exactly the way I remembered it, but too late now. All I could think of was to throw Smokey into some water, or keep rolling him in a snow bank to keep his neck chain cool. It ought to work, if he cooperated.

No liquid water nearby, so it would have to be a snow bank. There were plenty in the shady areas, from previous snows. When we passed a nice big one I stopped and persuaded Smokey to sit down with the remnant of his chain resting safely on deep snow. It began to sink in immediately.

"Cicéqi, I'm going to keepff Smokey here until the chain has fallen away from his neck. I'll keepff rolling him in the snow so the chain stays cool, pffut he may pffanic and try to run away. Will you helpff me if that hapffens? You don't have to use any Medicine Pffower if you don't want to. We can all sit on him if you like! Think of it as a game. If Smokey gets away, he dies and you lose. If the chain falls off without hurting him, you win. I offer a pffowl of milk for each of you as pffrize!"

How could they refuse an offer like that? I think the Pups would have held down a wounded rhinoceros for me. As it turned out, I didn't need their help at all. Smokey was puzzled at first, but soon he realized what I wanted and cooperated fully. I just had to nudge him now and then when he was distracted by the puppies hanging on all over him.

The bolt rusted through before the rest of Smokey's chain did, but we were all covered with thick, grainy rust mud by then. Smokey was neither frightened nor injured, and had no idea of the danger he had just escaped.

We proceeded then to a magnificent steeplechase of a run, and the Pups cheated at every opportunity. So did I, but they were better at it. No one was keeping score, though. They knew they had already won their bowls of milk.

"You're a lot more fun than you used to be! I hope you stay this way," Cicéqi exclaimed at one point. She was hopping about like a chickadee—eyes flashing and tiny teeth everywhere. I felt old, trying to keep up with her.

We returned home near dusk, tired and filthy. The rust mud didn't rub off of our fur as well as regular dirt did. Maybe that's why it's so good for paint. My feet were clean, though, and I left no significant footprints in the house as I gathered up a plastic milk bottle and five bowls. I put the bowls out first, laying them in a neat row on the porch, well separated. Dividing the milk into five precisely equal portions was harder. I did my best, but the Spirit Pups could not be satisfied.

I gave up on it, finally. "This is as even as you're going to get from me," I declared. "You can decide among yourselves who gets first choice." That got them off my back, but precipitated a heated internal squabble which I left them to conclude on their own. "Come on, Smokey. You and I don't get any at all, so don't even think apffout it.

"Pffy the way, I suggest you consider yourselves full and sleepffy after you finish your milk. There won't pffe any other food for you today."

I stood guard at the base of the porch steps, keeping Smokey away while the Pups sorted things out, then took their rewards with ecstatic single-minded intensity. Some of them were making a sound almost like purring as they drank. I didn't think it would be a good idea for Smokey to try pushing in and taking any just then.

When the Pups were done I let Smokey inspect the bowls and give a last lick or two, then picked them up to put back on their shelf. Milk bottle went in the outside trash can, and the rest was up to the Papillios. Maybe they would think of a plausible explanation for the disappearance of a half-gallon of milk and a twenty-foot steel chain. They might not even notice the milk.

It was dark again when I heard the Papillios' truck engine, but the sky was absolutely clear with a strong afterglow in the west. Stars were everywhere—already brighter and closer than I had ever seen at Sunbow. Still too early for Moon.

Smokey and I began to worm our way out from the pile of Spirit Pups, but they all got up with us and we moved as a seething, ragged pack over to the cattle gate. As before, the Pups waited until they were almost in the headlights, then burst away in all directions like a flock of frightened birds. This time, none of them were caught in the light. Smokey and I sat down by the gate latch like loyal dogs. I would have had the gate open already for John or Mooney. My pleasure! All I could do for these humans was wait and act hospitable.

"Smokey—you're loose again! Your head must be smaller and softer than I thought. Guess I'll have to tighten that chain another link. Can't believe it. You didn't hurt yourself, did you?"

Ernie got out and started going over Smokey's head and neck while the truck was still idling at the gate, so I skipped over to Nana's side and scratched at her window. She rolled it down and I stuck my head inside to lick her face enthusiastically, front paws on the window edge to steady myself. It was a comfortable position I could hold forever. Not like balancing on my hind legs.

"Coyote, dear—we've got to stop meeting like this! My husband will find out." She was teasing me, not speaking softly at all, and Ernie could hear every word. He had finished with Smokey and was pulling the gate all the way open, so I had to jump down to let Nana drive forward, and ended up helping Ernie close while she continued ahead to park.

Smokey and I gave him a proper greeting—licking and nuzzling his face from both sides, then curling our two bodies around him like a pair of male grunion I saw once on television. Ernie would be the female, since he was upright.

Ernie struggled free and pushed on toward the house while Smokey and I nipped and pulled at his clothes. Nana had taken the opportunity to escape without hindrance, and was already inside. I continued up onto the porch to get in too, but Ernie stopped me at the door.

"No way, Mister. You're too filthy! I can see that now.

"You know, Coyote, I think Nana and I have been had. You're a juvenile delinquent who's already corrupted our poor Smokey, and we didn't even know. Don't try to deny it! I can read your face like a book. 'Guilty until proven innocent.' That's my motto for the likes of you! So I brought you a bone. Nana! Could you hand over those two soup bones? I'm being attacked by wolves at our door, and I need them now or you'll have to find another vet student to support!"

If the humans' plan was to get us out of their way while doing chores, it was a good one. I worked on my bone up to and then after dinner, although both of ours disappeared during the night while we were asleep. Probably ended up in one of the Spirit Worlds, or some such place.

Nana was the one who fed us that evening, and she gave only a cursory flashlight search for the chain before continuing on with the rest of her duties. "It'll turn up in the morning," she told us. "Don't run away, please."

Smokey and I didn't run away, but we did leave home. Our doghouse collapsed shortly after we entered it, while we were still circling and pushing against the walls to make ourselves comfortable. That was quite a surprise, since we had both treated it much more roughly just the night before when we burst out to investigate Fox's activities. The house had felt quite solid, then.

This time a few gentle stretches and bumps sent the walls toppling outward and the roof clunking down onto our shoulders. No harm done, except to the house. We just moved out and settled down together in the cold, cruel outside world a few feet away. Didn't really make that much difference to us.

Next morning no one said a word about missing milk, and explaining the collapsing doghouse was easy. All the nails had rusted away to nothing. Must have been substandard quality.

The humans never did come up with a satisfactory explanation for the missing chain. I think the collapsed doghouse and lack of daylight rather hampered them in that regard. They had left for work in darkness and haste — waving flashlights here and there but never closely investigating the missing snow or the rust-stained, trampled dirt which marked the place where Smokey's chain and steel anchor post had been. They never saw the straight, deep, rust-caked groove his chain had melted into the snow-covered rangeland as far off as one could see, nor the big and little paw prints swarming over it. That's what I saw the next morning when I tried to look at it as a human would, but Nana and Ernie had missed most of that. In the winter they only saw their home by Sun's light on weekends, and this was a Thursday morning.

"All right, you guys," Ernie had told me as he stepped into the truck with Nana. "The chain is gone, and we don't have another one. You have two choices—you can behave yourselves, or you can get yourselves shot by the neighbors. Let me know what you decide." Then Nana started the engine and they drove away.

We didn't get in trouble. No, not us. I was tired of getting caught, so I didn't, and the steaks we stole were delicious, and poor Smokey was corrupted even further. Not the Pups, though. They're beyond corruption.

High clouds oozed in all during that day, and snow was falling by nightfall. That was very convenient, as there were a good many tracks on the ground I didn't mind seeing the last of. Especially the ones from our steak raid to the Papillios' northeast neighbors. The chain trail and associated oddities were covered up too.

Ernie came home with a bag of galvanized nails, and set to work on our doghouse first thing. The job appeared to be an easy one for him, except that something was the matter with his tools. "Huh! What's with this hammer? And the pliers, too! Never had a rust problem like this before—not out here, at least. It's worse than at the beach! Guess I'll have to keep 'em in a box with some Dri-rite, or something. What do you think, Coyote? D'you suppose that old chain just rusted away? Nah."

Poor human. They do have trouble understanding things, sometimes. I began to howl softly and politely, inviting him to join in with me. Howling always makes me feel better, and I thought Ernie might be one of those humans who could benefit as well, like my family at Sunbow.

"That's right, Coyote, sing it out! I've-got-them-rus-ty-ham-mer-bluuues..."

Then he laughed, and howled properly. Smokey joined in too, of course, until we were all interrupted by Nana.

"Hey! You animals cut that out and get back to work! We've still got a million chores to do. We haven't even started the feeding yet."

We all stopped howling, and Ernie resumed hammering on the doghouse. It didn't take him long to finish, and when he was done the thing looked as strong as it had ever been.

169

My visit with the Papillios settled into more of a routine after that. They didn't bother to buy a new chain for Smokey, and I kept him out of trouble to make sure they didn't regret it. The Pups manifested frequently, and I could feel they were close, even when I couldn't see or smell them. We didn't try any more Science lessons.

The Papillios really did have a nice place, and I relished the open sky—didn't miss the trees much at all. I missed Lazytail, though. Passionately. I might be doing anything, and then suddenly I would think of her and go all melty inside, and just stand there dreaming with my eyes open.

The Spirit Pups read my thoughts without scruple, and Cicéqi often teased me about my infatuation. "What's all this fuss about mating, anyway? Your turn will come!" One time she changed her body to be mature, in full heat, and just my size. She even got the scent right, and as she pressed up against me I thought my heart would burst from beating so fast and hard.

I was on her in a second, grasping with front legs and getting myself frantically and clumsily into position while she braced her legs and held as steady as... It couldn't be true! I had never done this before, but I was so ready... Kept trying and missing, trying and missing, until at last I felt the tip slip into her. Instantly I began to thrust forward, and she disappeared.

Cicéqi didn't really disappear, but rather shrank so rapidly it was near the same thing. I pitched helplessly onto my nose and onto her, felt her wiggle out from under me, caught my balance, and stood up. Cicéqi and the others were sitting in a circle around me, laughing with their tongues. Cicéqi was a puppy again.

"You're not supposed to do that with your children, Father! Or so some say. And do you really want me pregnant right now? Our offspring can be rather... interesting. One day I'll tell you story of you and me and Fox, and the first jackalopes."

I couldn't think at first—stared straight ahead for a minute like I'd been cow-kicked, then finally understood.

A fine joke indeed. At my expense, of course. I was not amused, and showed it.

"Oh, Coyote, you'll get your wish soon enough. We like these feelings too, and we'll share yours when the time comes, but the time is not now. Let's go for a run!"

Chapter 18

I was at the Papillios' almost two weeks altogether, but it seemed much longer. Snow came now and then, but mostly the weather was clear and cold. Never as cold as on the first days, though, and sometimes it would thaw for a few hours during the middle of the day.

The sky was clear when Mooney came for me, with a strong breeze from the northeast. It hadn't snowed for a few days, and the roads were open, but it was still dark when she arrived. The arrangement had been for her to meet with Nana and Ernie at the university so she could follow them home without getting lost.

Moon was in the sky again—evening sky now—her whisker-thin, growing crescent chasing Sun closely as he set. Eleven more days and Mr. Burrey would be running on four feet again, if Fox didn't catch him first.

I thought about being aloof and cold to Mooney when she emerged from her van, but when she touched me I couldn't help myself. In a moment I was tasting tears on her face, along with my favorite jojoba and almond oil lotion.

"It's good to see you again, Stinky. Sorry John couldn't be here too, but he and his boss had a long, unpleasant talk about chronic absenteeism, and he needs to be good for now.

"So. They tell me no one caught you getting into trouble. How skillful of you! We'll make a politician out of you yet."

No need to answer that one, even if this were a talking time. I just continued to rub and nuzzle her in the traditional manner, which was all I wanted to do anyway. Smokey watched from a safe distance, but he didn't seem upset. A good start.

Mooney and the Papillios were already through with their own greetings, and they soon finished with me and got to work on chores. When they were done I pushed into the house along with Mooney, and no one stopped me. In passing I noted that the porch boards were even looser than usual, and the steel door hinges were in a terrible state. Suspiciously rusty.

"You've already had your dinner, Stinky, but you can share a little bite with us too, if you like." I gave three exaggerated nods like a circus dog, and the other humans laughed.

"How many tricks does he know?" Ernie asked.

"Oh, quite a few," Mooney evaded. "He comes up with new ones all the time. Has he really been well behaved?"

"Yes. It's almost uncanny—like he knows what you're saying. It's been kind of a weird time in general, though."

"I'm afraid to ask, Ernie, but I guess I should. What's been weird?"

"Oh, like there's been people on the property, but no footprints in the snow; animals acting strange; things missing or breaking down for no reason—that sort of stuff. Sounds kind of like the start of a ghost story, doesn't it? But I don't want to scare you. It's lonely out here, but we like it. Nothing happens that you need to be concerned about. That's just for the movies."

Mooney looked sympathetic. "Don't worry about me. It's you I feel guilty about. You've done me a big favor by taking care of Sin-Ka-Lip, but you should know that if anything strange has been going on, it's probably his fault and it'll go back to normal as soon as he leaves. I'll spare you the details. It's kind of a hippie, alternate consciousness sort of thing. You know how we are."

"Don't put yourself down, Mooney," interjected Nana. "Vet students and lab techs can be just as flaky as anyone else. You'd be surprised what we might believe!"

Mooney laughed, "So don't tempt me! Get me started, and who knows what I'd end up saying. Never could keep a secret. Anyway, if there's been strange stuff going on, it's not dangerous and should stop as soon as we leave. Don't worry about it."

The humans kept telling each other not to worry. *Interesting. Should I? Nah, that would be too cruel. Still…*

"Mooney, what is Coyote doing? I've never seen him act that way before!"

I was staring at the front door with ears aggressively forward and tail straight back. Slowly I curled my lips and started a low growl, like there was something quite nasty on the other side. I lifted my hackles, but couldn't quite fake a good fear-scent. No matter. The humans couldn't tell the difference.

Ernie was the male, and the biggest human, so there was no question about who would have to check the door. He stood taller, pulled his shoulders back to look as large and strong as possible, put his hand on the knob. I hung back like I was scared to go with him, and lowered my tail a bit.

Ernie opened the door boldly enough, and stepped out onto the porch. Nothing there, not even Smokey. Suited my game perfectly.

"Hello? Is anyone there?"

Ernie stood on the porch for a time, called out again, then came back inside. I stayed where I was and continued to stare at the door after it was closed, growling softly with each exhalation—a wheezing growl, with a strident edge to it that almost scared me. I'm pretty good at that sort of thing.

After a time I shifted my focus to the left, as if the object of my attention were circling widdershins about the house, releasing emanations of horror only I could detect. Rover had picked up the spirit and was helping me by standing on the sofa back with fur fluffed, ears back, all the usual. She had even begun to roll out some of those soft, insane little cat moans that make you want to back away very slowly and carefully.

All conversation had stopped. The humans were staring at me, fascinated. I could feel their Presences contracted closely around their physical bodies, quivering with tension. I tried to expand my own Presence—made myself a room-sized coyote, pressing them against the walls—then bigger still. I threw myself outward beyond the walls as far as I could go. It was something I had never thought to try before.

Nana shuddered. "It's awfully close in here. Maybe we should open a window for a minute." But no one did.

I shifted attention again, locking my gaze onto the back door. I stiff-walked over to it and reached my nose slowly, so slowly, for the knob, then jerked away and skittered back to the center of the room, hackles up even more, tail curled tight between legs. I changed growl into whine, still softly with each breath.

Ernie opened a closet and pulled out a shotgun, which I saw by rolling my eyes without turning my head away from the back door. The gun looked dusty and old, like it hadn't been fired in years. I decided the game had been played far enough, and prepared to relax.

I felt a Presence outside the house.

It was not human, it was not one of the Puppies, and it was not friendly. That's all I'll say about it for now. I would really rather not encounter one again.

I produced the real fear-scent then. No trouble at all. Stopped whining and stared outward in utter silence. It was beyond the kitchen window now, still circling the same way I had pretended to start it. Soon it would be back at the front door.

Ernie was searching deep in the back of the closet—finally came out with a box of shells, and loaded the shotgun. None of us went near the door.

I had stopped trying to puff up my Presence or otherwise toy with such things, but a different kind of strange thing happened then. Suddenly I felt cut off, the way my hearing goes when I get water in my ears. I could hardly feel the humans around me, and lost touch entirely with the thing outside. I think my physical hearing was affected as well.

I wasn't sure if this new development was good or bad, but that didn't matter. No way was I going near that door, and my humans obviously felt the same. We waited.

The numbness lifted as abruptly as it had come over me, so that I started, and the humans did too. The strange Presence was gone, but it took some time for Ernie and me to work up sufficient courage to leave the house and investigate. For the first time in my life I was glad to smell a gun close by. It was quiet outside, and bright enough for a human to see. Moon was almost set, but the cloudless sky and the snow gave her all the help she needed. Smokey was not in evidence anywhere, and Ernie called for him. No response.

Something was wrong with the doghouse. Normally it would be the first thing one saw when opening the front door, but now it was gone, or broken down. I glided forward to investigate.

There's a type of cheese called 'String Cheese' which Mouse is fond of. Sometimes she'll tear it apart into bundles of fibers, then pull those fibers apart too. That's what had been done to the wooden boards that made up our doghouse. No claw or tooth marks, no marks from human tools, just a bird's nest of twisted splinter-strips the size of wheat straws. A kicked-open bird's nest. Even the hard-frozen earth beneath and around the house had been dug through and thrown outward, but not by claws or tools. The dirt looked more like a loaf of bread that had been plucked at idly by the fingers of a human child.

"Oh, my."

Ernie was staring at the doghouse remains. He already had a fine fear-scent going, but it grew even stronger as he stood there. My feelings exactly.

There were no new tracks, and no new scents besides those of broken cedar and disturbed soil. I felt no magical effluvium at all, but I was still just learning about that sort of thing. This lesson was not a pleasant one.

We left the doghouse behind and walked past the human house toward the paddocks. They were empty, and broken down on the far side. No sign of horses anywhere. I wondered at the time why I hadn't heard them crashing through the fence—didn't come up with the hearing block idea until later.

The owl and beaver were still there, sort of. They had not been overlooked by our visitor, and they were quite thoroughly dead. Even I felt pity for those two.

We went inside to report to Nana and Mooney, but I soon slipped out again. 'Upset' is far too mild a word for the way they were feeling, and fear-scent choked the house. They had already started one of those endless, go-nowhere human discussions, and I needed to find Smokey.

His track was not hard to follow—paw prints deep and well spaced. He had been in a hurry, as was proper. I settled into a fast lope, ready to go as far and as long as I needed to. No way could that pup leave me behind! Soon I noticed Cicéqi and the others running beside me. Hadn't seen them arrive. As usual.

I stopped to ask Cicéqi if she knew anything about our visitor, but she beat me to it.

"I can't believe even *you* would be stupid enough to summon a *Ga`at!*" Her voice and posture carried such a conflicting set of signals I gave up trying to sort them out, except to note that they were mostly negative. I was not pleased with the situation myself.

"What's a *Ga`at?*"

"Never mind what a *Ga`at* is! What were you doing summoning one?"

"Acting out of ignorance, as you all seem to want me to do. Are there any other stupffid, deadly things you'd like to warn me apffout now, or would you rather wait until later? Just what did I do to pffring it over, anyway? I was only trying to pfflay a joke on the humans pffy pffretending there was something dangerous outside. How could that summon anything?"

"You were mocking them—saying, 'Behold! Here stands Coyote in the World again, frightening his friends to feed on their fear like a blood-sucking gutworm of a *Ga`at!*'"

"I said all that?"

"You didn't have to. The *Ga`at* know how you feel about them. Exposing yourself as you did could only mean an insult and challenge, and one of them came for you. We didn't want that, so we shielded you and your friends. We used the fur you had shed in the doghouse as the base for an illusion, so the *Ga`at* thought that's where you were, for a while. *Ga`at* are not very bright, and not good at perceiving this World. In the end it decided you were not really here at all—just the illusion. Another Coyote trick. Sorry about the owl and beaver. They were outside our circle of protection, and not free to run away.

"That's all you need to know about *Ga`at*. Please don't tease them any more. The *Ga`at* may be slow and stupid, but they really are quite dangerous. You've ruined this house for the humans. *Ga`at* are not good at crossing over into this World, so once they've been shown how to get to a particular place, they tend to keep coming back to that place."

"I see. Thanks so much for the tipff. I had no idea soul-eaters were so common."

"The *Ga`at* are not soul-eaters. They just kill you slowly, feeding on pain and fear and despair. When they're done your soul is free to go where it will."

"That's nice of them, pffut I'm not sure I can learn to accepfft that."

"You never did."

"You mean... there's something good apffout the old me? That's wonderful!"

"We think so. But don't let it go to your head. You're still basically a jerk."

What a put-down. I lowered ears and tail, struggling to absorb the unexpected insult and put it behind me, but then I noticed something funny about Cicéqi's posture. She was teasing me!

Enough of that!

I leapt sideways to bump my shoulder hard against Cicéqi's, then grabbed her throat as she went down, and held her pinned to the ground in proper coyote style. She lay limp and rolled her eyes up to look at me, also in proper style, so I let her go after a short time. She jumped up to lick my face with frantic puppy kisses while pushing her head and shoulders up under my neck.

"That was fun! Let's do it again!"

Suddenly the others were pressing around me eagerly, and we joined together in another greeting session. Spirit Creatures are weird.

Eventually we caught up with Smokey, comforted him, and turned him around, but we never got him all the way back to the house. He balked about a mile out, and wouldn't approach any closer. As I said earlier, he's quite a sensible fellow.

I persuaded the Pups that staying with Smokey to keep him company was not forbidden as long as it was their own idea, and they laughed. "That's what we were planning to do all along!" they told me, as if those words had a special meaning for them, and were another fine joke on me. I didn't mind, just thanked them and loped rapidly back to report to Mooney.

Mooney was upset that I had run off into danger, but couldn't say anything in front of the Papillios. When I got her alone I rushed to start talking first, to distract her.

"The danger is pffast for now. I can feel it. I found Smokey, pffut he won't come pffack all the way. Can you get in the van and come helpff me? Maypffe he'll go inside."

The van trick hadn't worked for Lazytail, but that didn't mean the idea was worthless. Mooney agreed, eventually, after repeated assurances that it really was safe to go outside. We left with the Papillios phoning all their neighbors to track down the horses. It was almost midnight, which I thought was rather late for humans to be doing that sort of thing, but I guess they couldn't help themselves.

One of the gate hinges broke while Mooney was opening it to take the van through, but she managed to prop the thing up behind her so it didn't fall over. "This gate is shot! Rusted clear through. They'll just have to buy another one, I guess. Come on Stinky—you'll have to point out the way for me. You want to run, or ride?"

"I think I'll ride this time. I've done enough running for tonight."

We got Smokey into the van eventually, but it was not easy. Mooney had to turn off the lights and walk quite a distance away before he would go near it, and even then he wouldn't go inside. I could bully him all I liked, but that's not the same as making him go where I wanted him to. I think if it had been just me and Mooney we would have failed in the end.

I lost patience finally, and spoke with words, "All right, Smokey, this is it! If you won't get in the van, I'm sending Mooney pffack and we'll spffend the rest of the night right here where we are. I hopffe you realize this means no pffreakfast for us."

Smokey couldn't understand me much, but the Pups could. My comment about breakfast had been for their benefit, since I always shared my food with them when the humans weren't looking. They didn't need to eat a lot, if I reminded them about it.

Smokey gave a sudden, surprised yelp and looked to his flank. His hindquarters were at an odd angle—as if something invisible was pushing him while he braced himself against it. He began to take reluctant, mincing little side steps toward the van, then darted suddenly forward, or tried to. He only got a foot or so before running into something else invisible, and then he was being pressed from all sides, herded gently into the van. That's the way it looked to me. I don't know how Mooney perceived it. Moon had set, and I don't think a human could have seen much.

I slid the side door closed myself, and called Mooney back. "I've got him!" Then we both went in through the driver's door, opening it just enough to squeeze through one at a time.

I went to join Smokey in back. He was pressed into a corner, but didn't really smell that upset. He wasn't frightened of the van, just hadn't felt like entering it.

When we got back to the house, Smokey wouldn't leave the van. He did become upset—stayed pressed into his adopted corner and whined frantically when I tried to leave. "I think I'll spffend the night here, Mooney. Why don't you go inside and try to get some sleepff?"

"Okay. I'll go in now, but I doubt any of us will sleep tonight. I'm still planning on leaving at first light, though. That's in just a few hours. You sure it's safe out here?"

"Yes. The thing is gone, and I pffromise to make a lot of noise if it comes pffack. Also, it's slow. Smokey and I can run away if we need to."

"Stinky, what do you know about all this? You've been playing with magic, haven't you?"

"Not on pffurpffose, honest. I'll tell you all apffout it, pffut it would take hours. I met Fox! He tried to kill me, pffut we're friends now, and he sent some spffirits to pffrotect me. I think we're safe for now, pffut I'm worried apffout these humans. I think they should move away from here right away. You will talk to them, won't you? Tell them you think that thing may come pffack."

The next day was a Saturday, so the Papillios could devote themselves to putting their home back in order. The horses hadn't been found during the night, but first light brought a phone report that they were in custody, with minimal injuries. They had run almost twenty miles.

"Mr. Blevens says he can keep them for a few days until we get things back together here. They're too spooked to touch yet, but there are no flies this time of year, and the cuts will heal fine on their own. Tilly threw a shoe."

"Well, she needed to be done anyway," Nana replied resignedly. "I'm just glad it wasn't anything serious."

Nana was out in the yard when Ernie gave his report, so I could hear them easily from my station in the van. I had only left to shit and pee, and Smokey hadn't even done that. He wouldn't eat his breakfast, either. Smokey whined quietly at the sound of Ernie's voice, so the man came over to us again.

"Come on Smokey, buck up! You can't go on like this." Ernie squeezed past me to sit on the steel van floor beside Smokey, massaging his shoulders tenderly. Smokey leaned into his hands and groaned, but he wouldn't get up when Ernie grabbed his scruff and gently tugged. We had already been through this several times.

Ernie left to help Nana with the paddock fence, and Mooney came out to visit. It was way past first light, and she was ready to go, but she didn't want to pressure Ernie about the wolf.

"Did they pffelieve you when you told them apffout their danger?"

"Oh, they believed me, but we humans don't just move out like that. It's even worse for them. Where would the put all the animals?"

"If we take Smokey they'll pffe down pffy four. That's all the outside ones excepfft the horses." Quite an attrition rate, and all my fault, in a sense.

"I'll talk to them one more time, and I will offer to take Smokey, but the rest is up to them. We're leaving this morning regardless."

"Yes, Mooney. I can't argue apffout that, pffut pfflease make sure they really understand. They can leave their stuff here for now, pffut they and the other animals need to go today, and the house should pffe destroyed."

"That's a lot to ask of a human. Are you sure about this?"

"Oh, I'm sure, and you are too. What if you had pffeen out with the owl and pffeaver last night?"

Mooney went on to join the Papillios at the paddock fence. They had already fixed the broken section, but were investigating the other rails closely. I saw Ernie kick one, not very hard, and it fell off.

They stopped working and began an intense discussion with Mooney. This time I paid attention and heard most of it. It was just as Mooney had tried to explain to me. They believed her, they were frightened, they wanted to move, but they couldn't afford to. Money again. These humans were just as broke as Mooney, and paying even the simplest bills was a feat they were not certain of repeating each month.

When the three humans came over, I knew what Mooney's report would be. "Alright, Stinky, it's time to go. We'll be taking Smokey with us, and he can stay permanently if he gets along. You should like that. Nana and Ernie will find a new place as soon as they can."

Not a good enough answer, but no surprise. I had already decided what I would do next.

"Yes, Mooney," I answered distinctly. Sun was shining full on my face, and they all could see my mouth and tongue move as I spoke.

I turned to Ernie. "Thank you for your hospffitality... uh, *hosss*-fffit... for your food. You cook excellent steaks, and I liked the pffack rupffs too."

To Nana: "I will always remempffer our meeting together in the truck, pffut I must leave you now. I think your huspffand suspffects something." This was a serious occasion, but I couldn't resist trying to making a joke out of it. If I weren't a coyote I'd be ashamed of myself.

Stunned silence. Of course. I was almost learning to like it. Mooney spoke first.

"Coyote! What are you doing?"

She called me Coyote!

"These pffeopffle need to have things expfflained to them, and I thought you could use some helpff." The other two humans still hadn't moved or spoken. The expressions were hard to read, but I certainly had their attention!

"Well, Ernie, don't you have any questions? I don't supffose you've met a talking coyote pffefore."

"Uh, no."

"Is that all you can say? You watch Star Trek. What would Capfftain Pfficard do?" Ernie still seemed stuck in silence, and I was going to prompt him again, but then words broke loose.

"Well, what do you expect? Of course I've never met a talking coyote! Have you been doing this all your life? Why didn't you mention it before? And what do you know about all this stuff that's been going on?"

Ernie shut up as suddenly as he had started, like he was surprised by his own words. Nice response, though.

"I am Coyote. The Pffeopffle are always making fun of me in their stories. I'm their favorite character—the clown who is sometimes downright nasty, sometimes a hero. You met my friend Fox last week. He's like me, pffut more respffectapffle. A little."

I had heard these things said about me but I had never repeated them aloud. As the words left my mouth I knew they were true.

"I am here on a quest that has nothing to do with you, pffut I made a mistake last night and now this spffot is too dangerous for anyone to live here any more. The creature that visited us last night may come pffack from time to time over the years, pffut I will not pffe here, and so my Medicine Pffowers will not pffrotect you as they did last night. That is why you must leave now, and pffurn the house so no one else can live here."

"Did you say *burn it down?* That's crazy! I'll just explain to the police that a talking coyote told me the house was haunted and had to be destroyed. I'm sure my landlord will understand and not press charges. Maybe I'm crazy already. Nana! Am I crazy?"

"No, Ernie. No more than usual. Your delusions are just speaking out loud this time."

Nana was still looking at me. She hadn't turned her eyes away, even to answer Ernie. "I just can't believe this. You can't know what this means to me! To see real, living magic right here in front of me. In broad daylight..."

Her voice faded to nothing and she continued to stare at me like she wanted to eat me. I did understand how she felt, though. I think I must have stared at Fox that way when I first met him.

Enough of this stuff. The humans would require time to adjust no matter what, but Smokey was suffering and we needed to be going.

"I've only spoken to four humans pffefore you two. I may talk to others some time, pffut mostly not. It's too confusing for everyone.

"Pfflease listen. Last night I tried to scare you all as a joke. Just a joke. Good one, too! I pffretended something horripffle was outside, pffut then there really *was* something. Something even worse than what I was imagining. It's called a *Ga`at*. If you meet one again you'll pffropffapffly die unless you can run fast and far. I've pffeen told they like to come back to a pfflace they've pffeen to pffefore. That's all I know apffout *Ga`at*, pffut it's enough for me. And enough for Smokey, too! I never saw the *Ga`at* pffut I pffet he did, and he won't even come out of the van. I don't think your horses will like it here any more either.

"Mooney says it's time to go, so we'll leave now. I like you pffoth, and I don't want you to die, so *pfflease* find a new pfflace! I'm very sorry apffout your house, pffut if you're not too mad at me I would like to see you again sometime."

It was Nana who made the decision official. "We'll do as you say, and no, we don't hate you for what you did. The situation is way beyond that." She paused again, "Real magic, right here in front of me." She moved up shyly to touch me, and I let her. Treated me like I was made of glass or cobwebs.

"Yes, Nana, I'm real, and my left ear really itches, way down inside where I can't reach it. Why don't you use one of those wonderful long, soft fingers to scratch it for me?"

Ernie spoke up suddenly. "We can take the animals to school! We'll use the horse trailer to move them. There's plenty of room in the exotic animal ward, and I have a key. Dr. Hendricks will be mad, but she'll forgive me if I have a good enough story, and she'll keep the Dean off my back. Naomi and I have plenty of friends we can stay with for a little while. We can do this if we have to. We've just never been evicted by a demon before. Only regular landlords."

"I'm not quite certain, pffut I think demons are a lot worse than *Ga`at*. I hopffe none of us ever meets one."

"You're serious, aren't you? How much of this magic stuff is real, anyway? Should we believe every single thing we've ever heard, no matter how dumb it sounds?"

"I don't know. I'm just learning, myself. As far as I'm concerned I'm just eleven years old, almost. It's a long story, and I think Smokey needs to pffee more than anything. I know how he feels. I really am sorry apffout spffoiling your house. I had no idea this would hapffen."

Ernie smiled and shook his head, then opened his mouth to speak, but Mooney interrupted.

"Okay guys, I know it's weird and rude for Stinky and me to just drive off after totally messing up your world like this, but that's what we're doing. It's going to take you a while to learn to deal with it, if you ever do, but my friend here has invited you into one very exclusive club! Come see us at Sunbow if you decide you want to join."

Then she slid the door shut, closing me and Smokey into the back of her van, and a moment later she was starting up the engine. Just like that. I love Mooney. At times she's almost as practical as a coyote.

The second gate hinge broke when the Papillios opened up for us, and the middle part was collapsing too. Through the rear window I could see them each holding up the broken gate panel with one hand and waving goodbye with the other. Lost and scared, but I think joyful too, in a strange sort of way. I hoped they would choose to visit us some time.

We stopped in empty, snow-covered wheat fields a few miles out to let Smokey do his business. Mooney had me put a rope on him but it wasn't needed. He had left his fear behind at the Papillios' place, and finally wanted breakfast. I had brunch.

Mooney took the freeway home. She said it was longer, but Highway 12 had more ice and too tough a grade for the old van. I certainly won't argue that one! Cars zipped past us the whole way, and Mooney had to add oil to the engine each time she stopped for gas. We reached Seattle at dusk. Or rather, we reached the south part of it. We could have continued south and skirted the worst of it but Mooney went the opposite way on purpose—drove us clear through the center before turning back and resuming our journey. She said it was something I ought to see for myself—her words could never describe it properly.

Mooney was right. I keep trying to describe it but the words won't work properly for me, either. They're all just faint, distorted echoes of the real thing:

Big.

Smelly.

Big.

Noisy.

Big.

Urgently, pleasurelessly busy.

Big.

I simply cannot understand how even humans would choose to live there, yet John tells me there are more humans in Seattle than there are coyotes in the whole world. Then he tells me Seattle is only a medium-sized city. Humans certainly breed well for animals with such small litters.

Seattle and the other cities had us for over three hours. Mooney smelled terrified, and the other cars surged past on both sides like river water around a rock. Seattle was the worst, of course, but just when I thought we were free of it Tacoma grew up around us, and Olympia after that.

182

Finally even Olympia had passed behind, and we were free. Dark woods lay beside us now, and the road was mostly empty. Mooney broke long silence.

"Sin-Ka-Lip, there's something I need to tell you now, before we get back to Sunbow. You're not going to like it."

I felt a shock like jumping into cold water. *Is Lazytail dead?*

"What is it?" I said in a tiny voice. I don't even know if Mooney heard me over the engine noise. She continued regardless.

"You won't be going back to school with Mouse. The School Board has determined that you're a dangerous animal, and cannot be allowed on the premises."

I was braced for tragedy, and I got an insult instead. Had to think it through before answering.

"This is racism, isn't it?"

"Excuse me, Stinky. I didn't quite catch that."

"This is racism. You and John talk apffout it all the time for humans. The School Pffoard is pffeing racist against me pffecause I'm not a dog."

"Well, I hadn't really thought of it that way. There was a report that you snapped at one of the kids, and a group of parents put together a petition to get you out. The School Board did what bureaucracies always do, and that's the end of the story."

"Mooney, you know that's not true. That pffoy stepffed on my foot. Hard! I couldn't helpff myself, pffut we pffoth apffologised to each other and we're still friends. I know he's not afraid of me. I can smell it. Very few of them are afraid of me."

"That may be true for the kids, but there's a group of parents that doesn't feel that way at all. They're really upset. And there's been some stock killing going on. Some of those parents are saying you, or Lazytail, are probably responsible."

"I wasn't even there! You've had me away for two weeks!"

"Details like that are not important. No one in town believes me much anyway, especially after that attempted drug bust. I'm just that crazy Sklarsen hippie bitch who owns a hundred million dollars' worth of trees, and gets the land taken away for taxes because she won't log it. If they only knew I talk to spirits and animals too!"

"Is it really worth a hundred million dollars?" I was just beginning to learn the mysteries of mathematics, but the basics were coming in clearly enough. It seemed to me that one hundred million dollars was an awful lot of money.

"Maybe more. Those big peeler logs are hard to get now. It drives the mill owners crazy to know there's a huge stand of them just fifteen miles out of town, doing no good besides providing shelter for a bunch of worthless animals. 'There's the Park,' they say. 'Who needs more than that?' Sometimes I think the whole drug raid thing was a plot to pressure me into selling out. Paranoid, ain't I?"

"I don't know. It makes a lot of sense to me, pffut I supffose I'm pffaranoid too. I'm a coyote. Pffaranoid coyotes live longer."

We stopped talking for a while. Both of us had some things to think about. I spoke first.

"Did Lazytail miss me?"

"Did she! She and Mouse have both been pining away for you, you jerk. Me, too. We three ladies just sit around and sigh for a raunchy old dog we're better off without. Maybe Smokey will help take you off our minds. He's much younger. And cuter, too, don't you think?"

"He's pffeautiful, pffut not like me. I am New Coyote! I'm the god of the coyotes, and no one can match me." If she liked to think of me as vain, let her gnaw on that one! I had my reputation to grow into, after all.

The Black Hills passed by like fog at night, and then we were in the Chehalis Valley, and then the Wynoochee. Mooney wouldn't let me open the window much, but my nose was jammed into the crack at the top, smelling home. It was raining, of course. We had left snow and ice behind us in the Cascades.

Lazytail and Mouse both heard the van coming and met us out on the driveway. Lazytail was spinning in tight circles, whining frantically, and giving piercing little half-barks. I jumped out and fell on top of her before the van even came to a stop.

We tussled and sniffed and nipped and peed—all the usual things. I wanted them to go on forever, to lead Lazy on a run through the woods that we would never forget, but Mooney brought me up short.

"Sin-Ka-Lip, aren't you forgetting someone?"

Mouse! I rushed over to nuzzle her hands and lick her face, and she grabbed me in a hug that squeezed the air out of me.

"Hffuhhfff!" That's the closest I came to words, just then. Sometimes they're more trouble than they're worth.

We dragged Smokey inside to keep track of him, and I kept the humans up late telling them my story. The whole story this time, skipping nothing. Mooney interrupted me many times. She was clearly displeased with some of the choices I had made, and even more displeased with Mr. Burrey's part in things. I think she felt he had done it all deliberately.

"Stinky, I just didn't have a clue! I would never have let any of those things happen to you, even if I had to lock you up in a bomb shelter! Oh, I don't know... but how could I stop them? Coyote dear, I don't think I can protect you against stuff like this. I want to, but I just can't!" She had that crying sound in her voice, and I moved over close to let her hug me if she wanted to.

"Yes, Mother. I know. We'll just have to try and pffrotect each other the pffest we can. I think there will pffe more like this."

I didn't worry about myself. Death had never really frightened me that much. Not like it did the humans.

"Mouse, are you afraid? I've learned that I attract magical things, and some of them are dangerous. Maypffe it would pffe pffetter if you didn't live with us any more."

"No! Don't ever think that! I'd rather die with you than go back where I was!"

Mouse had just blown her amnesia story big time, but Mooney didn't say anything. She pretended she hadn't heard. Interesting.

I had wanted to share some time alone with Lazytail after talking with my humans, but Lazy and Smokey were long since asleep on the kitchen floor, and I was tired too. Smokey had tolerated the new humans quite well as long as they pretended not to notice him.

"Excuse me, pffut I think we've talked enough now. I need to sleepff."

Mouse had been staying in Mooney's room while I was gone, and she wanted the three of us to join them there. Mooney agreed for some reason, and I managed to get Smokey in with only token obstruction from him. I did make the humans put on extra blankets so they could open the bedroom window completely. Without that it would have been just too hot and stuffy after sleeping for two weeks out in the snow. Longer for Smokey.

I waited until everyone was settled, then cuddled up close to Lazytail. Her heat fragrance was still with her, as strong as when I had left. It made me feel excited, and sentimental, and incredibly horny. Next morning we would experiment together to see if she was truly, completely past her season, but this was a time for sleeping. Too bad I wouldn't be remembering my dreams.

I felt the Pups join us just before I fell asleep. Don't know how they arrived, couldn't hear or smell or see them, but I knew they were close.

"Welcome to Sunpffow," I murmured softly.

Thank you, Father. We're glad to be here.

Hot oatmeal in the morning—lots of oatmeal. Lazytail appeared to have come to terms with it, and ate with relish, but Smokey wasn't so sure about this new flavor of breakfast. We mixed some dog food in with his gruel and he liked it fine that way. I wouldn't admit it to anyone, but I kind of enjoyed mine too. I grew up on the stuff.

It was Sunday morning, so Mouse would be home all day. Looked like the rain would continue all day too. No matter. The humans needed exercise so I got them started right after breakfast. That means we were walking out the door an hour later. I don't know how they ever get anything done with all that bathing, dressing, and combing. Uses up the whole day if you include cooking, cleaning, dish washing, and chores.

I walked with Mouse, of course. No one could guide her like I could. Through the hand resting on my shoulders I could feel her Presence, as strong as it had ever been. I could sense the Spirit Pups too. They were close by, watching. After a time I tried calling to them.

"Cicéqi! Are there any rules against showing yourselves to my humans? They would really like to see you, and they have all sorts of food in the house you've never tasted pffefore. We're having fried tofu and rice with fish sauce for lunch. I pffet you've never tried that!"

I heard a rustle in the bracken behind me and whipped around just in time to see Cicéqi emerge. I heard similar rustlings all around, and in seconds the five Pups were among us. All were dry except for moisture just starting to bead on the tips of their guard hairs.

"What's a Tofu? Is it hard to catch? I've never seen one before." Cicéqi gave only the briefest of greetings, like we had hardly been separated. She didn't greet the new humans at all, but I knew she was watching them.

"Tofu is not an animal. It's a food the humans make. It's like cheese, excepfft it's made from soypffeans, not milk." I wondered why she needed to ask me these things if she could read my mind. Maybe she didn't bother all the time.

"Oh, we remember now! Tofu is a traditional Asian protein staple rich in vitamins and minerals, with natural macrobiotic enzyme activity that facilitates micronutrient absorption."

"You took the words right out of my mouth. Tofu is kind of pffland, too, pffut the fish sauce helpffs. Fish sauce is made in Thailand from little fish they pffut in a pffarrel to rot. You'll like it."

"Interesting. There's nothing like a human for inventing new ways to eat. Are you going to introduce us now?"

"Of course. Would you like to do it human style or coyote style?"

"Human style. They have on too much clothing to do it the other way. These humans 'shake hands,' don't they? We will 'shake hands' now."

Cicéqi walked over to Mooney, sat down, and moved to lift her left front foot, then switched quickly and extended her right instead. Mooney extended her right hand and shook the paw gently and without hesitation. "I am pleased and honored to meet you, Cicéqi. I've heard your name mentioned in the stories. My name is Mooney. Sin-Ka-Lip has chosen me to be his Human Guide during his quest to learn the power of the White People. I'm not sure I'm worthy of this, but I try."

"We think you're doing an excellent job, Daughter! So very earnest— just like your grandfather—and Father speaks most highly of you. He has never had such fine manners! We've already had one 'Science' lesson together, and it worked well. We created a new Teaching Song that has never been in this World before. It has very interesting effects on things made from Iron. Did Coyote tell you about it?"

"Yes, he did. I'm not sure you realize how powerful a magic that is!"

"Oh, we realize. Perhaps better than you do. But wait! You must meet my Brothers and Sisters too, and we must not forget our Mouse!"

All the Pups 'shook hands' in turn with the two humans, and each said a few words of greeting. Then they moved off in a group and paid their respects to Lazytail and Smokey in the more traditional manner. Finally I intervened to get us all moving again. I had offered them lunch, but there was no need to quit our walk early for it.

We encountered no cougar marks, but Broke Ear and Fluff Tail had wandered through more than once. There was no sign that Princess or her siblings had been with them. Worrisome.

Chapter 19

Mooney and Mouse were busy cleaning up lunch when I finally got my chance to be 'alone' with Lazytail. There were only Smokey and the five Spirit Pups to watch.

I tried mounting as soon as we were out of view from the kitchen window, and things went well at first. Lazytail was affectionate and cooperative—seemed to like the game just fine until I had everything in place. Then she sat down.

Damn.

Let me tell you that nothing, but nothing, gets accomplished in this business until the female is good and ready. You can whine all you like.

Well, it looked like the mating business was pretty much over. Maybe next year. Time for a run. Lazytail and I had a lot of fine country to show our guests. Might even catch something to eat.

We didn't encounter any game, but we did find Princess. She was thin and weak, and almost out of her parents' territory. On the margin, actually. Where two territories come together there's always a strip that neither party is quite sure about. That's where you go to rest when you don't have land of your own. You don't get beaten up so often, but there's not much to eat, either.

Princess was skittish, but she knew me well enough to let me approach when I left the others behind, and soon we had renewed our friendship. I still had food in my belly, so I gave it to her and she ate gratefully. It was the least I could do for an old friend down on her luck. Every coyote has to leave home some day, and it's a sad, risky time.

When we moved on again I was not surprised to see Princess following us. It was a sensible choice on her part, since we were a very well-fed pack, with one friend in it already. She would tag along for a bit to see how we treated her.

I had never worried much about whose territory I was crossing; I went where I liked, and no one ever bothered me. Princess was not so fortunate. She had not abandoned her old range by choice, and she hesitated and almost left us when the time came to go back that way. I gave her a few yips of encouragement, and that's all it took. Princess was following us again.

Closely now, and furtively; constantly alert for the approach of trouble. I lagged behind the others to give her courage.

Sunbow is my own personal territory. Just a few dozen acres, but all mine. Princess knew all about it, and as she crossed the boundary her footsteps became light and her tail and ears sprang upward in gay relief. Not that we coyotes ever hold our tails up that high. It's quite indecent the way some of the dogs carry them—especially huskies and chows and such. You can see everything in full view with the tail curled up like that. No sense of propriety at all.

"Mooney! Pffrincess followed me home. She's really hungry, and I think she has worms. Can I take her some food?" If Mooney said no I would do it anyway, but I thought it would be nice to give her a chance to agree, and perhaps berate me a little if she liked. She just sighed.

"What's one more mouth to feed? It's all nothing compared with what I owe the tax assessor. Let her be our guest! You know where the worm pills are kept. Probably you should dose everyone, including yourself. Do you suppose Spirit Pups need to be wormed?"

"I don't know apffout that. Let's not."

"Suits me. As usual, I'm over my head with this stuff. You too, eh?"

"Yes."

Princess knew about dog food. Unfinished bowls of dog food are one of the things we coyotes look for when we check out a house. She bolted it all down, including the worm medicine I had pushed into a lump of cheese on top. Afterward she wandered off into the brush, but I knew she would not go far.

Cicéqi and company disappeared after dinner, but Princess came back later for extra food, and she used a word!

"Morrre."

One of the two I had taught her. I always knew that pup was special.

189

Chapter 20

Next day was a Monday, and Mouse went to school without me. She had been slipping rapidly behind while I was gone, and I didn't think that would change much, at least in Mrs. Stanford's class. I felt angry thinking about Mouse all alone there, and I felt guilty, too. And lost. Mooney had become accustomed to doing her chores without me, and I was needed more by my new canine family, which was finding new and creative ways of getting into trouble.

Just before lunchtime Princess killed one of Mooney's hens right there in front of me, then proudly brought it over to lay at my feet. The hens ran loose in the daytime because predators are supposed to be too shy to attempt daylight attacks. Princess obviously felt that my invitation to join us included hunting privileges.

Lazytail and Smokey eyed all this in pleased speculation, while I glared helplessly at Princess. How could I teach a wild coyote not to kill chickens? I could only drive her away, and I didn't want to do that.

"Mooney!"

Princess jumped at my voice, then snatched up the chicken and trotted off into the woods with her prize held high. Lazytail and Smokey followed after her.

"What is it now, Stinky?"

I explained about the chicken with some trepidation, but I was not going to conceal anything. That chicken would be missed, and someone had to take the blame for it. Mooney was irritated, but not as much as I thought she would be. "Lazytail already killed two while you were gone," she admitted. "I was kind of expecting this."

We had chicken and dumplings and canned green beans for dinner that night, and Mooney ate some chicken too. She's only mostly vegetarian. The rest of her hens went into the freezer.

"Damned if I'm going to let you just kill them all one by one. These are *my* chickens."

"Pffut, I didn't kill any!"

"Same difference. You would if you thought you could get away with it. I'm only removing further temptation."

Mouse was distraught that evening, and the special meal did little to cheer her up. The school day had been rough, and when she asked to sleep alone with me neither Mooney nor I could refuse, despite our misgivings about leaving the pack unsupervised. We should have paid more attention to those misgivings.

In the morning I smelled blood on Lazytail's fur. Smokey's, too. Calf blood. This time I didn't say anything to Mooney.

After Mouse left for school I went out by myself to follow their trail, and the slugs didn't even follow me—just draped themselves around the farmyard in a contented meat-stupor. They hadn't even bothered with breakfast. *Shit.* I never thought I would be the one to get hot about rule-breaking, but killing stock could get us all dead.

At least they had left Mr. Bell's place alone. The trail led south past the Gundersons' ranch to a little farm which was hardly a farm at all. Mooney calls those people 'Gentlemen Farmers' with a kind of disgusted tone to her voice. There are a lot of them in the valley, and their places are often well worth investigating during night rounds.

I had been hoping to find the carcass and drag it away before anyone could examine it, but I was much too late for that. Several humans were there, and one of them was a Deputy Sheriff. That's what his car said, at least. A couple of dogs were nosing around too, so I left in a hurry.

I decided to tell Mooney after all, but when I got back she was holding a letter in her hand, and had that angry-helpless scent to her. "I can't believe this! They've sent me a writ already! It should be another year before they get to this stage."

I wasn't quite sure what a 'writ' was, but I could tell it was something bad, and so I moved up cautiously to comfort her. "Maypffe John can fix it," I suggested hopefully.

"This is not John's problem! I'm a grown woman. I can take care of these things myself."

"Yes, Mother. I know. What are you going to do?"

"Well, I can donate it all to the Nature Conservancy, or I can log it. I don't like either choice much."

"Can't you log it just a little? Compffared with what you have, it wouldn't pffe much, would it?"

"Of course I can do that, and I will, too, but it's against my principles, and I'll have to take back a lot of things I've said over the years, including some promises. Damn! But I don't want to just give it up! This is my land. I gave up everything else to keep it the way it is."

There were no words good enough to answer that one, so I didn't—just tried to be companionable and supportive. I was glad she had come to a decision at last. After a time I gathered courage enough to tell her about the calf killing. We would all be needing Mooney's help soon, and she had to be ready.

"Mooney, there's another pffropfflem I need to tell you apffout. I think Lazytail and Smokey killed a calf last night."

"No! Oh, Coyote! What am I going to do with you? It's not one of Mr. Bell's, is it? I could never face him."

"No, it's not Mr. Pffell's. It was at one of the little farms just pffast the Gundersons'. The one with the pffoat in the driveway."

"Ugh. Mr. Hubert! He's hated me for years now—ever since that time I almost got him voted off the School Board. He'll have the Sheriff here first thing.

"I think maybe it's time for you to go on another walk, kid. A long walk with your friends. See you at dinnertime. And Stinky, *please* keep them out of trouble!"

Mooney had a good meal waiting for us—a big pot of beans with one of the chickens boiled up for flavor. No Sheriff or anyone else had come by Sunbow while we were gone. Cicéqi and company showed up just as dinner was being served.

"Where have you pffen? I was looking for you out in the woods."

"We stayed here. Mooney was so worried about the Sheriff, we thought she might need some help. Besides, we haven't seen a Sheriff since OldCoyote was killed. He doesn't like Sheriffs, and sometimes he would let us play tricks on them. There was one I switched ears with for a week or so. That was the best. I crept up to him while he was asleep, took his off, and put mine in their place. I thought Old Coyote would die laughing when he saw me trotting back with a pair of human ears on my head, and it was worth it even though they weren't much good for anything. They didn't hear very well, and they wouldn't even turn properly. And... *uhgg-ly!*"

"I didn't know you could do that." These Pups seemed to think of me as dominant, but I didn't feel very dominant just then.

Cicéqi nipped me playfully on the cheek. "You're so much fun to tease! So serious! Of course you don't know what we can and can't do. We're not supposed to corrupt your sweet, empty little mind. Too bad your Children are so unreliable, isn't it? And to think we used to be the stable ones! You were much worse. It's a strange life, being the Rule-Breaker. Hard to tell if you're not doing your job well enough, or maybe doing it too well. And it hurts! The Laws don't like being tested."

"What hapffened to the Sheriff?"

"Oh, he went off to live by himself, away from the other humans. He didn't want them to see him, for some reason. A pity. I thought he looked much better with a nice set of coyote ears on him. He was more polite, too. I made him apologize for some things he had said, and he hardly fussed about it at all. Coyote could do anything he wanted after that, as far as our Sheriff was concerned. When he was in human form, of course. They all tended to shoot us on sight the rest of the time. Except the Sheriff. He didn't do that any more."

"So you can pffe a human too? I saw Fox that way once."

"Father, don't you listen to *anything?* None of us could ever be human, even if we wanted to. But we can put on a nice show! You could, too, if you had your memories back."

"You mean Fox was just using an illusion to look human?" The thought made me angry for some reason.

"Not at all! Let me show you. In a minute."

All the others had finished eating and were eying our bowls covetously, so Cicéqi and I got to business. Afterward I followed her behind the goat barn and she turned one of her paws into a hand. A small, perfect child's hand that even smelled human.

"Fox never smelled like that."

"Fox didn't want to. He likes his scent fine the way it is."

Cicéqi reached forward with her little hand and pulled one of my whiskers until it hurt. "This hand is as real as you are. Don't you doubt it." Then the hand was gone, and once again I didn't quite catch the change.

"I can take the shape of man or woman, child or adult—and other animals as well. I can live with them, mate with them, sometimes even be content with them for a time. And if I do mate, one or the other of us will get pregnant. Without exception—almost without exception—and certainly regardless of my wishes in the matter. That is the oldest and most powerful Magic of all, and cannot be denied. And it's true for you as well, even as you are now—no need to change form. It's a part of your nature that can never be taken away.

"I could live with the humans, and fool the humans, but still I would not be human, and my children would be only half-human. We do that from time to time, and they usually turn out quite well. Lots of coyote blood in the People! Keeps them strong, and clever. And by the way, such children always take the form of their mother at the time of conception, and the Old Magic will not allow shape-shifting while pregnant. It's for our own protection."

"Why are you telling me all this?"

"We know you better than Fox does. He doesn't realize how far you've already drifted from the old ways of thought."

"I see. I guess."

"Come. Let's go inside your 'house'. We want to sleep with you and your human friends tonight."

Mooney and I tried to teach the Pups to play checkers, and it was hopeless. They understood the rules because I did, but they couldn't keep themselves from cheating. It's hard to put up much of a game when your opponent can read your thoughts, so Mooney and I played while the others watched.

Later, Mooney and Mouse dragged a mattress into the living room and we all slept there together. All ten of us. With our bean dinner, it was a good thing the window was open.

Chapter 21

The phone rang while Mooney was driving Mouse to school, but I didn't answer it. I never answered the phone myself, but I was quite content talking with John when he was on the line. The speaker phone setting was best, but not actually necessary, and with Mooney's coaching I had learned how to dial a telephone by holding a pencil in my teeth. It was not so hard, and Mooney seemed to think it a useful skill.

"The phone rang while you were gone."

"I'm not sure I want any calls right now. They'll try again if they really need me, and I'm not expecting—"

The phone rang again while Mooney was talking, and she answered reluctantly.

"Yes.

"No, not any more. Coyote is staying with friends in Eastern Washington, near Pullman, and the other one has disappeared. I think she was hit by a car or something.

"No, I don't think she would just go feral like that. If she were alive, she'd be coming back here. She really liked it at Sunbow—ask Mr. Gunderson.

"Yes, of course you can come over. I'll be glad to help any way I can.

"Okay. That would be fine. I'll be here." Mooney put the phone down carefully and turned to me with a tight, closed expression.

"That was Sheriff Pickworth. He's taking a personal interest in this stock-killing case, and he wants to check out the Sunbow area. That man scares me. When he was pushing me into the police car during the drug raid he almost pulled my arm out of its socket—said it was an accident. He says he's already hired a couple of professional hunters, and one of them has dogs. Walker Hounds trained for cougar and bear, but he says they'll run down anything he wants them to.

"Well, I guess you'll need to be going now. Sheriff will be here right away. Be careful! And remember—don't come back until it's dark! Sorry about lunch, but I'll have a nice dinner waiting for all of you." She gave me a good-by hug then pushed me away, and I took my pack out of there.

I was going to take us all on a grand tour of the lower valley, but we were hardly out of Mooney's wood when we were spotted by a log truck—

came on us unexpectedly, in a section where the trees had been cut so recently there was no brush to hide behind. The truck actually stopped while the driver watched us scuttle off into better cover, and I heard him talking on his radio. Log trucks don't stop for anything, and it gave me a bad feeling.

Right away I led us back into Mooney's Wood. There are no roads there, and it's posted against trespassing. We didn't need a long walk anyway —might as well hang out and take it easy for the day.

We did that, and it was rather pleasant. There had been no rain that morning, but the huge trees were still dripping slowly from the night's rain and the moss we lay on was saturated, along with who knows how many feet of rotten logs beneath it. Thousands of years' worth, maybe. It was still too early in the year for mushrooms or flowers, but these woods are active all year in a cold, slow sort of way, and the moss was growing just fine. It didn't seem to mind freezing from time to time, just got back to business as soon as it thawed again.

A raven peered at us from close above, not trying to hide. I returned its gaze idly and upside down, showing a full expanse of muddy belly fur as I writhed luxuriously on the moss and hemlock needles. Lazytail lay half-asleep beside me, smelling like herself, her season, and the moss and ferns and dead leaves and beaver pond mud we had run through.

Magnificent scents! I could never tire of them.

"Hey, raven!" I called up jokingly, "Have you come to join our pffack? There's always room for one more, pffut you must pffe strong and clever to keepff upff with us, and you must learn to sing pffropfferly, like this." I began a mocking rendition of the Beatles' Hard Day's Night without using words—just howls. The others joined in with a standard howl chorus, and the raven flew away after landing a dropping almost inside my open mouth. Ravens are remarkably intelligent, with a Totem similar to me in many ways. I looked forward to meeting him someday.

As our howls died away I heard a faint sound from the west—from the way we had come after being seen by the log truck driver. It was the baying of hounds.

Lazytail and Smokey paid no attention but Princess and I jumped to our feet and listened intently. Cicéqi and the other Pups did too. That sound could mean great danger for us.

Coyotes and wolves are superior to dogs. No question about that! We have to be. We're smarter, tougher, and generally healthier when not dragged down by parasites, malnutrition, and badly-healed injuries. That said, I must admit that some dogs can outperform us in some ways. I'm a superb runner, but if I raced on a track with greyhounds I would finish last. Lazytail's jaws are strong, but there are dogs whose jaws are stronger. Hounds are bred to chase things until they become exhausted, and that's what they do.

Humans kill bears and cougars with hounds, and if those hounds were on our trail, and in good shape, one of us might die. The slowest one of us.

The slowest one would be Princess. There was nothing wrong with her that a few weeks of good food wouldn't cure, but she had only been eating well for three days. She kept up with us fine, but that didn't count. We were only fooling around, and those hounds weren't.

Princess was the first one to move, and I was right behind her—heading downstream and straight toward Sunbow. That was fine by me. It was only four miles away, and we could use it as sanctuary if we got there ahead of the hounds. I knew Mooney would protect us somehow, even if the Sheriff was still there.

Princess and I never even got close to Sunbow. Those hounds had a fresh, clear trail to follow, and they were already nearer than I had realized. And they were good.

Smokey and Lazytail left us behind, but I stayed back with Princess, and the Spirit Pups did too. Yes, I know, a regular coyote wouldn't have done that. Oh, well.

Princess tried her best but the baying grew steadily closer and more urgent, and finally there came a savage, triumphant ring to it that I had heard before: humans call it 'belling'. Those hounds knew they were almost on us.

Princess put out extra speed, and we gained on them for a time, but she couldn't keep it up. Even I was beginning to feel a trifle winded. Panicked, too—just a touch.

"Do you want to end this game yet?" Cicéqi asked. "You don't smell like you're enjoying it much." She didn't sound tired at all.

"If that's—offer of helpff—pfflease do!"

"Okay."

Cicéqi and the others turned as one, like a school of small fish, and streaked back the way we had come. Their movements were impossibly swift —like Mr. Burrey's and mine had once been—and they were out of sight in an instant.

I stopped, and Princess kept going, and I was alone. After some hesitation, I followed the Spirit Pups.

I never saw those hounds, but I heard a lot. First were the sounds made when they sighted the Pups. Proud, and frantically excited, and absolutely thoughtless of danger. Hounds will attack anything when they feel that way. In quick succession followed the sounds of a very, very short fight, a few seconds of panicked yelping, and silence. The yelps had been from the throats of hounds, and some of them had stopped suddenly, in mid-voice.

I met Cicéqi first. She was trotting back toward me with a collar around her neck that almost dragged upon the ground. It *would* have dragged if she had not been holding her head so high! That collar was so big she could have wiggled her whole body through it. Cicéqi stopped in front of me and lowered her head to slip it onto the ground at my feet. It was a radio tracking collar, and it was half-soaked in dog blood.

"That was good."

Her pale fur was groomed to perfection, without wound or stain except for a faint ring of blood on her neck which had rubbed off from the collar. She smelled like herself, except for her breath, which smelled of hound dog. All parts, not just the blood.

A moment later I had six collars in front of me—each one with a radio transmitter, and each one more or less bloody. One Pup had come back wearing two of them. The hound threat clearly was over.

Six radio collars! That must have been one valuable hound pack. So sad.

"What did you do?" Relief and pride and apprehension churned through me.

"We protected you."

"Yes, I see that, pffut what did you do with the dogs?"

"We ate them."

"Ah, yes. I see. Do you mind if I go pffack to smell for myself? We can leave the collars here for now."

"Of course, but there's nothing much left. We didn't think you liked dog, so we didn't save any." Cicéqi had that teasing look about her again, and the others did too.

Sure enough, there was nothing much left. Blood and other body fluids soaked into the moss, and the ground torn up by a violent scuffle. Nothing more.

"So you're saying you just... killed and ate them all?"

"What else should we have done? You wouldn't want us to waste all that good meat, would you?"

"Pffut, there were six dogs here, and each one four times your size! How could you do that?"

"Oh, Father, don't act so dumb. You know the answer to that!"

I shut up.

The human would be coming soon, intending to shoot whatever the hounds had not already killed. We had to prepare for that. They made a fine game of it after I explained how the man could use 'Science' to locate each collar no matter where it was hidden.

Cliff face, blackberry thicket, wedged into the back of a log truck, on top of one of Mooney's taller trees—one was even slipped over the head of a sleeping farm dog. I heard them all described in detail that evening, and they were all good. I gave mine to Wynoochee on a floating log, which was not such a bad idea either.

When I got home I smelled 'Sheriff Pickworth' all over the farm compound, and in the kitchen too. It was the same man who had spied on us just before the pot raid. I told that to Mooney, then described our dispute with the hounds.

"Stinky, do you really expect me to believe those little pups killed and ate six full-grown Walker Hounds?"

"I pffelieve it."

"Yeah, I know. I do too. Wished for magic in my life, and got my wish. Lucky me.

"Well, I guess you're better protected than we thought. Good thing. Sheriff Pickworth took plaster casts of the paw prints around Sunbow, and he says some of them match the ones by that calf kill. He wants to set up a stake-out here with the other hunter. The one who doesn't use dogs. This hunter likes to sit up in trees and wait for things to come to him."

A tree hunter! They're even worse than the ones who run hounds. If the wind is wrong you can walk right up to one without a clue. Humans call them 'snipers' when they're hunting other humans.

"Was the Sheriff mad when you told him no?"

"I didn't tell him no. I said the hunter would be welcome during the daytime, and I'd feed him lunch, too."

"Mooney!"

"Oh, Coyote, don't you fuss. You can't even *be* here in the daytime right now. It's a lot better for us to know where this guy is, and I might learn something, talking with him. Don't come close unless my bedroom light is on. You can see it from South Ridge."

"Yes, I know. Mooney, how long will this go on?"

"As long as it has to. I don't like strangers around here either, but I'm not going to let you get killed, despite what your friend Fox may say. Even 'Crazy Mooney' has her limits."

We slept all together again, except for Princess, of course, and we left before dawn with a good breakfast in our bellies. Princess was getting used to Mooney, and didn't bother to hide while her share was being brought outside. We stayed in Mooney's Wood the whole day.

I saw the hound hunter. He had no dogs with him, and I would have followed him around except that I didn't trust Smokey and Lazy to stay out of sight. I didn't trust the Pups, either.

"Can we kill him, Father? Please? Or if you like, we could just play some tricks on him."

"No!"

I thought for a minute, and changed my mind, "Well, maypffe you could follow him and scare him a little. Noises, and stuff like that. Pffut don't hurt him, and don't let yourselves pffe seen!"

That hunter was a brave man. The Pups say he located the cliff side and treetop collars, and actually recovered the bramble thicket one, but I don't think he had a very nice time of it. He left long, long before dark, and I never smelled him again. Later I heard he quit his contract that same day.

The other hunter had a much more pleasant time. Mooney told me he wandered around Sunbow for hours, checking our tracks and so forth. Finally he proclaimed that Sunbow was a favorite spot of ours (big surprise) but we probably didn't come by much in the daytime. He set up a couple of platforms anyway, sat on one for a few hours, had coffee with Mooney, and left. He would come back next day with a goat to stake out. Mooney showed me where the platform trees were.

"He really wanted to set up at night—thought it strange I wouldn't let him. But everyone knows how crazy I am. I think he'll be setting up on Weyerhaeuser land or Mr. Bell's place, so I wouldn't do much after-dark wandering. He has a night vision scope."

"Mooney, what am I supffosed to do? Just sit around in the woods all day and then come home to sleepff? I'm getting pffored!"

"I'd go with you!" said Mouse. "I'd rather be bored from doing nothing than bored from knowing nothing."

Mouse had not been in our thoughts a lot the last couple of days, what with the hunt and all. She didn't complain, or even talk as much as usual, but she was having her own problems. I kept hoping the friendly humans around her at school would help us out—talk to the School Board, or something—but nothing much was happening as far as I could tell. I thought maybe they weren't as friendly as Mouse and I had believed.

"Tomorrow is Friday. One more day till the weekend. Maypffe we can meet somewhere on Saturday. John will pffe here too."

"Yeah. That would be nice. If it's not raining too much." Mouse sounded so depressed.

"I recognize the scent of the hunter you had here today," I proclaimed, changing the subject. "He's the Elk Skull man. He's a terripffle shot." That was a lie, I knew. Lazytail and I had never given him a proper chance.

"Don't test him!" Mooney ordered sharply. "Don't try any damn fancy stuff until we get things straightened out. This type of a hunt can't last long. Soon they'll shoot a dog or two, declare victory, and quit. Make sure it's not you."

It didn't seem to me the hound dog hunter would feel like declaring victory, but I didn't say anything. My humans were gloomy enough already. Maybe the hunters really would quit before long.

Nothing bad happened on Friday. Quite the contrary! Friday, February 2, 1990 became a very special day in my life. That's the day Lazytail and I lost our virginity together.

We were in the higher, westernmost part of Mooney's Wood, near the last of the beaver ponds. The open water allowed for a view, and Sunlight too, if Sun happened to be shining, which he was. A sharp breeze from the north sent small dark-bellied clouds scudding along fast and low, almost at treetop level, and the sky above them was clear. Delightful day.

I was resting next to Lazytail—sometimes dozing, sometimes awake. Cicéqi lay by my other side, also seeming asleep or half-asleep. The others were scattered about haphazardly, but none far away.

Cicéqi spoke—softly and dreamily. "She's ready, you know."

The Spirit Pup must have slipped a few thoughts into my head with those words, because I understood instantly what she was talking about. Lazytail was not out of season at all. She was just entering the second half of her 'split-heat' or 'wolf-heat'. Funny I hadn't thought of it before, and a great joke on Mooney. Lazytail never had been ready, not even while I was gone. Now she was.

I didn't move, but my heart began to hammer. Cicéqi spoke again, this time with words alone.

"I have some advice for you. Will you take advice, or shall I save my breath?"

My mouth was dry. I licked lips and chin and nose, then answered meekly, "I would pffe very hapffy to have some advice. What can you tell me?"

"Lazytail is as horny as you are. She has been for quite a while, but her body needs to loosen up and stretch enough to hold you, and that's just not possible until the proper time. That time can be today, if you both are careful and gentle. Don't just push and bump your way in, like you've been doing so far. That's the traditional way of it, I know, but she's still not ready for that kind of treatment. You would only drive her away like you have before."

"Pffut if I don't pffush, how am I supffosed to get inside?"

"Ah, that's the secret. You don't have to. All you need to do is climb on top and get things lined up correctly. Lazytail will do the rest. And remember, don't push! At least, not at first. Let her choose the pace, and she'll allow you in a little at a time as she realizes it doesn't hurt any more."

"That's it? That's your advice?"

"That's all you get right now, and all you need. Lazytail is looking forward to this as much as you are.

"Now, about our payment..."

"Pffayment?"

"We've helped you out. Now it's time for you to do the same. A little thing, no trouble at all. We want to share this with you. We can feel you from where we are, but that's not as good. We want to be inside."

I knew what she was referring to. OldCoyote supposedly kept these creatures inside him almost all the time. We were made for each other. Supposedly.

There was only one proper answer, and my nervousness had nothing to do with it.

"Yes. Of course."

"Good. We will start now. First, you must open yourself to us. *Let me show you how...*"

I can't describe well what Cicéqi taught me to do. It was mental, and spiritual, and physical too. A sort of unfolding and dropping of barriers, but only for that which was already a part of me. I don't think I ever could have learned it on my own, but I will never forget it either.

As I held myself in that certain way I could feel the Presence of the Pups more clearly than ever before. The others were approaching slowly from all directions, and Cicéqi was already rubbing her head and shoulder against my side. Suddenly that whole part of me felt warm and wet, like I had been splashed with dishwater or blood. The feeling lasted only an instant, and when I whipped my head around to look, the fur was dry and Cicéqi was gone.

"Father, pay attention! We need our turns too!"

I complied.

The four remaining Pups came in, and something else as well, although I didn't really notice it at the time. I was rather overwhelmed, after all.

I looked around bemusedly. Just the four of us left—Lazytail, Smokey, Princess, and me. Flesh and blood, one and all. Sort of.

They were all staring at me—intently but without fear. All standing, now. I got up and sidled over to Lazytail, then slipped my muzzle under her belly to stroke it gently from beneath. She always likes that, even when she's not in heat. This time she arched her back and shuddered, then stretched herself long. I know exactly how she felt.

We traded rubs and nuzzles and licks as we had so many times before, and she held steady as I climbed on top, also as before. I think she enjoyed the feeling of my weight resting on her, front legs embracing her waist like the arms of a human. *I* certainly enjoyed it! This stage never lasted long though, because I would always be working away with my other end, and she would sit down and twist away when I began to make progress. I hadn't realized I was hurting her—thought she was just changing her mind. Again.

I took Cicéqi's advice, moved slowly and oh so carefully, slipped into the right spot with little fumbling. I was getting good at that part. I felt Lazytail shift as if to sit down and I froze, holding myself in position with the tip only barely inside her.

Lazytail was surprised, I think. It had never gone like this before. The game was still fun. She stood still at first, just like me. That was a joy in itself, standing together like that, except that it was so hard for me to keep still, especially when she began to relax and move against me ever so slightly. Just a little bit forward, my body seemed to say; she won't object. I began to tremble with the effort of holding myself back, but I did succeed, and we stayed that way for a time. Suddenly, without any warning I could detect, Lazytail began to push against me in a kind of tentative, backward stretching motion, and I felt myself sliding into her. I lost track of everything besides the sensation of that small, slow movement. Nothing else could ever be so important. When she stopped I was farther inside than I had ever been before, and she showed no signs of wanting to move away.

Sometimes parts of you seem to work without instruction from your head. I still managed to keep myself from pushing, but I had no power to stop the series of rhythmic, pleasurable contractions which began then. They weren't even in muscles I knew I possessed.

I couldn't stop myself from twitching strongly with each contraction, but that didn't seem to cause a problem. Lazytail squeezed back in response. Another stretch, and another—less time between each one—then I lost control at last and thrust inward, my hips bucking frantic-quick while Lazytail pushed eagerly back against me, taking me all the way inside. Still bucking I swelled up within her and Lazytail yelped at the strange sensation, tried to step away... and failed. *What have I done?* In panic I pulled back and Lazytail sat down... or tried to... but she couldn't do it. *We* couldn't do it.

My wolf would not be sitting down unless I did, now. Just like that we'd got ourselves 'stuck' as the humans say.

We caught our balance and pressed close again, quivering, quickly coming to terms with our sudden irrevocable intimacy. Lazytail had yelped just that one time, in surprise not in pain, and already she was squeezing me in a grip neither of us could possibly break. That grip was not painful. Far from it! I licked my nose in bemusement, and Lazytail did the same. So this was what mating was like. Not bad. Not bad at all! I got down from her back and swung around so we stood tail to tail, still attached to each other. I don't know why. We all do that. Instinct, I guess.

We stayed that way for a long time. I don't know how long. Time didn't matter. Nothing mattered except each other. Probably looked pretty boring to Smokey and Princess, or maybe not.

We stayed together for a long time, and it was good.

Different from my fantasies. Better.

Those blissful slow contractions kept on coming by themselves, mostly in synchrony with the ones I could feel from Lazytail. Kind of hypnotic, actually. I hear it's a dangerous time—enemies can sneak up on you, and even if you see them it's hard to run or fight with eight legs. I also hear that extreme fear can cause a quick loss of erection and immediate release. Makes sense.

No such problem for us. Nothing but friends around us, and nothing worth thinking about besides each other. We did it all over again a couple of hours later, but after that it was time to start back toward Sunbow.

Lazytail was in wonderful spirits—even more frolicsome than usual on the way home. So was I. She kept sneaking close to jump on top of me— sometimes to try and knock me over, sometimes to hold on and pretend I was the female and she was the male. I would hold steady for her, then sit down suddenly to make her lose balance. Several times she almost persuaded me to join her in a third mating, and finally we did, on South Ridge. Glorious view of Sunbow and Wynoochee in the northeast, Sun setting in the west. Not that I paid much attention to those things.

Chapter 22

Mooney was cross with me for being late home, but she didn't stay mad for long. She had news to tell. Or rather, she and Mouse both had news.

"Mouse, why don't you start? Tell him what happened at school today. All I know is what you said to me. I still can't believe they really got suspended! I thought that sort of thing didn't happen any more."

"Mooney! Do you want me to tell it or not?"

"Sorry. I'll shut up."

"Thank you. Well, Coyote, you know how we've been thinking our friends didn't care about us? Well, that's not true. When you were gone to Pullman, that was okay, but when I told them you wouldn't be allowed in school at all any more, they just couldn't believe it. None of the teachers had said anything. If I hadn't told them, they still wouldn't know why you weren't coming any more.

"They talked about it and talked about it, and finally, during afternoon break, David and Leroy said we needed to stage a protest."

Mouse paused for a moment, smiling. "It was a real protest, like Mooney talks about! They said I shouldn't go with them—it wouldn't be right. So I went to Mrs. Seeley's room like I was supposed to, but I listened carefully, and I heard a lot. Mr. Sawyer's office is just down the hall.

"I think there were only eight or nine of them who actually had the nerve to cut class and go. They had a 'sit-in' on the hall floor in front of the office, but it didn't last long. I don't think they even had a chance to talk. All I heard was Mr. Sawyer telling them it was totally unacceptable behavior, and every one of them was suspended for the day. He said their parents were being called to pick them up. I thought I liked Mr. Sawyer, but he didn't sound very nice just then. And he wasn't fooling, either. The kids stayed in the hallway, and I heard their parents come in one by one to pick them up. Some of them were really mad. Nothing like this has ever happened before."

Mooney spoke up suddenly, "That's the way it starts, you know. No one thinks it's important—or working, either—but it gets people to thinking. If Mr. Sawyer weren't such a nice man we could really get something going. But Mr. Sawyer isn't the problem—it's the School Board. And Mr. Hubert. He was against us even before he lost that calf."

"You know, Leroy is the pffoy I supffosedly tried to pffite. It's kind of a joke for him to get in troupffle trying to helpff me. I guess."

There was the usual conversational pause, and Mouse started to say something, but Mooney told her to hush for a minute. She was thinking.

"I've got it! We'll call in the newspaper. They love stories like this. 'Student suspended for trying to protect vicious seeing-eye dog!' No, that's no good. Better try again. We'll think of something. Couldn't hurt, anyway."

"What couldn't hurt?"

"Publicity. School Board members love it and hate it. They need to be seen doing good, kind, productive things so they can get re-elected, but they hate being criticized. We'll explain how Mouse was brought all the way from Seattle for the special learning environment at Sunbow, but it's all being spoiled because she's not allowed to take her Guide Dog to school. You don't mind, do you, Mouse? It's the first good idea I've had on this."

"No, Mooney, its all right. I know what you're trying to do. Just don't ask me to talk in front of a bunch of people, okay?"

"Okay. Good. I'll get right to work on it.

"But, totally off the subject, where are your pups, Stinky? I thought they'd be rolling on in by now, but I don't see them yet. Aren't they hungry tonight?"

"I don't know if they're hungry or not, pffut they're here already. The Pffupffs are inside me." I nosed my belly and stole a peek at Lazytail's. Maybe I had some puppies hidden in there, too.

"Inside you? Like in the old legends?"

I nodded. "Sort of."

"I don't think I want to know."

"Mooney, I didn't transform them into turds, or anything like that. We agreed we're not going to do it that way. They just—went inside. They're pffart of me now."

"Okay. If you say so. Don't mind me if I'm slow to catch on. I'm only human, after all.

"How do you take five pups inside you, anyway? They're small, but put all together they outweigh you."

"I don't know. They didn't tell me. Cicéqi says I'm not supposed to think that way."

"Well, that is our plan," Mooney concurred. "Hope it works. I guess this means I can put away the other food bowls, doesn't it? That's a relief, at least. Those pups are real gluttons. Worse than you." She tousled my head and ears for a minute, but wouldn't go for the belly rub. That was okay. My belly had already had a good workout.

"What do you think, Mouse? Should we believe this guy's story? You know how reliable his word is."

"Yes, Mooney, we can always believe him when he's being unbelievable. He's not clever enough to lie then."

"Pffut if you don't pffelieve anything I say, then I'm unpffelievapffle all the time, so you always have to pffelieve me. I think."

"See, Coyote? You're just not smart enough to handle it. Take a rest." That was from Mouse. She wasn't as submissive as she used to be.

"Now here's my news," Mooney interjected. "It's not so important as Mouse's, but I thought you'd like to hear it. The hunter was here again. You call him the 'Elk Skull Man,' but his name is Kelly Perkins. He said the other hunter quit. 'That guy's not from around here,' he said. 'What can you expect? Someone stole his damn dogs and he blames it on spirits. Let me tell you, there's no way no spirit's gonna take a radio collar and put it up top a two-hundred-foot hemlock. Not that I'm saying there ain't no such things as spirits, mind you. I seen a few things as makes you wonder, now and then. Just this winter I seen some things around my place as makes you wonder.' He stopped talking then. I think he was waiting for a little encouragement, but I wouldn't give him any. He probably wanted to talk about you."

"Aw, Mooney! I would have liked to hear what I looked like. Maypffe you can ask him tomorrow."

"Maybe, but I doubt it. I don't think I like him much. He chews tobacco and spits it all over the place."

"Yes, I know. I smelled it." He had left a fair bit around Sunbow, but none by his tree platforms. Not a dummy.

John showed up later that evening. I gave him a hero's welcome, and Lazytail joined me. Smokey was too shy, and refused to approach.

"Don't worry apffout Smokey," I said. "Mr. Pffuffey is the only human he's ever trusted right away. He'll pffe okay if you give him a little time."

Silence.

Mr. Burrey was not popular at Sunbow any more.

"Well, I like Mr. Pffurrey! It's not his fault he's pffossessed pffy an evil spffirit!" Mooney would be able to understand that. She was always making excuses for people who had problems. She even said communists were just human beings like everyone else. That's not what Mouse and I heard at school! I thought anyone who could speak kindly about communists should be able to handle a soul-devouring werewolf. I said so.

"It's not the same thing," Mooney and John replied together. Should have known.

"Okay. Forget it. Anyway, we'll pffropffapffly never hear from Mr. Pffurrey again."

The phone rang. It was Mr. Burrey. I hate coincidences.

Mooney gave him a piece of her mind, and almost hung up on him, but she didn't do that. Hanging up is not Mooney's style. She gets mad, all right, but she always lets you say your piece. Then she demolishes you. I don't talk back much.

Mooney listened, then began to look worried, even sympathetic. She excused herself to Mr. Burrey, covered the mouthpiece, and turned to the rest of us. "Now that I know about the werewolf curse, he wants to talk about it. He says it's giving him a lot more trouble this month, more than it ever has before. He says he should hardly feel it at all this early, but it's already on his mind a lot, and he's afraid he may be dangerous when the full moon comes. 'May be dangerous.' Ha!

"Pardon me, Mr. Burrey? Yes. I thought you probably heard that. Well, I guess so. Yes you can talk to Stinky, but it'll be on the speaker phone setting, so John and Mouse and I will be listening too. Okay.

"All right kid—it's for you."

"Hello, Coyote? Can you hear me?"

"Yes, Mr. Pffurrey. How are you doing? We're all fine here." I don't mind talking on the phone, but I wish I could smell the person I'm talking to. It never seems quite real to me.

"I'm fine too, I guess. For now. Listen Coyote, how much have you told them about me?"

"I told them everything I can remempffer, pffut I'm sure I missed a few things. You're not mad, are you? I thought they needed to know. Also, it was getting too confusing, and Mooney knew I was hiding too much. Don't worry. They won't hurt you or get you in troupffle."

"No, Coyote, I'm not mad. Your people really do have a right to know. If you feel you broke any promises of secrecy, please consider them forgiven. It makes things easier for me now, anyway.

"What I need to know is, what were your impressions when we did that *Neulebskar* ceremony on the Solstice? Did you feel we were doing white magic or black magic?"

"I don't know, Mr. Pffurrey. I know you're talking apffout good or evil, pffut I've run into quite a pffit of magic lately, and it didn't seem to care either way. Excepfft the *Ga`at*. That one seemed pffretty evil, I guess—pffut you wouldn't know apffout that. You were already gone pffy then. You know I'm not too clear apffout good and evil for just regular living! How can I tell apffout magic?"

I paused, then added, "So what's with the *Nolef*—with that rat sacrifice thing? It didn't seem to do much, as far as I could feel. Maypffe a little quiver of something. I don't know."

"Well, the reason is—you remember that trilobite fossil? Well, it seems to have picked up some sort of an aura. My hand tingles when I touch it, and it's hard to put down. I think it has become a talisman, but I don't know if it will help me or hurt me. What do you think?"

"Well, I... Mr. Pffurrey, I just don't know! What do you think, John? You know apffout Medicine Pffower."

"Peter, I can't help you much either. I was never trained for anything like what Coyote described to me. My people don't do sacrifices, only symbolic offerings, and that's not the same thing at all. My gut feeling is to leave the thing alone, or better yet, destroy it. But maybe I'm just prejudiced. Of course, I'm not too thrilled with Fox's plans for you either. You need help, all right, but I don't think we can give it to you. I guess you'll have to track down some of those other contacts you were telling Coyote about. Good luck!"

"Yes. Well, thanks for your help and understanding. I really do appreciate it. I'll keep you informed. And don't worry—I plan to be far away from Sunbow when the full moon comes! Thanks again. Bye."

Chapter 23

That night I heard a goat kid bleating out by Mr. Bell's place. It sounded hungry and scared. And angry. That went on for hours, and then I heard a single rifle shot. Big rifle. I knew it had to be the Elk Skull Man. Some serious yelping followed that shot, and I recognized the voice. It was Jake, and he sounded hurt, but not dying. That is, his voice didn't get weak and fade away like he was dying, but clearly he thought he was.

Everyone woke with the gunshot, and Mooney called out to me from her bedroom. "Stinky, don't you dare go outside! I don't care *who* that is — you're not going anywhere!"

"Don't worry, Mooney. I'm not going anywhere. Pffut I know who that is. It's Jake."

"Jake? Kelly Perkins shot *Jake*? Oh, boy, Mr. Bell is going to be pissed! He loves that worthless old dog. I can still hear him yelping. Wonder how bad he's hurt?"

I have excellent ears, but Mr. Bell's place is too far away to hear a regular human conversation, only yelling. Yelling is what I heard before long, and there was a lot of it. Afterward a truck started up and drove away, and the bleating went with it. Jake had already shut up. The night remained quiet after that, but we all had trouble getting back to sleep.

Next morning was crisp and cold—colder than it had been for a while. All the mud was frozen again, so it was good walking weather for the humans. I'm not sure quite how the decision was made, but somehow we slipped from breakfast preparation into preparation for a major expedition into Mooney's Wood. Mouse was coming too, and Mooney had dragged out the machete.

My feelings were distinctly mixed. I loved to share my favorite spots with the humans, but Lazytail and I had other plans in mind for the day. Keeping myself off of her during the night had been a considerable trial for me, and she was not restraining herself at all. Mooney had scolded Lazytail twice for being a tease, and I couldn't believe she hadn't caught on yet. Lazytail and I smelled like each other, but the humans missed all that.

Mooney packed a lunch, and we hiked a long way in before stopping to eat it. Afterward the humans stayed to chat and admire the forest, and

Lazytail and I arranged to get 'lost' for a time. Of course, Smokey and Princess managed to be there too. I was never alone much any more.

I heard Mooney calling while we were together, but that didn't seem nearly as important as what we were doing just then. Mooney was rather irritated when we finally got back. "I've been calling for half an hour! Where have you been?"

"Out in the forest. Sometimes we need to pffe pffy ourselves, without humans. I wouldn't leave you here." Mooney and John wouldn't admit it, but I knew they were both hopelessly lost. Without me they would have had to follow one of Fry Creek's branches back to Sunbow, but it would have been a long, wet, nasty walk for them and twice as bad for Mouse. We had come in through a maze of game paths, and I had chosen all the best, so that the machete had hardly been used at all.

"Oh, I know. I just wish you'd come when you're called. Even human children do."

I went into submissive posture. "Sorry, Mooney." I wasn't sorry, but it seemed the expedient thing to do. I don't think Mooney was fooled.

Mooney said it was time to head back for Sunbow then, but to me it felt too early for that, and I said so. "Maypffe you can tell us a story first," I suggested.

"Stinky, you know I'm not any good with stories. You tell one."

"Oh, I don't know. How apffout…"

"I'll tell a story." That was Mouse, speaking. Mooney and John and I were stunned.

"Yes, pfflease," I suggested. "I've never heard a story from you pffefore."

"Okay, I'll try. You probably won't like it though. I don't.

"Once upon a time, there was a little girl who lived with her mother in a big apartment building in Pasadena, California. The little girl had never met her father, and she didn't know who he was. Her mother would never tell her. She didn't care that much, because her mother loved her dearly, and that was enough.

"The little girl and her mother had a nice apartment and all the things they needed because the mother sold drugs for a living. She told her daughter it's a dangerous job, but the pay is good. The little girl didn't like the strange people who would come to her apartment sometimes, but there was nothing she could do about it, and it had been even worse before, when her mother was a hooker. Most of the time she didn't see the people, because she had to stay in her bedroom while they were there.

"One day the little girl heard her mother arguing with two men who had come over. That happened sometimes, and it always frightened her. This time the voices got very mean, and there were gunshots. Three fast ones, and then two slow ones. The shots were not very loud, but they were real. Guns with silencers sound like that. One of the men told the other one to cut it out, she was dead already. Then they told each other they might as well check for stuff and money.

"The little girl had a fire escape outside her bedroom window, and she knew she should go out that way, but she was afraid. She was afraid to stay, and afraid to go, so she just opened the window and waited there.

"When the two men came into the room they didn't notice her at first, but then one of them did, and he said shit, a witness. The other man was the one who had the gun. He started to point it at the little girl, but she got out through the window before he could use it.

"While the little girl was running down the fire escape, the man with the gun called down that she should run away, run away, run far, run fast; it didn't matter because he would find her no matter where she went. He would be waiting for her when she least expected it, and he would kill her. He would find her and kill her. Then he laughed and laughed, the way people sometimes do when they're on drugs.

"The little girl went to her best friend's house and borrowed some money for a bus ticket, but she didn't tell anyone where she was going, not even her friend. She went to Seattle.

"In Seattle she was lost and scared and cold, and a policeman tried to stop her and talk to her. The little girl's mother hadn't trusted policemen, and the little girl didn't either. She tried to run away, but she slipped on some ice and hit her head and died. The end."

Now, that was a story. I could understand what Mouse was saying, but how do you respond to something like that? I didn't even try. Mooney did, though.

"Is that a true story?"

"No. I just made it up. I have amnesia, so I wouldn't be able to remember something like that. Now, let's talk about something else. Please."

We talked about other things, but I don't remember what they were. That story kept worming its way through my thoughts, and it made me feel sick and angry. Not at Mouse, of course.

Mouse felt different on the walk back. Not happy, but relieved, like she had accomplished a difficult task that was very important to her. I tried to send back a feeling of pride and approval, and I think I succeeded.

Sun began to fade behind a thin, opalescent overcast during our walk home. Almost looked like snow again. I voiced my thoughts about that, and

John seemed surprised. "Don't you guys ever watch the weather reports? They've been talking about it for a couple of days now."

Mooney replied for me, "Our schedule's been all messed up. To be quite honest, I've been good and disgusted with the outside world lately, and sometimes the news is more than I can bear. Is it a big storm like last time?"

"No. We may not get any at all out here, but I think I'll move the truck down to the road tonight, just in case. It would be a very bad idea for me to miss work Monday morning."

We got back to Sunbow before dark, but that was okay. Mooney said the hunt was off for the weekend, and there are several ways to approach the house without being seen from Mr. Bell's place. She walked ahead anyway, just in case.

We had failed to encounter any Tofus on our expedition, and so were forced to feed on steaks and mashed potatoes with butter and sour cream, which John bought and cooked himself. Mooney didn't complain about the meat at all, except to criticize John for his extravagance. She ate a full meal, herself. Maybe the episode of the chickens had affected her more than we realized.

After dinner, Mooney worked up the courage to call Mr. Bell and ask him about the shot during the night. He told her Jake had been bothering the stake-out goat, and got his tail shot off. Shot clean off, on purpose. Hadn't even had to go to the vet—just slapped on a dollop of Bag Balm and wrapped it up, no problem, it would heal just fine. Most hounds had their tails docked anyhow. Still, it irritated him no end, and he sent that feller down the road. He could go shoot someone else's dog.

"So this is your 'terripffle shot,' is it? You stay away from him, Stinky. Do you hear me? If that man points his rifle at you, it won't be your tail he's aiming at!"

"Yes, Mooney.

"Mooney, there's no one else out hunting us tonight, is there?"

"No. There's only Mr. Perkins, and he's not going anywhere. He said so himself."

"Then it's safe for us to go out for a run, isn't it? We really do need the exercise. You don't mind, do you Mouse? I pffromise not to let any of us get hurt!"

Mouse nodded her head. She didn't want me to go, but I know she didn't want to seem over-dependent. Mooney and John reluctantly agreed as well.

Free! Hardly out of sight before Lazytail and I were at it again. Both of us fast and sure this time—we didn't have to be careful at all any more. The pleasure was just as intense, though. Maybe better. Afterward we raced each other north, along the river road. Lazytail and I left the others behind right away.

It's a long run to the elk skull cabin, but we were there before I realized it. You can see it from the road.

All the inside lights were off, which is pretty typical for a human house at one in the morning. Yard was lit up like a parking lot, though, and the glaring mercury lamp hurt my eyes. How I hate those things! The urge to play a trick was so strong, I think the Spirit Pups may have been messing with my head. Or maybe not. Maybe I'm the one who influences them. Whatever.

Smokey and Princess joined us as I stood there, thinking. It had to be something fast and safe. Safe for all of us. And special. A good trick has to be special.

Television gave me my idea. Horror movies often show beasties tearing through walls to get at their victims, and this place would be easy. Cedar siding is neither strong nor hard, and one can do a lot of damage with teeth and claws.

Good, wide old-growth boards, cracked and twisted from exposure to the elements—I chose a place where one corner had popped away and braced myself, ready to sink savage teeth into the soft, defenseless wood. Kelly Perkins' bedroom would be on the other side of this wall. Had to be.

Ready…

Go! I bit down hard, twisted viciously, and a paw-wide strip split free from the main board. I walked away, and the strip came with me, but it didn't come quietly. Splinter-crack, nail-shriek, gurgling, bloodthirsty growl—the board and I were not being quiet at all!

Rush back, grab again, pull away. Again. Third strip torn free, one board almost gone, time for the claws. My mouth was full of paint chips and splinters anyway. Those claws couldn't remove wood as well as my teeth, but they contributed quite adequately in their own way—sent out sinister, frantic scrabbling sounds as they skittered over the shattered remnants of siding board, ripped through the tar paper beneath, and raked across the wood strips and plaster nubbins of the room's inner wall. It was easier than I had thought it would be. Plaster chunks popped loose with each stroke, and I think with a few minutes' work I could have dug my way clear through. I didn't have minutes, though. This man was dangerous, and I needed to be out of there before he had a chance to respond.

I heard crashes from inside, and curses, and a thud that made the wall quiver beneath my claws. Finally the bedroom light came on.

Time to bid farewell. Long, low howl, hammed up Hollywood style, then words, with deliberate enhancement of my voice's natural unhuman quality, *"We have come for yoo-ooh, Kel-ly Pffer-kins! In the da-arr-ki-ness we will... wa-it."* Howl repeated, quavering and demented, then out of there, full speed. I knew the others would follow me.

Morning was Sunday, and the humans slept in, so I did too. That was fine by me. I rather prefer staying up all night and sleeping during the day. John woke me.

"Hey, Coyote! Would you and your friends like dog food for breakfast, or eggs and sausages?"

Tough decision. "Eggs and sausages, pfflease."

Mooney objected, "John, would you stop it? Sausages and eggs are too rich. They'll give them diarrhea, and they're too expensive. You're not made of money just because you have a good job."

"No, but I have enough to buy treats for my friends."

My kind of man!

The snow had finally arrived—five or six inches on the ground, and still falling heavily. Hypnotizing stuff, in the morning light. Mouse watched it through me for a time, then left to put on her heavy clothes. We furry ones ran outside straightaway.

Lazytail and I found a nice spot behind the machinery barn where we could be alone together, but Mooney must have been getting suspicious because she discovered us there shortly afterward, butt to butt.

"Coyote! What are you doing?"

Dreamily I answered, "What does it look like were doing?"

"I can see what you're doing! Stop it!"

"We can't. We're stuck." Mooney's discovery didn't seem to count as deadly danger. So far. At the moment it was more of a distraction.

Mooney was silent for a minute, then began to chuckle quietly. "My little boy is 'stuck'. Are you enjoying yourself?"

"Yes, Mooney, pffut I'd enjoy myself even more if I didn't have to keepff talking."

"Well, *excuse* me! I guess we'll just have to 'talk' later.

"I suppose you'll tell me you're just an animal, and you don't know any better."

"Yes, Mooney."

"If you're really feeling bold you'll tell me I had my chance when I sent you away to Pullman. You might even say that Lazytail doesn't care who the father is, as long as her pups are loved and cared for. There's all sorts of things you might say if you were brave enough."

"Yes, Mooney."

"Well, consider them said. Who am I to stand in the way of true love? Come on back to the house when you're done." Mooney left us, then.

This was a feeling time, not a thinking time, and I felt very, very good. No more hiding from Mooney! When we were done, Lazytail and I rushed back to her for a hug and greeting session, and everything was okay.

Mouse and I made another snow shelter, bigger and better than the last one. This snowfall was easier to pack, even though there was less of it, and Mouse was working more efficiently.

I wasn't very efficient at all, but my water bucket runs were not all that critical to the project. I think Mouse was sending me off to get me and my pack out of her way more than anything else. She could have simply used the hose. She never complained about how long it took me to dance back with my sloshing, half-empty bucket. Finally I ran off into the woods and didn't come back at all. Until lunch.

The shelter was finished then. Mouse pulled me away and around so we could admire it together from all angles.

"That's a good one, alright. You could last out a real blizzard in that."

"Yes," I agreed. "Or if the roof were lower you could use it to have pffupffies in. Excepfft that it would melt too soon."

Mouse looked at me strangely. "I thought you were supposed to dig a tunnel in a dirt bank for that, or use a hollow log or something."

"Yes, that would pffe pffetter, I guess."

Chapter 24

It was cold again by Sunday night, and the snow plow still hadn't come, but John was able to get out by following the ruts from other vehicles. He had brought chains with him. After he was gone, the phone rang. Mooney answered it.

It was Leroy's mother, and she was calling to offer help. To offer help! I couldn't believe it.

"She says her son is really upset about you being kicked out of school, and she agrees with him. She thought the whole sit-in thing was silly, but the kids, at least, are supposed to act childish. Leroy is not a troublemaker, and it really irritated her to have him treated like one."

"Yes, I know," Mouse interrupted. "That's what I was trying to tell you. Everybody's talking about it now. Even the teachers. Mostly they're on our side. Mrs. Seeley's room is next to the staff room and I can hear them through the walls sometimes. You know, I think even Mr. Sawyer is actually on our side, even though he's acting like a dork. I heard him say he was doing fine until the School Board butted in and started ordering him around. He said if they try that trick again he's going to apply for transfer to another district.

"He also said it would be nice if Mr. Burrey would come back to work. He's on emergency personal leave. Something serious, they say, but no one knows what. It was his help that got the program started, and people listen to him."

"Mouse! Why didn't you tell me this before?"

"I don't know. Sometimes I forget things. This was all stuff I heard Friday afternoon, after the sit-in."

"What else did you hear?"

"Oh, I don't know. Nothing, I guess."

"You're sure, now?"

"Yes, Mooney. I guess. I'll tell you if I think of anything else."

We slept that night, and Mouse went to school next morning with tips from Mooney on how to foment further student unrest. When Mooney got back she prepared to do the same with parents, and my pack and I went out to make ourselves invisible. As we were leaving, Mooney took out the garden hose and tried to melt away as many paw prints as possible. Especially those leading into the house.

"I'm not sure how well this is going to work, and it's going to make one hell of an ice slick, but there's not much choice about it. Hope no one comes over today."

"Me, too. Pffut we'll pffe okay out in the woods."

"Yeah, I just bet you will. Don't wear yourselves out, and try to think noble thoughts. We don't want those pups turning out like their father!"

We didn't wear ourselves out. Only a little. And I did try to think noble thoughts, except I'm still not quite sure what that means. We napped a lot between our nobility practice sessions, and made a fine day of it.

I had us at South Ridge well before dusk, and we headed down as soon as Mooney's bedroom light went on. I was curious about how the campaign had gone.

"Nothing much on the school protest front, but I heard an interesting tale from Mr. Perkins today. That man was seriously frightened, night before last. Says he was attacked by evil spirits." Mooney eyed me pointedly when she said that.

"Spffirits? I don't know anything apffout spffirits attacking Mr. Pfferkins." I held tail and ears high in a parody of innocence, so that Mooney knew I was teasing her. My voice gave a clue or two as well.

"So, you don't know anything about evil spirits, eh? Well, what *do* you know?"

"First, tell me Mr. Pfferkins' story. I want to hear apffout these 'evil spffirits'. Maypffe we need to pffut out some garlic or something, to pffrotect ourselves. Or spffinach. Evil spffirits hate spffinach. I'm sure of it."

Mooney almost laughed, but she stopped herself.

"If you're the 'evil spirit,' you're as stupid as you are disobedient. That man is not someone you should be messing with! Yesterday he put out traps and a trip-wire shotgun around his house. He even replaced the lead pellets with chopped-up silver coins. Old coins, made of real silver. No joke is worth that."

I cringed down ruefully, shocked and taken aback. Hadn't considered booby traps! I would definitely leave that place alone in the future.

"Sorry, Mooney. I never thought he would do something like that!"

"That's always your problem, Stinky. You're smart enough, but you never stop to think, most of the time. You just act.

"But enough of that—we've been through it all before. You'll be pleased to know your little performance was quite successful. Mr. Perkins said the Devil himself came for him that night, or something similar. In a malevolent, unearthly voice it demanded his soul, and with razor teeth and claws it began to tear through the wall of his house like it was so much rotten stump wood. Mr. Perkins said it would have gone right through that wall, but something stopped it in the end. He thinks it was the horseshoe he has nailed up above his bed.

"Mr. Perkins spent all day yesterday in church, and he even persuaded Reverend Moke to go to his house and bless it. He set up the traps afterward, 'just in case'. And he said he's probably going to quit the hunting contract he's working on with Sheriff Pickworth. He'll decide for sure later today."

"Hey! That's great! I didn't realize evil spffirits could be so pffersuasive. I'll have to remempffer that."

"Stinky!"

"Yes, Mooney?"

"Oh, never mind. Come on in—dinner is ready."

Rain came that night, cold rain with a little sleet. Turned the snow into slush. We all stayed home.

Tuesday we went out again all day, just to be prudent, but Mooney thought the hunt might be over. The only casualties so far had been Jake's tail, and that pack of Walker Hounds.

Mr. Bell came to visit while we were out. He told Mooney she shouldn't put herself to so much trouble trying to hide her animals from him. He said he might be a little slow, but he wasn't stupid, and no way could she keep him in the dark about something like that. Mooney says he smiled then, and told her not to worry. If her animals were calf killers he likely would have noticed it by now. As long as his herd was safe, she could count on him to back her up. He even agreed to conceal his knowledge of our presence at Sunbow—said he had already been doing that. He also mentioned that Jake's tail had got infected, and had to be trimmed off properly at the vet. He was thinking about asking Mr. Perkins to pay for it.

I guess Mr. Bell is not such a bad neighbor, all in all. And Jake, too. We certainly could have done worse.

Nothing much happened Tuesday night or Wednesday, except with Lazytail and me. We were pretty wrapped up in each other, so that all these intrigues felt somewhat unreal. I paid attention while Mooney or Mouse talked about them but when the humans were gone, all I thought about was Lazytail. I lost count of how many times we mated, but it was a lot, and we never tired of it. It was better than food.

Wednesday night was the first night of the full Moon. Only one month since Mr. Burrey and I had run together on the Palouse, but somehow that time felt far in the past, as if it were from a different life.

The night was rainy. Too cloudy to see Moon, but I knew she was up there, full and perfect. At first I kept running a paw over the top of my head and muzzle, folding the ear forward to reassure myself that it was still long enough. No problem. I was me, okay to relax, Fox's cure really had worked. I spent the night indoors, with Smokey and Lazytail and Mouse.

Next evening I learned there had been another stock killing: a mature Angus bull with his throat ripped out. That was more than a little unbelievable. Even a cougar would have trouble doing that, assuming it had the nerve to try. People do exaggerate, though. The farmer said he had killed the bugger; shot it while it was feeding, just before dawn. It had been a huge dog or wolf cross or something like that—too big for any full-blooded wolf that might have got loose. Dead, anyway. Gut shot real bad, blood everywhere, heavy blood trail into the woods. Never did find the body.

"That sounds like something Mr. Pffurrey might do, excepfft he tries to pffe a lot more careful, and he never kills stock. Also, he pffromised he would pffe far away right now." Mooney had just given me her report, and it had been pretty favorable except for that little bombshell. Kelly Perkins had definitely quit the hunt, the campaign to reinstate me at school was developing nicely, and Mooney had just found a land survey company that was willing to get the logging permit process started without any money up front.

"Well, I hope it wasn't Mr. Burrey, and I hope the critter was really killed. Otherwise they'll hire another bunch of hunters and start all over again."

"Would you like me to go over that way tonight? I can smell things out and tell you for sure what's going on. Don't worry, I'll be careful."

"No. You might leave paw prints, or a scent trail that can be traced back this way. Much better for you to stay home again tonight. I know, you've napped a lot today and you're not tired, but I don't want to be taking any chances we don't have to. You can go play with Lazytail out behind the barn, if you like. I won't bother you there."

Mooney actually winked at me then. Fickle creatures, these humans. Lazytail, too. She seemed to be losing interest in the mating game, and I knew what that meant—another night or two of fun, and then a year of celibacy. Oh, well. It had been wonderful while it lasted.

No sense wasting an opportunity, though. We had already eaten dinner. "Uh, thanks, Mooney. I think we'll go pfflay right now."

Moon rose while Lazytail and I were together. I could see her this time through a break in the clouds, and spared a few thoughts to wonder what would happen if the werewolf transformation occurred right then. I might still be susceptible, after all. Mr. Burrey had said the first night didn't have to trigger a change, but if the curse was active there would *always* be a transformation on the second night.

Nothing magical happened, though. Only the sharing-magic we had found in each other.

Chapter 25

Mr. Burrey came to us late that night, in wolf form. Strolled in through the dog door like he had every right. I awoke from the noise of the door swinging, but by then he was already standing over me, jaws positioned conveniently above my throat. Not threatening, just there. The trilobite fossil hung from his neck by a strip of leather, and there was something about that stone—something that caught my eye, and held it.

"Hello, Coyote. So nice to see you again. You're feeling healthful and strong, I trust?" He was speaking magically, like Fox and the Spirit Pups did, and like I could not. Lazytail and Smokey had awakened with me, of course, and had hackles up at maximum, fear-scent starting to fill the room. Me, too. Mouse stayed unmoving under the covers, but I knew she was awake as well. None of us made any noise. That never occurred to us.

"So, Coyote. You don't smell very sleepy. How about if we go for a walk together. Or a run. I think I could use the exercise, and there's a farmer I'd like to visit. I have some unfinished business I'd like to complete with him. And with you."

I remained lying the way I was, eyes still fixed on the trilobite fossil. Mr. Burrey had said it had become a talisman. No question about that! I could feel the Power in it. But what did it *do?* Very carefully I answered, "You know I can't give you much of a workout any more. Nothing can run like you."

"Nothing? Oh, I don't think so. You have some new friends now. They could give me a very fine workout indeed, I expect. If they get the chance. Come now: let us walk together." It was an order, not a request.

Mr. Burrey backed away from me and I got up very carefully, slinking down the hallway and out the dog door with the werewolf close behind. I was trembling violently and my legs were weak. When we were well away from the door, I heard it open twice more. Lazytail and Smokey were following us at a distance—Princess too, no doubt.

"Go where you like—I have no preference for now."

I had no preference either, so we just strolled down our driveway and onward along the center of West Wynoochee Road. I waited for him to do the talking, and he took his time about it. When he finally spoke it was with an elaborately casual voice—pretending to banter, but knowing he failed.

Taking pleasure in that failure. "I've learned a lot about my condition over the last few days. Or rather I should say, Mr. Burrey has learned a lot about our condition. I'm afraid I had to get rather firm with him about it."

My fear-scent had been fading with the walk, and the shivering had almost stopped, but both came back again, stronger than ever. How could I have missed it? This was not Mr. Burrey! Not speaking, anyway. The spirit had finally possessed him completely, and it was speaking to me directly.

"Is Mr. Pffurrey still alive?" I hated to ask, hated to initiate anything at all, but it seemed the thing wanted some sort of conversation from me, and I really did care about that man.

The wolf laughed, then. It should have been a pleasant sound, but it did not please me. Nothing should make a sound quite like that. Not humans, and certainly not wolves. "Of course he's alive. He would be useless to me otherwise. He's hardly even damaged. Just a little... diminished. Nothing he couldn't recover from in time. However, I am growing rather tired of this 'Mr. Burrey'. He has always been something of a disappointment, and I think I can do better. I spoke to you about it just a month ago."

"Uh, I'm sorry, pffut I don't remempffer ever spffeaking with you pffefore. I...

"You remember! I was inside you then, and I wanted to abandon the human. You... wouldn't *let* me." I really didn't like the way he said that last bit. For a moment I felt a touch of—something—that made the *Ga`at* seem homey by comparison.

"I was only trying to save his life," I ventured back oh-so-softly. Even that was too great a liberty.

"His life was not yours to save! It is mine!" The words were spoken fiercely, possessively. I stopped walking and threw myself down into submission position. Not that it made much difference what position I was in. He could demolish me regardless, and I had a growing conviction that he was just playing with me, that I would be dead or worse before dawn.

"I'm sorry, Sir. Should I call you 'Sir'?" I was fawning for all I was worth, and it seemed to please him.

"You could call me 'Lykos,' but I'm growing tired of that name, too. I think I prefer the name... 'Coyote'." I would not have thought it possible to feel greater fear, but I did, for a moment. Then it was gone. My terror didn't fade, it was taken from me, leaving me numb and confused. Nothing had changed, I was still in deadly danger, it just didn't seem to matter any more.

The wolf laughed again. "Most excellent! It's been a month since I tasted emotions like those. You're definitely worth the trouble. Now, I think —"

He never finished that sentence because we were both distracted by the sound of paws and claws approaching at high speed. It's a sound that cannot be ignored. Death may come that way. This time the sound brought Lazytail and Smokey, and Princess too. Black lips curled back in silent snarls, eyes staring white-rimmed in terrified bravery—they thought they were coming to my defense, but what they were doing was useless. Worse than useless.

I didn't need to think. Body already knew what to do, and acted. I leapt up and threw myself in front of Lazytail to block her approach, and I tried to stop the others as well.

My move was not the expected one, and it broke their rush—drove them all aside in confusion. I should have been helping them! They could smell how I felt. Why wouldn't I fight?

The werewolf was not idle. He stepped around me like I was a tree stump—moving almost languidly by his posture, but so fast he caught Lazytail while she was still off-balance.

A push to the shoulder and he had her down, teeth pinning her throat just as I had been pinned when he first met me. He hadn't even bitten her. Lazytail held still, just as I had that other time, and it worked for her as well. For the moment. I feared she had no 'use' for him except as food.

My terror was still gone, leaving me with a strange ragged clarity of mind. I had Power too, and I needed to use it this moment. *Now*. Before I lost my chance.

I summoned the Spirit Pups, or perhaps they summoned themselves. They were already with me, after all, sharing my thoughts and life. First hint of a call and they were all around me, solid and menacing as bears. Bear-sized, too. As one, they left me to attack—faster than I had ever seen them move before.

There was no real fight then. Fast as they were, it was still not fast enough for surprise. A flurry of action too rapid to follow, some crashing in the roadside brush, and then near-silence... only a few twig snaps heading off south and west. Soon those sounds were gone too, and we were alone. Just me and Lazytail.

Lazytail stood up shakily as I walked over to her. She was dazed and frightened, but unhurt. Smokey and Princess crept back while we were comforting each other, and joined with us. After a time my fear came back to me, and I was actually glad to have it. The effect might have been permanent, for all I knew, and I didn't want any part of me taken away, no matter how unpleasant or inconvenient it might be at times.

We were still not far from home, and I headed us back that way, still on the main road. This didn't seem like a good night for wandering.

It wasn't.

I almost made it back to Sunbow—was already on our drive—when he struck. No warning at all; didn't even hear him coming, just a massive shock to my leg and flip through the air in cruel, deliberate duplication of that first attack near Mr. Burrey's smokehouse. Tooth for tooth, motion for motion he matched it. Arrogant bastard. As if I needed proof of what he could do.

He held me a long time before speaking, long enough for me to feel the pain fully, and to fully grasp my position. I was helpless. This creature had defeated me; he could do anything he wished to me, and he did not wish me good things.

"I think it's time for us to review your lessons, little dog. Your progress so far has not pleased me. But before we start, a new lesson—a lesson about power: there is other magic in this World besides your Indian magic, your 'Medicine Power'. Stronger magic. You will learn to know it well."

Even magically, he couldn't talk well with my throat in his jaws, so before he spoke he had lifted his head up and away, causing the trilobite talisman to dangle before my eyes. It was mesmerizing—made me want to lift my head and touch it with my nose—but I didn't dare move. The wolf-creature noticed my stare, though.

"You like my new toy? You should. You helped to make it. Delightful irony, isn't it? Your own actions helped create the instrument of your defeat. Such a wonderful World we have been given! You and I will help make it even more wonderful. But enough talking. After tonight we won't need to bother with it any more. Why don't you just rest a bit, now? Your leg won't hurt so much that way. Probably you hardly feel it at all any more. In fact, I expect you can hardly feel anything, any more. Or move, either. Isn't that right, little doggie?"

He was right. I heard every word, but they sort of slid by me without sticking, like that time Dr. Benton gave me the ketamine shot. One big difference, though; that drug had made me lose interest in everything, but the magic stone made me lose interest in everything but itself. I stared fixedly—following its movements as the wolf slipped it off to lie on the wet gravel beside my head. Nothing else mattered.

I felt a touch on my thigh. The wounded one, of course. It was being licked. Not tenderly, as with care and cleaning, but more as I would lick the wounds on a kill before ripping them wider to begin feeding.

Thoughts came to me from inside myself. Not important, of course. Nothing was important.

Listen carefully, Brother: I will not be able to repeat this. The demon thinks it has beaten us, but we have a trick or two left, maybe. Be ready! That talisman of his has confused our Children and the others, so that they can't perceive where he is. That's how he escaped from them, and that's why no one is here now to help us. Watch carefully—soon will come a time when the talisman spell weakens. Destroy it then! Crush it with your teeth—do anything you can. Its magic will fail if the damage is great enough. I'll see to it that you get your chance. Good luck!

And… whatever happens next, know that I am proud of you. I have always been proud of you.

Teeth, then. Teeth inside me. The wolf-thing was settling its jaws precisely back into the wounds it had just made—easing in and then grinding down to the bone—clamping there like the pincers of an ant. It should have been agonizing, but it wasn't. Everything was numb and unreal. Everything except the trilobite talisman.

It was done, or nearly done, and I made no defense. I didn't even care at first when the struggle began inside me.

It was a thing of emotions. Emotions coming from within me, but not mine. Puzzlement first, then irritation, then anger. Anger more powerful than I had ever felt before.

I began to feel pain, again. It was not my own pain, but it might as well have been. It came from my belly, like a cramp—same place everything else was coming from. The pain was real. It mattered. I curled into myself and whimpered, forgetting the talisman.

Now I felt my *own* pain. My very own. It had been with me all along. A wolf had hold of my leg, and it hurt!

I could think again, sort of. There was something I needed to do about the talisman. I needed to… needed to bite it.

That was stupid! The thing was made of rock. Hard rock. I would break my teeth.

The pain was getting worse—that other pain from inside me. I felt panic, and despair. And triumph.

Mooney says I tend to act first and think later. She is right. I unclenched myself, scrabbled for the talisman with eyes closed, found it in an instant with the help of my whiskers, and took it into my mouth. It felt good there. Soothing. Satisfying, like food. I pushed it back with my tongue, back between the bone-breaker teeth. The strong ones. I bit down.

I bit down with all of my strength, knowing it would hurt, but trying not to think about it.

It hurt. Doing something deliberate like that is much worse than having things done to you. Your body feels betrayed, and lets you know all about it. The pain that consumed my jaws was truly worse than anything I had known before. I felt the two teeth shatter, felt the fragments tear and twist out sideways through the gums. I gasped, and retched, and spat out tooth chips and stone chips and blood.

Things happened very quickly then, and I missed a lot. All I could think about was my poor mouth. And my teeth! I loved those teeth.

Lazy and the others were there first—attacking the wolf from three sides. It released me to defend itself but it was slow. Dazed. It gave a token snap or two then tried to run away, and Lazy's teeth sliced deeply at least once before they all disappeared from view.

The turmoil in my belly pulled away from me somehow, and the feelings from it became less personal, but they didn't change much otherwise. The feeling of triumph was gone, but all the others were still there. A desperate struggle was going on right beside me, but it was a spirit struggle. I couldn't see a thing, and I didn't know how to help.

"Back away, Coyote!" It was Fox, and he had the Spirit Pups with him. I could feel the Presence of other beings too, but I couldn't see them. They formed a circle around me.

"Move! Now!"

I backed away—backed past Fox and the Pups, past the circle entirely. I was ignored.

The others closed in on the place where I had been, terrible in their wrath. Earth and Air sang with their power, and then they were gone.

They were all gone, everyone, and I was alone with my mangled mouth and leg. Had I done the right thing? Someone would come back to tell me soon, I hoped.

Lazytail came back first, with Smokey and Princess close behind her. There was blood scent on their muzzles, but they were unhurt. The blood was Mr. Burrey's.

Lazy wanted to tend my wounds, and I let her. Soon I would get up and continue toward Sunbow. Soon.

Fox came back. He looked tired and lost. "We won." He spoke slowly and almost doubtfully, as if he didn't quite believe his own words. "The demon is destroyed. It was a demon, you know. Not Lykos. I should take comfort in that."

"What is wrong, then?" I wanted to say, but I didn't even try. The pain in my mouth was too great. Fox noticed right away.

"I can help *you*, at least." He joined Lazytail in licking the thigh wounds. She had never met Fox, but she moved over respectfully as if she had always known him. How do they do that? Maybe someday I'll learn the trick too.

I felt a lethargy come over me, and I didn't fight it. If Fox was going to help me with his Medicine Power, he could do it any way he liked. I slept.

I woke a bit later, just a little while I'm sure, and I was cured. I knew what to expect, but so lovely to feel that it was true! So lovely. No pain, no weakness, and I wasn't even very tired. I ran my tongue over teeth as smooth and slick as ice cubes, and nuzzled a thigh as strong and handsome as it had ever been. "Thank you, Fox, Pffrother. Thank you very much."

"You're welcome. This is what friends and allies are for. I just wish I could do the same for your other self."

"OldCoyoteSpffirit? Pffut he's just a spffirit, isn't he? He's dead already! What could he do to get himself hurt more than that? What hapffened to him?"

"Don't you know? He's the one who saved you just now. OldCoyote is the hero who sacrificed himself to give us this victory."

This wasn't the OldCoyoteSpirit I thought I knew.

"A hero?"

"Don't be so judgmental! OldCoyote was a lot more than you realized. Such a loss. Such a great loss."

"Pffut what did he do? Was that OldCoyote I felt inside? I remember now. He talked to me. He said he was pffroud of me."

"Yes. The demon used that amulet to mislead the rest of us, but OldCoyote was already with you. He slipped in with the Spirit Pups that first day you mated with Lazytail, but you were unaware of him and so the demon, too, was unaware. OldCoyote had no Power to use in your defense, but he still had his guile. When the demon began to leave its old body OldCoyote placed himself in its path, and shaped himself to seem like a part of you. The demon was fooled, and entered him instead. Good for you, but not good for OldCoyote. Or for Lykos. Your Children are holding them together for now, but the damage is too great. We can't even separate them."

"What do you mean? Was his spffirit destroyed, or wasn't it? I thought you said a spffirit can heal itself."

"It can in a living body, sometimes. Even there it may still go mad or die. In the Spirit World it is much harder. Our spirits are created from life, and only when living can they change or grow. Or heal. OldCoyoteSpirit and LykosSpirit have no self-awareness left at all. If placed with a living host like you or me, they would be overwhelmed and absorbed. Best to do that anyway, though. At least we can save some of the habits and memories. You were closest to OldCoyote, so you should be the host. You'll receive the residue from LykosSpirit too, of course. Honor them both!"

"Fox—how can you stand it? Do you do things like this a lot?"

"No, Coyote, we don't. OldCoyote and I have dealt with more new ideas during this little life of yours than in the previous thousand years.

Enjoy yourself: you're at the center of it all now, and we're all watching you. You've always craved that sort of attention. May it bring you happiness."

"I already had hapffiness. What I crave now is to pffe left alone."

"Ah, Little Brother—you know you don't really mean that. Come. Let us do what we can for my oldest and best friend. I can't bear to lose him completely, even if it's just a certain twist of the ears or joke from you now and then. This way—it's easier if you stand in the exact spot where they entered into the Spirit World."

I hadn't realized Fox was so sentimental. I owed him so much— promised rashly what I thought he wanted. "I'll pffe Coyote for you! Tell me what he was like, and I'll pffe that way. I can't have changed that much."

Fox licked my cheek affectionately. "What you just said is 'OldCoyote' all over. You don't have to *try* to be like him. Just be yourself! But come. We must act now, or lose even more of what once was."

I positioned myself exactly where I had been when I destroyed the talisman, except that Fox didn't make me lie down again. He said standing was fine. Bloody fragments of stone and teeth still lay on the gravel just beneath my nose. I ran tongue again over the new, perfect ones Fox had made for me, and worried. The World is such an unstable place! Possible and impossible are not such easy concepts at all.

"Fox, why can't you just pffut OldCoyote into a new body without any spffirit in it? Then he could maypffe heal and grow pffack the way he was."

"I can't do that, Coyote."

"Why?"

"You don't know what you're saying. What's left of him isn't really a whole, complete spirit at all—just tatters. Not strong enough. Even if I could find a body without a spirit already in it, the body would die."

"Why?"

"Because a body cannot live if the spirit cannot help it. The heart would stop, and so would the breathing. Other parts would fail too."

"Why?"

"I don't know, they just do. Bodies always need to have a spirit with them, even before they're born. That's just the way it is."

"Where do the spffirits come from? Are they reincarnated?"

"Sometimes. In a way, that's what we did with you. Mostly they just seem to form out of nothing—new spirits that have never existed before. Or maybe the spirit-seeds come from somewhere else. It's one of the mysteries we lower-plane creatures don't understand very well."

"So what apffout the really little ones? There has to pffe a time pffefore they get their spffirits. What keepffs them alive then?"

"Oh, I don't know, Coyote. Why do you keep...

"No, wait a minute. That's it! Yes! The very youngest ones are not so dependent. We'll put them both into a new puppy—one so new it has no spirit yet. We'll *make* a puppy, just for them! Put OldCoyote and Lykos together in a living body with no distractions, and let them sort it out themselves." Fox's weariness had left him. He danced over to me, and nudged me with his shoulder.

"Step aside, Brother. You can relax for a bit while we make our preparations. I should speak with Wolf, first. That part will be tricky, and we can't do it without his help. Her help. She'll need to be female for this." Fox closed his eyes and took on that thoughtful look he had when he was speaking without words, and then his Presence was... gone. Fox still breathed—I could see the rise and fall of his chest—but I felt no life from him at all. Weird feeling!

Fox remained that way for several minutes, then abruptly roused himself. He turned to me and beamed triumphantly. No shortage of Presence now!

"Excellent, excellent! She has agreed, and she'll be here shortly. I was worried she might refuse to participate wholeheartedly in a project that benefits OldCoyote, but she says she'll do it for Lykos' sake, and she doesn't mind changing right now. She says it was about time anyway. That just leaves the Spirit Pups and Lazytail. Shouldn't be any problem there! But we'll let Wolf talk to Lazytail about her part in things."

Lazytail and the others had been standing by somewhat awkwardly through all this. They could tell that things were finally going well, but the details were beyond them. Of course, that pretty much summed it up for me, too. I wandered over and started a play fight to keep us occupied.

Lazytail had me pinned down by the throat when Wolf appeared. I think it pleased her to see that.

Formidable creature! Wolf was the size of a small horse. She glowed faintly, you could see through her just a little, and she was beautiful. I scrambled up to stand facing her, ears and tail down respectfully.

She growled "So you're the new, improved Coyote. I see you've started your career in true character by stealing one of my people and getting her pregnant. It appears you haven't betrayed her yet, though. She still seems to like you."

Wolf paused, staring down at me with cold eldritch eyes. "Well? What do you have to say for yourself?"

"Uh, greetings. Wel-welcome to my home. Thank you for coming to helpff us, Sir... ah... Wolf. What should I call you?"

"'Wolf' will be fine." She seemed to relax a little at my words. I had said the right things, so far, but the less said, the better. I waited.

At last she snorted softly and told me "Good. Humble silence becomes you, Coyote. You ought to practice the art more often. Let our Brother Fox claim the glory tonight! Gallantly he has led us to our greatest spirit-victory in long ages. Certainly our costliest! But that was not enough for him. Now he aspires to reverse even those grave losses! He says I'm to help save Lykos and Coyote through some new style of sex-magic that has never been tried before. That's a glorious plan—if he succeeds." She turned to Fox and asked him, "Don't you ever get tired?"

Fox laughed, "Not tonight! You know what's needed, Wolf. I thought it more fitting that you explain."

"Yes, I agree." She turned to Lazytail. "You are already pregnant, as I mentioned a moment ago. Most thoroughly pregnant! You have only four, but they've been quite well attended to. The pups are nothing, yet, but already they have spirits of their own. They should not be harmed, and we will not harm them, but Fox wishes to help you make one more. It will nurture his friend OldCoyote, and my friend Lykos. If Luck favors us, the pup may even be born alive.

"Fox feels he can do this, but it will require great Power. Fox and his... *friends*... the ones who serve Coyote... will make the Medicine using Male Power from Coyote and Female Power from you and me. You are not strong enough to do this by yourself, but I will be with you.

"This is a great honor we offer you! Step forward if you wish to accept."

Lazytail stepped forward. I think she understood every word. Magic, again. She touched noses with the phantom wolf and... it was gone. I still can't quite remember if it blinked out like a light bulb, or was drawn into her somehow like smoke into a vacuum cleaner, or something else. There was no doubt about what had happened, though. My Lazytail was now sharing her body with Wolf. Daunting thought!

I walked over to touch noses for reassurance. She smelled the same. I continued with the greeting ritual, even though we had been playing together just minutes before.

"Yes, Coyote. I'm still me. And I'm not planning to bite you." She spoke by Medicine Power, just like all the others. I didn't know whether to be happy or outraged. I had never been able to share words with her before.

I took my nose back to her front end. "Is it really you? Just you?"

"Yes, Coyote. Mostly. Wolf is lending me her Power, but she's trying not to overwhelm me with it. I won't be able to talk like this after she leaves. But I really *am* me! I'm ready when you are." She pushed her body close beside mine, and nuzzled my ear tenderly.

"Ready for what?"

"Why, ready to make another puppy! Weren't you listening? Come on now, Fox says time is important."

"You mean Fox wants us to mate again? Right here? Right now? In front of everybody?"

"Yes. And you need to put some real feeling into it. Fox says that makes all the difference. Now, come along this way. You know where we're supposed to stand. Let's show Wolf what we can do!"

We put real feeling into it, oh yes we did! Fox and Wolf and the Pups played us outrageously, possessing our poor bodies and remaking our innards gleefully who-knows-how, but at the time I was hardly in a condition to think about it. No words I try can describe to you the joy of what we felt together! Dawn was in the sky before we finished, and given a choice at that moment I would have died willingly, if that were the price to do it again. I felt dazed, and exalted, and exhausted.

I was not alone. My Spirit Pups were back with me, and Fox, Princess and Stormy and... *Lazytail*. Ah, Lazytail!

Fox was breathing heavily, and his eyes were shining, and he burned with triumph and elation. I could actually feel it on my face, like the warmth from a fire. "We did it! The pup is alive and strong. It will be long before we know if what we did was the right thing, but I have a good feeling about it. At one point I could distinctly feel higher-plane intervention. I was counting on that. Without help we're not really capable of completing a task like the one we started here last night, but I know about Coyote's special status, and I was hoping we would not be allowed to fail."

Fox turned to me, suddenly serious. "Never count on that help, Coyote! They don't like it when you become dependent or complacent. A charmed life is not all you might wish it to be, and with *two* Coyotes alive in the World, they may decide one of you is no longer needed.

"But enough gloom! We've won two great victories, and it's time to celebrate! Coyote will be our host. Wolf—will you stay long enough to celebrate with us? With all of us? I have it on reliable authority there are at least five chickens left in Coyote's freezer. At *least* five."

Lazytail answered, "Yes, of course Wolf will stay! She wants... she wants to inspect Coyote's home and mother. She says I always need to keep a careful eye on Coyote and on his... on his *family*. She'll be leaving some of herself behind, to make sure I'm properly taken care of."

We found Mooney in the yard by her van. She was dressed for heavy-brush hiking, and she had her shotgun under one arm.

"Mooney! What's wrong?" Lazytail and I ran toward her anxiously, leaving the others behind. Mooney jumped and almost lost her balance. She set the gun down carefully, and knelt down to crush me in her arms. "Coyote! Oh, Coyote... you're alive! And Lazytail! I was going over to Mr. Bell's to ask if he and Jake could help me look for you." She had to stop then, because her throat wouldn't work any more. She hadn't even noticed the others yet.

I wiggled free, and my wolf and I writhed yip-snuffling around her, pushing and rubbing in frantic greeting joy, but she quickly us. Stopped me, anyway. "Please, Coyote. Go to Mouse now. She needs you more than I do. I'll stay here with Lazytail."

"Okay, pffut look pffehind you. There's someone else you might like to meet. He's a friend of John's. His name is Fox."

Mouse was on the bed, covers over her head. I'm not sure she had moved from it since we left her there. She smelled of despair. Animals in traps smell like that.

"Mouse?" I nuzzled her hand, but she jerked it away. "Mouse, I'm sorry. I had to go last night. I had to! If I tried to fight here in the house, we would all have pffeen killed. All of us, even you and Mooney. Don't you understand?"

Mouse pushed the covers back and answered me in a raw voice, "Oh, I understand, Coyote. I understand that I failed you, just like I failed my mother. All I could think of was saving myself, but I don't deserve to live. I should have died myself. Go away. I can't stand feeling you here with me."

I backed away a little, but I didn't leave. "Mouse, I was very pffroud of you last night. You did exactly the right thing. You held so still he thought you were still asleepff, so he didn't pffother you. And you did the right thing for your mother! Your mother didn't want to die—pffut so much worse if you had died too! I *know* she'd say that if she were here with us! I think she'd also tell you it's time to stopff pffretending you forgot her. If I were dead, I wouldn't like that."

Mouse was quiet for a long time. "You think she wouldn't like that? I never thought of it that way! I don't want to disappoint her any more than I have already. Do you really think I should tell them?"

"Yes, Mouse."

"Okay, I will. But not now.

"Is there really nothing I could have done? I couldn't think of anything, even if I was brave enough to try. I should have at least screamed. Oh, Coyote! How did you get away? I knew he was going to kill you; I could feel it. But we'll be ready for him tonight! Mooney has the shotgun, and we can board up all the doors and windows, and wait for him right here. Just tell me what to do, and I'll do it. I'm not going to be a coward any more. I—"

"Mouse, it's okay. He's dead. Some of my magical friends came to helpff me, and they destroyed him, or at least the spffirit that was making him act wrong. I think Mr. Pffurrey may be dead, too." I had forgotten to ask Lazytail! So strange, that I could do that now.

"Come on. Out of pffed, you. You can feel guilty and worthless some other time."

"Okay. But I need to go pee. And wash up. You can go back outside until I'm ready."

"Why, thank-you-so-much," I said, and slipped my muzzle between the sheets to press a cold wet nose against her side. She screamed and I left, then, ears perked and head high. My friend might be dead but that didn't mean I had to drag myself around! It's possible to grieve and joke at the same time, and his soul had been saved, at the very least. I walked straight over to ask about him.

"Lazytail, did you kill Mr. Pffurrey last night?"

"No. We tried to, but he didn't stay slow like he was at first. He got away, finally, but we did hurt him." Mooney was looking very funny. Absolutely flabbergasted. We both ignored her for the moment, while Fox and the Pups sat innocently silent. Smokey looked lost and confused, as usual, and Princess was no longer in evidence.

"I should pffropffapffly track him down, now. He'll pffe awfully cold if he turns pffack in a pfflace where he doesn't have clothes ready. And humans can hardly even walk without shoes."

"Whatever. He tried to kill you. I no longer have any concern for his welfare." Lazytail had rather liked Mr. Burrey as a human, but I could understand her feelings. I didn't like being attacked, either. After a moment Lazytail amended, "Wolf says I shouldn't blame Mr. Burrey for what he did last night. She says the demon might have defeated even her, if she had faced it alone. Come on. Let's look for him together. We can have our victory celebration when we get back."

I turned to Mooney. "We have two very famous guests today. The cute, short, soft-furred one really is Fox. The real one. Our other guest is Wolf. She is visiting Lazytail in spffirit. That's why she can talk today. If you have any spffecial questions you've pffeen wanting to ask Lazytail, this is a good day to ask them. Also, they've invited themselves over for a victory dinner, for saving me. They would like chicken and dumpffflings. *All* of the chickens. Okay?"

"Uh, yeah. Sure. Whatever you say, dear. You're certain you didn't invite anyone else? No humans, I suppose?"

"No. Pffut don't forget the Pffupffs and me. We're famous too! And Smokey and Pffrincess. They're not famous pffut they like chicken as much as I do. Have I forgotten anyone?"

"I doubt it, but I'm sure I'll hear about it if you have. Chicken and dumplings, eh? With this many hungry mouths it may turn out to be dumplings and chicken. Whatever."

Mooney turned toward the house. "Here, let me get that backpack I made for you. I have sweatpants and a sweatshirt and a jacket that should fit, and rags and a roll of duct tape for his feet. That should get a naked human home well enough. I sure wouldn't mind if you could spare the time to explain what's happening, but if Mr. Burrey is out there freezing his buns off, I can understand why you're in a hurry. Good luck! Oh, and a jar of peanut butter. Good trail food. I'll loosen the lid for you, so try to keep it right side up. I don't want peanut oil dripping out on the clothes."

The trail was blood, with very little rain during the night, so it was an easy one to follow. Mr. Burrey's blood led us all the way back to where he had parked his van. The van was still there, and so was Mr. Burrey. He was lying under it, and he was still a wolf. Still a wolf, and in full daylight! Moon had set long ago. He looked a mess. Wet, bloody, tired, scared. And confused —I'll bet he was! By unspoken agreement my companions hung back to let me approach first.

"Mr. Pffurrey? Mr. Pffurrey—we're not here to attack you. Can I come closer?"

Peter Burrey nodded, silently, then he did something I had never seen him do before. He dragged himself out from beneath the van and rolled over, exposing his belly in submission to me. He'd done that often enough in play but that doesn't count. This was the real thing.

I walked up and took his neck between my jaws, squeezed it gently a couple of times, then snuffled over to investigate the wounds. There were a lot of them, and they needed stitches. A few deep ones too, maybe. "Can you walk? Would you like some pffeanut pffutter?"

He took the peanut butter. All of it. Then he stood, achingly, and looked for a puddle to drink from. He hadn't said a word. After he was done drinking I asked again, "Can you walk a long way, or should I get Mooney to come here for you?"

Mr. Burrey didn't try to speak with words. He just lifted his head to look me in the eyes, nodded, and started slowly back the way we had come.

The trip home was long, and rather boring. Mr. Burrey and I did it all at a walk, while the others ranged widely, sweeping in to check on us from time to time. It was early afternoon when we arrived back at Sunbow.

I wanted to present us all favorably to Mooney so I stopped us at Fry Creek before we reached the house. "Alright, everyone in excepfft Mr. Pffurrey! That means you, too, Mr. Fox-god, you. No victory dinner if you're muddy! I guarantee you won't pffe apffle to dodge that rule!"

Mr. Burrey watched silently from the bank but when we were mostly done he edged over and began to enter, slowly. His skin twitched strongly as the glass-clear water slipped into one wound after another, and curls of mud and blood twisted away from him down current. He dipped his head and shoulders under the water, shook himself, and repeated the process until his fur and wounds were as clean as they would get.

The aroma of stewed chicken and vegetables was everywhere, even by the streamside. Maddening. The source of it all was one of Mooney's commune pots—almost big enough to hold me, and with its own separate propane burner. Mooney was not taking chances about running out of food. We all hurried over that way as soon as we were finished washing.

Mouse was waiting there with Mooney—hadn't gone to school at all, obviously. If this didn't count as an excuse to stay home, I don't know what would.

"Well, you folks certainly took your time! Aren't you hungry? It's a good thing I didn't put in the dumplings yet. I'll do that now. Is Mr. Burrey okay?" Mooney had not yet noticed the new wolf in our midst.

"Mr. Pffurrey is hurt, pffut he can walk. He'll need to see a doctor today."

"That's not surprising. But no—that spell is supposed to heal his wounds, isn't it? Whatever. I assume you got him to his van and he was able to drive it safely."

"No. He was already pffy his van, pffut he couldn't drive it. We pffrought him here."

"Here? That had to have been a long walk! You should have got me to go pick him up! Where is—oh, dear! Is that you, Peter?" Mooney had never seen Mr. Burrey as a wolf before. She had only heard my stories. She believed them, certainly, but that's not the same thing.

"Why are you still a wolf? It's not full moon any more! Not until tonight. I thought this thing didn't happen in the daytime. Stinky! What's going on? Please? I am totally, totally lost this time."

"I'll tell you if you keepff working on the dumpfflings. None of us has eaten since yesterday. Excepfft Mr. Pffurrey. He ate the pffeanut pffutter."

I told of the night's events, taking my time and doing it properly, as John would have. I had Fox and Wolf in my audience, after all! And the Spirit Pups.

Mooney seemed rather upset that Mr. Burrey had not turned back into a human at dawn. Considering all that had happened, I thought just getting us all out of it alive was accomplishment enough. I said so.

"Yes, Stinky, I understand all that. But don't you realize, this change could be permanent! The demon is destroyed, Lykos almost destroyed. Who's going to change him back? Maybe it will fade in a day or so, when the moon is less full."

"Yes, Mooney."

"You don't really care, do you?"

"Well, no. Not really. I don't think Mr. Burrey does either. He once told me the only thing that pffothered him apffout the werewolf curse was losing control and killing things he shouldn't. I think that was from the demon. Now it's gone."

"But Mr. Burrey is human!"

"Yes, Mooney."

"Oh, forget it. Whatever else is going on, he needs medical help. At least the vet is cheaper. We'll go there as soon as dinner is finished. Oh! I forgot. Peter can't have dinner! His stomach needs to be empty for the anesthesia. You understand about that, don't you Peter? You might throw up and inhale it into your lungs."

Mr. Burrey nodded his head sadly.

"You won't be offended if I take you to the vet, will you? I'm sure your regular doctor would have a hard time with this." She smiled for a moment, then realized what she was doing and made herself stop.

Mr. Burrey shook his head, then tried to speak.

"Ooo-kkayy.

"Ffve-ta oo-kkay.

"Fvet oo-kkay."

"Yes, Peter, I understand you fine. Coyote used to talk like that when he was first learning. You're saying the vet is okay as far as you're concerned. But I'll have to ignore you now for a little while. This dinner serving is going to take my full attention. I'll be back with you as soon as I can."

The victory dinner was not formal. Most of us were talking animals, but we didn't talk much. There were no speeches, yet it still felt as if the meal had great symbolic importance. On a hunch, I nosed a small dab of meat and gravy from my bowl into a clean one and presented it to Mr. Burrey. He looked me in the eyes for a moment, then lowered his head to lick the bowl empty. Fox and the others seemed pleased, and Mooney pretended not to notice.

Mooney wanted me to go along and help her with Mr. Burrey, but she also wanted me to stay behind to keep the others in line. Lazytail solved the problem for her.

"I'll keep them out of trouble." Still so strange to hear words like that coming out of her! "Wolf needs to rest, as we all do, but she can do that best in her own body. She says she was pleased by her visit here, and she won't treat Coyote and his... won't treat Coyote like an enemy until he deserves it again. She says Coyote was a most excellent lover! Oops. Sorry. Wolf says not a lover. She would never say a thing like that. No way. She says partner. Useful and politely acknowledged magical colleague, that is. Wolf also says I should let my season pass without mating any more, no matter what Coyote or I want. It might disturb the work that was done last night. She is leaving me now. Farewell."

"Lazytail?"

She rushed over to reassure me she was alright, but she didn't use any more words. Just my Lazytail again. Who needs words, anyway?

We left with Fox joking that he shouldn't be any trouble at all, with Mouse and Lazytail to keep him in line. He was planning to nap anyway — might even stay for a visit. The Spirit Pups had disappeared right after they finished eating.

We met Dr. Benton during business hours this time. He seemed much happier to see us that way.

"More wounds, eh? And another 'shepherd cross' dog. I should have known. What a monster he is! Friendly, though. Yes, Furry Feet — don't take it that way. I know you're not really a monster. I just meant you're very big and impressive... there, that's better. These wounds are remarkably clean! Did you wash them?" Dr. Benton was talking to Mr. Burrey as he said that, but Mooney answered him.

"No, but Furry Feet did. All my dogs have to jump in the creek and rinse themselves off before they get fed. I don't like muddy dogs in the house."

"Really! I wish my other patients were so cooperative. I'm rather surprised he went in with wounds like these. It must have hurt! I'll get right to work on this new 'dog' of yours as soon as I finish my last appointment — another half-hour or so. Even with antibiotics there may be quite a bit of drainage, and possible delayed healing. Nothing serious, though."

"I can't tell how glad I am to hear that, Doctor. I feel partly responsible for Furry Feet getting bit up like this. Not that he didn't have it coming to him."

"Excuse me?"

"Hmm? Oh, sorry about that, Dr. Benton. I didn't really mean what I just said. No dog deserves this." Mooney didn't apologize to Furry Feet, though.

"By the way, Dr. Benton—Furry Feet can be a little hard to handle sometimes, but he'll be fine if Sin-Ka-Lip stays with him. Is that permitted?"

"Of course! We're always glad to see Sin-Ka-Lip!" Dr. Benton turned away from Mr. Burrey and gave me the attention I deserved. I wasn't supposed to get an exam, but I could tell Dr. Benton was doing that as we greeted each other. Most humans don't peel your eyelids and lips back, sniff your ears, and palpate your genitals while saying hello.

"Speaking of wounds, I can't help but remark on Sin-Ka-Lip, here. He's in superb shape, as usual. Not only has the fur grown back flawlessly, but I can't even find any scars. That fight injury he had last fall was not trivial! There should be major, permanent scars from it, but I can't see or feel a thing. Like it never happened."

"Oh, it's nothing, Doctor. Just more of that hippie metaphysical stuff. 'Magic,' if you will. Nothing you could believe in, and it doesn't always work. Today we want Science. Do it your way—use all the drugs and machines you like. I'm tired of magic."

"Uh, yes. If that's the way you want it. But I really would be happy to listen to some of your 'hippie metaphysical stuff' some time. Normally I change the subject when I hear that line, but it's different with you. I'll try not to pry, but please let me know if you change your mind."

"Okay. I just might, sometime, but not today. I still need to sort out some things for myself! But I want you to know that I really appreciate your patience in all this, and I do trust you. It's just that the situation is very complicated, and it's hard to understand any of it without knowing all of it. I don't suppose that helps much, does it?"

"No, not really, but thanks anyway. Now—I need to get myself moving again or I won't have time to work on Furry Feet before my staff goes home. I won't need your help today like I did last time, but you'll be able to visit first thing tomorrow morning, and I'll call right away if there are any problems. Bye."

I tried to nap during Mr. Burrey's surgery, but I couldn't do it with so many powerful noises and smells around me. I gave up after a time and pressed myself against the chain link kennel door, tensely waiting. We had adjoining kennels so I had a good view as two small women staggered in with Mr. Burrey on a stretcher, set him down heavily, gently rolled him off onto a pad of folded blankets, and propped him into a comfortable position with chest down and neck extended. Mr. Burrey was a patchwork of square shaved areas—one for each wound. Half his fur was missing, and he looked horrible. Still, the wounds were cleaned and stitched, and to me they looked like they would heal well. And the spring shedding time was not far off. Soon we would all be looking horrible.

As they attended to him the humans joked about Furry Feet in a crude but friendly way, remarking that with all those bite wounds in the hindquarters it was a wonder he hadn't lost his nuts in the fight. The doctor should have castrated him when he had the chance—keep him out of trouble like this in the future. I wondered if they had said the same things about me when I was asleep, but then remembered it had been late at night. Just Mooney and the vet.

The clinic was beginning to close down, and night had already fallen when Sheriff Pickworth arrived. The dogs were quiet at that moment, so I heard every word. He was coming for us.

My belly clenched in panic, and the fur of my neck rose tingling up on end. How had he known we were here? Mooney had trusted Dr. Benton! I unfastened the kennel latch and prepared to... I couldn't think of what to do. It would be hard enough to get myself out, and Mr. Burrey was only just beginning to stir. I waited.

Sheriff Pickworth was arguing at the reception desk, really acting like a jerk. That seemed strange. Police didn't argue much in the movies. Not with regular people, at least. Regular people just did as they were told. Maybe the clinic humans had not called him after all.

Dr. Benton came back to where we were. He smelled seriously upset. "I hate lying like that," he muttered to himself. "Hate it." He was going to say more, but I spoke instead. "Dr. Pffenson, we can't go with Sheriff Pffickworth. He'll kill us! Can't you helpff us? Pfflease? Mooney said you're our friend!"

Dr. Benton's expression changed from anger and indecision to surprise, but his scent didn't change—wasn't time for it, even if it was going to. Scents are not always that specific, anyway.

Dr. Benton looked at me then. Really saw me.

"So you talk, too. I should have known. I suppose you're expecting me to go through the whole 'reality shock' routine now? Sorry, but we don't have the time. I was planning to get you out of here anyway."

Now it was my turn to be astonished. I had never thought he would react like that!

"Nancy is stalling the Sheriff right now. When we get you two out of the building she'll let him do a search. I don't suppose your friend can walk yet, but let's try anyway. He's a real pain on the stretcher, and I don't want to involve the others any more than necessary. Does he talk too?"

"Yes. A little. Pffut he understands just fine. Mr. Pfur... Furry Feet! Wake upff! We have to go now."

Mr. Burrey opened his eyes, but he didn't move. He had a confused, frightened look—hardly awake at all. Like he was in a nightmare with his eyes open.

"Here, let me help. I hate to disturb them when they're coming out like this, but..." Dr. Benton stopped talking as he opened the kennel door and began to massage Mr. Burrey's head, neck, and back. Then he rolled him from side to side, letting him fall over gently each time. Two or three rolls and he was trying to stand up, which the doctor let him do. He took a leash down from the wall, slipped it on, pulled gently. Mr. Burrey sat down.

"Excuse me, Dr. Pffenson. He doesn't know apffout leashes. Let me try."

The back door was quite close to us, and the staff parking area just beyond that. Together we half-carried, half-pushed Mr. Burrey out of the building and into Dr. Benton's car. It was a station wagon with the back seat folded down, and the two of us fit there quite comfortably. All the windows were at my level, so I even had a view.

At first the roads were unfamiliar to me, but then we came to country I knew. Up ahead we would cross Wynoochee on the Geissler Road bridge— already an easy lope home.

Dr. Benton spoke after we crossed the bridge. "I know I'm not very experienced with this sort of thing, but I think we're being followed. There are headlights behind us that don't come closer even when I slow down, and now they've crossed the bridge, too. Most of the traffic goes the other way. I've never been there before, but I know Ms. Sklarsen's place is not much farther up this road. Maybe it would be better if you walked the rest of the way. If that's Sheriff Pickworth behind us, I can keep driving and lure him away from you. I don't suppose you know how he found out you were at my clinic?"

"No, I don't. That sounds like a good pfflan, though! Stopff where you like and we'll get out as quickly as we can. We know the way from here. When things quiet down I'll ask Mooney to invite you for a visit. Thank you very much for your helpff!"

Dr. Benton found a nice gravel shoulder with good cover nearby, crunched quickly to a stop, then flung his door open to run back and help me with mine. I pushed Mr. Burrey from the inside and we had him spilled out in seconds, with Dr. Benton and his car gone scant seconds after that. He had to keep moving so our follower wouldn't become suspicious. My job was to get Mr. Burrey and myself out of sight before he caught up with us.

We succeeded with half of that. Our follower did turn out to be Sheriff Pickworth, and we were out of view when he reached the turnout, but he was suspicious after all, and pulled to a stop no more than thirty feet from where Mr. Burrey and I lay hidden.

I could have disappeared quietly enough, but not with Mr. Burrey. He was still barely able to stand. All we could do was stay where we were, hoping the human would lose interest and drive on.

He didn't drive on. I guess police are taught to carefully search places where suspicious vehicles pull over for no apparent reason. Sheriff Pickworth knew this game better than we did. He rolled slowly forward along the entire length of the turnout, finally coming to a stop beside a big wooden power and phone line pole. He flicked his car searchlight through the bushes a few times, then got out and began to search the ground and the roadside brush more carefully—going over it inch by inch with the help of a hand flashlight. He didn't look in a hurry to leave, and if he kept up like that he would certainly find us. We weren't all that well hidden.

Why is it the folks I *really* don't want to deal with are the ones who most wish to find me? It seemed a little outside help would be exceedingly useful right then. If I could get it. Desperately I attempted to summon the Spirit Pups, calling to them without words.

"Children! My children! Come to me! I need protection!"

They came to me. How they do it I still don't know, but there they were.

"Shall we kill him?" "We won't eat him if you don't want us to!" "Okay, okay—we won't kill him." "We can do a trick!" "Not a gentle one, please." "We don't like him either."

I wanted to tell them to hush, but they were using the mind-speech so I guess it didn't matter. Sheriff Pickworth certainly didn't seem to notice.

"I was thinking of a trick. Not a gentle one. How about the Iron Song? It would be good practice."

"Oh, yes!" "The Iron Song!" "Do you just want to destroy his gun, or the car, too?" "It will be hard to save the car, but we can try." "Should we try?"

"No, don't bother. He can walk home. And anyway, I want to see what happens."

They began to sing softly—all of them—and they forgot to block me out. Or maybe they didn't forget. I heard it all clearly and it was a simple thing, really. So simple. I joined in.

Sheriff Pickworth heard us, or at least that part which could be heard with the ears. He drew his gun and turned his flashlight outward, toward the salmonberry thicket which concealed us. We finished our song and waited, all of us pressed low into the leaves and earth.

"Who's there? Come on out where I can see you!" He was trying to sound confident and authoritative, and not succeeding very well. Suddenly he realized how exposed he was, and moved back toward his car. If one of us had been a human with a gun, he would have been a very easy target.

He called out again from behind the car, then opened his door to get at something inside. The door hinges squealed loudly when he did that.

Just then the engine stopped. He had left it idling, headlights on, as police officers are fond of doing, and it stopped by itself—ran raggedly for a short time and then shuddered into silence. The headlights were still on.

Sheriff Pickworth turned the key to restart his engine but the starter made a horrible squealing sound that hurt my ears, and then no sound at all. The headlights went off shortly after that. It was a very nice car, with one of those computers that control everything, and I guess it didn't like our Song. Computers have little bits of iron here and there, I am told. Transformer cores and circuit breaker actuators were a couple that John mentioned. Little bits of iron rust faster than big bits.

The car was already dead, but Sheriff Pickworth didn't realize it yet. He was having trouble with his gun. It was getting hot—too hot to hold—and finally he was forced to set it down. He did that almost silently. Just a few muttered swear words. Muttered with great feeling.

He had stepped away from the car and was fiddling with his belt radio when the flashlight failed. Must have been a steel spring or switch part in there somewhere. Sheriff Pickworth was in the dark, and the radio didn't seem to be working either. I left our hiding spot to stalk him, or rather stroll up to him in the darkness. With the clouds blocking starlight, he couldn't see a thing. When I was very close, I spoke to him.

"Well, hello, mortal! Are your toys giving you troupffle? That's very sad. You humans do depffend on them these days!"

"Who's there? Show yourself!" He reached into his pocket and pulled out what looked like a knife, but he couldn't get it open.

"I am Coyote, and I'm standing right in front of you. I can see you just fine. Too pffad you can't see me. Don't worry. Moon will rise soon, and you'll pffe apffle to see again. Pffut you'll have light much sooner than that! Can you feel it yet? I can."

The human had been staring toward me as I spoke—unable to see me but knowing where I stood from the sound of my voice. Now he began to shift uneasily from foot to foot, then suddenly sat down on the gravel and began to untie his shoes, fingers jerking in his haste. I smelled scorched leather and rubber.

Some shoes have steel inserts in front to protect the toes when things are dropped on them. Sheriff Pickworth was wearing a pair like that, or rather, just taking one off. I wondered if he was wearing anything else with steel in it, but I was distracted by the car. It wasn't actually glowing yet, but the heat was intense, even from where I stood, and it stank of melting plastic. More than just melting. There was smoke coming out too.

Television cars always explode violently at the slightest pretext. John and Mooney hate that, and say it rarely happens in real life, but it looked to me like this car might be an exception. I wasn't sure whether the gas tank or the cartridges in Sheriff Pickworth's gun would go first, but I was far too close in any case. I began to back away.

"You know, Sheriff Pffickworth, that car of yours is getting very hot. It might even expfflode. I wouldn't pffe standing so close to it if I were you."

I could tell he was frightened and confused, but this new danger was one any human could comprehend, and it took precedence over all others. The man took my advice and stood up hastily, then began to step gingerly down the road, away from my voice and toward civilization. His gait was painful and uncertain, but quite rapid for a stocking-footed human in the dark. He kept his shoulders hunched as if expecting me to pull him down and slay him at any moment. Stupid human! Only cats play with their food in that way.

Okay, so coyotes do that too, sometimes. Never mind.

Sheriff Pickworth still carried his smoldering shoes in one hand as he stumbled away. They might even do him some good, once all the iron was rusted away. The toe parts would be burned off, but for a long walk home they were far better than nothing. I stood looking after him, gloating, and then remembered my own danger. Or rather—Mr. Burrey's danger. I could run away easily enough, but Mr. Burrey could not. I ran back to our hiding place and tried to nudge him to his feet.

"Come on, Children! You can helpff me with this too, can't you?"

"No! It's forbidden!" they all laughed, rushing eagerly to my aid. We had him safely clear in plenty of time—took him down the road toward Sunbow and away from Sheriff Pickworth.

When I thought we had gone far enough, I stopped to watch the car. Smoke was already bursting out from every opening, and soon flames became visible too.

The car exploded, then. Really, truly exploded, like a bomb. I guess that's what happens when gasoline ignites after boiling until the steel gas tank ruptures from the pressure. I had heard about shock waves, but never felt one before. It hit me in the chest like a surf breaker, and almost knocked me over. And my poor ears! Eyes were shot too. That car had been parked next to a wooden power line pole, and the fireball was considerably taller than the pole.

I stood there, stunned. Even the Spirit Pups were impressed. *"Your 'Science' really is rather powerful Medicine!"* Cicéqi remarked. *"We'll have to be careful with it."* If she had been using words I would not have heard her, my ears were ringing so.

The fire had not gone out with the explosion. Bits of burning car were everywhere, and the power pole was burning too. That pole carried high voltage and phone lines for the whole valley, and it looked like we might be losing them again. Oh, well. That's what repair crews are for.

I stood there in the center of the road, admiring the destruction I had wrought, and when my vision had cleared a bit I saw Sheriff Pickworth staring back at us. He was well beyond the car, and had not been hurt by the explosion, but he was still close enough to see us clearly with all the new firelight around.

Mr. Burrey was not ready for it, but I hustled him into the heavy brush anyway. No way was I going to leave him near that road! Fortunately the movement helped his drugs to wear off a little more, and he was able to keep on walking until we made it home. John's truck was in the yard when we got there, but the house was mostly dark—just some candlelight coming from the kitchen window. Power really had failed, but the weekend had begun. It was Friday night.

I told them all about Sheriff Pickworth and his car. Everything. They were suitably impressed, especially the humans. "Don't you *ever* try stuff like that near Sunbow!" Mooney said. "I'd like to tell you not to try stuff like that at all, but it is the purpose of your quest, after all. But maybe you could wait a bit. Until you're older."

"And wiser, too. Presumably," laughed John. "Don't hold your breath, Mooney."

Chapter 26

The power came on later that night, but failed again before morning. I could tell by the sounds the refrigerator made and then failed to make. No matter. We were getting used to power failures, and there was the generator if we really wanted electricity. I was planning to do as little as possible on Saturday, and that's what I did. It's what we all did.

The Saturday morning newspaper had a front-page story about a county employee who had collided at high speed with a power pole on West Wynoochee Road, totally destroying his car but emerging miraculously unhurt. The incident was under investigation, but the reporter's usually reliable sources suggested that extreme negligence and possible intoxication were involved. There had not even been any skid marks. The name of the employee was being withheld pending an official report. The article also mentioned that power restoration might be delayed slightly, due to the surprisingly poor condition of the neighboring poles. The steel insulator supports and cross-member bolts were rusted so badly they had come apart. It was almost as if the wires had fallen down from their own weight, rather than being knocked down. The damaged pole was badly charred, but still standing.

We had a call from the Sheriff's Department that afternoon. It was not Sheriff Pickworth, but someone higher up—some sort of commissioner. Mooney said the man was very polite and apologetic, and wanted to know what sort of dealings she had had with Pickworth. I was standing beside Mooney as she heard all this, and she was clearly at a loss about how to answer best. Finally she settled on aggressiveness.

"I'm afraid Sheriff Pickworth and I have never gotten along very well. I think he was responsible for getting me falsely arrested when those marijuana plants were found out this way a year or so ago. Since then he watches a lot, like he's just waiting for me to do something illegal. I've been so worried I sent my dog to friends in Pullman when those stock killings started a month or so ago. I was afraid he might get blamed for it, and nothing I could do to prove he's not a killer.

"A pack? No, that's silly. I don't have any dogs here at all right now, much less a pack. Just ask my neighbor, Robert Bell. If I had a pack of vicious dogs he'd be the first to know about it. He runs a dairy, and there are calves around there all the time.

"You already have? Good. See what I mean?

"Yes, I know. Don't mention it. Is there anything else I can help you with? I really do want to get this resolved so I can bring my own dog back. I don't have a man here most of the time and—well, you know how it is. I'm only a woman and I just don't feel *safe* out here by myself without any protection.

"Oh, come now! Did he really say that? I hate to sound disrespectful, but that's not the sort of thing I'd expect to hear from a County Sheriff! We may be rural out here, but we're at least moderately civilized. Magic is for children, not police officers.

"Yes, that's what I think too. In a way I'm sorry for him—but he's caused me so much distress—all I really want is for him to go away, or at least leave me alone.

"Press charges? Of course not! Like a lot of people out here, I'm a bit of a hermit. I try not to bother my neighbors, and hope they won't bother me. It sounds like you have the situation well under control. I'll testify if I have to, but please don't call me in unless you really need me.

"Good! I'm so glad to hear that! I can't tell you how much of a relief it is. I think I'll probably bring Sin-Ka-Lip back this weekend.

"Okay. And please let me know if I can be of any further help. Bye."

Mooney put the phone down, and turned to us exultantly. "Sheriff Pickworth has been suspended! I'm not the only one he's been treating like dirt, and it looks like his bosses are trying to get rid of him. That car accident last night was just what they needed, but he's making it even easier. He's claiming the car was destroyed by magic, and I'm responsible. He says I'm a witch, and I have several familiars who help me, and other humans as well. You're one of them, John, and also Dr. Benton. He thinks Mouse has been badly corrupted, but might be saved if she's removed from my influence right away. What do you think, Mouse? Is it too late for you?"

"You bet!" she laughed. "I like your familiars too!" She was holding Fox in her lap at that moment, stroking him like a cat. He seemed to be enjoying it. The Spirit Pups were not with us.

"Okay, but never say you weren't warned! I'm such a bad influence—just like old times. Eh, John?"

John put on his pompous tone for her. "I wasn't with you in the 'old times,' but I can believe you were as bad an influence then as you are presently. Coyote chose well when he called you to him. So guide him now. What will be the next step on his path?"

"Oh, stop it, John! You know I don't have a clue. That man told me the hunt is definitely over, anyway. It's been a great embarrassment to the department—all that fuss and expense, and the culprit was finally shot by a farmer! Oh, by the way, I keep forgetting to ask. Was that you, Peter?"

Mr. Burrey nodded his head, "K-yess. Waas mee. Ssorrr-ee." A simple nod would have done the trick, but I guess he wanted to practice his talking. His skill was developing rapidly now that he was a wolf full-time.

Mr. Burrey opened his mouth to speak again. "Kk-y-ot ssk-ool nnoww. Goo-da ti-i-ma. Mm-onday."

"Monday? The day after tomorrow? I don't think we're ready for that yet. I wanted to write some threatening letters to the Board, then put together a proper rally with cameras, and reporters, and all that good stuff. If we goad them hard enough someone's sure to say something stupid. Then we can *really* nail 'em!"

"Nn-o. Nno fi-i-ght. Ffet-terr ee-see wway firrs-ta. Go ssk-ool Mm-onday. Nno ffuss."

"Do you really think so? That would put quite a burden on Stinky and Mouse! They'd have to defy the school authorities without actually triggering a police call, and without much support from the rest of us."

"Goo-da trry. Lless thrr-eta. Lless aann-gerr. Go aa-lone."

"Okay. You're the one with the psychology degree. If Mouse and Sin-Ka-Lip are willing, we'll do it your way. What do you think, kids?"

Wonderful. Just my favorite thing to do. March up to a pack of hostile humans and pretend to be nice. Even harder for Mouse! Still... that was nothing compared with fighting demons...

"Yes, Mooney. I won't pffite or growl no matter what. Mouse has the hard pffart, anyway. Can you do it, Soft-Heart?"

Since the *Neulebskar* incident I had been using that nickname for her sometimes. She didn't seem to mind.

"I can do anything!" she answered fiercely. "There's nothing can scare me more than I've been scared already. I won't let it!"

Her answer pleased and surprised us all, although I couldn't help but feel it was a little grandiose. There are some things that will always be able to 'scare' me. Or worse. And Mouse too, I doubt not.

I didn't express those opinions, of course. That would have been a put-down of the worst sort. We had both come so far in the last year—maybe we could do this, too.

"Okay, then it's settled," Mooney proclaimed. "I'll take you both to school just like we used to, and we'll see what happens. We can brush out Stinky's fur and put on a new bandana so he looks as silly and innocent as possible, and he can work on his tail wagging and panting. You can do it, Snookums! Just pretend you're a Labrador!"

Yeah, right. "Fox, are you sure this was really all my idea? Pffefore I made myself forget apffout it? I must have pffeen crazy!"

"Yes, Coyote. You've always been crazy. It's a tough job, but someone's got to do it. The extra benefits are nice, though." He slithered around in Mouse's lap so her hand would be stroking his milk-pale belly fur. It's very convenient to be soft and small and cute. I was jealous.

Chapter 27

Sunday was dedicated to more resting and socialization, and then it was Monday. John was gone, and we were on the road to school. Time to assert ourselves. It was a rather new feeling for me, actually. Most everything before had been reaction—danger came to me and I tried to get out any way I could. Usually with help. This was something we didn't *have* to do. If I told Mooney and Mouse I had lost my nerve, we would simply turn around and drive home. I could hang out with Lazytail and Smokey and the Pups, and Mr. Burrey and Princess too. I'd be so busy keeping them out of trouble, I wouldn't care about school any more. Fox was keeping an eye on them now.

"Mooney, what are we going to do with all of ourselves? Smokey doesn't have any sense at all apffout what is really dangerous and what is just scary, and Lazytail wasn't any pffetter, pffefore Wolf joined with her. And the Pffupffs are always looking for troupffle, and Pffrincess only knows how to pffe wild. How do we keepff track of them all?"

"Don't ask me! You're the one who brought them all home. Mostly against my wishes. And you're the one who got Lazytail pregnant, *completely* against my wishes! She'll double your problems in another couple of months. Much more than double, if OldCoyote is born alive! You should be damned grateful if they let you back in school again. That leaves your home problems for me to handle, if I can. I think I'll save all the bad ones for you. 'Just wait till your father gets home,' I'll tell them. You need to savor your new role, after all."

Comforting words! Maybe it was time to change the subject. "I was kind of pffusy on Friday. Did you hear anything new from the timpffer survey compffany? John told me you were really worried apffout how to get things started, since you don't have two pffennies to rupff together."

"John said that, did he? How tactful of him! Well, you'll both be pleased to know that I did get a call from them on Friday. They said they had some very interesting news to tell me and wanted me to come over right away, but I said that was impossible; it would have to wait until Monday. I'll be going there this morning if our plan for you and Mouse is successful."

Our plan was successful. Ridiculously easy, in fact. My absence had given every student and teacher plenty of time to come to a decision, and

Mouse's distress and poor performance without me had made that decision easy for anyone with a heart and a brain. In the end there was no contest at all. Only Mrs. Stanford resisted. And Mr. Hubert.

We were standing in line when Mrs. Stanford arrived to lead away her class. Admirers surrounded us, petting me and welcoming us both, but Mouse and I stood at attention, faultlessly disciplined except that Mouse had her hand on my neck instead of the harness grip. Mooney was far away, in the parking lot, trying to keep herself inconspicuous.

"Children! Get away from that creature! It's not supposed to be here! Mouse—what in the world are you doing? This is a dangerous animal, and it has been specifically forbidden to come onto the school grounds! Remove it immediately!"

Mouse and I cowered for a moment, then forced ourselves to stand up straight. Mouse swallowed several times, then spoke in a hesitant, cracking voice, "I'm sorry, Mrs. Stanford, but I can't send him away. I need him here. I can't do it all without him. I just can't!" Her voice changed from cracking to crying at the end of that, but she stood firm. She stank of fear, but she held firm.

I could tell even Mrs. Stanford was moved, but she hardened herself. "I'm sorry, Mouse—rules are rules, and I can't allow you into my classroom this way. You have to understand."

Mouse braced herself to argue further, but she didn't have to. Mrs. Seeley just happened to be standing close by, and spoke on our behalf. "I'll take them. Mouse and Coyote can help me with kindergarten story time, and then we can try out a new math tutorial package I just received. They'll be no trouble at all."

"I'll thank you to mind your own business, Mrs. Seeley. Mouse is my responsibility in the mornings!"

"Not if you won't let her in your classroom! Come on this way, you two. I need to get you settled in before the others arrive." Mrs. Seeley turned on her heel and began to walk briskly toward the main building and her own room. She didn't look back, so she didn't see Mrs. Stanford standing there with her mouth open like a fish mouth. I saw, and so did every single kid standing there. I had never heard them so silent! Mouse still had her hand on my back, so I got us into motion right away. We left Mrs. Stanford behind without a word.

We had a visit from the principal during story time, as Mrs. Seeley no doubt knew we would. She had stationed me within a cluster of exceedingly small humans, and two of them were actually sitting on me. They all petted and poked and tickled, and I wasn't quite sure how I felt about such liberties, but I knew my assigned role: tail moving, tongue moving, ears up—kiss those babies 'til they giggle! That's what Mr. Sawyer found when he entered the room.

Mr. Sawyer didn't speak when he came in—merely leaned against the back wall and observed until the period was over and the kids were sent back to their regular room. He didn't say a word to spoil the story. It was a legend about how Coyote killed a monster that had swallowed everyone (Animal People) in the world, and how he cut the belly open to free the Animal People, then cut the carcass into pieces and used those pieces to create the People (Human Beings). It was a version I had not heard before and I listened carefully, wondering which parts were true.

Mr. Sawyer hadn't come to learn about the Coyote of legend, though. He was there to talk about me. "Mrs. Stanford is very upset with you," he told Mrs. Seeley. "She says you flouted the Schedule Plan, and undermined her authority in front of the entire student body. She also says you undermined *my* authority by letting this animal come onto the school grounds after I said it could not be allowed here. This is not the sort of behavior I would expect from either of you. Is it true?"

What a silly thing to say. Of course it was true! He was looking straight at me as he said it. Still, he didn't really smell that hostile. I took a chance and approached him obsequiously, licking his hands and trying to be friends. He responded favorably, getting down on his knees and rubbing my ears with both hands.

"Oh, don't bother to explain yourself, Jeanette. I know what's going on, and I support you on it. The School Board had no right to make me get rid of Coyote against my judgment like that, and I've had plenty of time to see the results of that action. I will not make the same mistake again. Coyote stays, even if they fire me for it. The School Board can hire and fire me, but while I'm here I'm in charge, and I will not compromise myself further.

"Excuse me, Mouse. Normally I don't discuss subjects like this in front of students, but this seems like a special case. I know Ms. Sklarsen has been working to get a rally together, and I don't want to be on opposite sides from her. Perhaps you can serve as our mediator?"

"Yes, Mr. Sawyer. I'll tell her everything you said. I know there won't be any problem. All we want is for me to be able to use my Guide Dog like anyone else who needs one."

"Yes, I know. I can't believe I went along with them as far as I did. We'll have an emergency staff meeting about it today during lunch period."

Mouse and I heard the whole meeting. It took place in the break room right next door. Mouse had brought a lunch for us, and Mrs. Seeley let us stay in her room to eat it. With my official status still in question, that solved a lot of problems.

The details are not important. They bored me even then, except for the part where Mr. Hubert spoke. Mr. Hubert was the only School Board member attending. It was an emergency meeting, after all. Rather surprising that even he was able to make it, but his opinions were not surprising. He was pissed.

Mr. Hubert berated the principal right there in front of his teachers, which is not a smart thing to do to someone who is well liked. Voices rose in Mr. Sawyer's defense, and it became hard for me to sort out who was saying what. I did hear Mr. Hubert mention something about immediate termination, and then I distinctly heard Mrs. Seeley say the teachers would be compelled to strike, in that event. Others took up the word, and it had a remarkable effect. Basically it ended the argument. Mouse was placed under Mrs. Seeley's supervision for both morning and afternoon sessions, and it was determined that I was not really a vicious... dog. I was a Guide Dog again. Breed undetermined. How very kind of them.

Mooney had some interesting news for us when she picked us up from school. We had news too, of course, and we told ours first.

"That's delightful!" she chortled, "I knew things were going well when Mrs. Seeley took you in, but I never expected such a warm welcome. They actually threatened to go on strike for you! Of course, it was not so much concern for you and Mouse as it was rebellion against being bossed around so flagrantly. Still, I guess the system really works, sometimes. I'd mind my behavior, though.

"Now for my news. It's from the survey company, of course. Something I never would have considered. It appears that Weyerhaeuser has been illegally logging part of our land for the last seventy years or so. A major survey irregularity occurred back then, and it's only just been uncovered. You might have noticed it yourself, Stinky, if you thought more like a human. Or a lawyer."

"Go on, Mooney—we're waiting. Don't draw it out."

"Aw, you're no fun! Won't you take a guess?"

"No. And Mouse won't either. Isn't that right, Mouse? If you and the other humans took seventy years to figure it out, I certainly won't pffe apffle to in a few minutes! So—what is this survey error, and what does it mean?"

"It's simple, really. The wording of the original land grant defined our property as the entire drainage of Fry Creek. That's easy to write, and they did it that way a lot in the old days. The problem comes when you want to be more specific. Surveyors come in to establish the boundaries exactly, and they place permanent markers along the way. The survey crew which marked our western boundary was either lazy or in a hurry, and they made a lot of curved lines into straight lines, because straight lines are so much easier.

"The end result was that a sizable chunk of our land was cut by the old Twin Harbors Logging Company, which was later bought out by Weyerhaeuser. That land is on its third growth now, and Grandpa never received a penny in cutting fees. Now that I know about it, I don't have to log anything myself. All I have to do is sue Weyerhaeuser! Won't even have to sue them, most likely. With a case like this they should settle out of court. That would save everybody a lot of fuss, and prevent any bad publicity for them. If they cooperate, we could be through with it all in a few weeks!"

"And… that's it? Life-crushing insurmountapffle pffropfflem solved… by a simpffle phone call?"

"Yeah, pretty much. If it works out the way I'm hoping. Wish me luck, Stinky! And… changing the subject now… while I was in town I traded hot cookies for some more worm meds for you. Chewy Chicken Flavor, the kind you like."

Humans! What an annoying, unpredictable, unfathomable species they are! Why do I even hang out with them?

Because I'm annoying, unpredictable, and unfathomable too? Must be. Can't think of any other reason.

"Good luck, Mom. Thanks for the meds. I love you too." Epilogue

Weyerhaeuser paid off all of Mooney's back taxes and penalties, and promised us an adequate yearly lease payment for continued use of the disputed land—just enough to pay future taxes on the main parcel. The Weyerhaeuser attorney explained to Mooney that her case was not all that strong, really, but he had been directed not to give her a hard time if she let Weyerhaeuser share the credit for her conservation accomplishments. Mooney complied without protest. Weyerhaeuser is not such a bad neighbor, and they do care a lot for their trees, in a corporate sort of way.

The Papillios have found themselves a new place to live. They're caretakers at a horse ranch, and get free rent and horse boarding in exchange for light duties. Most of their animals have been adopted by the vet school, and they say things are a lot easier for them now. They lost their security deposit, though. Their old house is in a shocking state—collapsing from its own weight and completely uninhabitable. It's not valuable enough to be worth repairing, so no one will ever live there again. Just another abandoned Palouse farmhouse. Haunted, too.

Lazytail is getting very big around the middle, and she'll be whelping soon. We both know she'll be delivering her pups in the house, but we've been digging a den anyway. It's a lot of fun, and Princess helps too. She's the one who showed us how to choose a site where groundwater doesn't seep in.

Lazytail decided she liked being able to talk, and she's been practicing simple words, just like Princess does. I think Smokey may take it up too, one of these days. He certainly listens carefully. And no, I don't know why they can learn to talk while others can't. I suppose it's some sort of influence I have on them. Or maybe that DNA virus John used on me is contagious. I don't know much about these things, and John doesn't know as much as he pretends. "That virus never acted quite right after Fox messed with it," he tells me. Fox says don't blame him—before their project together he never even knew what a virus was, or DNA, either. His kind has quite different ideas about how physical bodies are made.

John and Dr. Benton have done quite a few tests on us and found nothing unusual. No virus, no unusual DNA patterns—even Mr. Burrey has just the normal seventy-eight chromosomes one would expect in a wolf, coyote, or dog. He's wolf through and through, not just some human monster with fur and teeth.

Mr. Burrey's wounds are all healed, and he's fine except for his bad haircut, which is already half shed out. The rest of us are starting to shed too. Quite a mess, and itchy, but soon over with. Mr. Burrey talks all the time, and helps Mooney with the chores, and keeps track of the others when I'm at school. I don't know what we'd do without him. Mooney uses his van now, too. It's not a Volkswagen, but it's newer and it runs much better. Mr. Burrey says she's welcome to it, and all his money too, if she wants it. He says he wishes he could give her more, but he lost most everything when Wynoochee took his house, and there was no flood insurance. He got a nice income tax refund, though. He helped Mooney forge his signature on the check, and it was just enough to pay off his credit cards. The van was already paid for. He had Mooney notify the school district he needed more personal leave, and might not be able to go back to work at all. They said he should apply for disability, and so sorry, but they would have to hire a new person for his position. No hard feelings.

Fox became bored after a few days with us. He's gone now, and he never said a word about the Pups and me breaking so many of his rules. Expected it, I suppose. The Spirit Pups are gone too—or rather they've gone back inside me for a rest. That's what they said, but I think they were bored too. No problem with that! Boring is just fine, as far as I'm concerned. I think I like boring. It's safe.

Mouse let herself recover from her amnesia, which triggered quite a bureaucratic fuss. A very nice FBI man came and took fingerprints, photographs, and notes, in that order. Mouse had to go to court several times but she says they didn't treat her badly. Eventually she received several boxes of personal items and another box full of court documents. She has a name and a Social Security number now, but we all still call her Mouse, and she still lives with us. She has no relatives who care about her.

Some of her toys and other things are damaged, because there was a terrible fight in her apartment after she left it. The man who yelled at her on the fire escape had frightened the neighbors, and one of them called the police. The men were too stupid or drugged to surrender, and both died there. Mouse's fear had been for nothing. She had run away from nothing.

When the boxes first arrived Mouse took out all her things, and her mother's things. She laid them out and stroked or held each one of them, then put them carefully away. She hasn't touched them since. Not even her old toys. She says she doesn't need them any more—she has me. In the daytime, anyway. At night I belong to Lazytail. The hard part is finding time enough to sleep.

I can't say things have returned to normal. I'm not quite sure what normal is. Still, my belly is full—our bellies are full—and around me I see no danger or active enemies. What more could a coyote wish for?

We will see.

Tricks of the Light

Michael Bergey

Coyote awoke to the tingle of powerful Medicine coursing through his bones, and opened his eyes to behold the smirking, supercilious visage of Fox.

"I've been dead again, haven't I?" he sighed.

Fox smirked even more broadly, licked his nose with a languorous, laughter-trembling tongue, and nodded cheerfully. "Yep-yep. Big mess this time — couldn't find one tooth next to another!"

With some effort Coyote heaved a lean, dun-colored body onto four lanky, sand-colored legs, and surveyed his surroundings blearily: Grass beneath his pads — fresh summer prairie grass poking up through scattered glass shards and sun-bleached splinters of old pine. Nearby stood the stark chimney and debris-choked foundation of a burned out cabin. Coyote pawed at a pine fragment, sniffed it over with meticulous care, and sighed again.

"Yes, I remember now. I was trying to discover the secret of dynamite. There are these soft, waxy-tasting sticks, see — and little copper peg things called blasting caps, and a thin sort of rope they call fuse. Humans worry about the sticks, but it's those copper pegs that keep giving me a hard time! Especially the ones marked 'Acme Powder Company.'"

"I see," Fox laughed. "You've been playing with dynamite, and so far all you can tell me is what it tastes like. Common sense suggests a little human advice might be in order here."

"I don't *do* common sense. Common sense is for simple mortals. I'm above such things."

"Yes, Coyote, dear. Of course you are. You're the god of impracticality. Would you like something to eat?"

"Yes, thank you very much! And thanks for bringing me back to life. I don't know what I'd do without you."

"I was bored."

Coyote raised his nose to drink in the rich scents of fox musk and plains dust and grama grass and . . . "Pork ribs! Barbecued pork ribs with mashed sweet potatoes and pecan pie! Imagine that — snow on the ground when I had my little accident, and now it's summer already. How late in the season are we?"

"Today is the Fourth of July, nineteen hundred and three by the White Man's calendar. I could have brought you back when I found you last week, but I waited a bit so I'd have something nice to steal for you."

"Nineteen hundred and three? Like in... the new century, and all that? I've been dead for five years! What have you done with my Spirit Children?"

"Spirit Children? Hold on—let me remember . . . *Spirit* Children . . . Spirit *Children*—oh! You mean Cicéqi! And those other shape shifting troublemakers she hangs around with! Why do you insist on calling them your children, anyway? We both know they're really—"

"Fox!"

"They're fine, Coyote. How could they be otherwise? I feed them spirit-energy when they ask for it, and they take care of themselves the rest of the time. No doubt they'll turn up before long. Here, have a pig bone before they come and claim it for themselves!"

Coyote ate ravenously, consuming the lion's share while Fox stood back at a discreet distance, watching. "Er... excuse me... would you like some too?"

"Perhaps. If it's not too much trouble." Coyote stepped away from the feast while Fox ate until his belly would hold no more, then he drifted back to sniff out any missed scraps. Afterward the two canines settled down to rest companionably in the ashy dirt beneath the shade of the cabin's chimney, panting softly from a surfeit of summer heat and food.

"So, Sin-ka-lip my friend—now you're alive again, what are you going to do?"

"No more dynamite! I've had enough of that shit. If it were springtime I could go courting..."

"*If* it were springtime! When that spring rut kicks in we can talk about courting. 'Til then we're both wasting our time. Let's go make trouble with the humans."

"Works for me!"

*****

"Ah, Fox—just *feel* the power of that unbelief around us! There's enough *ixhicoláha* here to melt an illusion-shirt right off your back! Good thing we stole real human clothes to wear."

"Yes, Coyote. Of course I feel it. What I don't understand is how you can enjoy the sensation. Stinking iron steam monsters! I hate railway stations. Can we leave now?"

"Leave if you like. I'm going to talk to that man by the big stack of packing crates. Half the *ixhicoláha* in this station is coming from him! He looks so impatient, and *so* self-important. And take a gander at that hat he's wearing! It's all round on top, like a river boulder—and just the color of my ear fur! I wish I had a nice hat like that. Do you think he'll give it to me?"

"I doubt that very much. But please—don't let me stand in your way! You talk to him, and I'll ditch these clothes and go hunt jackrabbits. Or maybe cats. Did you notice that fat tabby tom lurking behind Jason's Idle Argonaut Tavern?"

"Yes, I did. You save some for me, you hear?"

"Bring beer, and I'll consider it." Fox ran one hand through a shock of blatantly red hair and tested the air with a sunburned, liberally-freckled nose. "Or cat whiskey. I smell a moonshine still nearby." He pointed toward one of the clapboard warehouses sharing a railway siding across from their platform. "It's in that one," he proclaimed confidently.

Coyote sampled the air with his own nose, and carefully scrutinized the structure in question. "Yes, that's the one," he agreed, turning back toward Fox.

Fox was no longer in evidence. "Fluffy show off," Coyote muttered, and returned his attention to the round-hatted man. Coyote feigned disinterest and wandered away, drifted back, admired his chosen prey from all possible angles before committing himself to the final approach. In addition to his admirable Bowler hat the human sported a magnificent handlebar mustache, a travel-stained but worthy broadcloth coat, and a watch. The man's watch was of gold, like the wire frames of his glasses, and seemed to be a part of him, he consulted it so frequently. This consultation brought him no apparent pleasure, however, no matter how often he repeated it. The watch hands' slow movements seemed, on the contrary, to infuriate him.

"Howdy, pardner! New 'round these parts?" Coyote extended a leathery, coffee colored hand for shaking, and received no response. The man didn't meet Coyote's eyes at all—merely cocked his head to one side as if listening to something far away, then consulted his watch again. Smiling sadly, Coyote reached forward to stroke the watch face with gentle fingertips and the man absently pulled it away, consulted it one more time, then shook it doubtfully and held it to his ear.

"Somethin' the matter with yer watch, mister?" The human's pale gray eyes roved vaguely for a moment, stopped, locked with Coyote's golden ones. From whence had this strange *Indianer* appeared so suddenly? And such eyes! He had never seen golden eyes in a human before. He must photograph this man! The primitive races are often sensitive about cameras, of course, so he would have to be careful how he asked—

"*¿Señor? ¿Habla espaniol?*"

"Oh! Excuse me! Please pardon my rudeness. I speak English quite well. How may I be of service to you?"

"Oh, I'm fine, I reckon. Just bein' neighborly. Are you waitin' for someone?"

"I'm waiting to meet my local guide," the round-hatted man replied. He fiddled distractedly with the stem of his watch, held it to his ear again, then reluctantly tucked it into a small, watch-sized pocket in the front his trousers.

"What's his handle?"

"His handle? I don't believe I understand."

"His name. What's the name of the man yer waitin' for?"

"Zebediah Foster. Our correspondence clearly indicated he was to be here at my arrival, with a dray wagon."

"Zeb Foster? Nah—name don't ring a bell, but that don't mean nothin'. I've been out of touch for a spell. Dead to the world, you might say. But if yer lookin' for a guide, I can do it. Me and my pardner, Todd Reynard, if he feels so inclined. We're crackerjack guides when the mood strikes us, and we know right well how the land hereabouts is put together—had our paws in the project from early on, so to speak."

The man extended his hand. "I will consider your offer, Mister..."

Coyote reached forth his own hand, and shook vigorously. "Latrans. Kay Latrans."

"It is a pleasure to meet you, Mr. Latrans! I am Herr Doktor Professor Wolfgang Eisenhertz-Sklarsen, representing the *Universität zu Berlin* on photographic expedition to this fascinating land of yours. You may address me simply as Dr. Sklarsen, if you like. If you'll do me the honor, we shall discuss your kind offer in more detail over dinner this evening. In the meanwhile, perhaps you could recommend to me a reputable—"

Professor Sklarsen's words were drowned out by a sudden cacophony of shouts and crashes from the direction of the Idle Argonaut. Glass shattered as a heavy whiskey bottle departed the premises through a dusty-curtained side window, and seconds later a magnificent, white Stetson hatted red fox flew out through the same opening. The whiskey bottle burst wetly when it hit the street but the fox landed gracefully—despite a neck stretched high and twisted sharply askew to maintain a bite-grip on the elegant but very much not-fox-sized headgear balanced across its back. The fox paused for an instant to readjust its load, then leapt forward and raced down the road directly toward Coyote and Dr. Sklarsen.

Humans swarmed ant-like from the tavern entrance as the fox streaked up the steps to the railway platform, circled Coyote and the professor in one mad, frolicking, heavy-hatted dash, and with a vigorous snap of its spine launched the hat through the air to land neatly on Coyote's head. The fox shook itself briskly, bowed briefly but deeply in Coyote's direction, and lifted its muzzle to favor the neighborhood with an impassioned cascade of ear-piercing yips and howls.

"Fox! Cut out with the barking, will you? You'll draw their attention here!"

The fox smiled, nodded happily, and made itself one with the darkness beneath the foundation beams of the cat-whiskey warehouse.

"Hey, you! Injun! Gimme me back my hat!"

"What hat?"

"*That* hat, you butt-sniffing son of a bitch! The one that's sitting on top your head. The one with my name on—er, maybe not. I ain't got around to that yet."

Coyote straightened his lanky form to its full, not-inconsiderable height, and regarded the interloper down the length of a disdainful, splendidly well endowed nose. The man smelled of horses, and old sweat, and young whiskey. Much whiskey.

"Clearly you are drunk, sir," Coyote informed him coldly. "I've sired a bitch or three in my time, but I'm not the son of one. And I never laid a hand on your hat. Please go away."

The man began to roll up his sleeves while simultaneously attempting to maintain balance on a pair of treacherously unsteady legs. The operation was not going well. "Liar! You sent your pet fox to steal it from me. That hat was brand new! I just bought it this morning."

"Fox? I don't see any fox here. And anyway, if I wanted to steal your hat I wouldn't send some useless animal to do it. I'd wait until you passed out drunk, and take it then." Coyote removed the Stetson from his head, inspected it ostentatiously, and brushed an imaginary fleck of dust from the brim. He turned to the professor. "It *is* a nice hat, isn't it? And just my size! Fox is always so good with those little details." In one fluid movement Coyote snatched away the professor's fawn Bowler and settled the milk-white Stetson in its place. "Well look at that—it's your size too! Would you care to trade, Dr. Sklarsen? You can take this one home with you as a souvenir of your journey to America."

"Didja—did you say . . . Sklarsen?"

"Why, yes, indeed I did—and a right friendly chap he is! He's traveled here all the way from Berlin just to take pictures, and his guide never showed up so he's going to hire me instead! Isn't that right, Dr. Sklarsen?"

"But—*I'm* his guide—I'm Zeb Foster! You know me, Perfesser—you wired me the money to get everything ready, and I did. I got the wagon, and the supplies, and I been waiting all day for your train to arrive, and—"

"Did you pack an extra hat?"

"No! I didn't! That hat cost me twenty dollars, and I'll roast in Hell before I give it up."

Coyote looked thoughtful. "Never been there, myself."

Zeb opened his mouth to reply, shut it again, scratched his neck in bemused concentration. "What are you talking about?" he offered at last. "What place is it you've never been?"

"Why, Hell! You were saying you wanted to go there and I said I'd never been, myself. Seems a right popular place though. A good number of my friends have lit off that way, and folks often suggest I take myself there too. Perhaps when the cold weather settles in this fall—"

"Excuse me, Mr. Foster. Clearly this hat is your rightful property. Please take it with my compliments." Dr. Sklarsen retrieved his Bowler from Coyote's head and extended the Stetson courteously in Zebediah's direction. The man snatched his hat away, slammed it down on his head, glared balefully at Coyote. "And *you* can be moving along now, Injun. Next time I won't let you off so easy."

"But no no, Mr. Foster! I must insist that Mr. Latrans remain with us! Your tardiness and intoxication have distressed me deeply, and I fear we may need to reconsider some aspects of our relationship. Mr. Latrans—please accept my provisional tender of employment, effective immediately. We will begin by instructing your assistant, Mr. Foster, on the proper transport and storage of modern photographic equipment."

*****

Professor Sklarsen extended his willow branch far out across the stream side shallows, just managing to snag and draw in the mold-fuzzed fish carcass drifting there. "Ah—*Saprolegnia!* How curious to encounter it here, of all places. Mr. Reynard, kindly return that poor *Cambarus diogenes* to its burrow. Have you even been listening to what I've been teaching you? Please recite to me the path taken by waters from this creek as they wend their way to the sea."

Fox brandished his writhing crayfish in Coyote's face one more time, tossed it casually into deep water, then raised himself to his entire five foot two inches of height and assumed a solemn, self-important expression suspiciously similar to the professor's own. He paused a moment for silence, and began to recite: "Currently we're admiring and photographically recording the exquisite beauty of Mad Marmot Gorge—a strangely unknown (except to more-than-naturally gifted guides such as Mr. Latrans and myself) yet truly excellent geologic feature of the Eastern Ramparts of the Colorado Rocky Mountains. From where we stand, Mad Marmot Creek bursts free from his mountainous beginnings and sidles southward to join inconspicuously with the river you call Arkansas. From there the combined waters flow eastward across the plains, passing through Pueblo, La Junta, Las Animas and Lamar here in Colorado; Dodge City, Great Bend and Wichita in Kansas; Ponca City and Tulsa in Oklahoma; then Fort Smith and Little Rock in Arkansas before giving themselves to Mississippi just upstream from Arkansas City. From that junction Mississippi snakes his way sinuously southward through Vicksburg, Baton Rouge and New Orleans before discharging his dark, silt-laden waters into the boundless Gulf of Mexico."

"Very good, Mr. Reynard! Your powers of memory are astonishing! Do you have, perhaps, a bit of Teutonic blood in you? By your surname and red hair I'd consider you to be French, but—as we all know—the races of Europe share a rich and extremely complex history."

Fox raised up a sunburned hand and critically scrutinized the mud and freckle splattered back of it. "In sooth I was trying for the Irish," he said. "But I suppose I could be French, *si vous préférez*. Now—what were you attempting to tell us about that rotten fish you find so *fascinant*?"

Professor Sklarsen shook his head in bemusement. "Mr. Reynard—and you, too, Mr. Latrans—if the pair of you would deign to turn your mental gifts to productive use there is no limit to how far you could go in the pursuit of... whatever it is you actually want from life. I wish you both the best of luck in those endeavors, whatever they turn out to be. Now, where were we? Yes . . . fungal hyphal necrosis. This fish—a previously unreported variant of the western blue sucker, if I am not mistaken—bears a luxuriant growth of *Saprolegnia,* or "cotton mold." Saprolegnia is a pathologic fungus which invades and proliferates within the fish's mucoid epithelium—relentlessly draining critical nutriments and vital energies until the fish perforce succumbs to its pernicious effects. Many times these fungal hyphae continue to grow even after the fish's death, sometimes—as in this specimen— eventually covering the body in a fur-like blanket over a centimeter thick. This fungal coat is the foundation for amusing reports of "furred carp" and "furred trout" which make their way into otherwise well-founded traveler's stories from time to time."

Fox and Coyote locked gazes for a moment, then Fox tilted his head to one side and favored the professor with a wide-eyed, ostentatiously innocent gaze. "I'll show you one."

"I beg your pardon?"

"I'll show you a furred trout, if you like. You can feel how cold the water is here at the mouth of the gorge. Up above Mad Marmot Falls the waters are so frigid even the fish in them need fur! Would you like to photograph one?"

"Of course not! What sort of fool do you take me for? Only mammals can grow fur. Fish most emphatically do *not*." Professor Sklarsen glanced up at the sky and brought out a brand new but rather ordinary-looking brass pocket watch for consultation. He frowned, raised the watch to his ear, shook it irritably. "*Verdamtes Steppenschmutz!*" he muttered, and put the watch away. "I'm sorry, Mr. Reynard. You and Mr. Latrans have served me extraordinarily well so far, but I'll have to decline this particular suggestion. We need to be in Colorado City by tomorrow evening, and we'll miss our train if we don't strike camp before the light fails. Mr. Latrans will carry the emulsion plates and—Mr. Latrans? Where has that man gone off to? Answering a call of nature, I suppose. Mr. Reynard, while we're waiting you can assist me with—Mr. Reynard? Mr. Reynard! Where are you? Don't be long, if you please! We still have a considerable amount of work to do before it grows dark."

*****

"Coyote—wait up! What are you plotting *this* time? As if I couldn't guess."

"Us unedjicated country fools is gonna show the boss-man a interestin' fish."

"Are you crazy? You know we'll never find a furred trout down here below the falls! They like it best in the high country, in the snow-melt rills."

"I'll do it."

"You? Do you *like* getting killed? That trout is hardly likely to survive the photographic process. Call your Spirit Children! They'll get one for us."

"No time. And anyway, they may not be ready to grant me any favors just yet. We had a bit of a falling out shortly before that incident with the dynamite. Sometimes I suspect—but never mind about that. It's not so dangerous, really. I'll stay in the water and look handsome, and you keep the professor on dry land where he belongs. Why would he want to leave his camera, anyway? It seems to require a great deal of attention from him."

Coyote removed and carefully set aside shoes, socks, thick khaki trousers and a rather fancy-looking red plaid Pendleton shirt, and began to step gingerly out into the stream shallows. "Arrgh! This water is freezing! And the rocks are slippery. Damn worthless human feet—why do I bother with them?"

"Because you're jealous of the humans, and like to pretend you're one of them?"

"Never! I play at being human because they need reminding of how it ought to be done, and because it's a way to put uppity foxes in their place.

266

Honestly! White skin and red hair—and *freckles!* Whatever were you thinking?"

"I was thinking we foxes roam the world now and you coyotes are still confined to a single continent. I was thinking I have many worshipers with red hair and freckles. Do you? And why is this human getting you so worked up? Just walk away, if you dislike him so much. Or kill him."

"He has power! We both feel it. He could have been a mighty shaman."

"He *is* a mighty shaman."

"Yes, and his magic—his Science—is poison to us. He symbolizes all the others who are destroying our world. I will change him."

"Coyote, don't fret so. Science is but a fad, and it will pass like all the others. Time is long."

"Perhaps. Or perhaps our time is running out. I am the Changer. I will change this man, or die trying."

"As you wish, comrade. Any last requests?"

Coyote pretended to notice his nakedness for the first time, feigned embarrassment, then favored his partner with an obscene parody of a military salute. "Yes, sir, Mr. Reynard, sir. If I fail to survive this mission, promise you'll keep me out of Zeb's frying pan! I know I need to be taken with a grain of salt, but that man would serve me up with ketchup and beans. I know he would." Coyote smiled, closed his eyes, and slowly filled his lungs with sweet mountain air. He held the breath within himself for a time, savoring it, then with a deep sigh he allowed it to slip away. His body sagged, then toppled backward like a felled tree—splashing extravagantly and sinking promptly when it struck the calf-deep water. It did not come up again.

*****

Coyote awoke to the tingle of powerful Medicine coursing through his bones—and the chest-thumping greeting-assault of five over-enthusiastic coyote puppies.

"Welcome back, Father!"

"We missed you!"

"And we forgive you, too."

"Almost."

"Fox invited us to a peace-offering-dinner with you!"

"There was more than he could eat all by himself."

"We *love* furred trout—can we have dinner with you again sometime?"

Coyote carefully extricated his pelt from the frantic tangle of puppy paws and tongues and teeth making free with it. "Uh, thanks, kids—so glad I could be of service. It's good to see y'all. Fox!"

"Yes, Coyote?"

"You could have at least *tried* to protect me!"

"I did try! But you nearly beached yourself showing off your otter-like soggy sleekness for that man—and there were stream boulders everywhere. Can you blame him for picking one up and whacking you on the head with it? When I realized what he was up to I splashed out after and tried to trip him up, but it was too late. Your doctor moves fast, for a human!"

"So then you all sat down together and ate me for dinner, right?"

"Of course not! Coyote—if you could have seen Dr. Sklarsen's face you would have died laughing! He laid your poor carcass out on the beach and photographed you until he ran out of plates, then kept poking at you and babbling about impossible this and impossible that—setting you down and picking you up a minute later to peer at some simple little part he had already looked at a dozen times. Finally he threw you over his shoulder and marched off for camp—commanding me to fetch my partner and secure the photographic equipment without further delay.

"So I did! I foxified myself and followed along behind, and fetched you when a rough spot forced him to set you down. That was a couple of hours ago, and he's been crashing through the brush ever since. I think he's lost now—do you hear him calling?"

"Fox, this is embarrassing. I don't think my Spirit Children have ever eaten me for dinner before! It sets a bad example. Cicéqi, promise me you won't do that again!"

The smallest coyote pup—a female—sidled up to Coyote and licked him obsequiously beneath the chin. "But you were delicious, Father! And Uncle Fox only needs a little scrap to work his resurrection magic. A bone or two would have been enough, but to show our respect we saved *both* your testicles! And an eyeball for luck."

"Uh, right. I suppose that makes it all better. Was I really delicious?"

"Oh, yes! And so big! I don't know how Uncle Fox managed to drag you away all by himself!"

"Hmmpf. I'm strong enough when I need to be," Fox reminded her. "Come on Coyote, shake a leg! It'll be dark soon and we need to secure ourselves some clothes and equipment—and a professor."

"Can we come along too, Uncle Fox? We've never smelled a real professor before!"

"He's nothing special, Cicéqi—smells like fried onions and moustache wax and photographic chemicals. You haven't missed much."

"What's a photographic chemical?"

"It's—it's hard to say. Coyote! You answer! She's your minion, so—"

"We are *not* Coyote's minions!" snapped the male pup to Fox's left.

"We're his *partners!*" growled the female to his right.

"Sometimes he *forgets*, it's true," offered a thoughtful voice from behind Coyote's left flank.

"But we *remind* him," purred the toothy muzzle lurking by his right ear.

"Come along, then, sweet Children!" Coyote responded hastily. "I wouldn't think of leaving you behind! Just don't let yourselves be seen—and don't break anything unless I tell you to!"

*****

Professor Sklarsen restlessly prowled the flat, boulder-strewn banks of Mad Marmot Creek—straining his eyes to penetrate the morning-sun-dappled waters and perceive, perhaps, the faint fleeting flicker of a furred fin. As he searched he talked—babbled—to the human and not-so-human entourage trailing along behind him.

" . . . and so *kraftig*—so powerful! How could one small fox move so swiftly with such a heavy burden? The wretched creature was impossibly light on its feet, and seemed almost to be taunting me as it ran off with that monstrous fish. I knew the fox must eventually tire, of course, so I continued my search in the hope I might stumble upon it and thereby recovery my specimen. Alas! Success had still eluded me when dusk forced an end to my search. Today we shall try again. Perhaps some fragment of the fish has been left behind, or a new specimen can be captured. Mr. Latrans, did you hear that noise?" The professor turned his head away from the stream side and listened intently. "There it is again! But no, it is nothing—merely the foolish yapping of a pack of coyotes. Such peculiar fancies we develop when we're overwrought! For a moment it sounded to me almost like demented laughter."

Zeb cleared his throat diffidently, and spat on the ground beside him. "It sounded kinda like laughin' t'me, too," he reluctantly affirmed. "Di'n't you say we'd be heading out to Colorado City today? If we strike camp now we can still make the night train, I reckon."

"I'll have to change my itinerary in light of this new development. Imagine—an entirely new fish family, completely unknown to science! No, no, no—a mere family will not do. We shall have to establish an entirely new *order* of fishes! *Tricho*... Greek for hair or fur... definitely it must have *trich* in it somewhere. *Trichichthyes... elegans...* or perhaps—dare I say it?— *Trichichthyes sklarsenii!*" More demented coyote laughter emanated from the nearby juniper scrub and Zeb spat again. He unslung his rifle and and checked the action for smoothness. "It ain't right," he muttered sulkily. "I seen spirits now and ag'in, but never like on *this* trip—and now they're actin' up in broad daylight! Kay! You hear 'em—why ain't you sayin' nothin' about it?"

"No one asked me."

"Well, I'm askin' you now. Ya got any good Injun tricks for drivin' the varmints off?"

"You should make them an offering of your fine cooking; that ought to do it. What do you think, Todd? Do the *paysans* of *Eire* have any special tricks for this sort of thing?"

"Be serious, guys! Them spirits can be dangerous when they get riled! And there's snakes here, too. I seen one yesterday when I was out gettin' the firewood."

"There's always snakes, Zeb. You know that."

"Yeah, yeah, there's always rattlesnakes and such. They don't bother me none. This was different. This was a hoop snake!"

"A hoop snake! Well, now—you don't see *them* much these days. There's nothing in this world deadlier than the tail-sting of a gen-u-wine hoop snake! And fast—they say a hoop snake can catch an antelope—even a *jackalope* when it has a steep enough hill to start from! Run fast as you like but it ain't no use—the serpent just rolls on behind until it's almost caught up to you, then snaps itself straight and flies tail-first through the air like a living javelin! Your only hope if a hoop snake is after you is to find a big tree to hide behind. The critters can't turn quickly when they're going along at a good clip, so you're safe that way. Sometimes they get mad and sting the tree, of course, which kills it instantly, like it was struck by lightning. Is *that* the sort of hoop snake you saw? Why didn't you mention it before?"

"I did. I told the perfesser right off, but he di'n't believe me. He says there ain't no such animal—nor spirits neither, for that matter."

"Mr. Foster," the professor replied distractedly, "I never denied the existence of hoop snakes! I merely explained to you they're not venomous, and they never form themselves into a hoop to roll along on the ground. 'Hoop snake' is a common colloquial term for the mud snake *Farancia abacura*—a large, handsome, red and gray banded creature which frequents riparian habitats like the one which surrounds us now. Is that, perhaps, what you saw yesterday? Please notify me immediately if you encounter one again, so I may capture and photograph it!"

"Hey, Spirits!" Fox called out. "Did you hear what the doctor said? He wants to photograph a hoop snake!"

"Fox—wait! What are you—"

"Shhh!" Zeb hissed. "Are you crazy? Don't you ever make fun of spirits like that! There's no telling what they might do!" The coyote laughter grew louder and was joined by the rustling of twigs and leaves, as if several small forms were rolling on the ground in helpless hilarity. Gradually the yap-laughter developed a strangely sibilant quality, and then laughter and leaf-rustle faded away altogether.

"Spirits," Zeb called out nervously, "Please don't pay no mind to what —"

"Mr. Foster, that will be quite enough!" interrupted Dr. Sklarsen. "Believe what you like on your own time, but at this moment you're a member of a modern scientific expedition, and your current credulous behavior is unbecoming of such a position. Jackals and coyotes are expected to yap from time to time, even in broad daylight! Come now—just ahead is the location from which yesterday's remarkable fish specimen was collected. I'll need your assistance in setting up my camera for some repeat exposures of the banks and stream channel. Mr. Latrans! Stand by, if you please, and await my further instructions. And Mr. Reynard... you stand by too."

*****

"Admit it! You're jealous you didn't think of the snake idea yourself!"

"Perhaps." Coyote twisted a branch from a nearby juniper and began to peel the bark from it with his fingernails. "*Collected*, my ass!" he muttered darkly. "Murdered is a better word for it!"

"Now, now," Foxed soothed, "you're not going to hold that small transgression against him, are you?"

Coyote snapped his juniper switch to the ground in a vicious arc— gouging a groove and throwing out a flat cascade of dirt and twig bits. "I am not—and will never be—a *specimen!*" he huffed.

Fox edged prudently away and eyed the nearby terrain appraisingly— paying particular attention to the bumpy but otherwise unobstructed talus slope linking the upper stream bluffs to the high bank on which they stood. "I think we're all specimens to the good doctor. And soon he'll have a pawful of hoop snakes to add to his collection! It seems likely to me they'll be making their move right away; don't you agree?"

Coyote glanced down at his mangled juniper branch, and tossed it away in disgust. "A-yep. I reckon we're all sittin' ducks, here. No hoop snake could ask for a more perfect attack spot! Now Brother Fox—I was jest *wonderin'* now, mind you—what do you make of that old cottonwood, yonder? Ain't she a fine lookin' tree? She's thick, and solid, and . . . and supposin' we was to sort of mosy a mite closer to her? Like . . . *behind* her? Just in case?"

"Really, Coyote! That's not very sporting, is it? Don't you trust your Spirit Children?"

"Trust is such a tricky word! You gave them the snake idea; you can be all sporting out in the open!"

"What are you afraid of? If you get killed I can just bring you back to life again! You won't feel a thing, they say. They say the venom's so deadly you're gone before you even know you're been done in."

"Fox my dear, dear friend—have you ever been snuffed by a hoop snake?"

"No, come to think of it . . . can't recall that I have."

"Don't."

"Ah. I see. Maybe you're right. Perhaps we should—Coyote! Did you hear that noise? Yes, there's one of them now! Is it Cicéqi, do you think?"

A ring-shaped object was rolling down the talus slope toward them. Sort of rolling. Imagine a unicyclist wheeling as slowly as possible along an unstable, hopelessly bumpy and very steep ramp—twisting violently to the right, to the left, and then to the right again in a valiant attempt to preserve balance under near-impossible conditions. Now imagine the rider gone, and the seat gone—and the pedals and spokes and hub. That is what Coyote and Fox saw. It was a memorable sight, and it brought them joy, of a sort.

"Fluffy show off!" muttered Fox, chuckling.

"Scaly show off," corrected Coyote. "You're the fluff-head!"

"We foxes *do* have a superior pelt, for all the good it does us," Fox graciously admitted. "Do you suppose mine is in danger now?"

"Not yet. That's Cicéqi for sure, and it looks to me like she's camera-posing!"

Slowly the hoop snake wobbled toward Coyote and Fox, then passed them with a friendly greeting-hiss and rolled on down toward the doctor, and Zeb, and the diligently rushing waters of Mad Marmot Creek.

"Dr. Sklarsen!" Coyote bellowed, "Can you spare us a minute o'yer time? I think we found us one of them thar loop snakes, or poop snakes or whatever you call 'em! This one's actin' mighty peculiar, though—must be matin' season or some such, I suppose. Anyhow she's big, and she's ugly, and she's headin' your way right now!"

A hiss of annoyance escaped the hoop snake's mouth and she straightened her course to build up sufficient speed for a graceful double loop around the astonished doctor, followed by a gentle spiraling collapse on the stream bank directly in front of his camera.

"Zeb! Quick—fetch me another plate!" Zeb remained rooted in place, and did not respond. "Zeb, it's just a snake! Please assist me now!" Zeb still did not move. In exasperation the doctor fetched his own plate cassette from the transport pack, thrust it firmly into the loading slot in the back of his camera, extracted the glass emulsion plate and made his exposure. Several times he repeated the process while the hoop snake happily posed before his camera—stirring only to present her sinuous jewel-scaled magnificence in new, possibly more flattering angles, or to wave her scorpion-like tail stinger in stern warning when approached too closely. When his last plate had been exposed the doctor slipped it carefully back into its light-tight wooden cassette, returned the cassette to its transport pack, and heaved the pack onto his shoulders. For a short time he permitted himself the luxury of merely *looking* at the frolicking hoop snake—admiring her simply for the the beauty and wonder that was herself—then he sighed regretfully, and called out: "Kay! Todd! Whoever of you is the best marksman, kindly borrow Mr. Foster's rifle and dispatch the creature now. Remember—you must be careful to avoid damage to the head and tail! This specimen is priceless, and must be kept as intact as possible."

The thought of sharing his beloved Winchester 1892 roused Zeb from his paralysis. With a smooth, practiced movement he unslung the rifle and cradled it ready for action. "I'm sorry, Dr. Sklarsen! The critter gave me a turn, is all. I'm ready now."

"Then by all means, sir, proceed!"

Zeb raised the rifle to his shoulder and the hoop snake promptly launched herself into the rushing creek waters, and was lost to view. Zeb's gun muzzle tracked urgently across the water for a time; then it slowed, and rose up into the air.

"Mr. Foster! Why didn't you shoot?"

"It was movin' too fast. You got to aim first, then shoot. 'Tain't right otherwise."

"Well, get that muzzle back down and keep trying! The creature may still rise to the surface and give you another chance. Todd, Kay—you patrol the banks downstream and mark where the snake comes back to land. Move!"

Coyote and Fox hurried downstream, and met their hoop snake behind the very first bend. She slithered silently from the sun-warmed stream shallows and spiraled up Coyote's leg to contemplate him through a pair of shining, serpentine eyes. "How'd I do, Father?" she inquired modestly.

"Adequately," Coyote admitted.

"You were wonderful, Cicéqi!" Fox enthused. "I've never seen such a gorgeous and frightening hoop snake!"

"Thank you! But you ought to have waited. If you think *I'm* frightening you should see the rest of me... of my Brothers and Sisters!"

A shout, a shot, and a strident shriek shattered the sylvan stillness and Zeb—burdened with nothing more than the clothes on his back—burst frantically into view. Seconds later Dr. Sklarsen—bowed beneath the weight of his precious camera and cassette pack—also made his appearance. The hoop snake flashed Coyote a fang-filled smile and slipped silently into the chaparral.

"Men, there has been a change in plans! Please proceed with me posthaste, as you are. We'll discuss the details later."

"What about our gear?"

"Leave it! I have my camera and plates, and everything else is replaceable. Come with me now!" Dr. Sklarsen didn't wait to see if his orders had been obeyed but puffed briskly downstream in the wake of his unencumbered assistant. Coyote and Fox remained where they stood.

"Well, now, Mr. Latrans—reckon we should risk a look?"

"By all means, Mr. Reynard! But . . . perhaps we ought to take our time about it. One can't be too careful, with hoop snakes! Cicéqi—are you still here?"

Cicéqi did not respond, so Coyote and Fox waited a few minutes, then began to work their way cautiously upstream. No hoop snakes were encountered, but they did discover five coyote pups scavenging beef jerky and salt crackers from the much-abused remnants of Zeb's rucksack. The pups were wobbling, and squabbling, and smelling strongly of cat whiskey.

"Cicéqi! Why the quick change-back? I thought you'd all want to be showing off your sinuous glossy snakiness for me!"

"Snakes don't like beef jerky and salt crackers. Coyote puppies do."

"Coyote puppies also seem partial to cheap rotgut moonshine! Did you save any for me and Fox?"

"Uh, sorry . . . there was only one bottle, and it wasn't even full all the way . . . but Zeb has more at camp! We left some of *that* for you! A little."

"Where's the bottle? Let me see for my—what happened to this cloth? It's not ripped; looks more like it was burned, or rotted or—is that snake venom?"

"Yes! Don't touch it!"

Coyote hastily snatched his hand away from the blackened, disintegrating fabric. "Yes, or course. Is there venom anywhere else I should know about?"

"I hit Zeb's rifle stock!" one of the male pups volunteered.

"I killed the tree they were hiding behind!" offered a female.

"I struck at Zeb's hat—"

"Not the white Stetson! I've had my eye on that hat for—"

"—but then I changed my mind and just knocked it off. You'll find it over that way—beside your pack."

"Did you strip that too?"

"No, we're still working on Zeb's. But we're done now! What's for lunch?"

"Beef jerky and salt crackers and whiskey. Hope you liked it." Coyote turned in a circle to survey Zeb's half-disintegrated pack, the blackened and eroded stock of Zeb's rifle, and one sadly assassinated cottonwood tree—the same tree he had recommended to Fox as a hoop snake shield. "Impressive! Do you suppose Dr. Sklarsen will listen more carefully to the next tall tale I tell him?"

*****

The day was a Friday, the hour was early, and the patrons of Jason's Idle Argonaut Tavern were in a frolicsome mood. Disparaging laughter and crude jests flew through the main hall as they made rough sport of one of their number.

"… and you says you seen hoop snakes and furred trout on the *same day?*"

"No, the hoop snakes was today. The furred trout was yesterday, and I never actually seen it with my own eyes. The doctor told me about it."

"Close enough! And jest where was it you encountered these mar-ve-lous critters? Did'ja say the place was called Mad Marmot Gorge? A day's ride from here and not a one of your buddies has ever even heard of it? Well lor-dy! Ain't never been a tracker like you before! Bartender! Bring Zeb here another beer! No, make it whiskey. The good stuff, mind you! We got some celebratin' to do…"

Just outside the crowd's circle of attention, Coyote and Fox savored their coworker's discomfiture while sharing bar space with two lagers of more than acceptable quality, a sad looking goldfish in a bowl, and a stuffed prairie dog. From the smoke darkened walls, many more taxidermy specimens stared down at them with dull glass eyes.

Fox lifted his beer, sipped just a little bit of it, set it carefully down again. "How much longer do you suppose he'll last?" he inquired.

"Hard to say. Long as they keep buying him free drinks, I suppose."

"I forget—was Zeb supposed to be keeping the gorge a secret?"

"Don't recall. Doesn't matter. None of them will ever—Fox! Did you see that? Over there—by the empty table—I think it's—" Coyote felt the gentle tickle of whiskers on his ankle, then the scampering prickle of rodent claws as an enormous wharf rat swarmed up his leg and onto his lap. "—a rat." The rat poked its head and shoulders between the buttons of Coyote's shirt, backed out when the rest of it didn't fit, then stretched its body upward to bring front legs and head to the level of the bar top. Whiskers quivering, it sniffed eagerly toward Coyote's beer and slapped the bar edge emphatically with one small paw.

Coyote reached forward to spill a little beer from his glass onto the counter edge, forming a foamy puddle just within rat-tongue-reach. He leaned forward to protect his new companion from casual view and the rat lapped furiously until the puddle was gone. It sighed, belched, groomed its face clean, then beamed up at Coyote with a bold, beady eye.

"Greetings, Cicéqi!" Coyote whispered. "Why no concealment magic? And why so large? Don't you think a wee little mouse would be easier to hide?"

The rat belched again. "Too easy! No sport to it. More beer, please."

Coyote let slip another dribble of beer, noticing as he did that Fox had also hunched himself forward, and was unobtrusively creating a beer puddle of his own.

"That's two of you. Where are the others?"

"Here and there. You'll notice soon enough."

Clinking sounds behind the bar brought Coyote's attention to a large rat dragging off an even larger bottle of something alcoholic, exotic, and expensive, and then a flicker of movement aloft led his eyes to the main taxidermy display where two of Cicéqi's pestilential cohorts were making improper overtures to a stuffed jackalope buck.

"'Hey! What's goin' on here?" Rat claws skittered and a dusty jackalope trophy crashed to the floor as the Argonaut's bartender stormed wrathfully back to his station.

"Lordy! Did you see that?"

"See what?"

"The ruttin' rats, thats what!"

The main hall had grown silent, and all eyes were focussed on the bartender. Fox drained his glass, then noisily slammed it down on the bar top. "More beer, bartender! An' it shall be free o'charge, if you please! 'Tis a year o'me life ye've taken from me! Nought but the merest breath of wind an' that moth eaten monstrosity comes crashing down from on high and near takes me eye out with its antler! I'll be expectin' a drop o' compensation for me sufferin', and that's for certain!"

"That wasn't no wind! It was a pack o'—"

"Hush!" Fox whisper-hissed. "Have you no sense, man? I didn't see any rats. How about you, Kay? Did you notice a rabble of filthy, disgusting, and no doubt illegal rats dancing about on the table tops here?"

Coyote drained his own glass and nudged it discretely forward for a refill. He peered diligently at the floor, under the nearby tables, and behind the bar. "Nope. No rats here today! Must've been a trick of the light—and the noise of that jackalope thing falling down. Looks like it hit pretty hard! One of the antlers has come off."

The bartender refilled the proffered vessels, then picked up his damaged jackalope and brought it into the harsh and unnaturally steady illumination of the electric lamp by his till. "Small harm done," he proclaimed after a moment's careful inspection. "A drop of Elmer's glue'll put 'er to rights. Sorry for your inconvenience, sir!" he added loudly for the benefit of his more distant and less rat-savvy audience.

Coyote sprawled himself across the counter to get a closer look at the jackalope, but as he did so the electric lamp flared suddenly, and grew dark.

"Damn! Why do I even bother with these newfangled things?" the bartender muttered irritably. "Gas lights are cheaper and a lot less trouble." He brought over a kerosine lamp, and Coyote continued his investigation under illumination of a more practical nature.

"Not a bad mount! Is it for sale?"

"No, all these trophies are just for decoration. Folk expect it—" Coyote extracted a large gold coin from his pocket and set it beside the jackalope. "—of us. This one is damaged, though. Might be about time for it to be retired."

Coyote gathered up his new-bought jackalope and its broken antler, and brought them back to his bar station. "Lookie what I got, Fox! Ain't he cute? He looks good enough to eat! Too bad the critters ain't real, like hoop snakes and furry trout and such. I'd love to introduce one to our professor friend!"

The bartender grunted ruefully. "They're real enough to put me back a ten-spot for a replacement! Got to do it, though. Folks'll be missing that one. But don't worry—you've more than paid your way so far. If you need another drink, or a bite to eat, just let me know. We got steaks, of course, and prairie oysters tonight for them that's fond of 'em. And if you need a room, or a companion..."

An annoyed voice intruded from Zeb's circle of admirers. "Bartender! You forget our drinks? Since when do Injuns and Irishmen get special treatment here?"

"Since they pay their way with cash money, that's when!" The bartender turned back to Coyote and winked conspiratorially. "Don't you give him no mind. This is an open bar and he knows it. Even Injuns can drink here if they watch their manners and don't get too drunk. You need anything, just give me a holler. My name is Jason."

The bartender busied himself with bartender things and later, when the man's duties had taken him elsewhere, Coyote felt the prickle of mouse claws scrambling up his shirt and onto his shoulder. Mouse whiskers tickled his ear and the distinctive bitter-floral-anise fragrance of absinthe wafted to his nostrils. "We could *make* them real, you know . . ."

"You could now, eh? *Real* jackalopes? That would be in the usual manner, I presume . . ."

"Yes, indeed! We already asked, and the Old Magic told us yes!"

"Already? My, we've been busy! Fox—did you hear that? My Spirit Children have invited me to a creation party! Care to join us?"

"Hmm... he *is* kind of cute... sure, I'll do it if I get to be the male."

"You were the male last time."

"Male spiders don't count! How did you ever talk me into that, anyway?"

"Just like we are right now. We argued, and you won."

"Fine. I'll be the jackalope buck, and you can give up shape shifting and strong magic for your pregnancy, then devote who knows how long to rearing our adorable little jackalope kits. Or fauns. Or faukits. Why do the humans call them jackalopes, anyway? Those are deer antlers on his head, not antelope horns. They should name them jackadeers, or stagbunnies or some such."

"Aw, Fox—don't be a grump! He's an interesting critter no matter what you call him. How about a wager?"

"What do I have to gain?"

"You'll be the progenitor of a whole new species! Isn't that good enough for you?" Coyote held up the jackalope for closer inspection. "Look at him! The humans love these guys! They're already telling stories about them, and they don't even exist yet. Think of what will happen when they're real!"

"What sort of wager?"

"We'll present ourselves just the way we are now, and the Old Magic will decide! No doubt it will choose the more manly of us to be the buck."

"No, your Spirit Children will cheat for you. They always do."

"Cicéqi! You won't do that, will you? Let Fox feel the truth!"

Fox reached forward to rest his finger tips gently on the Cicéqi-mouse. He tilted his head to one side as if listening carefully, then nodded thoughtfully. "Yes. I agree to your wager. We will present ourselves tonight—just the way we are—with no pre-transformations or other magical trickery."

"Excellent! May the best man win." Coyote banged his glass noisily on the counter top. "Bartender—Jason! How many of them prairie oysters ya got left? Never mind—I'll take 'em all!"

"What was that—prairie oysters? All of them? Got plans for the night, eh?"

"Could be..." Coyote leered surreptitiously at Fox and softly mimicked the grunting call of a whitetail buck in rut.

"Coyote! We agreed there'd be no cheating!"

"You said no *magical* cheating. Nothing magical about prairie oysters!"

"Right. Say, Jason my friend—what sort of tonics ya got here?"

"Tonics? You mean patent medicines? Well there's Coca Cola, of course —it's sweet and easy to down, and the cocaine infusion gives it a nice kick. And we have a couple bottles of Dr. Smith's surefire hangover preventative and breath freshener. That has cocaine too, but with a slug of opium to mellow it out. It's kind of bitter, but it does the job. And then there's—"

"No, I mean tonic like in—you know—like the prairie oysters, but stronger . . ."

"Oh! *That* kind of tonic! We keep Madame Bovary's confidential cordial for that problem, but we're fresh out right now. The only thing I got on the premises is... never mind."

"Never mind what?"

"It's good stuff, but you can't afford it."

"How do you know I can't afford it?"

"I know by the way you're dressed. Kenneth Lo's Lascivious Love Elixir is only for the—"

Clink.

"I'm sorry sir, but that's not enough—"

Clink, clink...

"Still not—"

Clink!"

"Yes, sir, that will do."

"Why, Coyote! That was very gentlemanly of you!"

"I'm not a gentleman. I bought it for myself. What good is gold if you can't use it to get what you want?"

"I have gold too! Here and there. I'll pay you back—"

"Do you have any with you?"

"No—"

"I do. Bartender, I'll have my tonic, if you please!"

With reverent hands Jason brought forth a small porcelain bottle sealed in gold foil and crimson wax. The label was written entirely in Chinese and featured a frolicking gold-leaf dragon of a blatantly male persuasion. Carefully he cut away the seals, extracted the cork, and poured out a tiny measure of dark brown, syrupy liquid. "That should be about right for a man your size. A little bit goes a long way!"

Coyote raised the glass to his nose. "Musky, aromatic, plenty of alcohol —smells like a pretty standard formula, but well brewed. What do you think, Todd?"

Fox took the glass, sniffed carefully, then tossed the contents down his throat. "I think it's pretty tasty for a love tonic. Thanks, Kay!"

Coyote glared balefully at Fox and snatched up the bottle of Kenneth Lo's Lascivious Love Elixir. He raised it to his lips and drained the contents without pausing for breath.

Jason was shaking his head slowly and regarding Coyote with a pitying expression. He retrieved the empty bottle and glass, examined them ruefully, and set them in the empty wash basin behind the bar. "You shouldn't have done that," he said.

Coyote laughed. "Don't worry about me—I have an exceedingly tough constitution!"

"You'd better! I'll have to ask you to leave now—it's bad for business to have patrons die on the premises. The hospital is four blocks south of here, on the tracks just like we are. Dr. Lo's elixir kicks in pretty quick—I recommend you take yourself there while you still can. Tell 'em you think you've been poisoned and require an emetic right away. Up with you, now! Can you make it out on your own feet, or would you like a little assistance?" Behind Jason's back, and out of Fox's angle of view, a small grey mouse licked the last dregs of Lascivious Love Elixir from Fox's glass, shuddered, and scampered unsteadily out of Coyote's sight.

Coyote rose to his feet and favored the bartender with a gracious bow. "Thank you for your hospitality, Jason! You have been a thoughtful and honest host. Perhaps we shall meet again some day." He turned to Fox and shrugged his shoulder for him to come along. "Ready to face your fate, mate?" he whispered softly.

Fox shared a brief, commiserating glance with the bartender, gathered up the stuffed jackalope and its broken antler, and followed behind Coyote without a word.

The street outside Jason's bar was lit by a single gas light—and deserted except for a rambunctious pack of five mismatched street mongrels. The cool evening breeze carried the scents of sage, and absinthe—and estrus bitch strong enough even for human nostrils! Coyote sniffed the air suspiciously, snorted, then knelt down to hug a large, lanky hound dog with white fur and red ears. "You little tease!" he laugh-hissed. "I should mount you right here and see what comes of it!" Cicéqi flipped her tail aside and pushed her flank hard up against Coyote's chest. "I dare ya!" she taunted. Coyote began to unbuckle his belt but the other dogs pushed between them singing: "Jackalopes! Jackalopes! Don't forget the Jackalopes! Follow us, follow us— seize your fate now, while you can! Come this way, to the riverside! It's dark among the willows of Arkansas' bank, and he's prone to flash floods this time of year. The humans won't bother us there."

Coyote rose to his feet and looked from Cicéqi to Fox, and back again. He was breathing heavily, and shifting his waistband to settle over-tight trousers a bit more comfortably. "All right, all right—have it your way, but let's get on with it! *Someone* is gonna get humped real soon!"

Coyote marched off in the wake of his spirit-dog pack while Fox... Fox nodded to Coyote's retreating back, smiled sneakily, and broke the second antler from the stuffed jackalope he was holding. He thrust both antlers into his pockets, tossed aside the de-antlered taxidermy mount, and circumspectly trailed the prankster's parade and Cicéqi's entrancing scent.

"Coyote! Can't you see anything at all? Here—rest your hand on my back and I'll lead you along. Fox! Stay where you are and you'll have some help in a minute." Cicéqi led Coyote to a flat, dampish area abuzz with mosquitos and lit by starlight alone. She sang softly, a single long note, and the mosquito-buzz grew silent. "Ah, Fox! There you are. Are you ready?"

Fox removed his clothes and placed the deer antlers on his head, holding them firmly in position with both hands. He knelt down in the darkness and nodded toward the sound of Cicéqi's voice. "Ready!"

"Yes, I see you are!" Cicéqi laughed. "Ready, Coyote?"

Coyote felt dizzy, and his skin had grown exquisitely sensitive. His hand was still resting on Cicéqi's shoulders and he gave them one long caress, then stepped reluctantly away. He pulled off his clothing, lowered himself gingerly onto hands and knees, and closed his eyes in anticipation. "I'm ready," he whispered.

"Excellent preparation!" Cicéqi laughed. "You're both mindless with lust, and I am too! The Old Magic will be pleased." Cicéqi filled her lungs, paused, then breathed out a single sharp note that pierced straight to the marrow of Coyote's bones. Coyote gasped, transfixed, as the other Spirit Children joined Cicéqi in a Medicine Song that was complex, and playful, and shamelessly erotic. His senses grew dim and his thoughts began to unravel but he made no effort to fight the process—willfully abandoning himself to the dubious dominion of his five Spirit Children and their fickle ally, the Old Magic.

*****

Whispering willow-leaf-rustle... beguiling lust-musk-scent... tentative, snuffling tail caress... Eyes still closed, Coyote stretched forward and lifted upward at the touch—spine base tingling and ears flushing hot as Fox's velvety jackalope nose seized the opportunity to tickle its way into more sensitive territory. "Ah, Fox—you're too good to me. And such a gracious loser you are! No, don't stop! In a minute I'll return the favor. I love that new scent of yours! It's nice... so nice... never thought a jackalope doe would smell so much like a buck in rut, though. Old Magic has such a sneaky sense of humor!" Fox's delightful nuzzling paused for a moment and Coyote heard something rather like a stifled chuckle, then the nuzzle-strokes danced their way swiftly up onto Coyote's back, and a pair of powerful jackalope forelegs clamped themselves firmly around Coyote's flanks. Thrusting movements, a distinctly *intimate* touch, and—"Fox! What are you doing?"

"What does it feel like I'm doing?"

Coyote hopped free from Fox's amorous embrace and snapped open a pair of dark-sensitive jackalope eyes to behold the handsome, *antlered* visage of—"Fox? What—no! How did you do it? I drank enough love potion to excommunicate a convent!"

Fox raised a fluffy front paw to pat one of the antlers fondly. "Don't you recognize them? These are the antlers you bought from Jason an hour ago! Tell me please—speaking as the beauteous and fertile doe you have become—are they not irresistibly seductive?"

"No! Those are *my* antlers! Give them back!"

"Sorry, too late. But I have a different sort of horn I can lend you..." Fox nuzzled the soft fur beneath Coyote's jaw, then began to stroke his way up and behind her long, sensitive jackalope ears. Coyote nuzzled back, trembling, then jerked herself away. "Fox—I don't think I'm ready for this! Did I really lose the bet? I should be seducing *you* right now! I think I need a little more time..." Coyote twisted around to nose frantically beneath her tail, and Fox joined her in the exploration. "Time for what? You're as ready as I am! Assume the position, please." Fox stroked delicately with his muzzle and Coyote shuddered at the touch, then scrabbled to her feet and kicked out vigorously with all four of them—launching herself straight up into the air, then off into the willow tangles with great long zigzag leaps. She stopped, suddenly, for no particular reason, and Fox was right there beside her—pressing his shoulder against hers and forcing his chin firmly down across the top of her back. Coyote bunched up her haunches to leap again but then she hesitated, savoring the sensation, and yielded to the craving for just one long, sensuous stretch. When the stretch was over Coyote found herself chest down and tail up, with ears flattened in submission and rump elevated invitingly. Fox was on her in an instant, grasping her flanks again and probing his way competently toward the proper spot. "No—wait! I didn't mean it that way! Hold on a bit..."

Fox didn't answer, and Coyote couldn't quite muster the will to wiggle her way free. Fox's scent was intoxicating, and his missed thrusts maddening, and even as she protested she was adjusting her posture just that little bit to help—

"Uncle Fox?"

Fox stopped his movements, but made no other response.

"Uncle Fox, I can tell you're busy right now, but—"

"Yes! I am busy right now! Please go away. Coyote and I have a very important matter to attend to."

"Yes, we can see that! But there's another matter you must attend to first."

"What—"

"Defend yourself!"

The weight on Coyote's back disappeared, and she whipped around to find Fox in astonished confrontation with another jackalope buck.

"Cicéqi?"

"Nah—I'm one of the other minions. Put up yer tines, varmint!" The new jackalope poked tentatively at Fox's shoulder and Fox snapped his antlers down to parry the attack, then converted his defensive momentum into a powerful offensive lunge. His opponent was caught off balance but managed a hasty recovery before Fox was able to press his advantage. The two jackalope bucks strove in earnest then—clashing antlers and tearing great furrows in the damp ground with the strength of their leaps and recoveries. Feints and strikes became a blur of frenetic motion until the interloper was thrown helplessly through the air, landing in an untidy confusion of unbalanced limbs and upside down antlers. Fox leapt forward to thrust both antlers into the exposed belly of his opponent, but at the last instant he held back his strength so that the attack caused little harm. "Yield—or next time I won't be so gentle!" he demanded.

"I yield!" the defeated jackalope confirmed, and Fox stepped back to permit him to hobble away.

Chest heaving, antlers raised in triumph, Fox stood alone and victorious on the field of battle. He savored the heady feeling for a time, then turned his attention back to Coyote, his rightful—

"Uncle Fox! Can I play too?"

"Wait a minute—who are you? How many of you are there?"

"Five. We're always five. Or one. It depends on your point of view."

"But how many of you are jackalope bucks?"

"Five. The Old Magic got carried away and transformed us all. Defend yourself!"

Fox defended himself—testing at first, then tearing into the new intruder with an energy even greater than he had shown before. Two more jackalope bucks drifted into view but they didn't join the battle. Not yet. Coyote watched in apprehensive fascination as the current duel grew more intense. Many *many* years had passed since Fox and the Spirit Children had fought together! This contest was still a game to them, but—

"Do you like it?"

Coyote whipped around to find Cicéqi looming close beside her. Cicéqi in jackalope buck form.

"Do I like what?"

"Do you like being fought over like this? We hope so! It's a lot of work!"

"It is nothing of the kind! You silly males are fighting because you like it better than sex. Honestly! I won't say I volunteered to be the female, but its done now and I'm not quite foolish enough to spurn Old Magic's gift by changing that small fact. So here I stand—alone, outsmarted, flagrantly in heat and exquisitely available—and all Fox wants to do is play with his silly little horns."

"Antlers. Goats have horns, deer have antlers."

"And jackalope bucks have hot tempers!"

"Yes, it appears we do—ouch! That hurt! Did you see what Fox just did? Nice move! If he tries that trick again we'll have to... er... where were we? Yes—we were talking about sex. Well, you see... I tend to be female most of the time but right now I'm not and... with Fox and the rest of me so busy, and you just standing here all neglected and unappreciated... it seems... if it's not too much trouble... while we're waiting you could share that lovely warm place between your haunches with me!"

"Cicéqi! How can you—"

"Of course, I should have known—you didn't really mean all those things you've been promising me since we left Jason's bar. It was all just more Coyote talk, I guess..."

"Cicéqi! No! I *did* mean them!"

"Very well—if you *did* mean them—prove it to me now!"

Coyote sighed, not unhappily, and assumed the position.

*****

"Coyote, I still can't believe you just raised your rump and let Cicéqi take advantage of you like that. Taking advantage of you is *my* job!"

Coyote rubbed her cheek fondly against the shoulder of her valiant new jackalope mate. "You did well enough when your own turn came!" she purred.

"Yes, but when we made our bargain I never thought I'd have to share you!"

"That took me by surprise too. It all did. But the look on your face when you first realized what Cicéqi was doing to me... it was priceless!"

"I'll bet it was! I wonder if we'll ever figure out which of us is... how many kits does a jackalope kindle, anyway? Or is kindle even the right word? Or kits?"

"You can call them kits. I'll call them trouble. If the Old Magic shows its usual sense of humor I'll pop out a dozen of 'em—or one enormous, groin-splitting calf. I don't know why I persist in dealing with that—"

"Careful, Coyote!"

"—noble and powerful and sadly misunderstood co-creator of our World."

"And personal creator of you... and me."

"Yes, indeed! Whatever was I thinking? Let's change the subject." Coyote nosed wistfully at the ample equipment Fox now carried beneath his own tail. "How's that extra horn you like so much to share with me? Is it ready yet for another go?"

"Er... not quite yet. Soon."

"Oh, never mind, then. I'll just call over Cicéqi or one of the other—"

"Listen! Do you hear that voice? It sounds like Zebediah. Bars must have closed for the night."

'O bury me not on the lone prairie.'
These words came low and mournfully
From the pallid lips of the youth who lay
On his dying bed at the close of day.
'O bury me not on the lone prairie
Where the wild coyote will howl o'er me ...'

"Hey! He's singing my song! Coyote lifted her head to the starlit sky and let forth an eerie, jackalope-flavored parody of a coyote howl. Fox joined her, and other voices from the nearby darkness. Zeb's voice grew quiet.

"Zebediah!" Coyote called out in an unearthly, jackalope-banshee keen. "Zebediah—foolish mortal—you have awakened the Spirits!"

"Spirits! I'm sorry—I didn't mean to rile you up! Please, you just settle down easy-like and I'll git myself away from here right quick. You won't hear no more singing from me tonight, you can count on that!"

"But we like your singing! Sing us another song about coyotes! Or rabbits. You can sing about romantic rabbits, if you like. Or anything with antlers and a bad attitude."

"Well, uh... I don't know... can't say as I recall any songs like that..."

"None at all? That's very disappointing, Zebediah! Perhaps we're displeased with you after all—"

"No! Wait! I can sing *Home on the Range!*

285

Oh, give me a home where the buffalo roam,
Where the deer and the antelope play—"

"Jackalope!"

"Huh?"

"The words of your song are not quite right. Try singing 'Where the deer and the *jackalope* play.'"

"Are you joshing me? Fellas—I admit you had me suckered for a minute, but I'm on to your game now. Come out and show yourselves!"

Coyote crept forth from the darkness and stationed herself directly behind Zebediah's earnestly intent, if unsteady form. She snorted loudly and the hapless human whipped around in a panic, almost falling over in the process.

Zebediah noticed the small furry creature crouched on the street before him and sighed in extravagantly intoxicated relief. "Well, goll-ie! Just a gosh-derned jackrabbit! Go on, you—shoo! Why are you just standing there like that? You got rabies, or something? If I had my gun with me I'd—what's that?"

Fox had crept into the circle of lamplight and stood now close beside Coyote—ears flattened and antlers raised threateningly. Behind Zeb sounded a hiss like a hoop snake and the human twisted back to encounter five more aggressively antlered jackrabbits . . . or spirits.

"Uh-oh." Zebediah bowed his head and attempted—with limited success—to return his attention to Coyote without quite turning his back on any of the other apparitions. "Spirits—I'm truly sorry I've offended you. I swear I never meant to! Can I make it up to you somehow?"

Coyote rose to her haunches and regarded the human through a lambently lamp-lit eye. "Perhaps. That's a mighty fine new hat you're wearing! Would you care to part with it?"

A tragic, thunderstruck expression replaced the look of terrified awe that had previously marked Zebediah's features. Wordlessly he lifted his hands to his head, removed the cream colored Stetson, and carefully placed it on the ground. Coyote hopped forward and sniffed the hat carefully from brim to crown, then nudged beneath it and stood on her haunches with the hat balanced on the top of her head, and the brim dangling ludicrously at the level of her belly. "Hey guys," she called out in a muffled voice, "look! I'm a parlor lamp!"

Fox flipped the hat away with his antlers and pressed himself close against Coyote's flank. "And I am the spark that shall set you aflame!"

Coyote cuddled close for a moment, then curled around and ostentatiously investigated her nether regions. "Hmmm—seems to be a problem down here. My wick is missing, and I can't quite recall where I left it."

Fox insinuated a companionable foreleg across Coyote's shoulders and whispered conspiratorially, "You lost it in a bet, remember? But you can borrow mine!"

"You told me you're not ready yet!"

"Now I am. We jackalope bucks recuperate quickly."

"Zebediah!"

"Er... yes, Spirit?"

"Keep your hat for now. This irresistibly antlered jackalope buck will cover me instead. Carry on with your song, please!"

"Uh... sure... you bet... whatever you say. Just let me catch my breath a bit and I'll get right to it...

Oh, give me a home where the buffalo roam,
Where the deer and the jackalope play;
Where seldom is heard a discouraging word— "

"Yes, that will do. It pleases us. Sing it louder, though! Sing it 'til you get back to your room... or any other time you think we may be lurking about, and it will save you a worse fate. You may leave us now."

"Yes, Spirit—uh, Spirits, I'll do that—*And the skies are not cloudy all day...*"

"Fox—that was one smooth invisibility spell you used on the night clerk! I hardly felt it at all."

"Didn't take much. The man didn't want to see us—just like Dr. Sklarsen doesn't."

"Too true. Look—there's light coming out from under his door. I wonder if he's still awake!" Coyote backed up to the professor's hotel room door and thumped emphatically with a hind foot, filling the hallway with her thrumming cadence. The door opened immediately and a disheveled, wild-eyed Dr. Sklarsen confronted the interloping jackalope pair.

Fox rose to his full two foot six of height and inclined a majestically antlered head in greeting courtesy. "*Guten Abend, Herr Profesor!*"

Coyote sat up on her own haunches and nodded a leanly attractive but otherwise unremarkable jackrabbit head in the professor's direction. "Howdy, pardner!"

Herr Doctor Profesor Wolfgang Sklarsen did not return the greetings. He merely stood stood there in his doorway, a dazed expression frozen onto his countenance. Coyote and Fox waited on the threshold for a few seconds, then invited themselves inside for a look around.

Photographic plate boxes were everywhere, some of them open, and on the bedside table one particular plate was propped intimately close to a brightly-burning kerosine lamp. A jeweler's loupe, an empty wine bottle, and an empty cup also shared the table's surface.

Coyote hopped onto a chair and peered closely at the photo plate. "Look, Fox! It's Cicéqi!"

Fox hopped up and admired the photo plate as well. In exquisite scientific detail it revealed a close-field negative rendering of sunlit mountain stream boulders, a single flood-battered cottonwood seedling, and Cicéqi's scandalously impossible hoop snake form.

Click.

Four ample jackalope ears snapped erect at the sound and oriented instantly on its source. The source was Dr. Sklarsen, securing the lock on his door.

Coyote and Fox turned to each other and shared a lazy, lagomorph grin.

"Well will you look at that—the doctor wants to capture us!" Coyote remarked conversationally. "When I'm a scrawny, dirt-colored coyote everyone wants me to go away, but as a scrawny, dirt-colored bunny I'm just too popular for words!"

"Maybe *I'm* the one he wants. An antlered jackrabbit would make an excellent scientific specimen, don't you think?"

"And talking jackrabbits are not worth his trouble?"

"We're talking with the help of our magic. The professor probably can't even understand us."

"Zeb understands us."

"Zeb's an ignorant yokel. Our professor is of much finer clay. Hey! Professor Sklarsen! Can you understand what I'm saying?" Professor Sklarsen was staring raptly at his two jackalope captives, but he made no direct response to Fox's words.

Coyote laid her ears back in annoyance. "This human is dense," she growled. "I gift him with furred trout, hoop snakes—even create a new species just for his amusement—and he's still stuck in his old ways! Let's sing for him—maybe that will break through the walls. A human song. One he already knows. What's a good song for a slow-witted ivory tower escapee?"

"Once upon a midnight dreary—"

"I said a song!" Coyote hopped down from her chair seat perch and stood up on her haunches, neck extended and ears trailing gracefully down the length of her back. "Daisy, Daisy give me your answer do..." she began. Fox oozed up beside and pressed a testosterone-fevered cheek close against hers.

"...I'm half crazy all for the love of you..." he crooned in honeyed harmony.

It won't be a stylish marriage
I can't afford a carriage
But you'll look sweet upon the seat
Of a bicycle built for two!

Dr. Sklarsen hefted his wine bottle, eyed its implacable emptiness sadly, and set it down again. "What *are* you creatures?" he inquired plaintively.

"We're jackalopes!" Coyote and Fox replied in unison.

"Jackalopes. I don't think I'm familiar with the term."

Coyote licked a forepaw clean, then ran it carefully down the length of one elegant ear. "That's 'cause you're from Germany. They know all about us out here in the sticks."

"I'm not from Germany!" Professor Sklarsen admonished sternly. "I just work there. My homeland is Prussia."

Coyote eyed Fox mischievously. "Do you suppose he'd enjoy a visit to *our* homeland?" she whispered.

"Don't tempt me," Fox muttered in reply.

"I'm so sorry, but I didn't quite catch that. You were saying you're jackalopes weren't you? I assume that's in reference to the North American steppe hare referred to locally as jackrabbit? I must acknowledge there's a certain resemblance."

Coyote hopped forward to sniff the human's shoe and rub her chin fondly against his ankle. "Dr. Sklarsen, I'm so proud of you!" she gushed. "I never thought you'd learn to accept magical talking animals so easily!"

"I'm a scientist. I've been trained to have an open mind. Please don't insult it by speaking to me of magic and such rot. You're a clever puppet, perhaps—or a drunken hallucination of some sort. The truth will come to light eventually."

"If we're hallucinations, why did you lock your door?"

"It seemed a sensible thing to do at the time."

Coyote hopped back up to her chair perch and braced both forelegs against the delicate milk-glass base of the professor's table lamp. "Since you're such a sensible fellow, perhaps you'll sensibly open that door again before I cover your floor with broken lamp bits and burning kerosene."

Dr. Sklarsen opened the door, and the two jackalopes utilized it immediately. When she was safely in the hallway Coyote turned back to the professor and waved a flippant forepaw in his direction, then nudged Fox with her shoulder and turned to go.

"Wait!" Dr. Sklarsen cried. "It was a mistake to try to hold you. I admit that. But I've released you now. Will I see you again?"

"Perhaps you'll hallucinate us again if you drink enough wine. I recommend Jason's tavern, just a couple of blocks south, on Main street. Nice atmosphere there, much better than drinking alone in your room. Tell the bartender Kay is doing just fine, and took no harm from his elixir overdose."

"Kay? As in Kay Latrans, my guide? Do you know him?"

"Intimately. I am Kay."

"And I'm Todd!" Fox added brightly. "Kay may be—occupied—for a while, but I'll be in human form and back to work in a few days, just as soon as we've concluded some important business together. See you then!" Fox bumped Coyote sharply with his shoulder, knocking her over, then sank claws in carpet and hurled himself down the hallway and around a corner in three tremendous bounds. Coyote recovered her balance and scrabbled after him an instant later—shouting something about burying her hat on the lone prairie when she caught up with it. Dr. Sklarsen stood staring after the apparitions for a long, *long* time, then bemusedly shook his head and returned to his room—where he went to bed, but most definitely not to sleep.

*****

"Greetings, Dr. Sklarsen! How you keeping, my man? Did you miss us? Do we still have a job?"

Wolfgang Sklarsen lifted his gaze from the beer glass before him and beheld Todd Reynard in human form, fully if dustily clothed, and unremarkable except for the lanky, insolent-looking jackrabbit—or jackalope —perched on his left shoulder.

"You certainly took your time!" he replied in a tight, strained voice. "This is the last night I was going to wait for you. My photographs are on their way to Germany even as we speak—along with that curiously corroded stock from Mr. Foster's rifle—and I'll be taking the first morning train north. Mr. Foster is gone already. He has left in my care a gun, a hat, and a story no man but myself could possibly believe."

Without waiting for an invitation Todd entered Dr. Sklarsen's bar booth and seated himself across from the professor. "You're ready to travel? Excellent! Kay and I have something really special to show you this time!"

"Did you say Kay? Kindly tell me where Kay Latrans is at this moment."

The jackalope creature leaned forward on her shoulder perch and glared across at the doctor. "I'm right here, you idiot!" she hissed.

Dr. Sklarsen inhaled deeply, then emptied his lungs in a long, heartfelt sigh. Looking straight at Kay he remarked softly, "I was afraid you were going to say that. Why aren't the people around us paying attention to you?

Are you a hallucination after all? Am I going mad, perhaps? That would be a convenient way for me to deal with this situation."

Kay looked sidelong at the doctor and twisted her features into a truly disturbing parody of the Cheshire Cat's grin. "But we're all *mad* here!" she purred. She held the pose for a moment but, sadly, chose not to fade conveniently away. Instead she drop-hopped smoothly to the table surface and glide-hopped forward to nuzzle Dr. Sklarsen's hand. The hand jerked at her touch, but did not pull away.

"Nah nah nah, Professor," the jackalope soothed, "don't you fret none. The other humans aren't noticing us because we're just not very... interesting... to them right now. It's a little trick we spirits use when we don't wish to be bothered. When you want that glass refilled you should let us know, 'cause I don't think Jason is going take care of it anytime soon!

"Now—we were going to tell you about the next great thing for you to photograph. You'll never guess what we have in mind for you you this time!"

Wordlessly Dr. Sklarsen removed his glasses, polished them with a spotlessly clean handkerchief, carefully settled them back in place. Sadly he shook his head and returned his gaze to the small furred entity before him. "I agree," he sighed. "I'll never guess. Please tell me."

Kay rose to her haunches and gazed earnestly into the professor's pale gray human eyes. "Sasquatch!" she whispered breathlessly. "We're going to guide you to Sasquatch! This time of year he's usually way out of reach in the high country, but he has this irresistible craving for—"

"No," Dr. Sklarsen interrupted. "Thank you all the same, but I think I have all the mystery I can possibly handle standing right here before my eyes. Sasquatch will have to reveal his secrets to some other, more intrepid explorer."

Kay's ears drooped for a moment, then stood up jauntily again. "So I'm all the mystery you can handle? That's nice, I suppose. What dark secrets would you like me to reveal? Do you yearn to blast your enemies with unspeakable curses? Travel to the other Worlds? Shape-shift? I can't shift myself right now, but I'm not entirely without resources. Mr. Reynard, for example, is quite gifted in that field, and this tavern would provide a most convenient locus for the magic. Our surrounding here have a delightfully credulous ambiance to them—not at all like that... difficult... train platform where we first met. If your soul is driven to truly understand this World, you really ought to try scenting it through a different nose."

"Perhaps we should begin with something a bit more prosaic. I'll need to photograph you, of course, and perform a proper physical exam, and then —"

Kay flopped backwards onto the table top, splayed wide her haunches, and slipped both front paws coyly behind her neck. "Oh, Wolfgang!" she crooned in a sultry voice, "I thought you'd never ask! Go ahead—*examine* me—I don't mind."

"Stop that!" Dr. Sklarsen snapped. "It's obscene! I would need more privacy and much better light to examine you properly. And even that won't do me any good. I'd have to bring you back alive—or ship home your dissected and preserved corpse—before my colleagues would accept my report."

Kay shifted back into the traditional hunchbacked lagomorph sitting posture, and rocked her ears demurely to Todd. "Did you hear that? The doctor wants to be alone with me—and he's going to carry me off to his lair in Berlin!"

Todd laughed, "I think your virtue, such as it is, is safe enough with him! And anyway you're out of heat now, and will be until your kits are born. Why don't you go with him? Berlin is a wicked, wicked city, almost as bad as Paris. You'll fit right in there."

"Fox... er... Todd, you know I don't like to be away from my people for long. I get homesick."

"That's not homesickness, it's hunger. If you like I can tag along and feed you the life energy you need."

"Hmm—that *is* a thought. Is Berlin really that wicked?"

"Well, you know the human cities are all about the same when it comes to that—but the European ones have had more time to practice. And they have some really excellent restaurants!"

"Wolfgang—promise you'll take me to Berlin!"

"I beg your pardon?"

"Silly human—you know you want to! Promise me."

"I really don't think I can—"

"Promise me!"

"Very well, I promise you shall visit Berlin if it is within my power to make that come to pass."

"Excellent! Now Todd, you must promise to come along!"

"Of course, my love! You do plan to wait until after our children are born, I hope."

"Yes, of course. We jackalopes should overrun Colorado first and save *der Rheinland* for later. But look! The doctor's glass has gone dry! Surely he'll be wanting another without delay."

Dr. Sklarsen's gaze shifted to his empty vessel and he sighed, resignedly. "Perhaps another beer would not be out of place," he admitted.

Kay sniffed the glass rim and nodded appreciatively. "Yes... nice brew! I think I'll have one for myself. Todd, love—perhaps you can find it in your heart to spare a coin for a thirsty doe who's just a mite short of change. I've misplaced my clothes, it appears, and all my money—"

"—is right here!" Todd laughed, patting a trouser pocket. "You don't think I'd just walk by and leave all your lovely gold lying out there in the coyote willows, do you?"

"No, I don't think that. I saw you take it."

Todd laughed again, reached out to pat his jackalope bride fondly on the rump, then firmly nudged her forward until she fell-jumped off the table edge and scuttled into the darkness beneath it. "Jason!" he called out sharply, "Can't you spare a little attention for your old buddy Todd?"

Jason rushed into view immediately. "Excuse me, sir—I'm so sorry!— how did you get in here without—"

"Never mind about that. I'm here now, sharing a round with my good colleague Dr. Sklarsen. And dinner too, if he's amenable. We'll have three more of what the doctor is drinking, and a couple of steaks, and some vegetables or salad, if you have any."

"We have corn and potatoes—"

"Yes, that will do nicely. Please keep the butter separate, in a side dish."

"Yes, sir. We'll have that for you right away..." The bartender hesitated, opened his mouth as if to say something more, then thought better of the idea and bustled off to secure the requested items.

Dinner arrived promptly, and Kay hopped lightly from floor to bench to table top as soon as privacy had been restored. She was not alone. As she rushed to make acquaintance with her beer glass five enormous cockroaches scuttled down from her back and infested the mound of mashed potatoes on Todd's plate. Kay ignored her chitinous consorts and buried her muzzle in beer foam. Todd leaned back with a wry smile and permitted his new guests to feed unmolested. Dr. Sklarsen sat rigidly immobile, regarding the tableau before him with an expression of horrified nausea.

Kay lifted her head for air, belched happily, then carefully groomed foam remnants from face and whiskers. She caught Dr. Sklarsen's expression and clucked sadly. "Now, now, Dr. Sklarsen, weren't you telling me last week that all of Mother Nature's creations are worthy of our reverence and respect? I seem to recall you were saying something of that sort, but perhaps my memory is playing tricks again. Memories are such fragile things."

Dr. Sklarsen nodded stiffly at the jackalope's words, but he did not offer any of his own, and the expression of nausea did not leave his face.

Todd waved the cockroaches away from his plate. "Go on, you!" he laughed. "You've had your little joke. If you want to share dinner with the doctor you'll have to dress for the occasion. Something cute and furry would be nice. And small. I'll not be buying any extra food for you!"

The cockroaches scuttled along Todd's left arm and out of view beneath the table, and moments later five small brown weasels returned by the same path—immediately sinking five sets of needle sharp canines into the edge of Todd's steak. "Excuse me," he interrupted, and sliced away a modest chunk of meat for himself—abandoning the rest to a squabbling and extravagantly toothy fate.

"Please, Doctor—eat! None of us will molest the food on *your* plate. It wouldn't be polite."

Dr. Sklarsen poked at his steak for a moment, then abandoned the pretense. "I suppose you're going to tell me the cockroaches and weasels talk too," he sighed.

The five weasels lifted their heads and fixed the doctor with a single, multi-orbed stare. "We do!" they squeaked as one, and resumed feeding.

The jackalope had been observing Dr. Sklarsen's distress with an expression curiously akin to sympathetic fondness. Now she glide-hopped carefully forward—sedulously avoiding the tangle of carnivorous and potentially deadly weasels—and politely nuzzled the doctor's hand. "We've been very hard on you," she admitted sadly. "It's all my fault, you know. I was annoyed, and determined to make you see a wider world. I've done that, I believe. If you wish we will leave you now, never to disturb you again."

Dr. Sklarsen's hand lifted, hesitated, then began to scratch tentatively behind the jackalope's jaw. She pushed her neck firmly into the movement and folded her ears down in pleasure at the touch. "I'll take this as a request not to leave quite yet," she murmured.

"No, please don't leave!" he begged. "If I've gone mad it's not your fault. Teach me more!"

Kay shook herself and stood up on her haunches, facing the human eye to eye. "As you wish! But first you must tell me—what is your favorite animal?"

"Favorite animal?" Dr. Sklarsen looked thoughtfully to one side for a moment, but not quite far enough to lose track of the table full of strange creatures before him. "I do not believe it is proper for a scientist to have a favorite animal. All living things are equally fascinating to me."

Kay nodded politely, but looked more than a little skeptical of the professor's statement. "Very well then, what was your favorite animal when you were a foolish child—before you became wise and important like you are now?"

"Mock me if you like—I'm merely telling you the truth as I perceive it. I had several favorite animals while I was growing up, but the wolf was my most consistent favorite."

Kay's tail snapped up in alarm at the professor's words, and she backed away, nervously. Todd and the spirit-weasels appeared unconcerned. Amused, perhaps, but not actually concerned. Todd extended his hand across the table, and Dr. Sklarsen shook it in automatic response. "Wolf, you say?" Todd inquired brightly, maintaining his grip on the doctor's hand, "Really, now—I never would have thought it! You strike me as more the raven type— but very well—wolf it shall be!" Todd's expression grew distant and strange... and rather frightening.

"No, Fox! Wait!" Kay called out. Todd relaxed his grip, and Dr. Sklarsen snatched his hand back hastily.

"Really, Kay—what's got into you? Weren't you asking me to initiate our doctor into the mysteries of shape shifting?"

"Yes... but let's not use the wolf form. The magic might draw his attention here. How about something simple and safe, like a fox?"

"Foxes are *safe*, says the delicious-looking jackalope!"

"That's not what I meant! It's just that right now Wolf and I are not... getting along."

"You've been gone for five years! Whatever it is you did to Wolf—don't you think he'll have calmed down by now?"

"Let's not put him to the test, if it's alright with you. And besides—the doctor will be a tough patient. Why not work with your natural strengths?

"Kay! Are you questioning my power?"

"Of course not! I was merely—"

"Good. Doctor, may I have your hand, please? Kay has just helped me to determine the most fitting choice for your initiation."

Dr. Sklarsen kept his hands firmly on the table top before him. "First tell me what you're trying to do!"

"Isn't it clear yet? At your request, Kay is attempting to teach you some of our strange ways. She feels the experience of a different point of view would be a good way to start. Don't you?"

"Yes, but—"

"Dr. Sklarsen, if any of us intended you harm, you would be harmed! We do not require your permission for that. Now—kindly give to me your hand, or bid us depart your presence."

The spirit weasels had ceased their squabbling and were peering at the doctor with an eerily intent gaze. Dr. Sklarsen turned to the jackalope creature and met the same reception. He averted his eyes and lifted one hand from the table surface, clenched it into a fist, released. It was a good hand—

strong, and generous, and full of skill. It had served him well for many years, and with luck and proper care it would serve him for many more. *Wolfi, you fool—you don't have to do this!* Dr. Sklarsen clenched his fist again and whispered to himself "No, I don't." Then slowly he opened the hand, examined it carefully front to back, and offered it humbly to the strange being who called himself Todd Reynard.

Conversation ceased in Jason's Idle Argonaut Tavern as every man in the building felt... something. A tingling change or wavering it was—or perhaps a simple earth tremor. Earth movement was the consensus, in any case, when conversation resumed a moment later. Proponents of the earth tremor theory were supported by the sudden appearance of a confused, no doubt quake-dazed jackrabbit which skittered frantically from table to table until it discovered the saloon doors and darted out of sight beneath them.

*****

Massive late-season thunderheads mounded high, to the southeast. They were larger and darker than the others had been. And closer. These ones might even deliver the moisture they promised. A rain-scented wind gust worked loose a lock of Dr. Sklarsen's hair—his perfectly normal human hair—and Dr. Sklarsen tucked it back with a perfectly normal human hand. Rain would be welcome, of course. Rain was always welcome in these lands except when it came on too strongly, and burst out through the arroyos in savage flash floods. Dr. Sklarsen scanned the sagebrush flats before him with a keen, gray, glasses-free gaze—pulling down the wide brim of Mr. Foster's white Stetson to better shade his eyes from the oppressive late morning sunlight that still bathed his part of the landscape. It was a practical hat— well adapted to this harsh climate—and he was growing rather fond of it. Dr. Sklarsen decided he would purchase another for himself if Mr. Foster—or Kay Latrans—ever returned to claim this one.

No movement. The search was pointless, really. No desert animal stirred voluntarily in such heat, and in any case he had failed to make a sure identification of Kay's kit... or *his*... in days. Jackrabbits aplenty populated the flats before him but they all sort of looked alike to his human eyes—even his new, perfect ones—and as for his nose . . . Dr. Sklarsen sighed, and turned away. Best to resume his vigil in the cool of evening, and utilize this time to struggle once again with his expedition report. He settled himself comfortably in the shade of the supply wagon, opened his photographic diary to the most recent entry, slammed the wretched thing closed again. Perhaps he should simply strike camp and be on his way. The kits were weaned, and fat, and already lightning-swift—and how could he pretend to guard them when he couldn't even recognize them anymore?

Only one kit each! And both of them males. Much heated discussion had followed the event, and the resolution had been most unexpected, involving six new jackalope females—none of which had been Kay—and Dr. Sklarsen to guard the kits once they were weaned. Dr. Sklarsen in *human* form, with all his possessions retrieved from storage intact—and guilt-gifted with a fine new wagon and mule team to boot! So strange... to be looking down at the strange hare-creatures again, rather than sniffing them nose to... nose.

"I'll be back soon," Kay had promised, gleefully flourishing his brand new jackalope antlers—*just the way Todd had flourished his*—and lasciviously eyeing his harem of newly crafted jackalope does—*just the way Todd eyed me!* "—and I'll have another surprise for you then!"

Wunderbar. He was not sure he could handle another one of Kay Latrans' surprises. Perhaps he should make his exit now, while the roads were still passable. The wagon was packed, the mules well fed and rested, and he could have the whole thing in motion with very little effort. A good photographer could earn his way anywhere, and doubly so out here in this strange, empty land where the people were so refreshingly free with their money. Dr. Sklarsen surveyed the wagon's contents again, and frowned. Emulsion plates, chemicals, flash powder, developing tent, food, water, formaldehyde— The formaldehyde would have to go. It was valuable, in its way—a special formula of the highest purity, and with the latest buffering chemicals, shipped to him at great expense by his colleagues in Berlin—but it was too heavy for the long journey he had in mind, and he would never use it in any case. The *Universität zu Berlin* would not be receiving any shipments of preserved hoop snakes or furred trout from him, even if he again chanced to encountered such creatures. They might be somebody he knew! And as for pickled *jackalopes*... he shuddered at the thought.

Dr. Sklarsen sighed again, and began to slide the formaldehyde drum toward the open end of his wagon. It was a large drum, too heavy for him to lift with just the strength of his own arms. Once he pushed the thing off he would never be able to put it back without help. Very well, so be it. He dragged, balanced, raised his eyes to the horizon one more time, and detected movement.

It was a coyote—a big, handsome one, most likely male—trotting toward him in full view, with tongue lolling extravagantly from the heat.

Dr. Sklarsen's eyes narrowed, but the only movement he made was to shift the formaldehyde drum a centimeter back from the wagon's edge. A week ago that coyote could have slain him with a single bite, and even now it posed a deadly danger to his... son. Still he bore the creature no animosity, and would do nothing to harm it if it continued on its current path. The coyote had a right to walk this land—far more right than he did! That opinion had been formed long before his... *peculiar*... recent experiences.

The coyote halted and crouched, ears fixed on some small noise in the brush.

No—not here! Hunt anywhere else... but not *here!*

As Dr. Sklarsen's gaze locked on the coyote his hand reached back and closed upon Mr. Foster's newly restocked and repaired Winchester 1892. The cartridge was levered in, gun raised to shoulder, safety released. The coyote pounced forward, tail waving happily, and a small gray form could be seen wiggling between its front paws.

Dr. Sklarsen fired.

*****

Herr Doctor Profesor Wolfgang Eisenhertz-Sklarsen signed the final transport papers, entrusting his valuable and extremely heavy specimen drum to the uncertain mercies of the Atchison, Topeka and Santa Fe Railway shipping clerk. "Cover letter?" inquired the man in a bored but kindly enough voice.

"I beg your pardon?"

"Your paperwork's fine, far as I can tell, but folk usually like to send a letter with their packages. You can tuck the envelope in this pocket right here, if you've a mind." The clerk eyed the acrid-smelling formaldehyde drum dubiously. "Unless you already got one tucked in there."

"No, nothing in there but my... specimen. I thank you for your offer, sir, and if you'd be so kind as to provide me with some paper and an envelope, I'll implement your suggestion right away."

*Never did finish the report—have to tell them **something**. Kay! If only you had come to me first...* Dr. Sklarsen accepted the proffered writing materials and turned quickly away. The tears were coming again, and he could not let them show. *Kay, Kay—whatever, wherever you are—do my human promises mean anything to you? Are you even truly dead? I wish you well, in any case. Enjoy your journey to Berlin.*

Dr. Sklarsen dabbed furtively with his handkerchief and in a firm, precise hand with only the tiniest amount of trembling he wrote:

> *Dearest Wilhelm,*
>
> *It is with the most overwhelming sadness and chagrin that I must report to you my failure to secure the fish and reptile specimens requested, and in addition my inability to provide you*

with a coherent account of my activities and expenditures as your field representative on the North American Plains Photographic Expedition. I am deeply humiliated by this lapse on my part, and shall take this opportunity to tender, in response, my immediate resignation from the Academy. This is a personal decision on my part, and in no way intended to reflect unfavorably upon you, or my many other treasured associates. Please do not attempt to respond to this letter. You shall not be hearing from me again.

The canine specimen enclosed herein is offered as partial— and, of course, ridiculously inadequate—compensation for my numerous failings in my primary endeavor. The specimen appears to be a previously unrecorded subspecies of **Canis latrans**, *as you will no doubt confirm upon close examination of dental and cranial morphology. If subspecies status is confirmed, please consider my suggestion of* **maii** *as the subspecies modifier. And also—as a personal favor to me, the last one I shall ever ask of you—please do what you can to keep the enclosed Stetson hat permanently together with the type specimen. It is a bizarre request, I realize, but I bid you respect it in any case, if you can find it in your heart to do so.*

With fondest regards, Wolfgang.